# Midlife CHAOS

## Sue Hawley

ISBN-13: 978-0-9997678-1-8

Cover designer: James Price, The Author Market

Interior Layout: Deena Rae; E-Book Builders

Dedication

This book is dedicated to both of my parents. My mother who loved to read and my dad who loved a good story.

# Acknowledgements

I want to acknowledge and thank my sister. She is still the first to read any of my manuscripts. She laughs in all the right places.

I also acknowledge Janine who is the last person to read all manuscripts before they depart for the editor. She ensures my characters stay true to themselves.

I acknowledge my friend EW, who answers any and all questions pertaining to law enforcement.

And finally, I acknowledge my kids. Without them, I probably wouldn't have all the stories and the sense of humor I developed in order to survive raising all five of them.

*Midlife* CHAOS

# Chapter 1

The time in the early morning before I'd had my first cup of coffee was always dangerous for anyone wandering too close to me. My husband, Andy, had learned throughout our thirty-plus years of marriage to steer well clear until the third cup was almost finished. To be fair to Andy, ever since our four boys had finally finished college and left the nest, I usually stayed tucked in bed until I heard his morning shower water running. I also made sure I never mentioned his recently acquired and annoying habit of singing happily while the hot water poured over him, allowing him to blissfully believe the sound of running water somehow deafened the god awful noise. Menopause had only enhanced my bad attitude, making my morning process increasingly treacherous for others.

I sat in my favorite kitchen chair, sighing with relief as the first few sips of the caffeinated beverage slid down my throat. I was a firm believer the first cup of fresh, steaming-hot coffee was the best taste in the world. I loved the peace and quiet of early morning as I peered out of the big window next to our well-worn kitchen table. The beautiful old window gave us a view of a large yard bordered by woods. This year, the leaves had sprouted on the trees by mid-May, signaling winter was finally behind us. My tulips had so far survived the deer, and the pink flowers on the bush I had planted years ago were in full bloom. I was never good at remembering what I planted or even quite when I planted it. But that didn't keep me from enjoying the beauty.

Shifting in my seat for better comfort, I jumped as the phone shrilled. Throwing a quick glance at the clock, I felt my stomach clench. I hoped it wasn't one of our boys calling to inform me of some horrible event. Seven o'clock was too early for a social call. Dread spread as I quickly grabbed the phone.

"Peg? Is it too early?" I heard Jack Monroe's voice greet me.

"Jack? What the hell?"

"I know you're probably still on your first cup, but this is important," he quickly informed me.

The tightening in my stomach had turned into full-fledged knots. Jack Monroe was our chief of police in Bath, Ohio, the small township where we lived. We had known each other for decades. We had endured years of PTA and school functions while raising our kids. Both families were grateful as each child graduated from high school and then college. A few months ago, we had become odd partners because of events that surprised both of us. We were close enough that Jack was well aware of my three-cup rule.

"What is it?" I asked, struggling to keep the rudeness out of my voice. I don't think I managed very well.

"I just got off the phone with the mayor."

"Uh-oh. It's too early for this," I moaned.

Hearing his sigh, I knew he wasn't any happier than I was with his sunrise phone call.

"I'm not even in my office yet, so I'm not thrilled either. But he asked for you to help on a case." He paused before adding, "For a friend of his."

I slumped back into my chair. "What type of friend?" I asked warily.

Our township doesn't have a mayor; instead we elect a board of trustees. Akron is the biggest city near us, and I knew Jack was referring to their mayor. I didn't like him much and was pretty sure I wasn't his favorite person, either. The last time we had dealings with one another, the situation did eventually work out, but it didn't mean I wanted to be on his dinner guest list.

"The type of friend we don't discuss on the phone," was the answer.

I felt the beginnings of a headache, which added to the knots in my gut, spelling trouble.

"What's so bloody important he's calling as the sun rises?" I asked with a touch of bitterness. Well, maybe more than a touch, but hey, I hadn't had enough coffee.

"It's a kid."

I put my head in my hand, feeling sick. I was a sucker where kids were concerned. But being a sucker could get you killed if you weren't careful.

"Whose?" I asked, pretty sure I wasn't going to like the answer.

Jack stayed silent a few moments and then said, "Anthony Spanelli."

I frowned, wondering where I had heard the name. Then it hit me. "Youngstown Spanelli?" I asked.

"Yeah, Youngstown," Jack said with a sigh.

Surprisingly, the Mafia wasn't only in New York City and Chicago. Hell, there was more than one type of Mafia—Italian, Russian, Irish, just to name a few. At one time, Youngstown was a hot bed of Mafia activity, but it had slowed down in recent years.

"I'm expected to go to Youngstown?" I asked in disbelief.

"Nope. This guy lives right here in Bath," Jack informed me.

"What? Since when?" This was news to me. Hearing we had Mafia in the vicinity did nothing to improve my mood.

"Not too sure; at least the past few years. I had no idea any of the Spanelli family lived around here until yesterday, much less in Bath," Jack said. "Have a feeling they were keeping it quiet."

"What's the story?" I asked with a sigh.

"His ten-year-old daughter was involved in a hit-and-run. She's alive but in intensive care down at Children's Hospital."

I realized I had been holding my breath only when I released it in a *whoosh*. Thank goodness she was alive; I don't think I could have faced a murder involving a child.

I could hear paper rattling as he checked his notes. "The incident occurred yesterday after she got home from school. She was riding her bike on Bath Road when a car hit her. At the time, we assumed it was a teenager hot-rodding down those hills."

Bath Road could be dangerous because of its twists, turns, and hills. It was a maneuverability test during winter months, and I avoided it like the plague.

"What's her prognosis?" I asked. "Are you driving and reading at the same time?"

"She's stable but unconscious. Mr. Spanelli told the mayor he's convinced it was deliberate. No, I'm not driving while reading; the car is parked."

"Good, at least you won't cause a wreck!" I snapped. A random thought hit my brain. "Did the dad mention he believed it was deliberate to the police yesterday?" I asked, suspiciously.

"Nope, not a word," Jack answered, his irritation vibrating through the phone.

"What exactly does the mayor expect me to do?" I asked, afraid I was going to hate the answer.

Jack remained silent. He was no fool.

I decided to wait him out and kept my mouth firmly shut. I could hear Andy finishing his morning routine, trying to give me time to hit my second cup of coffee. If he was lucky, I'd normally be on my third by the time he made it to the kitchen for his breakfast. Today, he would be doing himself a favor if he stayed safely out of harm's way.

I heard a deep sigh before Jack asked, "Any of your special friends contact you?"

I felt my eyes narrow. "No."

Silence greeted my answer. After a few moments, Jack asked, "Not even your dad?"

My shoulders slumped. My special friends happened to be dead. I'm convinced menopause was the culprit of the situation I was thrown into a few months back. One day, I was minding my own business, surviving hot flashes and night sweats. The next thing I knew, dead people were informing me I had to help them clean up crime in the area. The situation must have had something to do with disappearing hormones suddenly giving me the ability to see spirits and participate in conversations I would rather not have at all.

Sighing, I said, "Nope, not even Dad."

My dad had died when I was eight, and I missed him terribly as I grew up without his influence. My mother was not anyone's idea of stellar, and I felt his loss deeply. Thankfully, my grandmother had stepped in and protected me as much as much as possible. My recent involvement with a murder cases allowed me to suddenly have access to Dad. I loved being able to talk with him after so many years, and I was touched to learn from him he had been checking on me throughout my life. I would have enjoyed having him back in my life much more if I hadn't been in danger while solving the murder.

"I didn't expect that answer," said Jack. "I figured you would know more than I do by now."

I looked down at my now-cold coffee and moaned. "Let me finish my coffee. I'll see what I can do."

"Thanks, Peg," said Jack.

I could feel his relief and didn't blame him. The mayor was a pain in the butt, but the township tried to play nice with the big boys of Akron.

Andy rounded the corner as I hung up the phone. He glanced at it and then at me. "Everything ok?"

"Jack. Seems he needs my help. A little girl was hit by a car while she was riding her bike."

Andy looked at my coffee cup. "How many?" he asked.

"One, and I didn't even finish it before Jack called," I answered grumpily.

His lips pursed as he studied me. Grabbing my morning elixir, he dumped the cold mess in the sink, walked over to our coffee machine, and brewed a fresh cup. We had bought one of those new fancy brew-as-you-go coffee machines a while back, and I loved the darn thing. I thankfully took the offered cup and drank deeply, ignoring the scalding sensation. He puttered around the kitchen, making his toast and his own coffee, wisely silent.

When I had reached the bottom of the cup, I got up to make another. Andy grinned but remained quiet.

"Okay, here's the deal. I am going to drink my needed amount of caffeine, then go meet with Jack."

Andy nodded and continued to eat his breakfast in silence. I appreciated that he understood mornings were not my best time. He was a bit over six foot, while I was lucky to hit five foot one on a good day. We look like Mutt and Jeff, but weirdly, his towering over me gave me a sense of security. While he had stayed basically trim through the years, age and four pregnancies had left me just a little bit pudgy—well, pudgier in some spots than others, but I could still fit in my jeans comfortably if I stayed away from sweets. Sweet treats had a bad habit of bloating me like a Macy's Thanksgiving Day parade balloon float. It was quite unfair.

"Jack's surprised none of the gang has been here to inform me," I said.

Andy looked up at me, saying, "Maybe this isn't supposed to be one of your cases."

"I hope you're right," I said, sitting back in my chair.

Suddenly, the hair on my arms tingled. Damn it.

"Sorry I took so long," said Nana, out of breath, which is a little bit creepy, since she's dead. How could a dead person need a moment to catch her breath? Nana was my grandmother, and I loved her very much. But she started the new chaos in my life, so I think I might have been holding a little bit of a grudge.

"Hi, Nana," I said.

Andy looked up, surprised. Nana was one of the few special visitors in my life he couldn't see. He had been given the ability as a gift from a powerful ghost named Logan. He could only see spirits protecting me, and while Nana was not a threat, she was not part of my protection squad, which included Indians in the woods. It's complicated.

Nana looked around the kitchen. "I thought you'd have changed the wallpaper before I returned." She and I had picked out the cornflower-covered wallpaper together a gazillion years ago. I loved it still.

I ignored her comment, refusing even a glance at the fading, peeling focus of her attention. Even without enough coffee, I recognized a dodge when I saw one.

"So are you here about the little girl?" I asked.

"Yep. Sorry I didn't get here before now. There was turbulence," she said, avoiding my eye.

I frowned. "Turbulence? What do you mean exactly?"

Nana had a bad habit of answering a question half way. I had learned last time she was *visiting* I had to phrase my questions carefully.

"Have you even bothered to look at wallpaper samples?" she asked.

Allowing my eyes to wander over the mess she was referring to, I shrugged. "Nope. I told you before, I like it just the way it is now."

The wallpaper had been peeling for years, but I couldn't bring myself to replace the memories that were attached to the process of hanging it with Nana.

She sighed. "I know you have fond memories of our shopping sprees, pouring over samples. But, sweetie, it's long past its due date." She still wasn't looking at me, which increased my headache.

"Nana, what type of turbulence?" I asked, determined to find the truth.

Waving a hand, she said, "It isn't so bad. Your mother has riled up a bunch of her buddies and is causing problems."

I closed my eyes and took a deep breath. Mom had been trouble while she was living, and obviously death had not improved her personality. Last time I saw my mother, she was dead and still causing problems for both the living and nonliving.

"How 'riled up' are we talking?" I asked, not sure I wanted to know the answer.

Nana shrugged. "Enough I was late. Which reminds me, I need your help."

"Figures. I haven't seen you since I helped you last time," I snapped.

"Watch your manners," Nana said, distracted by her own thoughts.

I found myself smiling at her words, remembering how many times while I was growing up I heard the familiar phrase. My temper and ornery personality had justified her constant application of etiquette lessons. Studying her face, I hoped when I reached her age my skin was as smooth and soft as hers had been—and still was, since she appeared to me exactly the way I remembered her, gray hair and fresh perm included.

"You need my help?" I prompted.

Finally facing me, she said, "There's been a little girl hurt here in the township. We need to find the culprit."

"I am aware of the accident. Why are *you* involved is the important question?"

Her eyes wandered towards the window. Not a good sign. "Hmm?"

"Nana! Why?"

"The bigger picture," she said, waving her arms around in a circle.

Talk about evasive!

"I'm not impressed with the bigger picture. Last time, it almost got me killed!"

"Well, you survived, obviously," she said, eyes still inspecting the yard out back.

"Yeah, by about one minute!" I snapped.

Shrugging, she said, "This one may be a bit dicey."

I narrowed my eyes. "What would you call last time?"

"How were we to know the killer was on the police force?" she snapped.

Owen Wells. I had watched the kid grow up. He had been a model student and citizen. Everyone had loved the guy. He had become an excellent police officer; but it was all a cover for his criminal life. In the end, his insanity had become obvious, and we had discovered that knowledge almost too late.

The incident had led Jack Monroe, as chief of police, to institute stricter hiring policies. Every new hire now had to endure a psychological test, plus an extensive background check. The entire police department had been in shock, not to mention the township trustees. Jack was not reliving that nightmare, and township politics had, surprisingly, not risen to the surface, fighting his new procedures. Shows just how freaked they had been at the discovery one of their finest also happened to be a sociopath.

I shook my head, disgusted. "I still can't believe the spirit world doesn't have all the facts."

"We can't know everything! Precisely why we need your help," she pouted.

I studied her face carefully. What vital piece of information was she withholding this time? Maybe none of the dead people who were involved in the last case had actually known who the killer was, but even if they had a clue, the information had stayed within their ranks.

"Jack has already called; as soon as I'm dressed, I'll head over to the station."

Still distracted by the scenery, she said, "Whatever works for you, sweetie."

Andy had patiently sat there, waiting until I had a chance to fill him in on the conversation.

"Nana," I informed him.

"Yep, figured that much on my own," he said.

Turning back to Nana, I pressed for clues that might make this an easy case to solve.

"Anything you know that would help me? What makes this so dicey?"

Anything worse than last time would not be welcome.

She waved a hand. "You know, the crew in Youngstown."

I shrugged. "Yeah, so what? If it's a mob situation, the mayor will feel right at home."

I admit, the sarcasm felt good. Shoot me.

"He's not in the mob!" she chided. "And if I remember correctly, it was a mob friend of his who was responsible for saving you from Owen!"

She was absolutely, 100 percent correct. And I was thankful for the guy's skill with firearms. But it didn't make me a supporter of the mob just because he had whacked Owen with a bullet seconds before Owen's knife would have finished me off for good.

I glanced at Andy, noticing his concern. I didn't think the details of the current situation were going to alleviate it one bit.

"I heard you told the boys about your new career," she said.

"What a dodge! Yes, I told the boys. Andy convinced me it was probably the best decision."

Our four boys were grown and scattered all over the country. I had resisted explaining my newfound abilities to them for fear they would think I was either bonkers or menopause had finally destroyed me emotionally. I am thankful Andy had been on the phone with me, backing me up completely. They had eventually believed I now had the capability to see dead people— not *all* dead folks, merely the ones involved in solving problems. I'm not a medium like the ones on TV, communicating with family members of clients. Nope, and I'm thankful for that. That is not a lifestyle I'm interested in having. Hell, I'm pretty sure I don't even want the few showing up in my life now.

Nodding, Nana said, "Yep, that's the gossip on our side."

I cocked my head, frowning. "There's gossip over there about me? Who, exactly, is doing all the gossiping?"

She glanced at the peeling wallpaper again. "Hmm?"

"Nana! Who?"

She flicked her hand dismissively. "Oh, you know, some."

I began drumming my fingers on the table.

After a few moments, she said, "No one you know." She sighed. "I guess I mentioned you made a big impression solving those murders. Sorta the talk of the town, so to speak."

My mouth fell open. I made an impression? Wow. Was this good news or not?

She continued. "No one over here ever suspected that Owen fella; took us by surprise, I can tell you."

Discovering the spiritual realm could be surprised was one of the details about the afterlife that did not thrill me. My entire life I had counted on the fact heaven was perfect and all was known there. The many revelations that had occurred during the last investigation had destroyed my preconceived ideas. Andy, on the other hand, had been fascinated.

"Well, I have to get going. There's a big meeting I am required to attend," Nana informed me.

I sighed. Another set of facts that gave me heartburn. There were *meetings* on the other side—*social gatherings, clubs* to join, and *responsibilities*. Whatever happened to streets of gold and rest for the weary? The more I learned about what I thought was *heaven* the less I liked it. Go figure.

As she began fading from sight, she paused, saying, "Did I mention you have been assigned a helper?" Then she was gone.

A helper? Just what I needed. The helpers I had had last time drove me to distraction.

The air changed, and I whirled around to see who had shown up now.

Andy broke into a huge grin. "Hey, Bob. How's it going?"

Andy enjoyed Bob, who was among the ranks of the dead he could see, much more than I did.

"Hey, Andy! Good to see you," said Bob as he grinned.

Bob liked Andy. I'm pretty sure Bob was just a little bit afraid of me.

I plopped my head back into my hand as I watched the greetings.

Bob turned. "Hi, Peg. I should have been here earlier, but I know your three-cup rule. Been hanging back, but I saw your Nana and decided I might as well get started."

I hated to admit it, but Bob had improved greatly since I first met him. His wife, Elaine, and he were murdered by our hometown boy, Owen. Elaine was a horrible dead person, and I knew for a fact she was no picnic while living. She had run Bob's life, and death, completely. Once he became involved in the process of solving his murder, he had actually bloomed into a somewhat talented person.

I gave him a finger wave but remained quiet. I needed to give him time to get his thoughts together. If I pressed too quickly, he became flustered. Even this old dog could learn new tricks.

Bob glanced out the window. "You see anything in the woods? You know, 'the guys'?" he asked.

I frowned. He was referring to the group of Indians in the woods guarding me at all times. The catch was I could only see them if I was in some sort of danger. So if I *did* see them, I could officially begin to sweat.

I got up from the table and made my way to the window. I really didn't want to find out if my goose was cooked, but I forced myself to sneak a quick peak at the woods at the back of our property. Seeing absolutely nothing other than trees was a huge relief.

"Nope, no guys."

I noticed Bob relax. "Okay, good. Just checking. Better if we realize your danger level now rather than find out the hard way."

Andy and I exchanged quick glances. This didn't sound good.

"You expecting trouble?" Andy asked.

Shrugging, Bob said, "Well, you never know. Better safe than sorry."

I narrowed my eyes, studying Bob's face. "Do you have more information than you're telling us?"

Bob grew scarlet. I still hadn't figured out how a dead person could blush. There was no blood. My Mom turned pale the last time I was in her company, and it was the same principle. I shook my head.

"Bob, you might as well tell us if this situation has the potential to be a pain in my butt."

His eyes returned to the woods. "As long as you can't see the guys out back, we're good."

My headache returned in full force, and my stomach began turning somersaults.

Chapter 2

I studied Bob a few moments longer. There was something different about him, but I couldn't decide exactly what had changed. I knew breaking away from his dragon of a wife had bolstered his self-esteem. Getting away from Elaine would have helped anyone. He had stayed with her in the afterlife, even though apparently he wasn't obligated to stick with her over there. The rules and regulations concerning that side of life still confused me since nothing in the heavenly realm abided by anything I had learned here. We had it all screwed up from what I could gather. Andy loved discovering the workings of what I used to call heaven; I end up with knots in my stomach.

"What do you know that Nana is obviously not revealing?" I asked Bob.

Bob shifted his stance, his eyes skirting around the room. These were not good signs.

I opened my mouth to throw him a dose of snottiness when Andy chimed in.

"Hey, Bob. It's okay, man. Just tell us if there's a problem." Andy smiled kindly at Bob.

Finally, Bob's eyes met Andy's and he sighed. "Look, guys, I'm not supposed to give out sensitive information," he said. "It's sorta like a military secret."

*Oh, great. Now Bob thinks he's in a spy novel.* My head was beginning to bang like a drum.

Andy grinned. "Sounds a bit like a movie."

Bob returned the grin but shook his head. "If Logan gives me the okay, I'll tell you."

*Logan? Bob takes orders from Logan? Since when?*

"You working for Logan now? Full-time?" asked Andy. "How cool. A bit like a promotion. Congratulations!"

Bob's face lit up like a Christmas tree. "Yeah! He personally asked me to be part of his team. I couldn't believe it." He lowered his voice, looking quickly around the room. "Especially, you know, being married to Elaine."

Elaine had apparently gone over to what I call the *dark side* of the spirit realm. In other words, she was hanging out with my mom. Always up to no good, Mom was definitely working against our efforts to clean up our tiny piece of the world. I had no idea what the eventual outcome of world events would be, but Nana was convinced we had to work hard to prepare for whatever was next. I had once thought death would be the end of problems, but I'd learned that was not how life worked. It was a mess, in my opinion.

I closed my eyes, rolling my head around to relieve some of the stress I was experiencing. We hadn't even started working on this case, and I was already anxious.

"I know one thing for certain. It's a sure bet with Mayor Bennet Hayes involved it will be complicated. His connections with the mob world are questionable, at best," I said.

"Did you forget one of those connections saved your life a few months ago?" Andy inquired.

If it hadn't been for one of the mayor's connections, I would now be helping Bob in the afterlife. My dad and Logan had encouraged me to enlist the help of the mayor's friends, and it had been wise advice. When our rogue cop, Owen Wells, had tried to slit my throat, Antonio had shot him in the head. The nightmares had only recently subsided. I wished everyone would stop reminding me I should be grateful for the mob connection.

Sighing, I answered. "Nope. But it doesn't excuse his questionable involvement with those guys. If you remember correctly, I would never have been in harm's way if the idiot man hadn't hidden his son's involvement with a murder!"

Alex Hayes, the mayor's son, had been present when Owen killed Bob and Elaine. The mayor covered his son's tracks, thus hindering the investigation at the time. When Nana had shown up a few months ago, it was to inform me my job was to solve the murders. We had finally worked together with the mayor and solved it, but let's face it, owning up to the situation at the beginning would have been a wiser course of action. His political career had come before the law, which still pissed me off a lot.

Andy shook his head. "I'm grateful for Antonio's help. And I'd use him again if we need him."

My mouth dropped open. "What?"

"Peg, I want you around for my retirement years. Grandkids, vacations, all of it. It may take drastic measures if your involvement with the spirit world continues." He leaned back in his chair, looking me square in the eyes.

I was able to hold his gaze out of sheer stubbornness, but I have to admit, his declaration melted my heart.

"Fine. I'm getting dressed." I turned to Bob. "You stay here and keep Andy company. I don't need an audience to pull myself together."

Bob grinned. "I know better."

Andy laughed but squeezed my hand as I passed him on my way to the bedroom.

I could hear their chatter as I gave myself a quick once-over in the bathroom. Checking my roots for signs of gray, I shook my head. Better grab a box of hair color the next time I was at the grocery. I'd colored my hair for so long I couldn't remember what the actual color was eons ago. The air suddenly changed, which made my stomach clinch. Who now? It was never a good sign when a dead person showed up in my bedroom.

I slowly turned, dreading whatever spirit I would face. Elaine stood there, looking like she had recently eaten an entire bag of lemons. Great. Her husband was chatting with Andy, and I was stuck with super shrew.

"What do you want?" I demanded.

"So they've called you in for another case." It was a statement, not a question, which told me she knew more than was healthy for me.

"What business is it of yours?" I asked. I had learned during the last case Elaine was a major problem for me. Now that she was hooked up with my mother, it spelled mega trouble.

"You were lucky last time. I wouldn't be so sure this time will turn out so well for you."

I wanted to slap the sneer right off her face, but I was pretty sure my hand would glide right through her essence. Just because I could see them as solid didn't mean they *were* solid. The only spirit I had encountered to date who had physical capabilities was Logan. I was positive Elaine didn't have his skills, and I knew I didn't have the type of talent necessary to make contact. Too bad. I would have enjoyed watching her reaction if I had acquired the knack.

Changing the subject, and hoping to draw information from her, I asked, "How's my mom?"

She narrowed her eyes, watching me. She tossed her head, saying, "None of your business."

Nodding at her lousy answer, I said, "Well, Elaine, I don't have time for you. Leave."

She faded; I wasn't sad to see her go. Another fun fact I learned a few months ago is if I tell spirits to leave, they have no choice in the matter. They gotta go. *Works for me.*

I quickly finished my normal dressing routine with shaking hands. Sailing back into the kitchen, with a whole lot less confidence than I hoped I was conveying, I smiled brightly. Bob and Andy were still chatting but not about anything I considered important. Cars. What was the big deal about cars? You stuck the key in, turned it, and bingo! You had transportation.

"Well, Elaine showed up," I announced.

Bob grew pale, which was his normal response knowing when she was too near him.

Andy raised an eyebrow, sneaking a quick peak at Bob. Turning back to me, he asked, "Your mom with her?"

Andy was well aware of the problems those two women could generate. We had no idea what they were up to, even though my dad had tried nosing around, hoping to stumble across answers. I knew Logan was concerned, but it was one of the few arenas in which he had limited access. I was trying to picture exactly how this afterlife crap all worked, but so far, the little information I did possess wasn't exactly what I would call enlightening.

Watching Bob closely, I realized what was different. He had better clothes!

"Bob! You changed your look."

He frowned. "What?"

"I like it." I gave him the once-over, admiring the new shirt and jeans. Spirits choose how they appeared to the living and could change outfits, hairstyles, even age. My mother added perfume to her ensemble. While Bob had remained in his fifties, he had upgraded his wardrobe. He still had a disheveled air to him. I could tell his rumpled aura hadn't disappeared totally, but it was a definite improvement.

He glanced down, barely noticing his attire. Elaine's visit must have freaked him pretty darn good.

"Your dad helped me." This surprised me; Bob wasn't necessarily Dad's best friend. They had been in high school together, but I knew they hadn't been close buds.

"Well, it looks good on you," I said and smiled. I hoped my distraction would help calm him down.

He straightened a bit, saying, "Thanks." Looking at me, he asked, "You plan on seeing Jack about this situation?"

"Yep, on my way now."

"I think I should be there. I might be of some help."

He sounded doubtful, so I decided Logan had sent him. I was confident there was a high probability Bob wasn't exactly certain what his job was at this point. For some reason, Logan had taken Bob under his wing, using him where he could. The decision had actually worked in our favor last time. While the mayor's son was lying in ICU, fighting for his life after a brutal attack, Bob had saved his life by alerting Logan immediately when someone had tried to finish the poor guy off completely. It had come as a shock he had so much common sense, but wonders never cease.

I cocked my head. "Really? If you have better things to do, I could fill you in later."

Shaking his head emphatically, he responded, "No, I'll meet you there."

He faded quickly, leaving Andy and me staring at each other, surprised.

Finally, Andy broke our shocked silence. "What's up with Bob?"

Shaking my head, I said, "Who knows? It's obvious he's on edge. The question is, are the nerves from a legit problem or because Bob isn't allowed to give out information at this point?"

Andy didn't hesitate. "Mostly, not being able to tell you a thing. You make Bob nervous."

I nodded. "Yeah, he's a weird one for sure."

I grabbed my purse and began the process of digging for my keys. You'd think after all these years, I would come up with a better plan than tossing them in the bottom of my bag. It was amazing how much stuff I accumulated—grocery receipts, old shopping lists, gum wrappers and general junk. Every few months, I broke down and spent twenty minutes cleaning out the garbage. It must be that time again.

Feeling success as my fingers detected the cold metal in a corner, I grabbed them before the darn things buried themselves back among the clutter. Keys were sneaky little stinkers.

Glancing at Andy, I smiled. "Gotta get to Jack's. He's probably having a nervous breakdown while he's waiting for me."

Andy laughed and planted a quick kiss before I headed out.

The police station was about a mile from our house, so it was a quick trip. One of these days, I should really walk the distance; it would provide some much-needed exercise. I thought about this plan quite often, hoping the mere process of deciding which route to take would convince my body I was actually *doing* physical activity. So far, I was pretty sure I hadn't fooled my muscles.

I parked in the back, close to Jack's office. So much for a little workout for the legs. I scanned the area, and my heart sped up as I realized Owen used to greet me as I pulled into the parking lot. I could feel sweat forming on my forehead and shook my head to clear the memories. I made a beeline for the back door and quickly got my butt inside the building. I smiled at the dispatcher as I passed her cubicle. She nodded and waved and then returned to work. None of the employees were aware of my dead people problem, but they all knew about Owen's betrayal and the fact I was involved in his death. They didn't blame me, but it created a small amount of tension when I was in the building.

Walking down the hall, I heard Jack's voice booming from his office. "As soon as I have a chance, I'll be out there to talk with Mr. Spanelli." A pause and then, "Yes, I understand." A moment before I reached his office, the phone banged down with enough force to cause damage. Uh-oh.

"Hey," I said, sticking my head around the corner of the door. "You busy?"

Head in his hands, he used one to wave me inside. "Thank God you're here. The mayor has called me three times, and it isn't even nine o'clock yet." He sighed. "Coffee?"

"Not now. He's in a snit?" I asked, noticing the extra gray in his hair. Jack had a hefty build, not overweight, more like a linebacker for the Cleveland Browns football team. But he loved food, which could be a problem as age caught up with him.

"Oh, yeah. You'd think I had nothing better to do than pamper his friend." Jack shook his head in disgust.

"Simmer down, you are well aware he's mostly bluster. All bark and little bite." I comforted him the best I could.

"Yeah, but his little bit of bite can leave marks," Jack said, getting up to refill his coffee cup. He had a bad habit of drinking coffee absentmindedly, especially when he was irritated.

"Hey, Peg, I'm here," said Bob, from the corner of the room.

Gosh, I'd forgotten about him. "Bob's here," I informed Jack.

My remark earned me an eyebrow raise. I shrugged. "I think he's been assigned to help."

Jack shook his head. Bob was the least of his problems. "You ready for a little trip?"

"Okay. Where we going?" I asked, pretty sure I knew the answer.

"Spanelli's."

Yep, I was right. "Sounds good. You want to finish your coffee?"

"I'll take it with us," he said, as he reached in the bottom drawer of his desk and pulled out a travel mug with a Bath Police logo printed on the side. He quickly poured his cup of coffee in it and stood up. "Let's hit the road."

Once in his car, I asked, "Is this Spanelli guy still active in the mob?"

Jack shook his head. "Not anymore, at least according to him. It's why the family moved him here. To get him out of the family business."

I frowned. "Really? I didn't know you could leave the mob."

"The story I heard is he got sick and landed in the Cleveland Clinic. His father realized the health of his son was more important." He paused and then said, "I'm not sure the guy was too great of a mobster. The scuttle butt is he is a great dad and serious about family life." Frowning, he added, "We'll see if it's true."

I thought about this surprising information and then asked, "What was his job while he was working for his father?"

"He did the accounting," Jack said.

"The term covers a lot of ground. Cooking the books?" I asked.

Jack shrugged his shoulders. "Have no idea. Damn sure he wouldn't admit it to me if he was fiddling with the money. Would you tell a cop?"

I laughed. "Nope. But his daughter was hurt for a reason. Somebody is sending a message."

Jack nodded and then grinned. "He helps the mayor with his personal investments."

I snorted. "Not surprised. When did you learn all this information?"

"Been on the phone the last hour with some contacts," he answered, his temper flaring.

"Is Hayes leaning on you a little?" I asked, grinning.

Jack grimaced. "Mayor Hayes believes we owe him a favor. I'm not entirely convinced he doesn't have a point."

"*What?*" I said, my volume increased more than I had meant it to.

He sighed. "I hate to admit it, but without Antonio, you'd be…" He didn't finish.

I looked out the window, remembering those last few moments before Antonio shot a hole in Owen's head. Turning back to look at Jack, I said, "I know, Jack. But remember, we did him a *huge* favor by putting in a good word with the prosecuting attorney concerning Alex. His kid could have been in real trouble."

Nodding, Jack said, "Yep. But you'd be dead if it wasn't for his connections."

"And his son would be toast if it weren't for *my* connections!" I retorted.

Bob snorted from the back seat, which made me jump.

"Damn it, Bob. Remind me when you are here!"

"Sorry, Peg. Figured you'd know I'd be in the car."

Even Jack was surprised Bob had tagged along. He couldn't see him, and he forgot to ask if anyone was with us sometimes.

Jack slowed down, searching for house numbers on the mailboxes near the road. We are considered rural here, so all the mail boxes were usually positioned at the end of driveways. The mailman could stay safely in his vehicle delivering mail. He was probably thankful in the winter. The city carriers had to walk to each house to deliver mail to boxes mounted on the porches of homes. *Those poor people must be popsicles by the end of their routes.*

"There it is," he said, pointing to a long, curving driveway.

As we turned in, I spotted a humongous house, even for Bath. Obviously, this guy had money, and lots of it. I looked at the manicured lawn and beautiful gardens. *Must be modeled after villas in Italy*, I thought.

As we approached the house, I saw a tennis court off to the side of the property and a pool behind the courts. Wow. After Jack rang the bell, the door opened, revealing a middle-aged women dressed in a maid's uniform. I didn't know anyone still had servants; it made me feel a little as though we were in an old movie. Jack handed her his card and identified himself as the police chief. She didn't say a word but stepped back, allowing us to enter the house. We found ourselves in a huge foyer lined with carefully arranged art.

After the maid closed the door, she quietly left us alone, and I assumed she had gone to fetch Mr. Spanelli. It was a guess, considering she still hadn't uttered a word. Left standing there, I decided to sneak a peek at the art. A couple of Monets, a Picasso, and even a Von Gogh, were prominently hanging on one wall. I was a bit surprised anyone would have these paintings hanging this close to the front door. It would be so easy for an intruder to walk off with them. I was turning to signal Jack to join me at the wall when a far door opened. Not wanting to be caught snooping, I quickly stepped back to join Jack.

"Chief Monroe! I really appreciate your coming to the house. I would have come to the station, but I'd rather my presence in the township be unnoticed." Spanelli's face turned light pink as he explained.

While Jack was assuring him we didn't mind meeting at his home, I studied the ex-mobster. He was tall, at least six four and had dark hair, which curled at his neckline. He was nice-looking but needed to take advantage of the tennis court to get rid of the love handles forming around his waistline. Maybe watching Al Pacino all those years in the Godfather movies had formed an image in my mind. This man certainly didn't fit Pacino's image by a long shot.

"The mayor has told me you could help," he said, nodding in my direction.

I stepped back a little so I could look up at his face without straining my neck. Andy is tall, but Mr. Spanelli's height caused my shoulder muscles to ache.

"My mother will be able to aid in your investigation," he continued.

Jack shook his head. "No, sir, we can manage."

Spanelli wasn't listening; he eyes were locked on me, which made me sweat. "No, no. You misunderstand. I know she will help! She was a fantastic mother and grandmother. Surely you can understand?"

"Was?" It was the only word that had caught my attention.

His face became sad. "Yes, she passed away a few years ago."

Great. The mayor must have divulged information he promised would not be shared—ever. The ass.

Jack and I exchanged a look. Then I faced Mr. Spanelli. "I'm not sure what you've been told, but what makes you think your mother can help?"

He leaned down close to my face. "My friend, the mayor, told me in confidence you have abilities. I will tell no one."

Taking a step back, I closed my eyes, planning on ways to make the mayor miserable.

"Mr. Spanelli, we have found it works better for Mrs. Shaw to work her own way. We don't interfere."

"Yes, yes. I understand, but my dear mother will make herself known. I promise you this," he answered, confident of his beliefs. "Please don't think I want to obstruct a proven method, but I know my mother."

Deciding a change of subject was in order, Jack asked, "What makes you think your daughter's hit-and-run wasn't an accident?"

"Come with me," he said and motioned for us to follow. We entered his massive office. Looking around, I was bombarded with framed family pictures. They were on the walls, desk, and shelves; clearly this man loved his family. The cherry furniture filled the room but was not overwhelming. Someone with talent had decorated.

He walked over to his desk and pulled out a wad of letters from a drawer. Showing them to Jack, he said, "I have been receiving these for the past few months. It will prove to you it was no accident but a deliberate act."

"May I look at them?" I asked.

"Yes, please read them," he said, handing them over to me.

"Don't assume too much; they may not help."

He stood up straighter and said, "I have faith in you! They will give you clues!"

Jeez Louise, what did he expect from me? I was still on a learning curve, something the mayor obviously did not share with the man. I opened the first letter and noticed the pen had dug deep into the paper. I didn't know much about handwriting analysis, but even I could tell it was written in anger. Too bad it was written completely in Italian.

"Um, I need you to translate," I said.

The shock on his face puzzled me, until he answered, "You can't read them? The spirits aren't helping?"

I sighed. "Sorry." I held out the paper. "Please translate."

He shook his head. "If you are able to communicate with the spirit world, they will come to your aid. My mother will lead them to you."

Great. Another moron to handle. I was not going to convince him otherwise. I decide to back off. "Fine. I'll let you know."

Jack had remained quiet through this exchange, but now asked, "Is your wife at home? We would appreciate if she could answer a few questions."

For the first time, Spanelli's face closed. He frowned, asking, "How could she help? She is unavailable."

The sudden change in his demeanor alarmed me. He was definitely hiding something. We had been through this before when the mayor withheld what turned out to be vital information. I felt my anger on the rise. Jack must have sensed it also, because he said, "She may have noticed something or someone as she went about her errands."

Spanelli relaxed, saying, "She is not important, but if you believe she may have seen a clue, I will allow you to talk with her. She is at the hospital with Caterina, our daughter."

"Thank you," said Jack.

"Please forgive my manners. I will have refreshments brought in for you," he said.

I frowned at the sudden change in his manner, yet again. I was uncomfortable with his emotional state.

I was thankful when Jack shook his head. "Sorry, sir. We have an appointment soon we can't miss." Our host began to insist, but Jack stayed firm. "No, I'm truly sorry. The sooner we begin to study these letters, the sooner we find out who hit your daughter."

Slowly nodding, Mr. Spanelli said, "I appreciate your diligence in this matter. I do not want to hold up the special work of Mrs. Shaw." Taking my hand, he looked deep into my eyes. "The spirits will not let us down!"

I kept my big mouth closed, nodding with a small smile. We made our way to the door, thanking him for his help, and got out of there as fast as we could.

Once in the car, safely heading down the drive, Jack asked, "Well?"

"I think he's a little creepy," said Bob from the back seat.

I jumped. "Damn it, Bob! What did I tell you less than an hour ago?" I snapped. "I almost peed my pants!"

"Bob's still here? Did he witness any of our conversation?" asked Jack.

"Tell him I saw every bit, and I think the guy is nuts," answered Bob.

I rubbed my forehead, trying to ease the pain growing by leaps and bounds. "Bob thinks the guys is crazy."

Jack snorted. "Hells bells, so do I."

I shook my head. "It's obvious something is way off." I turned to face Bob. "What do you know about this guy?"

Bob looked at me and then turned to face the window. After a few seconds, he faded completely.

"Damnation! I knew he was hiding something! You mark my words, whatever information he's not telling us is probably critical."

"What's going on?" asked Jack.

"Bob left, which tells me he knows something important."

"It's not like Bob to keep anything to himself. If I remember correctly, he shares too much."

"He's working for Logan now," I informed Jack.

"Is it a good thing or not?" he asked.

I hesitated before answering. Logan was a powerful spirit and one I respected. But he had a bad habit of playing cards too close to his chest.

"We'll see," I said, sighing.

# Chapter 3

O nce we had returned to the security of Jack's office, I agreed to a cup of coffee. Maybe the caffeine would be the remedy for the headache determined to resurface. Both of us were silent as we sipped the steaming brew. Finally, Jack asked, "Well, what do you think?"

"About?"

"Spanelli."

I laughed. "Oh, he's into something up to his neck. Not sure what it is, but nobody receives so many threats without having his fingers in someone's pie," I said, indicating the stack of letters Spanelli had readily handed over to us. "Did you notice the artwork? Pricey stuff."

Shaking his head, he said, "Didn't bother. Figured they were prints."

"No way! I'm no expert, but they looked real to me," I said.

"I hate to say this, but I hope the mayor isn't involved in this wreckage." Jack sighed.

I opened my mouth to make a smart-ass remark and then snapped it shut. Jack was right; I still didn't like the mayor, but he had come through for me a few months ago without one ounce of arguing. Problem was, now he believed I owed him, I didn't like the attitude one bit.

I shrugged. "I agree, but if he is, I don't want to be cornered into helping cover his butt either."

Jack nodded, taking another healthy sip of coffee. He reached over, grabbed a couple of the letters, and tossed them to me. "You start on those; I'll tackle this stack."

I caught the letters and nodded. Settling back in the chair, I realized it was tons more comfy than I remembered. I glanced down and then looked up surprised. "Is this a new chair?"

Never taking his eyes off the letter he was scanning, he said, "Yep. Trustees had a few hundred bucks left over from our budget." He smiled, "You know the rule; spend it or lose it at the next budget meeting."

I spent the next few minutes squirming in the chair, appreciating the comfort level at any possible sitting position I could find. "Wow, this is really nice."

"Hmm? Oh, yeah, I know. I sat in about fifty chairs before picking that one."

"I didn't know you hand-picked the office furniture," I said, surprised.

"What?" answered Jack, finally looking up from the letters. "I usually don't bother, but since the chair was going to live in my office, I wanted something nicer than the junk those trustees would have chosen." He shrugged. "I had enough money to finally have a decent visitor's chair." His head bent back down to read.

Once I started reading my own pile of letters, I realized sweat was beginning to form on my upper lip.

"Um, Jack?"

"Hmm?"

"These are a little on the creepy side; more than the run-of-the-mill threats."

"Yep, I noticed." He frowned. Grabbing a pen and pad of paper, he started making notes.

"Think it would be wise to see if there's a pattern of some sort. Whoever is the author of these letters uses a few phrases I'm not familiar with at all."

"Because they aren't written in English," said a voice from the corner.

I looked up, surprised to see my dad leaning against the wall. Every time he leaned, I wondered how on earth he managed it since he wasn't solid. I did ask him once; he merely smiled.

"Hi, Dad," I still loved seeing him. He hadn't shown up for over a month, but I knew he was around somewhere. Being able to actually see him with my own eyes warmed my heart.

Jack's head snapped up, eyes searching the room. "Your dad's here? Where?"

"In the corner by the window," I said.

"Hi, Dave," he said and smiled. Even though Jack couldn't see any of the spirits, he enjoyed knowing they were around us.

I frowned. "We don't know Italian," I informed Dad.

He threw back his head and laughed. "Yep, I'm well aware."

"Then how are we reading these?" I asked, my temper starting to rise.

"Watch," he told me, disappearing.

"What the hell?" stuttered Jack. "I was reading along, and now all I see is gobbledygook."

"As long as I'm in the room, your mind will translate. When I leave, you can't." Dad reappeared, smiling. The ornery expression on his face told me he was thoroughly enjoying himself.

I narrowed my eyes, saying, "Not necessarily funny, Dad."

He laughed again, "Oh, sweetie. Just having a bit of fun while helping you two."

"Helping?" I asked.

He nodded, "It would have taken hours to find a translator Jack could trust, so I decided to help out a bit."

I thought back to the first time I met Logan. He had informed me while he wasn't speaking English, I *heard* English. In a weird, screwy way, it made total sense to me.

Jack had chosen to remain quiet. He learned last time it was easier in the long run if he waited until I bring him up-to-date once there was a pause in conversation with whatever dead person I happen to be dealing with at the time. Sensing a lull, he asked, "What's the deal?"

While I quickly explained, Jack's expression became admiring. "Pretty cool, Dave. Thanks. Can you hang around long enough for me to get all the notes I need?"

I shook my head. Jeez Louise, it didn't take much to impress Jack.

I glanced at Dad, "Well?"

He nodded. "Not much else to do now you're involved in my snooping."

My eyebrows creased. "Snooping? What are you talking about?"

Dad looked down at the letters we held. "We've had our eyes on the Spanellis for a long time, long before they immigrated to the States." He shrugged. "Guess they were a problem back in the old country."

"How long is long?" I asked, intrigued.

His eyes met mine. "A few centuries at least."

"Wow."

Jack couldn't hold himself back, asking, "What now?"

"The Spanellis have been under surveillance from the spirit realm for centuries."

Jack's eyes closed as he slumped back in his chair. "We are in for a mess, aren't we?"

"Probably," Dad answered. While I informed Jack of Dad's answer, I felt my spine tingle.

Dad straightened a little as Logan appeared. Great, just what I needed.

"Hello, Peg. Nice to see you again," he said, politely. The guy could teach etiquette classes; his manners were impeccable.

I hadn't seen Logan since the afternoon Owen had decided I needed to join my dad and his dead buddies. Logan only showed up when matters were important and needed his personal attention.

"Hello, Logan." See, my manners weren't horrible, most of the time.

He turned, acknowledging my Dad with a slight nod of his head. Dad returned the nod but remained quiet.

Turning back to me, he said, "You seem well. I am glad."

"Thanks." I liked Logan, don't get me wrong. But if he was here, I was probably not going to like my immediate future a whole lot.

Glancing at Jack, who clearly realized someone else had shown up, Logan said, "Please tell the chief I am also concerned about the Spanelli family."

"It would be easier if you told him yourself. I know you have the ability to allow him to experience your presence." I admit, my attitude was a tad ballsy, but I couldn't hold the words back. They flew out of my mouth totally on their own, with absolutely no help from my brain.

Logan stared at me a moment, then turned to Jack. "Chief Monroe?"

I swear Jack almost had a heart attack. I guess I should have checked for any health concerns he might have had before opening my big, fat mouth.

"Jack, breathe!" I commanded.

"I did not intend to frighten you, Chief Monroe. However, we need to work together concerning the Spanelli family," Logan said calmly.

Jack finally caught his breath and mutely nodded. His eyes darted in my direction. I shrugged. What could I say? Welcome to my world.

Logan continued explaining. "We have watched this family for centuries." He shook his head sadly. "It all began quite innocently; a young man trying to protect his family from politicians. I have grown to appreciate the fact many politicians usually cause more problems than they solve. I admit, it is only my opinion, and must not be taken as the opinion of the entire spirit realm."

Wow, a disclaimer. I almost laughed.

Jack continued to remain mute but nodded again. I, on the other hand, didn't stay silent.

"I totally agree! They ruin more than they repair."

Logan threw me a tight smile. Turning back to Jack, he asked, "Would you be willing to work together on this issue?"

Jack's mouth opened and then shut. He nodded. I figured he had no idea what to say, so he followed the old saying, 'Silence is golden.'

Dad had remained quiet throughout the exchange but now said, "Is anyone in the family trustworthy?"

Logan gave the question some thought, eventually saying, "Yes, some. However, they seem not to survive for an extended time." He smiled. "They work with us now, but they are limited in abilities."

This was interesting news, but from Logan's expression, I knew he had no intentions of expanding on the statement. I was bursting with questions, so I said, "If they are with you, can't they tell you family secrets which could help us here?"

He seemed amused at my question. "Most families have secrets, but the Spanellis have more than the average. The members we consider trustworthy were never given access to vital information while alive. On our side, it is difficult to see through the veils shielding that information."

Wow, learn something new every day regarding the dead cosmos. So even Logan couldn't penetrate certain areas of the other side. While I was aware of his rare limitations, I considered the fact unnerving; I wanted Logan to be all knowing. It made me feel safer.

Jack raised his hand. "Um, what type of help are you asking for exactly?" He glanced down at the letters from Spanelli. "I'm not sure what to look for in these." He held one up for our inspection.

"I assume they are anonymous?" Logan asked.

Jack rifled through them quickly. "Yeah, no signatures to speak of really. Signed, 'Beware,' which is no help."

"Think we might be losing something in the translation," chimed Dad from his corner. I noticed he had returned to leaning against the wall.

"Yes, I agree," said Logan. "Cannot be helped." He turned to Jack. "Chief, I will return. I want to warn you while you do not, at this time, possess the ability to see me, you will continue to hear me. I believe a signal to alert you is in order, and I will supply one next time. Thank you for your cooperation."

Before Jack could muster an answer, Logan was gone.

"He left," I informed Jack.

"Yeah, the air changed a little," replied Jack.

"Peg, I'm not sure where this will lead, but I'll be here as much as I can to help," said Dad.

"Uh, Peg, I can hear your dad, also." He frowned. "A bit of a surprise."

Dad nodded. "I was pretty sure Logan allowed the ability, since he allowed you to hear him."

Dad's eyes slid to mine. "I was impressed you challenged Logan to allow Jack to hear him. Shows guts."

"Ha!" I said. "It proves my brain cells don't always govern my mouth!"

Dad shook his head, chuckling. "Trust me when I tell you, I haven't witnessed many people talk to the old Indian the way you do. Refreshing."

"You don't think it will come back to bite me in the butt?" I asked.

Dad started to answer and then paused thoughtfully. "The old guy is pretty sneaky sometimes; he may retaliate in some way. But he would never allow harm to come of it, so I wouldn't worry too much."

Easy for him to say. It wasn't his butt on the line. I trusted Logan to save me from certain dangers, but based on last time, there were levels of danger he was more than willing to allow me to experience. Perhaps he thought it built character.

"Dave, what's with the Spanelli family making you guys so interested in them? Anything I should be aware of in case I happen to stumble onto a big secret? It would be nice to know in advance," said Jack.

"Well, I'm not sure how much Logan wants me to divulge. He hasn't exactly given me the go-ahead to fill you in on the details. Let me work on it, and I'll get back to you."

"It would help if all you dead folks would remember while time is nothing to you, it means an awful lot to us in the land of the living," I snapped.

Logan's perspective of time seemed to be more of a long-range one. They live in eternity. Clocks and calendars had very little impact on their existence. We poor slobs still possessing a heartbeat didn't have the luxury of ignoring the movement of the second hand on the clock.

Dad nodded. "I'll keep it in mind; can't promise Logan will bother with it much."

A thought struck me. "I forgot to mention Elaine showed up this morning. Is it significant or merely her habit of being a pain in the butt?"

Dad blew out air. *Can dead people do that stuff? Jeez.*

"Not a good sign. When was the last time you had seen her?" he asked.

Shaking my head, I said, "Not since Owen's case."

"You didn't tell me about Elaine," Jack said. "The woman gives me the creeps."

"My concern is Mom isn't far behind. According to Bob, they are as tight as two bugs in a rug."

Dad's frown deepened, which made my stomach flip. If he didn't like this news, how was I supposed to feel? *Bloody hell, I can't seem to get a break.*

Dad pointed to the letters. "Keep pouring over those; right now, they are our best lead."

I snapped my fingers as a thought managed to fly in my head. "Jack, what about Spanelli's wife? Can't we drive downtown to Children's Hospital and interview her?"

"Not a bad idea. He certainly didn't want us talking with her, did he?"

"Nope," I said and grinned. "And there must be a darn good reason he didn't."

"You two be careful. He may not be involved with the family business, but I wouldn't trust him," Dad warned.

"I agree," stated Jack. "Even though it's rumored he isn't active in the mob, there's definitely something he's hiding."

Jack filled his travel mug with a fresh cup of coffee, saying, "Let's get moving before Spanelli thinks to warn his wife we are interested in talking with her."

I nodded. Turning to Dad, I asked, "You coming?"

He shook his head. "I'm thinking of doing a little snooping on my side. It would be nice to know what your mom is up to."

I turned to join Jack at the door but paused as Dad said, "Peg, be careful. Your mother's friends are a bad bunch. And don't ignore the letters."

I nodded. Dad's warning made my stomach jump. This could be a mess if I wasn't extra careful. The question remained, *How do I accomplish the careful part if I don't have all the facts?* It had been beginner's luck last time, but I wasn't confident the luck would hold.

It was a quiet drive downtown to Children's Hospital. They had been working on the streets in front of and, just to cause extra problems, the streets behind the hospital. It was a nightmare maneuvering our way to the parking deck. Glad I wasn't driving. Jack made good time dodging the workmen, and we found a parking spot near the door to the bridge leading into the hospital.

We stopped at the information desk and asked for Caterina's room number. While the volunteer lady checked her computer, I glanced around the main floor. When my kids were little, the place had been in sore need of an overhaul. It had looked like a scene from an old movie—very sterile, very business like, and not kid friendly.

Now, the place had the feel of a children's book—bright colors everywhere, comfy seats scattered around, and the nurses wore brightly colored uniforms. Gone was the starched white nurses' garb, replaced with warmer, friendlier clothing. I nodded my approval.

"I'm sorry, sir, it is restricted information," she informed us.

Jack hauled out his police badge and asked for her supervisor. His professional attitude must have struck a chord, because she scuttled off to find someone higher on the food chain of authority. I didn't blame her one bit—no sense getting in the middle of a potential battle of law enforcement versus patients security. A few seconds later, a well-dressed woman emerged from the once-closed door behind the information center.

"Yes? How may I help you?" she asked.

Jack held out his hand, saying, "I'm the chief of police from Bath Township. We are investigating the hit-and-run that put Caterina Spanelli here. I need to speak with her mother and was told she was by her daughter's bedside."

She automatically reacted to Jack's outstretched hand, and while they were shaking, she sighed. "Is this official?" she asked.

"Yes, ma'am, it is."

Nodding, she said, "Please follow me." Turning, she headed for her office.

We exchanged glances and trailed behind her. Once inside, she closed the door and stepped around a couple of chairs to sit behind her desk. Gesturing at the padded chairs, she said, "Please make yourselves comfortable."

Jack frowned, but we sat. "I don't need a meeting, just a room number."

"Yes, I understand. We were informed by the Spanelli family absolutely no one, other than hospital personnel, were to enter the room," she said.

Jack took a deep breath, and I knew he was ready to explode. The woman held up her hand; apparently, she recognized the look on Jack's face from years of experience.

"I have every intention of disclosing the room number. I brought you in here to explain a few things."

Jack sat back in his chair, willing to hear her out. I made myself comfortable and noticed the chair wasn't as nice as the one in Jack's office.

"There is a private security man, hired by the family, sitting outside Caterina's door. I'm not sure if he is armed, but hospital policy forbids firearms on hospital property." She winced. "We've had problems in the past."

Jack nodded but didn't utter a word. Everyone in the Akron area remembered the *problem*. A man had entered the hospital in the wee hours, shooting two doctors and a nurse. His son had died of cancer, and he blamed everyone involved in the boy's case. The doctors had survived the attack, but the nurse had died. It had been a horrible tragedy, which stunned the city.

"Mrs. Spanelli's whereabouts at this time are unknown to us. We have strict rules concerning the ICU but were encouraged to bend them for this family." She paused. "To be honest, *encouraged* is the wrong word. *Ordered* is closer to the truth."

Jack nodded again, but this time he said, "The mayor?"

Her eyes widened. "Yes. You, too?"

Jack grinned. "Yep."

She leaned back in her chair. "I didn't introduce myself. Rebecca Dean."

Jack smiled. "Jack Monroe." He turned to me, "This is Peg Shaw."

I nodded, smiling.

"I'm not sure exactly how to proceed and honor the families' wishes."

Jack shook his head. "I don't need inside the room. I'm here to talk with the mother. If you could provide somewhere private, I would appreciate your help."

She nodded thoughtfully. "There is a doctor's conference room on the floor. If it isn't being used, you could talk with Mrs. Spanelli there if she is here."

"Sounds perfect," Jack answered.

"I need to warn you, this family is not easy to work with," Ms. Dean said.

"I've already talked with Mr. Spanelli. While he wasn't entirely forthcoming, he is working with us," Jack told her.

She shook her head. "It's not who I'm referring to." She sighed.

Jack frowned. "He's the girl's father."

"He isn't the one who's running the show. Mr. Spanelli from Youngstown is calling the shots," she said.

"Oh, hells bells," said Jack. "I didn't know."

"What does the guy have to do with the accident?" I asked. "Why is he allowed to butt in?"

Ms. Dean shrugged. "I do what I'm told. Mr. Spanelli knows Mayor Hayes, and when his call came in, the directors here were jumping through hoops."

"So the mayor is up to his old tricks!" I snapped. Turning to Jack, I said, "I told you I didn't trust the jackass!"

Ms. Dean grinned. "At least we understand one another."

"I'll talk with the mother, then figure out my next move," Jack told her.

"Bloody hell! I think a visit to town hall is in order!" I snapped.

"Peg, simmer down," Jack advised.

"Nope." Turning to Ms. Dean, I asked, "How far are we from his office?"

She thought a second and then said, "About six blocks."

I looked down at my loafers, wondering what my feet would feel like after a six-block trek. Figuring I would survive it, I said, "Jack, you talk to the mom. I'm off to see a mayor." I stood up, and marched out of the office.

# Chapter 4

I had no idea how long a city block was, but it was longer than I expected. By the second block, my feet were screaming at me. To add insult to injury, I felt a hot flash starting up. Good thing we were in early summer; if this had been July, I'd have wilted.

Finally arriving at city hall, I stomped up the gazillon steps and marched into the mayor's office. The same snooty secretary I met a couple of months ago during the last investigation maintained her silent guard.

I wiped the sweat from my brow and said, "I need to see the mayor."

She glanced up from her paperwork, frowning. "Do you have an appointment?"

Same question as last time.

"Nope. Tell him Mrs. Shaw is here," I snapped.

She obviously remembered me from the previous visit to His Honor and picked up her phone. Nodding at the voice on the other end, she hung up. "Come this way." Been here, done that.

I sashayed through the door and walked across the carpet, noticing it was new. Figures. People were being taxed to death, and his office had new carpet.

"Mrs. Shaw. How nice to see you again," he said, rising from his overstuffed chair, hand outstretched.

I ignored his hand and leaned against his desk. "What have you dragged me into this time?"

He looked surprised. "What do you mean?"

I plopped down in the chair in front of his desk, dropping my purse on the floor. I noticed his hair had gotten whiter and his waist thicker since the last time I saw him. "My understanding is you asked for me to be involved in a girl's accident."

He nodded. "Yes. I thought your special talents would come in handy. Is it a problem?"

I narrowed my eyes. "Why did 'my special talents' need to be involve in a hit-and-run?"

He sat back in his chair. "Mr. Spanelli has a strong belief in the spiritual realm. I assumed he would feel more comfortable working with you."

"It was supposed to remain a secret!" I snapped.

"Yes, yes. But,…" he paused, "Look, Mrs. Shaw, I already knew about his interest in the spirit realm. I didn't mean to mention your abilities, but it came up in conversation."

I glared at him, deciding how to cause the most bodily harm to the idiot without causing any trouble for myself. Finally forced to admit it wasn't going to happen, I continued with my rant.

"What about the guard at the girl's hospital room?" I demanded. "Certainly smells fishy to me!"

The mayor frowned. "Who's guarding the room?"

I hated to admit it, but he appeared completely confused. Certainly, he couldn't be so dense. Or could he?

I studied his face a moment longer. I reminded myself that a politician, much like an actor, needed to convince people of his sincerity. I decided if he was fooling me, he deserved an Academy Award.

"So you had no idea Mr. Spanelli from Youngstown put a guard on the girl's hospital room?"

"Youngstown?" he asked, growing pale. "Are you shitting me?"

Well, well, well. The skunk was outstunk; would wonders never cease.

"You really didn't know?" I asked suspiciously. I needed to be absolutely certain he was telling me the truth.

He shook his head, turning his swivel chair so he faced the window. His view was High Street on one side and Bowery Street on the other. His corner office allowed him to view either, but I realized he wasn't focusing on much of anything. I gave him time to gather his thoughts; I figured those suckers were scattered to the four winds with news the Youngstown mob was involved. Mayor Hayes had an obsessive desire to control his public persona; he wanted to hang onto his job. If the voters had proof he had questionable connections, it could make the next election dicey. No matter how much they liked their candidate, most folks didn't like to be taken as fools, or worse, gullible.

Swinging around to face me, he shook his head. "I swear I had no idea. Let me make a few calls." He reached for his phone, but I got there first.

My hand firmly holding the mayor's phone, I shook my head. I could see on his face he actually considered wrestling me for it. "Don't." I shook my head again. "Think this through." I used my free arm to indicate his office. "You managed to stay here all these years. How? It shocks me, to be honest. But you've kept this job by not being too stupid. This is the mob we're dealing with here. The real mob, not some second banana group. Serious people, with serious connections."

He held my eyes, hand still perched to grab the phone, for a few seconds more. Finally, he sat back in his chair. "How much do you know?" he asked.

"About what? The rumors flying around about your friends? The fact without turning a hair a few months back, the only thing I had to do was ask for protection and within hours I had armed guards at my house. I may not *know* anything that would stand up in a court of law, but I do know in my gut you play with iffy people. I know you're damned careful the public never has any facts or faces to go along with rumors. What I don't know is how deep in the mud your neck is or how blind of an eye you turn when it suits you." I sat back, chest heaving. I was mad, mad his stupidity could get my butt in a sling, *yet again.*

He held a hand up. "Okay, Mrs. Shaw. Calm down. You have a right to be upset. But I swear, Anthony is not involved with the family anymore."

"You willing to bet your life, political and physical? I don't have to worry about constituents; they're your problem. But I don't relish allowing you to withhold vital information that could place me in another pickle. Do you understand me? You've done it once, and I'm not in a hurry to play the game again."

Gotta hand it to the old boy, he allowed me my say and took it well.

"I hear you loud and clear. Believe me, I sent you over to Anthony's because I honestly thought you could help. He has been receiving threatening letters. I would hate to think they'd hurt little Caterina to get to him."

I nodded. "Yep, we know about the letters. I also know your friend is hiding something; just can't figure out exactly what it is. But the fact doesn't make me feel warm and cozy."

Hayes frowned. "Hiding something? Like what?"

"How should I know? But Jack agrees with me. Anthony has something up his sleeve other than his arm. The fact the head of 'family' called the hospital making demands tells me the idiot still has some contact."

He continued to stare at me, which was a little creepy. Finally, he sighed, saying, "I'll talk to Anthony. I'm positive he is out of the family business, but he may know something that would help you. Maybe his father was worried about Caterina. I would understand his feelings."

Nodding, I said, "If this was a normal situation, a grandfather intervening on behalf of his granddaughter wouldn't bother me. Problem is, this isn't what I consider normal. These people are still dangerous when pushed, and I don't want to be in the crosshairs if they piss off the wrong associates."

He reached for the phone and then pulled back his hand. "I need to be careful how I broach the subject with Anthony. I wouldn't want him to have the impression my trust in him has faltered."

I snorted. "Really? *That's* what you're worried about? Not hurting his feelings? Lord, save me from morons!"

His face turned a light pink, heading towards the red range. I must have hit a nerve with my statement. No surprise there.

"I don't appreciate your attitude," he huffed.

"Tough beans," I snapped. "Experience has taught me you don't always have great judgment."

He glanced down at his desk, his neck becoming splotchy red. Serves him right. What an idiot.

The silence in the office was deafening, but I was determined not to give him any wiggle room. Let him squirm. He finally looked back at me.

"I never meant for you to end up in so much danger. I was protecting Alex," he said.

"It's debatable, but let's stick to the problem with Spanelli. Whatever he's hiding may be a problem for both of us. You must realize your association with an ex-mobster would make headlines. You'd be in a pickle, and you know it."

Nodding, he said, "Yes, I understand your concern. Give me a few days to think about the best way to deal with him. His father's involvement is a problem."

I opened my mouth to respond, when I noticed Bob standing in the corner by the window. Frowning, I raised a questioning eyebrow, not wanting the mayor to realize we had a visitor.

"I need to talk to you," he whispered. Why he was being so quiet was a mystery. Mayor Hayes couldn't hear him, but it was how Bob thought.

Barely nodding, I stood. "Thanks for your time. Don't take too long. Remember, the longer we don't have correct information, the higher the chances are I'll stumble across something, or someone, I shouldn't."

Rising from his chair, he came around the desk. As he walked me to the door, he said, "I appreciate your coming down to check in with me. I'd rather not have these types of conversations on the phone."

"I bet," I answered.

With the door closing behind me, I turned to see Bob trailing after me. I shook my head, refusing to be seen talking to air. He learned from our last adventure I wasn't thrilled being observed having full-blown arguments with invisible beings. It wasn't fun knowing people thought you were delusional.

Once safely walking back towards Children's Hospital, hoping Jack hadn't forgotten me, I said out of the corner of my mouth, "You talk, I'll listen."

"Cool. Okay, here's the deal. Logan gave me permission to tell you some stuff."

"Oh, yay," I said, knowing his mind wouldn't register the sarcasm.

"Yep, thought you'd like it." I was right; he was clueless.

"Go on," I said, still cautious so no one would notice I was speaking to air.

"Well, Anthony Spanelli probably isn't as squeaky clean as you might think," he announced triumphantly.

I sighed. This wasn't news to me, but Bob was so thrilled to be including me on the information road from eternity.

"Not only that, but his dad has always been a real stinker. A bit crooked, if you get my meaning," he said.

I nodded, wondering if Logan had allowed Bob to give me worthless information on purpose, knowing it would make him feel important. Wouldn't surprise me. He understood Bob better than most people did. *Probably trying to build up his self-esteem*, I decided. It couldn't hurt and would, no doubt, help him. Bob wasn't necessarily easy to work with, but he wasn't complicated.

"You'll never guess what else! They are in the Mafia!" he announced with a great deal of glee.

*Jeez Louise. Thanks for nothing, Logan.*

"I thought you knew," I said, trying to remember if Bob had been with me during conversations with Jack.

"Well, I did suspect," he conceded. "I've found tons of proof!"

"Such as?"

"Spanelli has been the head of the family mob for decade. He runs a tight ship and does deals with everyone important."

According to Logan, they've had proof for centuries. I wouldn't let Bob know this bit of information. Better he continued to enjoy my assumed ignorance. I'd go along with Logan's morale-boosting for Bob's sake.

Listening to Bob had taken my mind off the six-block walk, and before I knew it, we were standing back at the hospital. I saw Jack waiting in the foyer and was relieved he had remembered I had driven in with him. It would have sucked to have to call a taxi, or worse, haul Andy away from work to get my butt home.

Walking up to him, I said, "Bob's here. He was given permission to share certain knowledge with us."

I stared directly into Jack's eyes, 'the go-along-with-this stare, hoping he would realize I was sending him a message. I hoped his parenting skills were still intact enough to receive those silent memos only parents recognize.

He must still be up-to-date on his skill level because his eyes began to twinkle. Even though he couldn't see Bob, he was aware of the personality I was dealing with. He nodded.

"Okay. Such as?" he asked.

"Oh, the fact we are now dealing with the Mafia," I said, quietly.

Jack raised his eyebrow and did a decent imitation of looking stunned. It wouldn't have fooled me, but Bob is another story.

"See, even the chief is surprised!" Bob declared.

I sighed. What could I do with this guy's enthusiasm?

Shaking my head, I said, "Also, Anthony's father is bad news."

Jack nodded and remained silent. I was positive he didn't trust himself to speak for fear of laughing.

"It's as far as we got." Turning slightly towards Bob, I asked, "Anything more I need to know?"

He frowned in thought. Finally, he said, "No, I think it's about all. But I'm sure as we proceed with the investigation, Logan will allow more information to be released."

Nodding, I said, "Okay. Anything else?"

Bob stood up straighter, "Not right now. I should get going. Logan has me running all over the place." He faded so quickly I didn't have a chance to tell him bye. *Works for me.*

Shaking my head, I turned to Jack. "He's gone."

Jack burst out laughing. "I didn't think I'd make it, but ya gotta give the poor guy a break. What's Logan up to sending him to tell us info he knows we have already?"

"I think he is building Bob's self-image. Living with Elaine for so long created some serious personality issues."

Jack shook his head, smiling. "He isn't a bad fella."

"Nope. Just irritating. How'd the meeting with Mrs. Spanelli go?"

"It didn't. She was napping. I told the guard we would be back later. I'm starving right now, though. Let's find some place to eat. You can share your visit with the mayor over lunch."

Sounded like a decent plan to me. Stepping outside, we glanced around.

"You know, Harlan's is right around the corner, I think. We can hoof it if you think your feet can manage." Jack grinned, looking down at my loafers.

At the mention of Harlan's, my mouth immediately watered. "I'd walk on glass for a chance to eat there."

Laughing, we started off. It was a warm day, not too hot, with a slight breeze. Dodging around the workers who were jackhammering the street, we walked the block in companionable silence. I love the smells of early summer—flowers blooming, fresh leaves on the trees. Too bad all I could smell was asphalt and sweaty guys.

The line at Harlan's was pretty reasonable, and as we waited, I said, "Wish Lou and Hy's was still around."

"God, yes! The place was fantastic," said Jack.

Lou and Hy's was a staple around Akron for decades. It was the best deli outside of New York City. Their sandwiches were so huge you couldn't move after gorging on one. But you had to find a spot in your belly for a slice of homemade cheesecake. Those suckers greeted you at the front as you entered the door. Barely able to pass by without ordering one on the spot, you would be ushered to a table with fresh, homemade pickles on it. It was a great eatery, but once Lou and Hy themselves were gone, the family had no interest in continuing the business. A chain pharmacy lived on the spot now, which broke my heart.

Once it was our turn to order, we did so, paid, and found a table near the window. We could enjoy the sight of concrete being jackhammered and cars carefully maneuvering around the mess. Great.

"Okay," said Jack, taking a sip of his iced tea. "How'd it go with the mayor?"

I shrugged. "Not sure I trust him much, but he seemed shocked the old man from Youngstown was involved. I also said Anthony was hiding something. I don't like surprises, and to be honest, I don't think the mayor was too thrilled to hear about a potential vote killer either. He has to be careful with the likes of the Spanellis; he's well aware it could be political death for him." I looked around, wondering what was taking so long for our sandwiches. I was starving—must be all the hiking around the city.

"What's the deal with the wife? You think she is dodging us?" I asked.

Jack shook his head. "Nope, but I can easily believe the guard is doing his duty and screening anyone requesting time with her."

I frowned. "Why? It doesn't make sense."

"Sure it does, especially a cop wanting to talk with her. They have no idea why I'm there. Probably wouldn't believe us if I had bothered to explain, which I didn't." He joined me in glancing at the counter, waiting for our number to be called. He must have been as hungry as I was; we'd had a busy day and it was only noon.

I had opened my mouth to complain when our number was called. Thank goodness. I stayed at the table while Jack grabbed our food. No way I was chancing leaving the table empty in this crowd; we would lose it for sure.

When Jack set the sandwich in front of me, I expelled a sigh of total contentment. The aroma of corned beef, sauerkraut and toasted rye bread was heavenly. The first bite is always the best; Ruebens were my favorite, and it was worth the wait. We had silently agreed not to ruin lunch with conversation and happily watched the traffic out the window while eating. Taking the last bite of pickle, I sat back, satisfied. Even my aching feet couldn't ruin my happiness.

Jack finished his sandwich and sat back, rubbing his ever-growing belly. "So much for the diet I started last week. But, hell, I'm not downtown very often; I couldn't resist the temptation!" He laughed.

Grinning, I said, "Yep. Once you mentioned this place, I was sunk."

"Okay, back to work. Let's see if Anthony's wife is *awake* yet," he said, rising from his chair.

"Wish they had cheesecake here," I sighed.

He raised an eyebrow. "The last thing I need."

I laughed. "Same here; let's go."

We didn't bother trying to have a conversation; the jackhammers made it impossible. Once inside the hospital, Jack grabbed my arm. "Let me do the talking. I don't want that temper of yours getting us killed in front of kids."

I grinned, shrugging my shoulders. "I can't help it if morons irritate me."

Jack shook his head, and we headed for the elevators. Pushing the button for the ICU floor, we braced ourselves for a possible confrontation. Jack obviously had more experience than I did dealing with people in these circumstances, so I decided his idea of keeping my mouth shut was the best way to handle the guard.

Off the elevator, I noticed how quiet the floor was and felt sorry for the families so emotionally spent as they watched their children fight for their lives. I sent up a quick prayer of thanks we never spent one second in a similar situation with our boys. I had no idea where the prayer actually went, since my previous ideas of heaven had been blown to smithereens.

We turned the corner, heading to Caterina's room when we became aware of a hushed argument in front of the girl's door. Uh-oh, this couldn't be good. Jack and I exchanged glances, and he reached inside his lightweight jacket. It was the first time I realized Jack was probably armed, and I felt shivers run down my spine. Jeez.

Jack reached for the badge that lived on his belt and flashed it at one of the nurses who was obviously trying to diffuse the situation. She looked frazzled, and seeing Jack's badge, she relaxed. "You can explain it to this police officer," she said to the man standing in front of her.

He turned around and I was stunned to find my old guard, Santino, was the man in question. He was equally as surprised and none too happy to find me involved in the situation.

"Hey, Santino, what's up?" I asked.

He was a big guy with dark hair and eyes, and his capacity to protect was apparent. I liked the guy, but that he was here wasn't necessarily a good thing.

He shook his head, annoyed, but smiled slightly. "Hi, Mrs. Shaw. Glad you survived our last meeting." He gave me a onceover. "Looks like you recovered in good shape."

I nodded, "Thank you. I'm fine. Don't want to relive the close call anytime soon, though." I was in no mood to rehash my near-death experience. "What's going on here?" I asked, pointing to the door.

He looked pained at my question. I was pretty sure he liked me too, so not disclosing the reason for his presence was making him uncomfortable. He looked over at the nurse and shook his head. Santino was not about to divulge sensitive information in front of an outsider.

Jack took the hint and informed the nurse we would take responsibility for the situation. Too bad we had no idea what the heck was going on. She didn't appear too thrilled but she nodded and stalked away from us.

I watched her turn the corner and then turned back to Santino. "Okay, what's the deal?" I asked. I had no time for the niceties of polite conversation.

Grimacing, he shook his head. "It's a wreck, let me tell you."

I didn't necessarily relish being dragged into another mess, but I pressed on for the scoop.

"The old man," he started and then stopped. "You know who I'm talking about?" he asked.

I nodded, sighing.

"Okay, the old man is furious Caterina has been hurt. He's been warning his idiot son for years about the possibility of an attempt on the girl's life." He shrugged, noticing my surprise. "Comes with the territory."

I was shifting on my feet; my earlier walk had done them in totally. Santino, noticing my discomfort, turned, grabbed his chair, and offered it to me. He must have remembered those homemade cookies I served them. It pays to have manners, as Nana always told me.

I gratefully sat, pulling my loafers off and giving my feet a break. Jack watched in amusement. It's not every day a mobster offers a chair and spills the beans at the same time.

"Don't tell Anthony I said anything. He would be furious," Santino warned.

"I don't want you to get into trouble," I said, concerned for my one-time bodyguard.

Jack shook his head, disgusted by my caring. I ignored him completely.

Santino grinned. "I'm not going anywhere. The old man is my uncle; I'm his favorite nephew."

I met his grin and nodded. "Okay, makes me feel better. So your uncle has been worried about the girl for a long time. Which explains why you're here."

Jack had been quiet so far but had questions of his own. "Why did your uncle believe the girl was in danger years ago?"

Santino shrugged. "In our business, family members are always at risk." He sighed. "Especially now with the younger group's arrogance. They don't understand traditions; hell, they don't respect them. It makes for wild decisions which have bad consequences."

I nodded, realizing for the first time that while I didn't agree with Mafia traditions, they had been doing business the same way for generations. It made them predictable, and everyone played by the same set of rules. It was changing and not necessarily for the good.

Jack pressed for more answers. "Why doesn't Anthony take the threats seriously?"

"Oh, he does. But that mother of his was looney. She convinced him her husband was making too much of the old feud."

"Old feud?" I asked.

Santino nodded. "You remember the Godfather movies?"

"Yep," I said. "I love James Caan."

"They weren't too far off the mark. The families have been around for centuries; it's a long story. But the short version is they have grudges. I personally don't hold a grudge, but the families have been good at it for centuries." He shrugged. "It's a way of life. You get used to it."

I felt my shoulders slump. What a lousy way to live.

"Do you feel the girl is still in danger?" Jack asked.

"Oh, yeah, absolutely. It's why she is being guarded," answered Santino. "She's a sweet kid, and we have to watch her carefully. One of the reasons Anthony was moved here was to protect her."

Wow! We were actually nudging information from a usually cautious man. But I felt Santino was holding back information; I decided not to push the matter right then.

"So he's still active in the family business?" I asked, hoping to sound innocent.

Nodding, Santino said, "Yep. Does all the accounting." Noticing Jack's expression, he put his hands up, saying, "All legal. He's a great accountant and has my investment portfolio very healthy."

He grinned at me. "Mrs. Shaw, he could get you and your husband set for life if you listen to his advice."

"I'll run it by Andy and let you know," I said, with a quick glance at Jack. He was fuming by this point, and I knew it wouldn't help his mood at all to hire Anthony as our accountant. I inwardly grinned, remembering a few minutes ago Jack had been worried about my temper. He looked as though an artery was about to blow.

"I have a few questions for Mrs. Spanelli. Is she awake yet?" Jack asked, teeth gritted and eyes narrowed.

Santino looked surprised. "Mrs Spanelli? She isn't here. They split up years ago. Who told you she was here?"

I watched the veins in Jack's neck begin to bulge. Throbbing soon followed. His face was so red, I figured his head would explode in a few seconds. He was speechless, but then, so was I.

# Chapter 5

I quickly took over to allow Jack time to simmer down. The last thing I needed was for him to have a heart attack, even if we were in a hospital.

"Jack was told earlier she was napping! Sure as hell sounds like she was here, to me!" I could feel the ice on the words as they left my mouth. Too bad. I liked Santino, but I wasn't putting up with lies from anyone this time around.

Santino frowned. "Antonio was here this morning, before him was Bill." He turned to Jack, "Did you speak with Antonio?"

Jack didn't trust himself to talk, so he shook his head. Since Jack knew Antonio from our last adventure, I was positive he would have shared that tidbit with me, had he actually talked with Antonio.

These guys were professionals; no way would they have slouched concerning the boss's granddaughter. I asked Santino, "Did you relieve Antonio himself or someone else."

Santino answered, "Antonio got called back to the office an hour before I showed up." He shrugged. "Happens all the time." He studied my face before asking, "You think there's something fishy here, don't you?"

I glanced at my well-worn watch the boys had given me one Christmas. They had been so proud of their selection. Andy swore he didn't aid in their choice, but I had my doubts. Adam was only about twelve at the time, so I know Andy must have forked over the cash for it, but no one owned up to the obvious. It warmed my heart every time I strapped it to my wrist.

"Jack, we've been gone a little over an hour. Santino has been here…" I glanced at him. "What? Half an hour?"

He nodded. "Yeah, about thirty minutes."

Jack's color was slowly returning to normal, and his bulging neck artery had calmed down. "It wasn't Antonio who was here. Some guy named Marco."

Santino nodded. "Yep, he had relieved Antonio but hadn't been here long."

I sat there, thinking through the time line. A nasty thought jumped into my head. "Sweetie, how well you do you know this Marco fella?"

Frowning, he thought a few seconds before saying, "He's been with us about a year. He came highly recommended." Shrugging, he said, "Seems like a decent guy."

Decent? They were in the mob, for Pete's sake. I almost laughed at the insanity of his statement.

My phone began singing at the bottom of my purse. Santino laughed as he heard the ring tone; the theme to Star Wars was happily announcing a call from Andy. Bryan, our second son, had changed everything on my phone the last time he was in town. Each family member had a specific ring tone now. Star Wars was one of Andy's favorite movies, so our son had chosen the theme song to be the ring for him. It drove me batty, but I had no idea how to change it back to normal.

Digging through the junk, I answered. "Hey, babe, what's up?"

"A quick check before I head into this meeting. You okay?" he asked. Since I was almost toast a few months back, Andy had developed the habit of checking in every once in a while. I appreciated his concern.

"Yep. Jack and I are down at Children's hunting clues for the case."

After a few moments of silence, Andy said, "Things working out?"

I smiled, "Yeah, it's fine." I noticed Santino signaling and looked up as he mouthed, 'Say hi for me.'

"Oh, and Santino says hi."

This too was met with silence. "You're with Santino?" I could hear a little strain in his voice.

"Yep. He's helping guard the girl." I said. "I'll tell him you said 'hi' back."

I heard a sigh on the other end. "Yeah, okay." A short pause before he said, "Peg, please be careful."

"No problem. Later, gator," I told him.

Another sigh. "Okay, I know you're busy. Call me later."

"Yep," I said, hitting the End button. I was with Jack, so what could happen?

Dropping the phone back into the cavern, I looked up at Santino. "How decent are we talking?"

"You really think he lied to Chief Monroe?" he asked, surprised. Shaking his head, he continued, "I don't think it's likely."

"Well, he sure as hell told me she was napping!" snapped Jack.

His face was beginning to darken again, so I said, "Santino, could someone else be guarding Caterina?"

Shaking his head and digging in his back pocket, he said, "We have to keep a log of events. We pass the notebook off, each shift." He was rifling through the pages. Pointing a finger on the correct page, he said, "See, Marco came on duty at ten this morning, relieving Antonio. No mention of any other person. It would have been in the log." He flipped the notebook closed.

Jack's mouth fell open, and I shook my head in wonder. How could a mobster not think someone could fiddle with the log?

"You trust the log book completely?" I asked, trying to be nice.

Nodding, Santino said, "The consequences of keeping a sloppy log aren't worth it."

I shuddered to think what those consequences entailed. I sat quietly, thinking how to break it to the guy someone probably *had* been a bit sloppy— sloppy enough to omit anything which would point to a problem.

Santino frowned, opened the little black book again, and checked through the pages. "What time did you say you were here earlier?" he asked Jack.

"About an hour and a half ago," Jack answered, teeth gritted.

"Odd," said Santino. "Should have been logged." His frown increased as he pulled out his phone. After a quick discussion with someone higher up the food chain, he shook his head. "We have a problem."

"No shit, Sherlock," Jack snapped.

"Have you actually checked on Caterina?" I asked, suddenly alarmed.

Santino's face paled. "Son of a bitch. Not part of the protocol." He turned, pushing the heavy door to the room open. Sagging in relief, he turned and whispered, "Still there. All the machines seem to be making the correct noises."

I got up from the chair and poked my head in the doorway. She looked peaceful as she rested.

A voice from behind me demanded, "What do you think you're doing?"

I turned to face the nurse we had witnessed earlier arguing with Santino. "Just checking," I said with a smile. My polite manner had no effect on her attitude.

"You aren't family! This is ICU," she snapped.

Jack's temper, already riled, was close to blowing. He grabbed his badge, shoving it near her nose. "I'm investigating this child's accident. If you don't like it, talk to your supervisor!"

She held her ground. "I am the supervisor!"

Jack didn't back down one bit. "You may oversee this floor to a degree, but you sure as hell don't control my police duties. Talk to the administrators; then come back. Right now, leave us alone unless you are performing your nursing duties."

She narrowed her eyes but turned and stomped away. Jeez Louise. Turf wars can be nasty.

Santino had wisely remained quiet through the confrontation, but broke into a wide grin. "Wow, Chief, I'm impressed. She's been a bitch since we arrived."

Jack turned to him, saying, "I wasn't trying to help you. I need the truth, and she can't help in that arena."

Santino's grin remained, but he held up his hands in surrender. "Okay, okay."

When the nurse had shown up, Santino had wisely allowed the door to the room to swing shut. We continued to talk quietly, not wanting to disturb Caterina in any way. She may be in a coma, but I didn't want to take a chance our conversation could complicate her condition.

Jack jerked his head at Santino's phone. "What did you find out?"

Santino studied Jack a moment, sizing up the situation. Making a quick decision, he said, "Marco didn't return to the office. It's protocol. Not following orders is a serious infraction. Remember," he said, turning to me, "we have all had military training. Follow the rules, take orders, and do the job. It's the way we operate."

"Personnel problems are your headache, not mine," said Jack. "What I want to know is why did Spanelli tell me his wife was here at the hospital?"

"How long have they been separated?" I asked.

Santino thought a moment and then said, "I've only met her once or twice, and I've been with the organization over five years."

"But you're family!" I protested.

Shrugging, Santino said, "It's complicated. I work for the organization but try to stay out of family problems."

*Organization.* What a polite word for the mobster family. It was not necessarily the term I would have used to describe them, but that was me. I was sure Jack would agree.

Jack's mouth fell open. "Over five years they've been separated?" He turned to me. "Spanelli failed to mention that nugget."

I pursed my lips. "I knew the creep was hiding something!"

I felt the air change and looked around quickly.

"Hey, Peg," said Bob. "Everything okay here?"

I nodded slightly. I tried giving Bob an annoyed stare; he knew better than to appear when I was with people outside the circle of those who knew about my new abilities.

Turning, he spotted Santino. "Hey, San! Good to see you again!"

I felt blood rush to my head. You could have heard a pin drop; the silence so thick you could slice it twenty ways.

Santino blushed, finally saying, "Hey, Bob."

"Bob's here?" demanded Jack. Pointing a finger at Santino, he said, "And that guy can see him?" Jack was fuming and I knew exactly why. Here was a gangster who had access to Bob's visits, and Jack, chief of police, didn't.

I turned to Santino. "You can see and hear Bob?" Shock waves still racing through my body, I turned back to Bob. "You never told me!"

Bob shrugged. "Wasn't allowed. Orders."

"Bob!" said Santino. "Shut the hell up!"

Watching this exchange, a light bulb went off in my head. I leaned closer to Santino, whispering, "You aren't a goon, are you?"

He stared down at me but remained silent.

"Nope!" declared Bob with glee. "Isn't it cool?"

"What the hell is happening?" demanded Jack. I waved a hand at him, "Shh," I said.

Santino closed his eyes in frustration. "Bob! You need to leave!"

Instantly, Bob disappeared.

Narrowing my eyes, I said, "Since when?"

He shook his head. "I'm not saying another word about Bob, other than I'm going to wring his damn neck!"

Jack's head swiveled back and forth, trying to make sense of our conversation. With Santino's last statement, he burst out laughing, obviously having connected the dots.

"Whew, boy! This just keeps getting better and better," he said, wiping the tears of laughter from his eyes.

I pulled us away from the doorway so we wouldn't disturb Caterina or bring the wrath of the nurse upon us.

"You work for the Feds?" I asked.

Shaking his head, he said, "Not saying another word about any of this."

"You alone, or Bill and Antonio your partners?" I figured it wouldn't hurt to keep asking questions; he might break protocol out of sheer irritation at my persistence. It didn't work.

Santino remained resolute in his objective, which was giving me the silent treatment. Ha! I had four teenage boys at one time; I could outdo any silent crap he threw my way.

I turned to Jack, "Well, this puts a different face on the situation." Facing Santino again, I asked, "How long have you been able to see Bob? I take it the other two have some sort of abilities. It's why you have this job, isn't it? Did you already know my connection with Bob when you were my bodyguards a few months back?" I could keep this up forever, and Santino finally realized the fact.

Sighing, he said, "Look, Mrs. Shaw, I really can't share any info with you. I will get back to you when I inform the boss you are aware of..." He hesitated. "...certain facts."

Jack chimed in, saying, "I know you can't say much. I appreciate your situation, but I will tell you one thing. Knowing you are probably not mob sure makes my blood pressure decrease."

I have to admit, I felt better myself. I didn't feel so guilty about liking the trio from the first time I met them. Okay, maybe not Antonio so much, but I did enjoy Bill and Santino.

Nodding, I said, "San, it does make me more comfortable."

"Yeah, but it's a problem. I'm not explaining anything until I check with higher-ups on the best way to handle Bob's screw up."

"Okay, fair enough. But what *can* you tell us?" I asked.

"I have no idea why Anthony didn't inform you of the separation. He and his wife have been separated for years. I'm not sure what he thinks he gains by keeping it secret. But I will warn you, his mother makes Elaine look like the girl next door."

"Elaine? You know Elaine?" I asked. Why I was surprised is a mystery, but it hadn't occurred to me Santino would know Elaine.

He closed his eyes. "Oh yeah, I know Elaine."

"And my mother?"

He hesitated. "I've said too much already. I'll get back to you with more if I'm allowed. Remember, this is under wraps, so please be discreet." He paused and then said, "The mayor has no idea, so you can't let it slip. Understand?"

Nodding, I said, "We'll keep your secret." A thought hit me, and I asked, "Andy? Can I at least let him know?"

Shaking his head, he said, "Not yet. Let me check with my boss. Please."

Sighing, I agreed.

Jack asked, "Any idea where we can find the wife?"

Santino tiredly exhaled. "Nope. When you find her, let me know."

"Dead?" I asked.

He shrugged, "No damn idea, and we aren't encouraged to poke around trying to find her." He hesitated and then said, "I will get back to you. Now you are aware of, um, things, it may work to our advantage to bring you into the situation further. But, again, I've got to check in with others first."

"Chain of command," said Jack absentmindedly.

"Yep."

Being nosy is part of my personality. Not having answers drives me nuts, which is also a personality glitch.

"Well, hell. We came back here to interview the wife. Since no one knows where on God's green earth she is, our job here is done. We might as well leave you alone and figure out what we need to do next," Jack said.

"At least we had a great lunch!" I said.

Jack grinned. "Yep."

Santino cocked his head, asking, "Where'd you two eat?"

"Harlen's," I said, my mouth watering at the mere mention of the place.

"Oh gosh. They have the best food!" said Santino. "One perk to working downtown is eating there."

"Yep. Not as good as Lou and Hy's but definitely at the top of the list," I said.

"Let's get going," said Jack.

Turning to leave, I said, "Don't forget your promise."

Santino smiled. "Something tells me it won't be possible."

I grinned at him and then joined Jack at the elevator. Waiting for an elevator is possibly one of the most irritating things in the world. While we stood there, Jack turned to me. "Well, we have a new wrinkle to the mix. To be honest, I would never in a million years have seen it coming."

I gave him a quick smile. "Neither would I, but the second I realized he could see Bob, I knew there's a lot to this puzzle we haven't be told. At least I don't have to feel guilty I liked those guys when I first met them."

He laughed. "If I remember correctly, Antonio isn't your favorite person."

"He's a strict rule follower, which is not necessarily a bad thing. He needs to work on his manners." I sighed. "But, to be fair, he did make the kill shot saving my life."

Jack grew red at being reminded he had hesitated and Antonio took the shot.

"I've been at the range twice a week ever since! If we ever find ourselves in a similar position again, I will be able to handle it without any help."

I patted his arm. "Jack, you've been sitting behind a desk for almost a decade. I'm not surprised you felt overwhelmed in the moment. I don't blame you, so stop blaming yourself. I wasn't hurt."

"I was afraid of missing and hitting you," he said.

I sighed. "How many times are we going to have this conversation? It worked out; I'm fine. Owen's not. End of story."

He shook his head stubbornly. "What if Antonio hadn't been there?"

"He was there; drop it!" I was tired of his self-recrimination; he needed to let go of any guilt.

He nodded, knowing by the tone of my voice I was not continuing the conversation. But I knew it wasn't over, and sooner or later, he would mention the mess again. I decided a change of subject was the best course of action.

"So are we going back to see Spanelli?"

He punched the down button again, knowing it wouldn't speed up the elevator; he did it out of frustration. "Nope. I think a little digging into their marriage is in order."

"Want me to call Bob or Dad to help?"

He started to open his mouth to say no but stopped and thought a second. "You know, your Dad would be the best candidate for the job. He may also know something about the mother. Santino mentioned she was a real piece of work."

"Holy cow, I forgot he mentioned her! Just what I need is another dead nut to handle. I hope to high heaven she doesn't bother me."

"I figured that morsel was not good news for you. For once, I'm happy I can't see these people. Well, except I can hear Logan. The guy is a little scary, know what I mean?"

I laughed as the elevator finally arrived, and the doors were creaking themselves open. "Yep, I know exactly how you feel."

Finding ourselves alone on the elevator, I said, "I'd rather meet Dad at my house. You want to be there, or you need to get to the office?"

He shook his head. "No way am I missing a meeting. The office can survive without me for another couple of hours. They can call my cell phone if anything crops up."

Nodding, I said, "Then, home it is."

Chapter 6

Once we maneuvered out of the thick downtown traffic, it was smooth sailing all the way to my house. My car was still at the police station, but I decided Andy and I could grab it later. Talking to Dad was first on the agenda; we needed to know more before we could safely proceed. We had learned last time the lack of knowledge led to big trouble, and I wasn't willing to take a chance if I could guard myself this time around.

"Coffee?" I asked Jack.

"Sure. When can you call your dad? I mean, how does it work?" he asked.

"Not too difficult, usually," I said and yelled, "Dad!"

"That's it?" Jack asked, surprised.

I shrugged. "Works for Bob."

"Hey, Twinkle Toes."

Turning towards the window, I smiled. "Hey, Dad."

"You two have your work cut out for you this time," he said.

I shook my head. "I don't need to hear you say those words."

"What?" asked Jack. "Doesn't sound good. For some reason, I can't hear your Dad. Why? I could hear him at the office."

I waved my hand at him. "Hush…Dad, we found out Spanelli and his wife have been separated for a few years. Did you know this?" I asked. What good were dead people if they didn't know this stuff?

"Sorta. We knew she wasn't living at the house, but we had no idea for how long." He paused before continuing. "Certain events are a bit fuzzy from our side; there are times it's not as clear as you might think."

My shoulders sagged. I shook my head, saying, "Not very reassuring. I need to know you guys have access to this type of info. I don't like the whole fumbling-along-finding-out-information-the-hard-way thing."

Dad nodded. "I understand, but we aren't all-knowing on our side of things." He hesitated. "It's complicated."

"Complicated doesn't begin to describe it!" I snapped. "Doesn't Logan have anything helpful to share?"

Dad grinned. "If he does, he hasn't told me." He cocked an eyebrow and said, "Have you tried Bob for help?"

"Ha! He works for Logan! I think he's enjoying his role as keeper of secrets."

Dad laughed. "Yep, sounds about right."

Jack erupted, "What the hell is going on?"

I turned to face him. "Not much help. Only thing so far is we have a tough road to walk on this one."

He sank back into the chair, shoulders slumped. "Not exactly what I was hoping to hear," he muttered.

I nodded my agreement before I turned back to Dad. "You must know something that will help."

He thought a moment, cautiously admitting, "I can share this much; Mrs. Spanelli may hold the key. Find her, and you discover what's being hidden."

"Oh, for Pete's sake, you sound like Logan!" I snapped.

Grinning, Dad said, "I'll take it as a compliment."

"Well, it certainly wasn't meant to be one!" I growled.

His grin faded as he grew serious. "Sweetie, I'm not sure what is going on here, but for some reason, we all have boundaries concerning certain people. I can't cross them, even for you."

I eyed him for a moment, and then I felt my body sag. "Damnation! We need help." I took a sip of my now-cool coffee and felt my face squish into a frown at the taste. I hauled my butt out of the chair and headed to the microwave. Once my coffee was happily heated back to a decent drinking temperature, I tried again. Much better.

"Do you know where on earth we can find her?" I asked.

Dad's grin returned. "Yep. I sense somewhere here in the township."

The township's original size was six miles by six miles, nice and neat. We had lost some land due to adjoining cities annexing bits and pieces, but most residents didn't notice the loss. The local schools were shared by our neighboring township to the north, Richfield. Even though we are quite small, last census clocked us just under ten thousand people; we liked the place. It was close to shopping, the highway, and culture sites, but we were still considered rural. I was not sure how much longer the status would last, considering they were building so fast I was surprised we hadn't busted at the seams.

"Thanks, Dad. Think you can narrow it down a bit?"

"Narrow what down?" asked Jack.

I threw him a glance, indicting he needed to cool his jets, and waited for Dad to answer.

"Haven't heard, but I am positive she lives here. She won't be in the phone book though; this family is security conscious and only uses cell phones."

Drumming my impatient fingers on the table, I asked, "Are they aware everyone is watching them?"

"Everyone who?" Dad asked, frowning.

"You, Logan, and my previous bodyguards," I answered.

His frown deepened. "What previous bodyguards? You mean the mayor's friends?"

"Yep. They aren't necessarily mob guys."

His eyes grew wide. "You've got to be kidding!"

Eyeing him suspiciously, I asked, "You didn't know?"

He shook his head. "No idea. Wonder if Logan is aware of the fact."

I snorted. "More than likely, since they seem to have a relationship with Bob."

"Bob?" He looked at the floor for a moment, thinking. "Certainly explains a few things over here."

"Such as?" I asked, intrigued by the idea Dad was out of the loop but Bob was included in some type of inner circle.

"How do you know they can see Bob?" he asked, ignoring my own question.

"Easy. Bob came to the hospital while Jack and I were trying to see Mrs. Spanelli, who incidentally was *not* there with her daughter. Bob looked over at Santino and, quite friendly I might add, said hello. What was the poor guy to do other than acknowledge Bob's presence?"

Dad leaned against the wall, deep in his own thoughts. Jack took the opportunity to be demanding. "What the hell is your Dad telling you? Can he help?"

After quickly filling him in on the details, while allowing Dad time to mull things over, I sat back when finished, out of breath. I really needed to exercise and get myself in better shape. If hurrying through a story can take the air out of me, I was in big trouble. I tried making a mental note, but my brain rejected the idea. It knew I wasn't going to follow through, so why waste time storing the information?

I watched Dad as he continued to lean. I still can't figure out how he does it. Let's face it, he doesn't have physical form, so how can he actually prop himself up on a solid object? One of life's mysteries, I guess.

Finally, his eyes met mine. "I'm positive you've managed to discover info no one imagined you could. Bob is an idiot."

I had to laugh. "Tried telling you guys last time. Everyone kept saying he had unrealized potential. Okay, it could be true, but he doesn't always think through situations."

Dad nodded. "He should never have acknowledged Santino. But to be fair, Santino should never have confirmed his existence. I'm betting both will hear from Logan."

"You're going to rat Bob out to Logan?"

Dad shook his head. "No need. Logan seems to always know when these little incidents occur. He's very sensitive regarding matters of security. I wouldn't want to be in their shoes."

I shuddered. Logan had helped me in the past and would probably help now. But the guy was scary as hell and loaded with power.

"What's your Dad think about Bob blowing Santino's cover story?" Jack asked.

"I think he feels sorry for both of them. Logan will deal with the situation."

Jack paled. Logan was the only spirit he could hear, except for Dad and with him, only the conversation in his office. His relationship with Logan was brand new, but he was wary of him. Actually, I think the entire crew of dead people hanging around gave him the creeps. Well, maybe not Bob; he was too goofy.

"Why can't Jack hear you this time?" I asked. Jack's impatience would only grow if we didn't get an answer soon.

Ignoring me again, Dad said, "You two need to find the wife. There are answers only she can provide."

"In what part of Bath should we start the search?" I asked.

He pursed his lips, saying, "Probably the opposite corner from her husband. They've got a huge battle going on between them. I'm surprised she came along for the big move." He shrugged. "Most likely because of the little girl."

"Caterina," I said.

He nodded. "Yeah, that's her name. Have you met the grandmother yet?"

"Nope, and I don't want to meet her—ever," I answered. "Her son seems to think she'll be hell-bent to help."

My comment gained a big nod from Dad. "Oh, yeah. You can bet on it. A little overbearing on the living side of things and not much better over here."

"Uh-oh. Shades of Elaine? I don't need extra bitches to handle. Elaine and Mom are quite enough, thank you," I said.

"Different from Elaine. And definitely a far cry from your mother. Possibly more powerful."

"Great," I said, landing my head onto my hand. "I have enough problems."

"Hang in there, Twinkle Toes. It's going to get interesting." He slowly faded, waving as he left.

Sighing, I turned to Jack. "All clear."

He nodded. "Figures. He didn't supply much help, did he? Any clue why I couldn't hear him?"

"Not enough. Mrs. Spanelli lives in Bath, but either he doesn't know exactly where or he can't say. He thinks she has answers we need." I sat lost in my own thoughts. "Wonder why Dad wouldn't answer your question. It's a little irritating."

Jack looked at the ceiling, thinking. "I'm sure he has his reasons. Bet the wife lives as far away from her husband as possible. Do you have a map of the township?" I was surprised he had placed the wife pretty much where Dad had—opposite side of Bath. Was it a guy thing?

"What makes you so sure?"

Shrugging, he said, "It's what I'd do." Ah, so it was a guy thing.

"Why stay in Bath? I'd move to a different town," I said.

Jack shrugged. "Maybe because of the girl."

"Who has custody?" I asked.

"Good question. Where's your computer?" Jack asked.

Glancing around, I spotted the laptop on the chair next to me. I shook my head, wondering why I had stuck it there; I must have been clearing off the table for dinner. I grabbed it, passing it over to Jack.

Once he had it up and running, he began typing.

"What are you doing?" I asked.

"Looking up court records to see if they have filed for divorce."

I felt my eyes widen. "I didn't know you could find so much on the Internet."

"Everything's on the Internet! It's scary sometimes. Have you ever Googled your own name?" he asked, waiting for files to load on the screen.

"No, why would I?" I asked.

"Try it; you'll have a heart attack. Your address, property owned, criminal record, and almost everything else that's considered public record… We think we protect our privacy, but our lives are online whether we like it or not."

"Jeez. I had no idea," I shook my head.

"Ah, here it is," he pointed to the computer screen. "Okay, let me type in their name."

The screen flipped to a new page. "No entries found."

"What does it mean?" I asked.

"They haven't filed legal documents. So no legal separation or divorce."

"Maybe they have some type of agreement between themselves."

"Or maybe he's blackmailing her over some past indiscretion," Jack said, still staring at the computer screen.

"Your mind flies to the gutter pretty fast," I said.

Shrugging, he said, "Crap happens."

Jack's fingers began flying over the keyboard. His face lit up like a Christmas tree, but glancing down at the screen, I couldn't decide what was so exciting.

"Yes!" he crowed. "I've got her address!"

Peering closer, I said, "How'd you manage?"

"Looked up the property tax records. Figured Spanelli probably owned the house where the wife was living. No doubt part of whatever deal he's made with her."

I looked at him with renewed respect. I doubt I would ever have thought of tax records. "Where does she live?"

He checked the screen for the address. Grinning he said, "Bath Road. I told you it would be across the township from the husband."

I sighed. "Bath Road is too confusing. It could be the section close to his street." Bath Road ran the width of the township. Some of the twists and turns were enough to make your stomach protest, not to mention how confusing the road was. It didn't straighten out until you were on the west side of the highway. Once there, it was a straight shot to the next county.

Writing down the address, Jack said, "Nope. On the east end, near the Falls." The Falls was shorthand for Cuyahoga Falls, the next big city east of the township. There was a fantastic bakery right off State Road over there, which I could never seem to bypass when I was in the area. I gain five pounds just walking in their door.

"Let's go and get this over with," Jack said, heading for the front door.

"Wait a sec," I said, frowning. "Shouldn't we call and see if she's home?"

"No way should we warn her!" he said. Glancing at his watch, he said, "The sooner we get moving, the better chance you'll have of being here when Andy gets home."

I shot a look at the clock and was stunned to see the time. The day was zooming, and I hadn't even figured out dinner yet.

Grabbing my purse, I said, "You've got a good point."

She lived on the winding section, and I was relieved when we finally found her address. My stomach couldn't have taken many more curves the way Jack drove.

We sat in front of the house, surprised by the quaintness of the place—not at all what I had expected. It was a century home, stained red with cream trim. The garage was tucked away in the back, accessible, yet hidden from easy view. It had obviously been kept up through the years, updated along the way by someone determined to keep the original architecture intact. No contemporary additions to ruin the charm of the property.

"Kinda small compared to her husband's place," Jack observed.

"No kidding," I said, staring at the charming house. I admired the garden, which obviously was not a professional job. Those tended to be boring, with run-of-the-mill flowers. Hers, I noticed, had clematis, salvia, dianthus and columbine, with oregano, basil, lavender, and rosemary interspersed throughout.

"She better watch the spearmint," I said. "The stuff takes over an area in only a couple of weeks."

Jack looked over to the garden. "Gosh, it's kinda early for a garden to look so good. Wonder what she's doing?"

I shook my head. "I work in my garden constantly; it never looks so lush at this point in the season. Too early."

Deciding we had sat staring long enough, Jack opened the car door. "Let's get going."

I nodded. "Yep. Want to ask her about the flowers."

He laughed. "We are here for more important information than her gardening skills."

"Yeah, but it won't hurt to ask."

He shook his head, smiling.

While he rang the doorbell, I wandered over for a closer look at the flowers. Some were in full bloom, whereas mine only held the promise of things to come. I turned at the sound of the door opening and saw a woman whose face held signs of emotional trauma. Uh-oh. I looked at the pale, but pretty face. Her dark-blonde hair was pulled back into a ponytail. On me, her style would have looked frumpy, but on this woman, it was enchanting.

She was a slender woman who probably never worried about jeans being too tight.

"Mrs. Spanelli?" Jack asked.

"And you are?" came the cautious reply.

Putting his hand out, he said, "Jack Monroe. Chief of Police here in the township."

She took a deep breath but shook his hand. "How may I help?"

Glancing in my direction, he said, "Mrs. Shaw and I are investigating your daughter's accident. May we come in?"

She didn't say a word, but stepped back, allowing us to enter.

"Your garden is lovely," I said, as I walked past her into the house. "How on earth are there so many blooms now?"

She allowed herself a small smile. "It's my secret."

She led us into a small but nicely decorated living room. The colors were soft, pale lavender, sage green with cream accents. I loved it immediately. The furniture was tasteful, yet it fit the feel of the century home completely.

"Please sit down. Coffee?" she asked.

Jack shook his head. "No, thank you." I could have smacked him; a cup of coffee sounded pretty good to me.

Jack didn't waste time but jumped right in with questions. "Not to be rude, but why aren't you at the hospital with your daughter? We were led to believe it is where we would find you."

She raised an eyebrow, surprised. "Not sure who told you, but I'm not allowed access to Caterina."

I felt my body stiffen. "Not allowed access?" I asked. "By whose authority?" I could feel my anger rising.

She gave me a quick, tight smile. "Her father's."

Jack gave me a quick look and then turned back to Mrs. Spanelli.

"Interesting, since he was the person who told us the hospital is where we would find you."

Nodding, she said, "Doesn't surprise me. He refuses to admit we are separated."

"Not legally, am I correct?" Jack asked.

"No, not legally. The family avoids divorce. So while we remain married, we live separately. I receive a monthly allowance, which is quite comfortable. I have everything I need financially. The only stipulation is I am not allowed to see my daughter."

"Oh my God!" I blurted out before I could stop myself.

She nodded. "I know. Ridiculous, isn't it?"

"How long since you've seen her?" Jack asked, making notes.

"Just over a year," she said. "We've been separated much longer, but the restriction was a recent addition to the arrangement."

I could feel the tears well. The thought of not seeing my boys when they were young was heartbreaking. Even though they were grown and living in other states, I found it difficult seeing their faces only occasionally.

Seeing my tears, she shrugged. "I had little choice."

"You should have a lawyer!" I said.

She laughed without joy. "There isn't a lawyer in the area willing to touch my case. I gave up and resigned myself to living alone. Well taken care of, but alone."

"Surely there are lawyers who aren't afraid of the family," I shot back.

Shaking her head, she answered, "When your family is being threatened, you do as you're told. I don't blame the lawyers. I blame Anthony."

"Is there anything you can tell us which could point us in the right direction? Catching the person who hurt your daughter is important."

She thought a moment, and then said, "I know there have been threats through the years, but I was never involved in the family business." She paused and then added, "I didn't know about the family back then, not until we were married."

"You didn't have a clue they were the mob?" I asked, incredulous.

"No. We met in college. I was a history major, and he was studying to be an MBA. He has a good head for numbers. He was charming and handsome. I fell head over heels." Sighing, she said, "It was a long time ago."

A thought struck me. "How about his mother?"

She grimaced. "She was difficult. Honestly, I believe she was the worst of them all. Cutthroat in business, controller of her household, and dominant in Anthony's life. She hated me, and the feeling was mutual."

"Somehow, you are the key to this puzzle," I said, remembering Dad's words.

She frowned and said, "I don't know how." But I had a feeling she knew exactly how.

Chapter 7

J ack brought the conversation quickly to a close, and we skedaddled out of there pretty darn fast. Once back in the car, Jack turned to me. "Well?"

Shaking my head, I said, "No idea."

"No dead folks helping back there?"

"Nope."

"Damn."

"Yeah."

He finally started the engine, and we drove out of the driveway, back onto the winding roads. I fought the car-sickness again, but my mind was busy elsewhere.

Once we turned off the twisting road, I felt better physically. But my brain wasn't a happy camper. Something was off, but I couldn't decide what seemed wonky.

Turning to Jack, I said, "She knows more than she's telling."

"Agreed. Any idea what?"

I shook my head, disgusted with the situation. "Everyone is holding back information. Even if it isn't worth a dime, I would feel better if we knew what they were hiding."

"Yep, which is the problem with any investigation. People hide secrets, and even if they aren't important to the case, it helps knowing as much as possible. Frees up my time; otherwise, I'm focused on finding out what they are hiding. Nine times out of ten, what they're afraid of telling us is pretty innocent." He shrugged. "Everyone has something they are either embarrassed about or convinced will make them look guilty. They create unnecessary problems for not only themselves but us."

I felt my face grow red, listening to Jack. I had my own secrets; they didn't amount to much, but I wouldn't want the neighborhood to know. Was it necessary for the world to know I fart my brains out while I'm weeding the garden? While it was a great way to relieve a gassy belly, it wasn't information I was willing to share.

Obviously not recognizing my discomfort, Jack continued, "I wish people would understand what is near and dear to them, isn't a shock to us. We've heard some bizarre stories through the years."

"Like what?" I asked.

"Remember Old Man Brewster?"

"He lived on Hametown Road. A hermit, right?"

"Yep. The old coot was a hoarder like you wouldn't believe. He had rubber bands wrapped around every doorknob in the place, tons of the damn things. I asked him why one time, and he told me 'just in case.' Just in case? In case of what?" He shook his head at the memory.

I smiled. "Those rubber bands weren't a menace to the neighborhood."

Jack grinned, "I know, but come on! His bathtub was full of newspapers. Never did figure it out, and I wasn't about to ask. Don't think he had bathed in years."

"He didn't smell bad," I said, thinking of the few times I had encountered the old guy. We sat lost in our memories for a few moments.

"What do you think Mrs. Spanelli is hiding?" I asked.

"Hell if I know. She seemed glad to get away from the family, but not to see your kid must be hard."

My eyes filled again, tears threatening to spill right down my face. Damn hormones must be acting up again. My emotions had gotten so uncontrollable in the last year, I had to mute Hallmark card commercials on the TV. It's bad when you find yourself sobbing over advertisements. I'd be glad when menopause was over; it's no fun.

"Why would she agree to such a ridiculous deal? It sucks!" I said.

"Either dealing with the family is horrible or she doesn't care about the kid very much."

"She didn't strike me as the type who wouldn't love her own daughter." I sat thinking about the woman. She hadn't shown much emotion when she had told us it had been over a year since she last saw the girl—no anger, no sadness, just resignation.

"You think the family has enough power in this area to scare lawyers away from her case? I mean, really, in today's world, the mob isn't as powerful as they were back in the forties and fifties."

Jack shook his head. "You'd be surprised. We have bigger problems today than the mob. They had their heyday, but you are correct; it is waning. Maybe they are itching to regroup and rebuild their relevance."

I looked out the window, frowning. "Where are we?"

Jack grinned. "Figured we'd hit up Mr. Spanelli again. His lies need to be addressed."

"Hey Peg, you headin' back to the Spanelli place?" asked a voice from the backseat.

I jumped, almost peeing my pants in the process. "Bob! Damn it! What have I told you about popping up with no warning?" I snapped.

"Bob's here?" asked Jack, surprised.

"Yes," I answered, gritting my teeth. "You better have something important to tell me, buster," I said to Bob.

"Okay, here's the deal. Logan gave me permission to pass on more delicate information."

I swear Bob was gloating; made me want to smack him upside the head.

"Go on," I snapped. "We don't have all day."

"They are still married, living separately."

I tossed my head back in frustration. Sighing, I said, "Bob, we know. We just came from interviewing Mrs. Spanelli."

Bob nodded his head. "Yep. I know."

I frowned. "You were there?"

His face closed down, which was interesting. In the time I'd known him, Bob had never been able to mask his emotions—a guy who wore his heart on his sleeve, so to speak. Keeping secrets was a newly acquired trait of his, which didn't make me happy. I wanted the old bouncing Bob back, the one who couldn't keep a secret to save his life—if he had a life to save. Wonder what type of punishment Logan would bestow on someone for spilling the beans. The thought made me shudder; if anyone could discipline a dead person, it would be Logan. The guy had formidable powers and I didn't want to be on his bad side.

"Bob?"

"Well, maybe," he finally said.

I felt my eyebrow go north. "Maybe? How 'maybe' are we talking?"

"Sorta maybe," he said, blushing.

I was going to have to ask Dad how, without one drop of blood, dead people can blush. Not something I had ever realized, not knowing any dead people until a few months ago. Live and learn.

Narrowing my eyes, hoping I conveyed my anger, I said, "You were there! I didn't sense your presence or see you."

He smiled widely. "I know! I'm really getting good at this stuff!"

I decide to ignore my irritation; getting info from Bob was more important than yelling at him.

"So what did you learn?" I asked, patiently.

"Her flower garden is awesome!" declared Bob. "Elaine's garden never looked so good." I had to smile to myself, hearing his dig at Elaine. Obviously, finding even a small element to criticize her about made Bob happy. Why not? After all the years she nitpicked at him, he deserved the pleasure of his observations.

"Yeah, I noticed the garden myself. Wonder how she manages to have it look so good this early," I answered.

"You know, when this case is solved, I'm going to do a little snooping at her house. She must use some secret ingredient in the soil," Bob said.

I opened my mouth so a snarky comment could fall out but quickly snapped it shut. I'd like to know what Bob found actually. It would be nice if he discovered how she does have such a great garden.

"Back to the case. Do you know anything helpful?" I asked.

He tilted his head to one side, saying, "I'm not sure this helps, but the missus and the mother-in-law hated each other. I mean *really* hated each other. I'm sure it's one of the reasons why the marriage went south. Her husband was a bit of an idiot, in my opinion."

My eyes widened in surprise. What did it take to make someone an idiot in Bob's eyes? Not to be mean, but Bob pretty much fell into the idiot category himself. No cruelty intended, just the bare facts. He was a goofball.

Not noticing my expression, he continued. "She is a lovely lady from what I've seen. Smart, pretty, and sweet." He sounded a bit wistful, making me wonder if he had a crush on her. Well, his crush on the lady was going nowhere fast. Bob was dead and she is still alive and well.

"Earth to Bob!" I snapped. "Do you know anything else about her?"

"Yep," he said, putting on a business attitude. "She gets over four thousand a month; plus he pays all the bills. That's almost fifty thousand, tax free, dollars a year."

"Wow," was the best I could do; it was a huge amount of money to stockpile.

"I know," he nodded his head. "Wonder what she does with all the dough."

Jack's patience was wearing thin. "What's he saying? Anything helpful?"

"Not really," I answered.

Bob looked hurt. "I've given you some good stuff here!"

"Bob, most of it we already knew."

"Well, I can tell you this; she's got a secret," he whispered.

Why on earth he thought he needed to keep his voice low is beyond me. I was the only living person in the car who could hear him.

"Okay, I'll bite. What's the secret?" I asked. Now we were finally getting somewhere.

He waved a hand. "Oh, I have no idea. But I know she has one."

My lips tightened into a thin line. If he wasn't already dead, I'd kill the little moron.

"How about finding out what the secret is?" I asked, sarcasm thick as molasses.

"I've been working on it." He pouted.

"Well, work harder. The secret is probably very important."

"Okeydokey," he said, happily. "See ya later, gator." He quickly faded, leaving my frustration level at all-time high.

Sensing we were alone again, Jack said, "So nothing good?"

I shook my head. "Nope, other than he knows she has a secret. Hell, we'd figured that much out for ourselves."

Jack laughed. "He means well."

I rubbed my face. "Why Logan uses him is beyond me."

Jack's face became serious. "Logan hired him because he saved Alex's life. If it weren't for Bob, the kid would have been toast, and you know it."

During our first case, Bob had alerted Logan someone was trying to kill our favorite suspect, Alex, who turned out not to be the culprit, while he was in the hospital fighting for his life. Without Bob's quick action, the poor guy would have joined Bob in the afterlife.

Sighing, I said, "I know. But sometimes dealing with Bob is rather like holding on to water. It slides through my fingers."

Jack smiled, "I know he drives you nuts, but his heart is in the right place."

I nodded silently, noticing we were almost to the Spanelli estate. "How are you going to handle this?"

The smile left his face, replaced with a grim stare Jack said, "Play it by ear. He lied, and I want to know what he thought he would gain. Let's face it, we easily found out she wasn't at the hospital. Why bother lying about something so quickly disproved? Doesn't make sense."

"Hmm. Good point."

Parking the car exactly where it had been a few hours before, Jack turned to me. "Let me do the talking. Don't allow him to get the conversation off track with his obsession about his mother helping."

"Sounds good to me. I don't want her help."

Chuckling, he opened his car door. "Let's get this over with."

I followed his lead, walking up the path to the front door. Before Jack could ring the bell, the door opened.

Mr. Spanelli, rather than the maid, faced us. "You are back. Have you found the person responsible for my daughter's accident?"

I frowned. Had he actually convinced himself we would have the case solved after a few hours? Was he a mental case? What about the whopper of a lie he spun about his wife being at the hospital? Had he been expecting our return?

Jack shook his head. "No, not yet. We have a few more questions first."

Spanelli stepped back, flourishing an arm to allow our entrance. "Please, follow me."

We walked behind him, back to his study. Nothing had changed in the past few hours, and I would have been suspicious if there had been any changes. He crossed the room and sat behind his desk. Ah, his attitude was definitely different this time around. He was all business, no emotional excitement in sight. Hmm.

Even though there were two chairs near us, Jack would not sit unless asked. We weren't asked, so we didn't sit. My feet were killing me; I needed to invest in a new pair of shoes. Too bad I hate to shop, such a waste of time.

"How may I help you?" he asked, his voice very formal. Maybe this wasn't the same guy we had met earlier. Did he have a twin? We probably should look into the angle; somehow, the guy had managed to change his personality completely in less than a day.

"You can start by explaining why you didn't think your separation from your wife was important information," Jack said calmly.

Spanelli ignored the question, turning to me. "Have you heard from my dear mother yet? She told me she would be talking with you soon."

My stomach lurched. He could hear his mother? Uh-oh. Either he actually could hear her or he was certifiably nuts. I shook my head, "Not yet. I'm sure she's busy."

He looked confused by my answer. I couldn't decide what had him baffled—that his mother hadn't contacted me or the possibility she could be doing other things in Deadsville. He didn't understand the other side of life the way I now did, and even I wasn't completely savvy to the protocol there.

His eyes slid back to Jack, since I wasn't being helpful in any way. "It is none of your business."

"I beg to differ," Jack answered, still calm. I would have ripped the guys lips off his face by now. I took advantage of their discussion, turning to look at pictures. I stepped closer to the framed items on the bookshelf, whispering, "Bob!" Nothing. I tried again, a little louder, but careful not to allow Spanelli to hear me. "Bob!"

Bing! The air changed, and Bob was standing next to me, not at all happy. "I was in a meeting!"

"Tough beans," I whispered, trying not to move my lips much. It's harder than you'd think. "Walk over to Spanelli. I want to know if he can see you."

Bob frowned, shrugged his shoulders, but did as I asked.

I turned to watch his progress, keeping an eye on Spanelli's expression. Bob made it to the desk, looking over at me. He shrugged again. I motioned for him to step it up a bit.

He yelled in Spanelli's face. It made me jump, but Spanelli didn't turn a hair. Okay, the guy thought he talked with his mother; hell, maybe he did hear her. But he couldn't see or hear Bob, which made me happy. At least I knew Bob could do a little spy work for me. If I thought there was something off the first time we met this man, now I *knew* there was some suspicious funny business. I just no idea what.

I tuned into their conversation, hearing Jack comment, "Mr. Spanelli, you led us to believe your wife would be at the hospital. Neither was she there, nor had ever been there at all. Upon further investigation, we discovered she has no access to her daughter—another fact you failed to mention."

While he was still calm, I noticed the veins on his neck were beginning to bulge slightly—not much, but enough to alert me that his mood was not improving the longer the interview continued. I quickly decided to intervene. With a glance at Bob, I nodded, and miracle of miracles, Bob got the silent message.

I don't know what exactly I expected Bob to accomplish, but I was stunned when he scooted over to Jack, took a deep breath, and blew in Jack's face. I had no idea he had improved his skills to the extent I was witnessing. Jack flinched, startled by the sudden breeze on his face. He opened his mouth to comment, but I stepped in quickly.

"Jack," I said, looking down at my watch with a grand flare, "I hate to interrupt." Ha! I was grateful to stop this conversation before Jack decked the guy. Trying to look meek, which I'm darn sure didn't work, I continued. "We need to scoot. I have to fix dinner for Andy."

Jack frowned, and he stared at me as if I'd lost my mind. Maybe I had; menopause does strange things to a gal. But in this case, I was certain getting Jack out of the house was the sanest move I could make. After a moment of glaring, he nodded.

Turning back to his adversary, he said, "We will talk later, Mr. Spanelli. Withholding information in a police investigation is a crime."

Jack turned, not waiting to be escorted, and stomped out of the room. I smiled at our host.

"Thank you for your time. I'm sure this is not the last time we will need to speak with you. You understand, of course?" I smiled such a sweet smile I felt my blood sugar sky rocket. Yuck.

He had been watching me carefully. I had no idea what he expected, but I certainly had not acted the way he had anticipated. I turned, following Jack out the door. Once outside, I found Jack standing by his car. Clearly still fuming, he said, "What game is the man playing with us?"

I shrugged. "We'll figure it out eventually."

"Yeah, but I hope we get to the bottom of this before it bites us in the ass."

I knew exactly what he meant.

Slamming the car door, he jammed the key into the ignition. Pausing, he turned to me, "What was the air hitting me in the face?"

"It was me!" said a voice in the back of the car. I wasn't surprised; I figured he had followed us out the door.

"Bob, he can't hear you." Facing Jack, I said, "Bob. I needed him to distract you before you went into orbit."

Jack started to protest and then grinned. "Yeah, I was losing it in there. Something about Spanelli is way off."

"Drugs?" I asked.

Jack thought a moment. Then he said, "You might be onto something. I've seldom seen a personality transplant as thorough as he managed."

"A little creepy," I said.

"Nope," said Bob. "He's always like that! He's nuts. I thought you knew."

My mouth fell open. Turning to Jack, I informed him of Bob's bit of news.

Jack and I stared at one another. It was not like we didn't suspect a problem, but it would have been nice to have actual confirmation earlier. I sighed, Jack shook his head, and Bob sat back, enjoying the ride.

Chapter 8

"What makes you think he's nuts?" I asked Bob.

"Hmm?" he answered. Not quite the enlightenment I had expected.

"Bob!"

"When did they expand the cemetery?" he asked, as Jack flew past Moore's Chapel Cemetery.

I looked up at the roof of Jack's police cruiser, exasperated. Hametown Road was home to a two-hundred-year-old cemetery, which had opened up for more burial plots a few years back. The road was also known for the hilly terrain, which made winter travel fun for the adventuresome—not necessarily the high hills Bath Road was famous for, but hills nonetheless.

"Over a decade ago! What difference does it make?" I snapped.

He frowned before answering. "On our side, these things become important." He paused and then continued, "Cemeteries hold secrets, family secrets."

I felt myself become completely still. Bob could be somewhat self-conscious, making extraction of information dicey. He could shut down completely if not handled with care. Surviving life with Elaine had left emotional scars, which obviously transferred to the afterlife. I secretly liked Bob and wouldn't be surprised if he knew it. We never discussed my attitude toward him, but the bottom line was, it was hard not to like the moron.

"What type of family secrets?" I asked, quietly. The question earned me a quick glance from Jack. I shook my head slightly, not willing to break Bob's concentration.

Bob, however, was on his own train of thought. "I wanted to be buried in that cemetery. When we bought our plots, there were none available there." He sighed. "It is such a lovely setting. Quiet, you know?"

I remained silent but nodded, realizing I could extract more information by allowing his mind to wander. I was thrilled, thinking I had possibly found a key to Bob's irritating personality. I hoped it worked.

He continued to look out the car window, watching as the houses flew by, which they did because of Jack's break neck speed. Jeez, he needed to slow down before my bladder protested and we had a puddle in the car, or worse. Neither scenario was appealing.

Jack frowned, not knowing what was happening, but I wasn't about to break the spell that had captured Bob.

We came to the stop sign at Bath Road. Jack flipped his blinker on for the left turn we would make, heading toward the police station. As we waited for the few cars to pass, Bob said, "The Spanellis have many secrets. Most of them are run-of-the-mill family stuff. You know, Aunt Gardina was pregnant when she married cousin Rico back in 1729. The kind of junk just about everyone has in the family lore. Nothing shocking today, but boy, oh boy, way back when, it was a huge scandal."

Nodding slightly, I was impressed with Bob's analysis of genealogy. When you think about it, probably everybody has dirt in past generations now lost to history. We didn't take the time to consider our bloodlines anymore. It was a shame, but even ancient history explained a little of who we were in the present.

"But the Spanellis have more secrets than most." He shook his head. "The family is spooky. Mental illness runs rampant, which is part of the reason those two are separated today. He's nuttier than a fruitcake."

"He suffers from mental illness?" I asked, more for Jack's benefit than my own need of clarification. Jack's head swiveled towards me like a shot. I needed Jack to know Spanelli was more than squirrely; he was truly unstable. Jack's mouth fell open, and then he snapped it shut.

"Yeah, it's one of the reasons the old man sent him here. Had to get him out of the way. He was becoming a problem."

Uh-oh. I didn't like hearing this tidbit of news. I'd already dealt with one crazy person, and he came close to killing me.

"So how long have you known about Spanelli's mental instability?" I asked, hoping my anger wasn't apparent. Bob was on a roll; the last thing I wanted to do was stir his insecurities.

Bob shrugged. "When you work for Logan, need-to-know is one of his rules. You didn't need to know, I guess."

Not able to contain myself another moment, I blew. Throwing my hands up, I screamed, "Logan decided I had no need to be aware of Spanelli's mental state? Who is he to determine what is best for my long-range health?"

Surprisingly, Bob remained calm. Maybe Logan was having a small effect on his ability to cope with me. Time would tell.

"I don't make the rules."

"Logan gave you permission to tell me?" I asked suspiciously.

"Um, well, not really. I made a command decision." He frowned. "You think I'll be in trouble?"

Trouble? Logan would kill him.

"A command decision? Could be a bit, um, risky."

He shrugged. "You mean more to me than Logan." He held up his hands. "Don't get me wrong. The guy is great, but he sure does play his cards close to his chest." He paused. "Sometimes a little too close, you know what I mean?"

My eyes watered. Wow, I had no idea Bob liked me so much. I was almost ashamed of my continuing irritation with him. Life is full of surprises.

"Thanks, Bob. I appreciate your telling me."

"There's more, but the insanity in this brood was starting to worry me. The mob part's bad enough, but when you consider Mr. Nutsville back there…" He shook his head. "I don't want you in danger's way unprepared. Last time was too close to being a disaster."

Maybe my hormone level was the culprit, but the tears flowed down my face. Jack glanced at me, concern clearly showing on his face.

"You okay?" he asked.

I nodded, knowing words wouldn't make it out of my mouth, unless accompanied with a gush of mushy emotion.

Bob seemed oblivious to my waterworks, for which I was grateful. No sense in him knowing what a soft touch I could be at times.

Wiping my face, a thought hit me. "So it's the secret his wife won't tell us?"

Nodding, Bob said, "Yep. Well, one of them. But this one is important; not sure what else she knows." He paused. "I'm pretty sure his craziness is the biggest factor."

Frowning as I dug for a tissue in my purse, I looked back at him. "Pretty sure?"

He matched my frown. "Yeah, at least I think so." His face suddenly clearing, he announced, "Well, gotta go. Lots of work to do, and Logan has me busy as a bee. Later, gator."

He quickly faded. I shook my head, wondering what punishment Logan would bestow on the poor guy. He had taken a chance, and the ramifications could be severe. I decided I would go to bat for him if Logan's discipline was too harsh.

Jack realized by my silence Bob had left the car. "Well, what did you find out? And what's with your crying?"

Sniffing, I said, "Bob took a chance by telling me the family has many nuts, which is the reason Spanelli was sent here, and it could explain his visit to the hospital. Must have been the psych ward."

"Okay, so why the tears?" he said.

Gosh, couldn't he let it go?

"Well?" he persisted when I didn't answer.

I took a deep breath. "Bob said I meant more to him than Logan." I paused and then said, "Logan is going to kill him for telling me."

"I think it may be hard to kill Bob, considering he's already dead." He grinned at me.

Shaking my head, I said, "I'm sure Logan knows a few measures of discipline we have never heard of before."

"Was that the big news? Or is there more?" Jack asked, as he pulled into the station parking lot, sliding into the space marked, 'Chief.' "Bob can take care of himself; the guy is more resourceful than we think. The insanity angle bothers me, though. Don't need another batty criminal." He shook his head. "Damn."

"There's more, but Bob clammed up on me. I suppose he figured he'd spilled enough beans for one day," I said.

Grinning, Jack said, "Yeah, but they were mighty important beans!"

"Glad you came back to the station. My car is still here," I glanced at my watch. "Guess Andy will have to survive on grilled cheese tonight. Too late to actually cook."

"Ah, hell, Peg. Go out to eat. Montrose is full of restaurants." Montrose was once a sleepy intersection: one gas station, one soft ice cream stand, a Ford dealership, and one grocery store. You could lie in the middle of the road most days and never get hit. Today, you'd be smashed flat in less than a minute. You couldn't throw a rock in any direction without hitting a fast-food joint.

"I don't know. I hate to waste money when I could have cooked myself," I said.

Laughing, Jack said, "Peg, these investigations take up your time. Give yourself a break."

I shrugged. "It's not like I get paid, which would help me justify spending Andy's well earned-money."

He shook his head, disgusted. "For Pete's sake." He reached back and pulled out his wallet, extracting two twenty-dollar bills. "Here, dinner's on me."

I felt my face flame red. "Jack! It's not like we can't afford to go out to eat!"

His stubbornness wouldn't let me off the hook. "Peg, the township should have paid you for your efforts concerning Owen. I brought it up in a meeting, but they all acted as though the entire scenario never happened. Too caught up with the township's reputation. Disgusted the hell out me."

"I didn't ask to be paid," I argued.

"Nope. But if we solve this case, I'm hiring you as our consultant."

My mouth dropped open. "What as? A medium?"

He shook his head laughing. "Nope. I have it all figured out; you know people, know the area, and damn well know the township. What the trustees don't appreciate, and let's keep this to ourselves, is the fact you have a direct line to dead folks who help us. I know Bob can be a pain, but he comes in damn handy. Your dad has been a literal lifesaver, and Logan knows all sorts of stuff, which guides us occasionally. Think about it, we would never have caught Owen if those ghosts weren't involved. Hell, we never even suspected him."

Stunned by the thought of being paid, I said, "I'll need to think about this. Let's see if we solve this case first. It's becoming muddled. A little girl is lying in a hospital, fighting for her life, with a dad who's mental and a mom living apart from the entire situation. Doesn't look good for our side."

Jack grinned. "I'm counting on the dead folks getting us across the finish line." He cocked his head. "Peg, how much 'cleaning' of our community do the folks in the hereafter expect us to do?" He held up his hands. "I'm not complaining, but it would be nice for a little clarification."

I wheezed out a moan. "Who knows? Logan isn't good with the whole 'sharing information' bit. Dad is almost as bad. Bob is clueless most of the time. And Nana only shows up occasionally to comment on progress." I frowned. "However, Bob seems to be in the know right now." I shook my head. "Who knows, once Logan realizes how much Bob has confided in us."

Jack looked out the car window, lost in thought. I stayed quiet, allowing him time to ponder. Uh-oh, I thought, watching a car whiz into the parking lot. What now? Jack hadn't spotted the vehicle yet.

"Peg, what if Logan is very much aware Bob isn't the most reliable person when it comes to secure information remaining under lock and key?"

Not taking my eyes off the now parked car, I said, "What? Everyone knows Bob can't keep a secret. Information explodes out of the poor guy eventually."

Jack looked smug. "My point exactly."

Surprised at this new line of thinking, I said, "Wow, maybe Logan wants us to know certain things but for some reason can't divulge the information himself. Who better to leak certain details? Logan probably figures Bob wouldn't be able to hold back. Puts a whole new light on why he has Bob working for him; he's using Bob's natural enthusiasm for his own benefit." I nodded, appreciating Logan's strategy.

"Sorta makes you wonder if even Logan has to play some sort of game over in Deadsville."

Jack nodded. "Yep, it would explain a few things which have been bothering me."

I frowned. "Like what?"

He sighed. "I've had a feeling in both investigations, we are being played." He held up a defensive hand. "Don't get me wrong. Maybe for the greater good if you consider the big picture. But played, nonetheless."

"Oh, God, don't tell me I've been snookered!"

Jack shook his head. "Nope. Not snookered." He paused. "Well, maybe just a little. But from their point of view, their assignment, which is to clean up this area, has to be accomplished."

"So being dead doesn't necessarily equate to being honest." I sighed.

His expression became irritated. "Hells bells, Peg, even I have to color outside the lines once in a while." Shrugging, he added, "It goes with the territory."

Glancing back at the car, I noticed the door finally opening. "Who's the guy?" I said, pointing across the parking lot. Might as well let him realize his archenemy was in the area.

Jack looked across the pavement. I couldn't catch what was said under his breath, but I'm pretty sure it was a really bad word. "Tom Newman," he answered, irked.

Shaking my head at his tone of voice, I asked, "What's he doing here?"

"His office is in the building."

"Yeah, so? Doesn't he have a day job?" Trustees didn't hold full time positions. They had jobs and do township business as a side interest. It probably makes them more in tune with life, since they have to live by their own rulings for the community. While they are politicians in a small sense, the size of the population kept them more honest than a bigger community. Our least favorite mayor was a good example of political shenanigans swept under the rug from the general public in a larger community. People couldn't stay on top of situations when the issues are more complicated than we face in little Bath Township.

"He's going to retire soon from his day job. He'll probably be here at the office more, and no one is excited about the prospect."

I laughed. "We can always get Bob to spook him."

Jack smiled and glanced back at Tom. "Guess I better see what the little turd wants."

"Yep. I'm heading home."

"Peg." Jack stopped me. "Run this by Andy. You know, Spanelli, Bob, Logan? Andy's a smart guy, and his insight may shine some light on the situation."

Nodding, I said, "Already on board with your idea. I'll let you know."

I watched him walk toward Tom, hoping he knew better than to blow up at the man. Tom Newman was an ass, but he had the capability to make Jack's life miserable.

Once buckled into my car, I heard a slight noise. The hairs on the back of my neck twitched, which is never a good sign. *Jeez, now what?*

I closed my eyes, hoping whoever had appeared would happily disappear. Opening one eye, I chanced a quick peek at the passenger seat. Crap, it wasn't empty.

"Hello, Peg," my visitor said. It was one of my spirit guides. I had started out really liking her, but getting to know her a bit more, I had revised my earlier opinion. She wasn't against me but not necessarily on my side. Logan was a wealth of information compared to her. If Logan played his cards close to his chest, she didn't allow you to know if she even had cards to play.

"Hey. What do you want?" No sense pretending. She hadn't appreciated Logan's willingness to help us last visit by giving Andy limited ability to hear and see people from their side of the aisle—well, not all people, only my protectors. But it had helped, and I enjoyed knowing he could talk with Bob and my dad, as well as Logan. Andy was smart and had insight I frankly didn't possess. I learned Logan made decisions based on the needs of the situation; this gal didn't much like those ideas. Too bad.

She smiled. "I'm not the enemy."

"You aren't necessarily in the friend column either," I snapped.

Her smile in place, she shook her head. "I have a job to do; that is all."

"Yeah, I have a sneaky feeling you played Nana for a fool, which she isn't."

"No, I merely relied on her love for you, and yours for her. We need you," she quietly said. "I have no regrets."

"You used her!" I said, shocked she had basically admitted to tricking a sweet, little old lady. Okay, maybe she was not naive, but not an idiot either.

"She knew the risks but had faith in you. She was correct in her assessment." Her eyes remained locked with mine. I looked away, not sure she couldn't use the gaze to some advantage. There was still a lot about the afterlife I didn't understand and I wasn't willing to trust. They could be pretty sneaky over there.

"I could have been killed," I said quietly.

Nodding, she said, "Yes, but you weren't."

I laughed without humor. "True. You didn't lend much help if I recall."

"Not my job, actually. Keeping you on task is my job. Not the same thing at all."

"So it's why you're here? To keep me 'on task?'" I snapped angrily.

"Yes," she answered simply.

I narrowed my eyes. "Does Logan know you are here?" One thing I did learn last time; her relationship with Logan was iffy. He clearly had the upper hand, and she didn't like it one bit.

She allowed her eyes to inspect the scenery but didn't answer. I wasn't surprised; when you corner people, their best bet is to keep their trap firmly closed.

"So he doesn't know." I stated. "I'm on task so why your visit?"

No answer.

I shrugged. "If you aren't going to share, then you might as well leave."

She turned to me. "This situation isn't as simple as the last."

"Oh, thanks. The last *situation* wasn't simple from my point of view!"

She sighed. "Compared to the present dilemma, it was quite easy."

My head sagged against the headrest. "Great. Just what I needed to know."

"Yes. I will leave you now."

She was gone in an instant. *Thanks for nothing, lady.* I sat there a few minutes longer, trying to calm my pounding heart. I was pretty sure her visit hadn't helped. I finally started the engine and made my way home, hoping Andy was there.

# Chapter 9

I was sweating by the time I had driven the mile to our house. Relief washed over me as I saw Andy's car in the driveway. I needed to talk with him about the case, but more important, I needed him to anchor my emotions. Dead people are such a pain to deal with.

He must have been waiting for me; the front door opened as I slammed my car door.

"I was wondering where you were! Don't scare me!"

I frowned as I approached him. "Scared? Why didn't you call my cell?"

He pulled me into a bear hug. "I've been calling the damn thing for hours. Couldn't get Jack, either. Where have you two been?"

"What?" I said, pulling away from the comforting hug. I began digging in my purse, knowing full well the blasted phone had maneuvered itself to the bottom of the pit. Finally snagging it, I checked the battery. Full. So what was the problem? I pushed a couple of buttons and then sighed. The ringer was off. I didn't remember turning it off at all.

I looked up at him. "Sorry, for some reason I muted it." Shrugging, I said, "Nice to know you were worried."

He gave me a pained look. "Peg, seriously. Please check in more often."

I gave him a quick peck on the cheek. "I promise." Arm in arm, we walked in the house. "No dinner though."

"We can always pick up something or splurge and eat at a real restaurant," he said. "Either way is fine with me."

"You need to grab something and bring it home," said Dad from the shadows of the corner. I threw back my head in exhaustion. "Hi, Dad."

I continued on to the kitchen, and Andy grabbed my hand tightly; I could feel the tension in his grasp.

"We need to talk," Dad said.

"Hi Dave," Andy said.

"Andy," was all Dad offered. I stopped, turning towards his voice. He stepped from the shadow, and I gasped. His face was a mess, the shirt he always wore was torn, and his hair stood on end. Andy stopped in his tracks.

"God, Dave. What the hell happened to you?"

"We have a problem," said Dad, walking past us and making it to the kitchen before us. Andy and I exchanged a quick glance.

"Since when can spirits get beaten up?" I asked.

"Since forever," was the reply.

Well, this was certainly news to me. My mental image of afterlife activity never included fighting. Well, maybe between the angels, the type of battle you read about in the Bible. But my dad in a fist fight? That never entered my head. But his appearance forced me to realize my vision of heaven was not reality. Once again, I found myself disappointed; being dead wasn't a time of rest. My hope the afterlife would somehow be better had been hanging by a thread, but Dad's appearance certainly snipped those remaining strands completely. Jeez Louise.

"You going to be okay?" I asked. I didn't know if you could cease to exist in these situations. Let's face it; he was already dead. How much worse could it get?

He gave me a tight smile. "Yep. It's not as bad as it looks."

I had a zillion questions but tried to hone it down to a couple. "Who did this? And why?"

"We still have to fight evil over here; you know your mother's on the wrong side. Right?" he asked.

I nodded.

"Okay." he sighed. "Didn't want to burst your bubble any more than necessary, Twinkle Toes."

"Oh, Dad," was all I could manage.

"Babe, it's why your work is so important." I started to argue, but he held up his hands. "Seriously, you need to realize we wouldn't have bothered you if your help wasn't paramount."

Feeling overwhelmed, I said, "Dad, I'm not sure what I can do." I waved my hands around. "It's too much!"

He shook his head. "Nope. You really *are* only given what you can handle. It's the rule."

"Ha! I bet Logan bends those rules constantly!" I retorted.

Dad smiled. "Yeah, but not where you are concerned. Why do you think you have your guards out back?" He pointed to the woods, where my Indians stood watch over me.

"It's a land thing."

"Nope, they don't have to be here. They *choose* to stay and watch you. They understand how vital the mission is at this point in time."

My eyes watered. Damn hormones.

"Why now?" I asked. I've pushed this issue in the past, only to be stonewalled. The dead didn't like the question, and it made me nervous how creative they could become to avoid answering.

"All you need to understand is we are at a crossroads. How this point in time plays out is what determines the next few centuries." He shook his head. "There's a lot of unrest, both on your side and ours."

"Dave, what do you need from us? You look pretty beat up, but I don't think a shower or beer is on your agenda," said Andy.

Dad grinned. "Wish it was possible. Both sound pretty damn good about now."

Andy returned the grin. "So what's the game plan?"

"Logan and I had a long chat," he began.

I raised an eyebrow, which he happily ignored.

"The Spanelli family is bad news, but the son is garbage. He even has his own father worried. He's volatile, unpredictable, and smart. When all three of those factors are working at the same time, it's a recipe for disaster. The kid has caused major problems within the family business and with the feds. Normally, we wouldn't be concerned; it's the law's problem. But his mother is now on our side of the fence, and she's stirring up as much trouble as your own mother."

I shuddered. Mom wasn't great in the land of the living; over there, she was a major player for evil. The spirit realm, from what I've been able to piece together, was pretty much what we saw here in many arenas—just a lot more power and influence. A spirit could easily manage to be all over the place in a matter of seconds so the person's sphere of influence wasn't tied down to a location like it was when there's a heartbeat.

"Whose side is my irritating spirit guide on? She drives me nuts!" I said.

Dad grinned. "She's fine. Logan trusts her but keeps her at arm's length."

"Yeah, she seems…" I paused, "…not really afraid of him, but cautious for some reason."

Dad threw back his head and laughed. "They are at loggerheads constantly. She's been around on our side for a really long time. Logan is a relative new comer, in her opinion. She doesn't like his abilities, but she does recognize he brought most of the power with him. Plus, while she has seniority, his influence far outweigh hers. I think it has become an ego thing."

"For her?"

"Logan isn't perfect, but his ego is in check. Most of the time."

Ah, so fault could be found in both. Their relationship was beginning to make sense. "I don't want to get caught in the crossfire."

Dad smiled. "Logan won't allow it to get out of control. He stays focused on his job."

"Dad, what about Bob?" I asked.

He frowned. "What about him?"

"He clued me into some facts about Spanelli. You know, the fact the guy is crazy and a huge problem. Not much more than you've shared today, but more than Logan probably wanted me to know. Is he in trouble?"

Dad smiled, shaking his head. "Don't worry about him. Logan knows what he's dealing with regarding Bob."

"So Bob is a useful idiot?" I asked, temper rising. Bob drove me nuts, but I felt protective. The realization stunned me for a second.

"Logan will deal with him fairly. Don't forget, Bob isn't an idiot. He saved Alex's life, and that alone was worth gold. Logan probably respects him more than you do."

His last remark stung me, and he was right. I hadn't really bothered to fold respect into my feelings towards Bob. His puppy-dog personality grated on my nerves.

Andy opened his mouth to comment when the doorbell rang. We all stared at each other in surprise.

"Don't look at me," said Dad. "Our side doesn't bother with doorbells."

Getting up from his chair, Andy said, "You have a good point!"

I waited until Andy was safely out of the room before asking, "How much danger am I in this time? Spanelli creeped me out today. He was helpful the first visit, but when Jack and I went back, it was freaksville. Almost as if we were talking to a different person altogether."

"Now you know why his father sent him away. Their connections in New York gave the old man an ultimatum: get the kid away from the business or suffer the consequences."

"Wow, sounds serious. But you didn't answer my question." I'd learned you really had to pin down the dead to get them to answer questions. They evaded constantly if you didn't watch them carefully.

Dad sighed. "You still have your protection. We may have to call in the heavy guns again."

My trio. I shook my head. "Not sure it will work this time. I found out today they work on our side but, I'm not sure who exactly is running their show. I'm positive the mayor has no idea; he'll have a heart attack if he ever figures out their real job."

Dad whistled. "Wow, news to me. Logan know?"

"Oh, yeah. Bob showed up at the hospital and let the cat out of the bag. I guess all three of them have abilities. Bob acknowledged poor Santino, and he answered."

Dad shook his head. "Santino should have pretended he couldn't see or hear Bob."

I laughed. "It would never have worked. There is no way Bob would have understood a silent warning. I can just see him if Santino hadn't acknowledged him. He would have gotten upset, asking why the poor guy wasn't talking to him. Santino must have instantly realized the situation himself; he wasn't happy."

"Logan probably wasn't thrilled either."

"No idea. Bob didn't mention any reaction from Logan a few hours ago when I saw him."

I could hear voices coming our way, and we stopped talking. Never knew who was coming, so it was better to be cautious.

As they rounded the corner, I recognized my neighbor's voice. Dad raised an eyebrow; I sighed.

"Look who's here," Andy said, grinning. Amy Branch had lived next door to us for over thirty years. Her husband had passed away years ago, and they never had children. I had no idea if it was by choice or they couldn't conceive. We had never become close enough for those types of conversation.

"I don't mean to bother you two, but thought I should inform you I saw some men here this morning," she said. I could see the concern on her face.

"Want some coffee?" I asked because I have manners, not because I wanted her company.

"Oh, no thank you. Wouldn't want to be a bother."

I gave her what I hoped was a kind smile. "No bother. Cream or sugar?" I asked, heading for the coffee brewer. I love my one-cup brewer, it allowed me to have a fresh cup quickly. No more pots of coffee forgotten and dumped down the sink.

"Oh, you have one of those new coffee brewers. I almost bought one, but they are *so* expensive."

I shook my head. "Not really. I waited until Macy's had a sale. We love it."

"Maybe I should keep my eye out for the next sale. Aren't the little coffee things expensive? I have to watch my pennies."

"We figure it evens out in the end. Now, back to these guys you saw. What made you worry?"

"Oh, Peg. They looked quite mean."

Andy and I exchanged a quick glance. "Mean? You need to be a little more specific." I smiled at her, hoping she didn't hear my irritation. She didn't.

"They were prowling around the entire property. I walked outside, hoping to scare them off, but they must not have seen me."

I pursed my lips, trying to decide whom she could have seen. My personal bodyguards, who I now knew were good guys? Or had Spanelli sent guys out here? Coffee done brewing, I set the steaming cup in front of her.

"Oh, it smells lovely, and so fast!" She took a tentative sip. With a look of surprise, she said, "Why, it's quite good." What had she expected? "I'm really a tea drinker to be honest. But this is delicious."

"Amy, did you call the police?" Andy asked.

"Oh, no. I don't like to bother them. They are so busy with all the crime we have now." She took another sip, obviously enjoying her coffee. Andy slightly jerked his head towards the cabinet. I knew what he was signaling, but didn't want to prolong her visit. He jerked his head again but more forcefully.

*Fine, you could entertain her*, I thought.

I got up and went to the cabinet, grabbing the cookies from my favorite bakery. I tried to make these little gems last, but no telling how many Amy would gobble. I snatched a small plate from the dish drain and put a few of my treasures on it. When I placed the goodies on the table, Amy's eyes lit up.

"Oh dear, these look scrumptious."

I sighed, smiling at her. "Enjoy."

"All the crime? I don't think we have a ton," I continued.

"Well dear, you did have a dead body here in the spring," she said, reaching for another cookie.

Yes, the dead body; she had me there.

I watched her eat my stash and noticed how frail she had become. When did this happen? Amy lacked height; she was probably less than five feet tall, about an inch shorter than I. But she appeared to have shrunk somewhere along the line. Her curly gray hair looked a bit disheveled, and her blouse had a few stains. Was she taking care of herself?

"Amy, how have you been lately?" I asked, concern seeping through in spite of myself, I realized she had no one to watch out for her.

"Oh, okay. I can't get around as easily as I once did; age catches up with you." She smiled brightly.

I glanced over at Dad. He had been watching her carefully. Hope it didn't mean she was going to join him anytime soon. He caught my glance, and grinned. "She's interesting."

"How long have you lived alone, Amy?" I asked, embarrassed I couldn't remember when Albert had died.

She focused on her coffee cup, finally looking up. Tears swimming, she said, "It's been almost fifteen years now. Your boys were still quiet young. How they loved running through the woods."

I felt my irritation rise again. The boys didn't respect property lines as well as I would have liked. The phone rang weekly, Amy reminding me their presence in her yard could be a problem. I never understood why it bothered her so much. They were usually playing pirates or knights of the realm, nothing that warranted a phone call. Adam had eventually mowed her lawn, seldom receiving any payment. Andy was a strong believer in taking care of neighbors, especially since she was a widow. I had wanted to pay him myself since her yard was huge, almost two acres of lawn. But Andy had vetoed the idea in favor of teaching a lesson in community spirit.

"Yes, they still roam around when they are home. Remembering their childhood, I suppose."

Nodding, she asked, "Have you noticed any reenactors around here lately?"

I frowned. "No," I answered slowly. "What type of reenactors?"

She vaguely waved her thin hand. "Oh, must be my imagination. Don't concern yourself with an old lady's wandering mind."

Uh-oh. Out of the corner of my eye, I noticed Dad's grin become wider. I shot him a look, but he shrugged, keeping his grin in place. Obviously, he was enjoying Amy's visit more than I.

"Seriously, Amy, describe what you've seen. If people are in the woods, we should be aware," I said. Surely, Amy couldn't see the Indians! I didn't want any more complications to my life.

"Well…" She hesitated and then continued slowly "they seem to be Indians." Her face became increasingly red as she talked. "I know they do reenactments down at Hale Farm, but I don't understand why those people would be in our woods. We're miles from there." She shook her head, "I think I must be watching too much TV."

What TV had to do with her eyesight was beyond me. She was correct; no way would reenactors be on our property. Hale Farm was our local historical village, and there were many reenactments that took place each year. But it *was* down in the valley, which was well over five miles from the house.

"How often do you see them?" I asked. My curiosity was growing by the minute.

"Oh, sweetie, I'm not sure exactly," she said. She glanced out the window and said, "Oh dear, there they are again."

My forehead broke out into a sweat. I dragged my eyes towards the window, petrified I would also see them, which would mean my danger level had increased to crisis mode. I had closed my eyes nanoseconds before they landed on the wooded area; now I slowly allowed myself to peer carefully. Relief flooded my body as I realized while Amy could see them, I could not. A whoosh of air rushed out of my mouth, and I slumped back into my chair. I chanced another quick glance and saw Logan talking earnestly to air. As long as I couldn't see them, I was relatively safe. Seeing Logan was normal— well, normal for me.

"What are they doing?" I asked Amy.

She concentrated, staring intently. Nodding, she said, "They seem to be listening to the tall one in front. I have no idea what he could be telling them, but they are quite attentive."

Logan must be giving some type of orders to the tribe who lived there. I saw Andy's concerned expression and understood he was wondering if the rule of imminent danger also applied to Amy. I shrugged and then looked at Dad. "Not sure," he said to my unasked question. It still gave me the creeps these dead people seemed to know what was floating around my mind, sometimes before I did. So unfair; a gal has the right to keep what's in her brain to herself.

I turned to Andy and opened my mouth to ask him if he wanted coffee, when Logan suddenly appeared. Looking around the room, his eyes stopped when they reached Amy. She had gone white as fresh snow when he said, "Hello, Amy."

Her mouth opened, shut, then opened again. She looked over at me, and her frantic expression alarmed me. I should have seen it coming, but somehow, I missed it. She slumped, heading for the floor.

Chapter 10

A ndy caught her before she totally hit the floor—at least he caught her head. The rest of her made it down before either one of us reacted. Andy cradled her head, waiting for me to run for a pillow so we could make her comfortable.

Once Amy was settled or had gathered her wits at least, I narrowed my eyes, turning towards Logan. "Since when can the old neighbor lady see you? Plus, the guys out in the woods? It scared her to pieces!" I was fuming mad, with a frail, little old lady, over eighty years in age lying on my kitchen floor.

Logan, stoic as ever, merely said, "It happens. Your second sight began suddenly and…" He gestured toward poor Amy. "So did hers."

"Well, I've never heard of second sight suddenly happening. Mine is one thing, but to frighten a wido— who is afraid of the world, I might add— is plain mean."

Logan shook his head. "I have no jurisdiction over these matters, usually."

Another nugget of information about the afterlife—jurisdictions. Who would have believed the hierarchy that existed over there? Plus the social clubs, group meetings, and on it went. I glanced at Andy, expecting his smile as another piece of afterlife puzzle slipped into place. I wasn't disappointed. His grin was wide, eyes twinkling. I caught Dad's grin also and shook my head.

Amy began to stir, and I leaned down, saying, "Hey, you okay?"

Her eyes slowly opened, relieved when she recognized me. She started to look around, but I said, "Keep looking at me. Don't look anywhere else!"

She frowned, fear beginning to fill her face. The last thing I needed was for her to face Logan again before she was ready. Seeing a dead Indian in my kitchen, dressed as though he recently participated in a reenactment of the French and Indian War, would probably knock her right out.

I shook my head. "Amy, it's fine. Listen, I'm going to explain a few things. Keep your eyes on my face!" I ordered as they began to wander, glad when she locked back onto my face.

"You aren't imagining anything. Hard to get used to, I know. I understand how you feel. Would it help if you saw someone you know? Like Nana?"

She shook her head, and I continued. "Here the truth. The reason you see Indians in the woods is because they are there. For protection. Um, for me. Oh hells bells."

She took a deep breath. "Peg? You see them?"

I nodded. "Yep."

She sighed. "Thank God. Okay, let me up," she said, trying to wiggle around, getting her body parts to coordinate their movements. "I'm good. Just need to get off the floor or my back will never be the same."

Andy chimed in, "Amy? You sure you're ready to move?"

"Yes. Ow," she said, as Andy pulled her to a sitting position.

"Amy, sit for a second to allow the blood to stabilize or you'll pass out," Andy told her.

Nodding, she said, "So I'm not senile?"

I smiled, "Nope. Or at least if you are senile, I'm right there with you."

She was still being careful where her eyes roamed, but she looked at me, saying, "When did it start for you?"

Sighing, I said, "A few months ago. I figured it was menopause."

She nodded once. "Makes sense. I started seeing them a few years ago, but it was only occasionally. Around the anniversary of Albert's death, Christmas, other holidays. I decided it was an emotional reaction."

"Yeah, I understand your rationale. Makes sense."

"A few months ago, the activity…" She paused. "Is that what it's called?"

"Why not? Works for me," I said.

"Well, it increased. Some poor murdered man who used to live in Bath, kept popping in and out. He always apologized, explaining he had overshot his destination."

I winced. Bob. Go figure.

Dad burst out laughing, causing Amy to jerk violently.

"Dad, be quiet!" I ordered.

"Your dad?" she asked, surprised.

"The one behind me is," I said.

"Oh, how nice. He died when you were little, didn't he?"

"Yes, and it is nice to have him around." I smiled at her.

Nodding, she asked carefully, "Um, who's the other one?"

"Logan. He is in charge of the guys in the woods. They help protect me."

She thought about the information and then asked, "Protect from what?"

This is where the story had to be handled delicately. I didn't want to scare the crap out of her.

"Well, I'm helping them clean up crime in the area. Wasn't my idea, but it seems the job is important."

"Okay," she said slowly. "I can see it would be important. But why you?"

"No idea; all I know is Nana was involved."

"Your Nana always was a bit, well...*out there*, if you know what I mean."

This statement brought laughter from both Dad and Andy.

Amy smiled. "I don't mean to be rude, but she scared me a little sometimes." After a moment, she added, "But she was so much better than your mother." She seemed to surprise herself with this comment and turned red. "Sorry," she whispered.

"It's okay. She's still a problem," I informed her.

The creases in her face become deeper. "Peg, I'm Baptist."

I shrugged, "Fine." I didn't care about her religion.

"Yes, well, we don't believe in this type of thing." She began to whisper, "It goes against everything I've ever been taught."

I sighed. "Amy, hang around here for any length of time, and your entire belief system will fly out the damn window."

"Oh, dear. I'm not sure how to handle this," she said.

Logan cleared his throat. I was sure he made noise to allow Amy to easily accept his presence. It worked; she looked his way, no fear apparent.

"Do not fret about your religious beliefs. Spiritual encounters seldom match those beliefs. Even your Jesus had encounters which did not match his religious teachings." Eyes twinkling, he continued, "I believe it led to a rather large dilemma for him."

Amy sat quietly, listening to Logan's short speech. Finally, she said, "Yes, I believe you have a very good point. Never thought about it quite your way." Looking him full in the face, she said, "Thank you."

Logan regally bowed to her, something he's never bothered to do in my direction. Jeez.

Acknowledging his bow with one of her own, she faced my dad. "Hello, Dave. It is nice to see you again."

"Hi, Amy. Sorry to hear about Albert."

She began to say something but changed her mind. A moment later, unable to hold back, she asked, "Have you seen him, you know, *over there?*"

Dad nodded. "Yep. Not much, you understand. We run in different circles. He's usually with his friends from church."

"Oh," she said surprised. "I wasn't sure they all made it. Bernie Crocker had an affair back in the sixties. I figured it would make him ineligible."

Wow. Wonder how she'd take the news there wasn't a hell. I decided now wasn't the time to delve into a theological discussion.

"Nope. Bernie's fine," Dad said, eyes twinkling. He winked at me.

"You know," she confided, "I was a little worried about Albert. He was such a miser. Never tithed properly. It's nice to know it wasn't held against him."

"Never came up in discussion as far as I'm aware," said Dad smoothly.

Well, hell. Of course it never came up in discussion! They didn't bother with our rules and regulations in the afterlife. They were too busy with their own!

"I'm so glad," she said sincerely.

Logan had studied Amy carefully, watching for signs of relapse probably. She seemed to be coping quite nicely as far as I could tell—well, ever since she had become coherent again.

"Amy," began Logan, "would you consider helping our endeavor?"

I narrowed my eyes, wondering what he was up to.

She looked up at him thoughtfully. "I'm not sure what I could do to help."

"I believe you would be a great asset," he told her.

I couldn't believe my ears! Over eighty and he was enlisting her aid? Was he out of his mind?

"Maybe I should think about it before giving you an answer," she said. Good for her!

"I agree. It could be dangerous at times, but I am confident you will rise to any occasion," he smiled.

She glowed at his remarks, reaching a hand up to pat her disheveled hair. Oh my stars, he was schmoozing her!

Cocking my head, I said, "You sure about this?"

He smiled and nodded. "Yes."

Man of few words when I asked a question, Shakespeare where Amy was concerned. Jeez.

Andy frowned, and I knew he was trying to decide why, exactly, I was irritated. I hated to admit it, but I felt a little bit of the green-eyed monster. Jealousy. Oh, dear.

I smiled widely. "Okay, then. I may have a partner. How convenient! She lives right next door!" I hoped no one discovered my feelings.

Logan smiled, shaking his head. I hadn't fooled him for a second.

"Andy, could you walk me home? I'll feel better in my own house," Amy said.

"Sure. No problem," Andy answered.

Smiling around the room, she said, "It was so nice to meet you Mr. Logan. Dave, I'm glad you are okay. Peg, thank you for the coffee." Looking at Andy, she continued, "And thank you for your aid. I'm ready to go." She waved her petite hand and turned to leave. Andy raised an eyebrow, shrugged and followed her.

I waited until I heard the front door close behind them and then whirled around to face Logan. The old fart had taken advantage of the fact my head had been turned and disappeared. My mouth fell open, and I swore. Glaring over at Dad, I said, "He has some nerve!"

Dad laughed, shaking his head. "Peg, you should be used to him by now. He manages things his own way; worked out pretty well for him so far."

"But to ask Amy! She's over eighty!"

"You're almost sixty," he said.

"Yep, twenty years younger," I snapped.

"Maybe Logan decided she needed to reengage with life. You notice her hair and clothes? She hasn't been taking care of herself the past few years."

I glared, but couldn't find room to argue with him. A little guilt was making itself felt as I realized it had been a while since we had checked up on Amy. Obviously, she needed some help. Maybe Logan was correct. Not a thought I enjoyed.

"You going to be able to have her help you?" Dad asked.

Sighing, I said, "What if something bad happens to her? I'd feel horrible."

Dad shook his head. "Babe, you aren't responsible for those events. She's coming to the end of her days on earth, but it's no reason for her not engaging herself. Don't you want to live life to the fullest?"

My eyes teared up. "Dad, of course I do."

"So does she. Allow her the ability to feel useful again. She and Albert didn't have kids, so she busied herself with church work, community service and township business. After Albert died, she slowed down, pulling away from her activities. Now, she needs you and Andy; she needs purpose."

I plopped my well-padded butt in the chair. Dad's words, a form of chastisement, hit me like a brick. It hurt, but he made sense.

"Yeah, you're right. Okay, I'll tell Logan."

Dad burst out laughing. "Logan doesn't need your permission. He'll do what he damn well pleases."

My shoulders slumped. "I know."

"Now, down to business. I've been nosing around on my side of the fence. Spanelli's ancestors are a real piece of work. They have formed a mob-like presence even over on our side." His head moved a tad, listening. "Hm, I'm being called. I'll get back to you as soon as possible."

He faded as the front door opened. "Hey Peg, it's me," Andy called.

I heard him making his way down the hall towards the kitchen. Turning the corner, he looked around the room. "Where'd everyone go? I wanted to talk with your dad."

"After sorta chewing my butt out, he got called away."

Andy looked surprised. "Your dad chewed you out? What about?"

I threw my head back, staring up at the ceiling. "My attitude about Logan asking Amy to help."

"Oh, Peg! Really? The sweet little lady needs purpose in life!"

"Oh, shut up! It's exactly what Dad told me!"

Andy laughed. "Nice to know he and I are on the same page."

I goosed him with my foot. "Thanks a lot!"

"Anything new with Spanelli?"

"Dad said his ancestors are pills over there. It's as far as he got before he was called. He actually used the word 'called.' Don't remember it ever happening before."

"Wow, better than a cell phone!" Andy laughed.

"Okay, I'm back. Didn't take long," said Dad, reappearing.

"I didn't expect you back tonight," I said, surprised.

Smiling, Dad said, "Bob had a quick question. Not sure why he didn't just show up here."

"Um, Peg. Are we eating tonight?" Andy asked.

I clapped my hands over my face. Dinner. How had I forgotten? I jumped up from the table. "Eggs and toast?"

"Anything, I'm starving."

"Can you cook and listen at the same time?" Dad asked.

Laughing, I said, "Dad, while the boys were growing up, I cooked hundreds of meals. I've listened to everything from book reports, whining about homework, all the way to many musical instruments being tortured while practiced upon, plus sorting arguments."

Grinning, he said, "Here's the bottom line; the Spanellis have caused headaches on our side for centuries. The family business may have started out to protect innocent people in the villages, but it changed rapidly. Nothing was done out of the kindness of hearts." He shook his head, disgusted.

Andy piped up. "I did a little research on mafia families. I was stunned how far back their history extends."

"Yep," said Dad. "Tradition is difficult to break."

"Tradition? How far back in history is the Mafia?" I asked.

"Way back," said Andy, as Dad nodded. "We're talking about many empires seizing control and inflicting great injustice and corruption."

"Sicily, correct?" I asked. "What was the big deal about a tiny island?"

Dad laughed. "History not your strong suit, I take it."

I felt my face redden.

"It's not so small; biggest island in the Mediterranean. You know Italy is shaped like a boot, right?" Andy asked me.

I nodded. "Yep, remember that much from geography."

"Right. Off the coast of the toe part of the boot is the island of Sicily. Smack-dab in the middle of the trade routes. Plus the fact the soil has been fertile for centuries, making it an important piece of property. Everybody wanted to own it."

"Trade routes? You're talking way, way back," I said.

"Couple of thousand years," said Andy.

I shrugged. "What's it got to do with the Mafia?"

"Everything. Romans controlled them for a long time, then Arabs, next came the Normans, finally the Spanish. Each empire favored the rich and powerful, taxing the poor but giving the wealthy breaks. The laws, where they existed, favored the powerful. Over time, people became resentful and formed their own forms of justice."

I raised an eyebrow. "Huh. Not much has changed through time."

Dad laughed. "People are people, no matter what the culture."

"So why did I need the history lesson?" I asked.

"You asked when the Mafia came into existence," said Andy. "The Mafia was a direct result of the unfairness of local governments, which were filled with the rich and powerful. The common man was treated badly, which spawned groups protecting the little guys." He shook his head. "People never learn."

"How so," I asked.

"There comes a point when normal, everyday people are fed up being treated like dirt. They band together in an effort to level the playing field." He shrugged. "Study history; it has a bad habit of repeating itself."

"What's this got to do with the Spanellis?" I asked, impatience growing.

Dad looked at me. "They were one of the first families to form."

"Ah. So their particular brand of 'family business' has been around for a long, long time." Light dawned. If the Spanellis history went back almost a thousand years, we were talking deeply instilled tradition.

"Not what we call the 'mob' necessarily, but the family itself, yes, has been around for centuries," Dad interjected.

"What about the family's insanity issues?" I asked, nodding at the clarification.

"Ah, another ball of wax," said Dad. "To retain their power base, the families intermarried, which as we now know causes genetic problems. This family started seeing issues as far back as the seventeen hundreds. They dealt with the problem as quickly as possible, but mental problems usually weren't recognized until adulthood."

"Which meant marriage and children had already taken place," I said.

Dad nodded. "They knew insanity was popping up in each generation, but they didn't know why. They dealt with the problem the best they could as soon as it was apparent." Shrugging, he said, "Didn't help in the long run."

"Is our Spanelli the only nut right now?" Andy asked Dad.

"As far as we know, alive, yes. But there could be more we are unaware of running around out there."

"So how did he get custody of the daughter?" I asked.

"Threatening his wife, probably," said Dad.

"Bob thinks she is the key to the puzzle," I told Dad.

"He may be correct, but the old man also knows the score. He won't help though; probably keeping his distance from the problems his son has created."

I tapped my finger on the spatula I was holding, glancing down at the eggs cooking. I reached over and popped two pieces of bread into the toaster. Looking over at the two men in my kitchen, I realized they were waiting for me to comment.

"What?" I asked.

Andy grinned. "What's going on in that head of yours?"

I smiled back. "No idea, it does its own thing. Never tells me anything."

Dad chuckled. "I wouldn't admit it if I were you."

Grinning, I said, "Okay, back to business. Knowing the facts about the Spanelli family allows an understanding but not a clue how to proceed. The wife isn't really helping, the husband is nuts, and the dead mother has thankfully not shown up to help."

"Much like the police, you need to feel your way through the situation. Get your bearings."

"Easier said than done! No idea where to start," I said, buttering toast.

"Jack have any ideas?" asked Andy.

"Nothing I've heard. He's fighting with Tom Newman as we speak."

"Uh-oh. Not good. Tom isn't the easiest person to deal with," said Andy, helping me get our plates ready.

"I'm outta here," Dad announced. "Eat your dinner, and get a good nights rest. I have a sneaking suspicion Logan has plans for your neighbor, and you'll be included."

"Dad! Wait…" I stopped talking as I watched him conveniently fade away.

# Chapter 11

The next morning, as I sat over my coffee cup in a stupor, Andy breezed into the kitchen. As usual, he glanced at my cup, asking, "How many?"

I held up one finger. I was pretty lethal in the morning. I hated the fact my mornings were horrible; those first few minutes before I dragged out of the bed are okay. But by the time I'd hit the bathroom, brushed my teeth, and pulled my robe on, I was a mess, wondering why I was awake. I couldn't remember any time in my life I was chipper first thing. Andy, on the other hand, woke up cheerful, full of conversation, and high on life. I wanted to kill him most mornings.

"Okay, sweetie," he said, planting a light kiss on my forehead.

Eyes narrowing, lips forming a slit, I glared at him with what I hoped were death rays. He laughed and proceeded to make his breakfast, whistling as he puttered around. I found myself planning his murder. This was our normal routine, and he wasn't offended, much less frightened.

The doorbell rang as I took another long sip of coffee. Frowning, I glanced at Andy, who shrugged but bounced happily down the hall to answer the door. I hated him and whoever was stupid enough to be at my front door at this ungodly hour. I winced as I heard Amy's happy voice.

"Is it too early?"

*God, yes*, I thought. Noon would have been too early to see her. I dragged myself out of the chair, heading to the coffee machine. I grumpily pulled another cup from the cupboard, swearing under my breath at her stupidity thinking sunrise was a good time to visit a neighbor. What was wrong with people these days?

"I hope Peg doesn't mind, but I needed to talk with her," Amy said as she rounded the corner, smiling her way into the kitchen. One glance at my face was all she needed. "Oh, dear, maybe it is too early."

Andy maneuvered around Amy, saying, "Just don't talk to her until she reaches her third cup of coffee, and you're good to go."

Eyeing the cup in my hand, she asked, "Third?"

I narrowed my eyes, and held up one finger.

"Oh, dear," she said.

I plopped down in my chair but did point to her cup, now filled with steaming, fresh-brewed coffee.

"Thank you, sweetie, but it's too early for coffee," she said.

I turned away from her, hoping she would take the hint. I honestly couldn't stand talking until at least two full cups of caffeine found themselves galloping through my veins. She would have to cope with silence.

"So Amy," began Andy, "what brings you over so early?"

I glared at him. He knew perfectly well I needed total quiet. He winked but continued talking, "I can keep you company until Peg reaches a safe level of caffeine."

Turning to face him, she said, "That fella Logan came by this morning."

I slowly placed my cup on the table and faced her. *Came by? He doesn't come by nicely; he pops in and scares the crap out of people. Just like the rest of my gang of the living dead.*

"Did he frighten you?" asked Andy, voice full of concern.

"Oh, no. He was quite kind. Actually carefully announced he was going to appear, his voice very soft. I had to strain a bit to hear him."

*Oh, really?* I thought to myself. *So she gets the kid glove treatment?*

Andy looked over at me, knowing full well I was pissed. Deciding to ignore me was the best way to go, he said, "Wow, really nice of Logan. He doesn't usually appear around here so carefully."

"I wondered if he was treating me differently. I decided it is my age; doesn't want to give me a heart attack," she said.

*Hmm, she probably has a point. No good enlisting her help, then killing her from fright.* I turned back to my coffee, determined to ignore the rest of the conversation. It wasn't easy.

"Well, how considerate of him," said Andy.

I could hear the grin in his voice but I refused to give him the satisfaction of glaring at him.

"Oh, yes! I thought so," said Amy.

Dear God, Logan wasn't necessarily considerate, more like a patient general, waiting for the troops to follow orders.

"Why did he visit you so early?"

"Well, at my age, you don't sleep much. I was awake, listening to the birds start their day. Such a lovely sound," answered Amy.

"Yes, it is. So did Logan have any news?" I had to admit, Andy was trying to find out exactly what Logan was doing, visiting Amy at the crack of dawn.

"Well, it was confusing, to be honest. He didn't say much other than I was to come over here when I finished dressing."

What? Logan knew damn well I was worthless this early in the morning.

Andy laughed. I turned slowly, giving him the death stare. He shook his head, laughing. "Peg, he knows you very well. Maybe he is attempting to help you revise your morning routine," he grinned.

"My morning routine is none of his damn business," I snarled.

Andy's grin grew wider, but Amy looked concerned.

"Peg, dear, I'll come back later." She glanced worriedly at my coffee cup. "Give you time to wake up and get yourself together." She looked over my old, worn out bathrobe critically. I loved my tired bathrobe, so I didn't like her expression. Yesterday, she didn't look so great herself.

Andy chimed in, trying to be a helpful husband. "Amy, don't worry about Peg. She's always a grump in the morning. Since you don't want coffee, how about a nice, hot cup of tea?"

I wanted to kill him. Visions of hiding his dead carcass floated in front of me as I watched Amy's anxious eyes quickly slide to Andy. Unable to decide, her fingers picked nervously at the buttons on her sweater—clearly, not a great decision maker. Her anxiety was increasing by the second, and I couldn't stand witnessing her indecision.

Sighing, I said, "Stay. Do not talk to me for another fifteen minutes."

Andy nodded encouragingly at Amy. "See? It's fine." He turned back, finishing the process of making tea.

No, it wasn't *fine*; I'm just a sucker. I turned back to the window, trying to ignore both of them.

Andy brought her tea over to the table and pulled out the chair for Amy. She gave him a quick smil and sat down. "Have you eaten?" he asked kindly. Oh for Pete's sake! Next he'll be offering to mow her damn yard.

Shaking her head, she said, "I was afraid of being late."

I frowned. Late? Late for what?

The air changed, and my head dropped as I realized for what.

"Oh, great! Amy's here!" said a voice entirely too chipper.

To my satisfaction, Amy jumped at the sound. Quickly glancing around, she spotted Bob. "I've seen you before."

Bob's face grew a slight shade of pink. "Um, yes. Well, sorry; didn't mean to frighten you."

I felt my eyes narrow. "Bob, you never told me you had popped in on Amy. What was the idea of scaring her?"

The pink increased, becoming nearer to red. "You remember at the beginning I was having a little trouble with the whole appearing thing?"

I nodded.

"Well, the first few times when I was alone, well, my aim wasn't real good."

Ah.

"But I got better."

"Yes, you did," said Andy, encouragingly. He threw me a dirty look, which I ignored.

"Amy, this is Bob Bradley. He and his wife were murdered a few years back. Peg helped solve their murder," Andy said.

Amy's eyes grew large as she studied Bob. "It was you!"

"Yeah, sorry about the mix up," he said.

"Why are you here?" I asked.

He gave my coffee cup a nervous glance. "How many?"

I held up two fingers as Andy slid a fresh cup of steaming brew in front of me.

He pursed his lips. "Whoops. But this is Logan's party. I just show up when I'm told."

Logan. I knew it!

The air changed again.

"Good morning," he said.

Everyone answered back but me. I wasn't in the mood for one of his meetings. His eyes dropped to my steaming cup of coffee. "I am sorry for the early hour, but we need to familiarize Amy with our work."

I glared at Logan. "And it couldn't wait another hour?"

Bob's mouth dropped open; he wasn't one to antagonize anyone, at least, not on purpose. He drove most people nuts just being himself.

Logan regarded me thoughtfully but didn't answer. Instead, he turned to Amy.

"Amy, the work we do is quite important. There is an element of danger, as Peg discovered earlier this year, but we work hard to maintain safety," he told her.

She listened carefully, her eyes never leaving his face.

"You recently acquired the gift of sight, and I am aware of the shock which accompanies your new abilities. It is normal at this point in time." He smiled down at her. "When I walked the earth, seeing a spirit was considered a great milestone for a person's spiritual development. Sadly, it is not the case in today's world."

She remained stock-still but managed a small nod at his words.

"The men in the woods protect you and Peg, so do not be alarmed."

"Okay," she squeaked.

Smiling kindly, he said, "You will be working with Peg from this point forward. I believe Jack Monroe will also be involved." He glanced at me, and I nodded.

Amy's surprise was evident at this news. "Jack Monroe? The chief of police? I had no idea!"

Andy laughed, "There are more people, but I'll let Logan guide you concerning others."

Nodding, Logan said, "Many people help; you will not be alone. But I must warn you, do not take any action yourself."

She nodded. "I'm not sure what I can do to help. I'm not a young person."

"Youth does not guarantee success," he answered.

Frowning, she asked, "Am I allowed to ask you something?"

He nodded.

"Does Albert help you?"

Logan's face became guarded. "No, he is not a candidate. I am sorry."

Amy became thoughtful for a moment and then said, "I'm not surprised. He always was a bit self-centered."

Andy had to turn his head to hide his smile. We knew Albert was a pain in the butt; everyone in the township was aware of the his ghastly personality. He argued with the town council about everything from road maintenance to snow removal.

Logan regarded her silently. Bob, however, said, "Ha! You don't know selfish until you've met my wife!'

Logan turned to face Bob, who turned a deep shade of red. "Sorry," he managed to say, chastised.

She looked at Bob thoughtfully. "I do seem to remember her. Elaine, right?"

Bob nodded but kept his mouth shut.

She looked at the ceiling, thinking. "Didn't she help Albert fight the township about the new horse trail they were trying to allow at the community center?"

"Yep, it was her," said Bob, trying to ignore Logan.

"Yes," Amy nodded. "I thought so. She wasn't a very nice person, was she?"

"You could say that," said Bob. "I never realized how mean she was until we got over to the other side. Just accepted her bad temperament."

Amy nodded again. "Yes, it is what you have to do to survive, isn't it?"

Well, hell. I was seeing Amy in a new light. Her marriage to Albert wasn't much better than Bob's to Elaine. Gratitude for Andy swelled inside me. I had taken his love and kindness for granted all these years. I felt my eyes water.

Hoping no one noticed the tears, I said, "So what's all this have to do with the Spanelli case?"

Logan turned to me. "Everything. I am aware you have gained knowledge of other helpers."

Bob turned red again; if this kept up, he'd stay red-faced permanently. Obviously, Logan had gotten wind of Bob's screw-up concerning my three favorite mob guys. Poor Santino.

"Yep," I answered, wishing my morning need for caffeine had been met.

"The information must remain confidential. More than their lives are at stake." I recognized a command when I heard one. He could have saved his breath. I was well aware that bit of news was a secret, even if Bob hadn't.

"Yep," I repeated. "No problem."

He nodded.

I jerked my head in Amy's direction. "So what do you want from Amy?"

Before he could answer, the doorbell rang again. Oh, for Pete's sake! I looked at Andy, who shrugged. Considering we had a kitchen full of dead and living people, not much was shocking him at this point. He pivoted and went to answer the door.

I raised an eyebrow at Logan. His eyes locked with mine, but he didn't utter one word. I had a sneaking suspicion he was well aware of the new arrival long before the doorbell announced we had more company.

I heard voices coming down the hall and recognized Jack's laugh.

Rounding the corner, Jack held up a hand in defense. "Peg, don't get your panties in a wad. I was told to be here, but I bear gifts."

I looked at his hands, filled with bags and a huge cup of coffee.

"Muffins, anyone?" he asked and smiled.

I reached for the coffee, ignoring the bag of muffins. The first sip was heavenly. Sighing, I sat back in my chair. "Thanks, Jack."

Grinning, he said, "When I heard what time we were to be here, I knew I would need a bribe to keep you from hitting the roof."

Andy laughed.

"I'd give anything to be able to drink coffee," said Bob wistfully.

Logan patiently endured the munching which ensued, not interfering with the social atmosphere. Once the last muffin had been snagged by Jack and Amy had a fresh cup of tea, he resumed.

"Since we are all here now, I will explain the plan. Amy, you were a high school science teacher. Correct?"

She looked surprised but nodded. "Yes, biology."

"Jack, you have many resources available to you no one else has access to, correct?"

Jack swallowed the last bite of his muffin before answering, "Yep."

If my old friend wasn't careful, those muffins would land square on his expanding waistline.

"Andy, you have a very analytical mind and will be an important piece in this investigation."

Andy nodded.

Turning to me, he said, "And, Peg, you have the capacity to antagonize people, who then respond in some unfortunate manner."

My temper flared. "I don't antagonize anyone!" I snapped.

Andy grinned, Jack choked, and Bob coughed.

"What?" I demanded. "Did I antagonize Owen? No, I did not! I never even suspected the little creep!"

"You were the catalyst that forced his hand. I will admit, those annoyed by you last time were mostly on our side of the veil."

"Yeah, and they scare me spitless! My mother being at the top of the list."

"Oh, dear," said Amy. "Your mother is involved?"

Ignoring her question, I glared at Logan. "That side of veil is *your* problem! I have absolutely no control over a dead person."

His eyes twinkled. "Very true; however, your talent of provoking elicits much-needed activity to flush their intentions to the surface."

My eyes became slits; I knew they had, because the only person I could see was Logan. My teeth gritted, as I said very plainly, each word enunciated completely, "I…do…not…antagonize anyone!"

"How would you characterize your investigating skills?" asked Logan, head tilted.

"I blunder along, with absolutely no idea what the hell I'm doing!"

He smiled slightly, nodding his head. "Correct. Your 'blundering' as you call it, creates anxiety in people when you step too close to their secrets. Whether you understand the fact is not my concern."

103

"You want me to change? I wouldn't know where to begin! I'm not trained to investigate crime."

"No, you are not, nor do I want you to change." He pointed to Jack. "He does though. He will guide you."

Jack looked startled. "Me?" he asked, pointing his finger to his own chest.

Logan nodded. "Yes. You have taught her much."

"Like what?" I demanded. "No offense, Jack," I said to him. "But you have to admit, even you aren't aware of any teaching taking place."

Amy had been watching the conversation with apprehension. Raising her hand, she said, "May I say something?"

Logan turned to her. "Yes?"

"Maybe Peg and I should take self-defense classes." Her timid voice wavered a little. "It was just a thought," she said, as my mouth dropped open.

Logan's eyes sparkled as he nodded. Looking at me, he said, "I believe it is a wise course of action."

Throwing my hands in the air, I asked, "And when do I have time for classes?"

Andy cleared his throat. "Peg, I think Amy has a good idea. After last time, we should have already signed you up for them." Turning to Amy, he said, "Way to go, Amy!"

She blushed, while I fumed. I didn't want to take self-defense classes—mainly, because I didn't want to believe I would ever have the need to self-defend. Sighing in defeat, I knew if I continued helping Logan's gang, those classes were necessary. Bloody hell.

"Classes won't help me defend against the dead," I pointed out.

"Correct. However, there are few on our side who have the capacity to harm you physically."

I shuddered, knowing the damage which could be inflicted would be from the living influenced by the nonliving.

"Fine." I looked at Amy. "You find classes to attend, and let me know when and where."

Alarmed at my suggestion, she glanced at Logan, who nodded. "An excellent idea."

"I thought this was a meeting about the case, not about my deficiencies and how to correct them."

Bob piped up, "Oh, it's next on the agenda. Logan's got it all planned out!" This proclamation earned Bob a slow glare from Logan. Bob slammed his mouth shut and looked at the ceiling, frantically ignoring Logan's displeasure. Good luck.

# Chapter 12

"The Spanelli family has been of great concern on both sides of the veil for centuries," Logan said. "Amy, I realize you do not have the facts of the current situation. Peg will explain the details later, but you will learn much from listening."

Amy nodded. She took orders better than I did; being married to Albert must have trained her well.

Logan continued. "We have observed their criminal activities through the centuries, identifying the leader in each generation. Our orders, until recently, were to merely nudge situations to keep them under control. The last century, when they immigrated to this country, became more serious. Their power has increased greatly, which was significant; they were extremely powerful back in Sicily." He paused, looking around at us.

Jack was hanging on to every word. Logan had recently given Jack the ability not only hear him but also to see him. Even though he knew they were around, seeing Logan for the first time had been startling. Jack obviously had become comfortable with the sensation of watching a dead person giving orders and making speeches.

"It was alarming they made their home base in Ohio rather than New York or Chicago," he said.

"Why?" Jack asked.

Logan turned to him. "It was proof they were receiving aid from our side." He shook his head. "Otherwise they would have remained in a larger city, where the Mafia was firmly in place."

"Not necessarily," said Amy quietly.

Logan cocked his head, gently smiling at her. "What are your thoughts?" he asked her kindly.

Absentmindedly rubbing her finger along a drop of coffee on my well-worn kitchen table, she looked up at him. "Why stay in a city where the competition is securely established? If it had been me, I would have moved somewhere free from interference. I don't know much about these types of people, but I have seen movies. They spend as much time fighting each other as they do fighting outsiders."

From their expressions, I could tell both Logan and Jack were impressed with her analysis. I hate to admit it, but so was I. The old gal could really work through a problem. Must be all the scientific logic she taught.

Logan gave her an appraising look, saying, "You have made an excellent point, and one we had not necessarily taken seriously."

Andy piped up with his own thoughts. "Amy's idea is great, but what if there is another wrinkle in this mess? What if there were associates in Youngstown who were more along the lines of silent partners?"

Logan beamed. "I am grateful for both opinions; they are quite perceptive."

Turning to me, he said, "Peg, do you understand why their involvement is necessary? This gathering…" He swept his arm around my kitchen, "…was to collect ideas." He shook his head, saying, "Our side of life has faults. Our observations and activities tend to be framed by our own experiences while living." He shook his head sadly. "Human nature seldom changes."

"I'm sorry, Logan, but I was under the impression my main concern was Caterina. Stopping the Mafia is way out of my experience," I said. "Hell, finding who ran down the girl is out of my expertise; adding the Mafia angle into my job description is…" I shook my head. "Outta my league entirely."

"There is much you do not know at this point," Logan said, his eyes locked with mine.

Laughing, I said, "Ya think? You haven't given us much to work with but hope we stumble across solutions as we bumble our way through these assignments." I hope he caught my frustration.

"We have people in place who will come to your aid at the appropriate time," he remarked, ignoring my irritation.

"Yeah, like my three buddies," I snapped.

Bob went white and then turned an interesting shade of red. He looked at me, pleading with his eyes. I guess he wanted me to shut up. Good luck with me biting my tongue.

"Yes, it is unfortunate you are aware of their allegiance," Logan said, allowing his eyes to slide over to Bob. When they had found their way back to mine, he continued. "However, the knowledge is now yours. I trust I may count on you to refrain from sharing it with anyone."

"I have no intentions of 'sharing' info with anyone; those guys saved my life. Even when I thought they were crooks, I appreciated the fact."

Logan nodded, satisfied with my answer. "I believe discovering who hurt Caterina will be an important key, one which allows our side to accomplish a goal."

I stared at him and then said, "Okay, I'll trust you know what you're doing. But finding the jerk who ran down a little girl doesn't guarantee you'll get the answers you want."

"We have made great progress. Thank you for your time," he said.

As he began to fade, I spoke up.

"Logan!" The fading stopped. "What's Elaine doing, popping up around here?"

He returned completely. "Elaine? When?"

Uh-oh. He had no idea she had been back here. Not good.

"Very recently. Couple of days ago."

His absolute stillness gave me shivers. At least it wasn't a hot flash.

Turning to Bob, he said, "Please find her whereabouts."

Nodding, Bob vanished. I heard Amy's sharp intake of air. She'd have to get used to this crap sooner rather than later. They came and went as they pleased, with little warning. Logan had been kind to her, but I wasn't sure the behavior would continue.

Facing me, he asked, "Your mother?"

"Nope. Haven't seen or heard her, but it doesn't mean she isn't lurking."

He nodded thoughtfully. "I will investigate. Thank you. Please advise me if either appear again."

"You got it," I said, as he faded.

The four us who had heartbeats sat silently, lost in our own thoughts. I, for one, was annoyed. Finding who hurt a little girl was one thing, stopping the Mafia was not an agenda I was prepared to tackle.

Jack finally broke the silence. Clearing his throat, he said, "Well, that was interesting." Not an original opening line.

Andy laughed. "Logan is a leader for damn sure. Wonder what he was like when alive?"

"Pretty much what he's like now. What I'd like to know is, *who* was he when he was alive? I know he wasn't the real Logan." I sighed. I had a feeling my curiosity about my tall Indian would never be satisfied. I'd bet money he liked to keep me guessing.

My statement silenced our little team once again.

"Not sure I want to actually know," Jack said eventually. "Might make me nervous."

I grinned at him. "Like he doesn't make you nervous now!"

Jack returned my grin. "Yeah, he does a little."

Amy had remained quiet, but now said, "Peg, I am serious about the self-defense classes. We're dabbling around formidable people. It could lead to real trouble."

Sighing, I agreed. "Yep, I know. Spanelli is scary, and I'll bet he's dangerous. Doesn't help the whole family has issues." Looking at Jack, I asked, "So how much of this do you think the mayor knows? Should we tell him his little friend is looney?"

Amy looked stunned. "The mayor? Of Akron? Oh, dear, is he involved?"

I slumped back into my chair. Damn, I had forgotten she wasn't up to speed yet. "Only a little. He knows Mr. Spanelli. At least, I hope that's the extent of his involvement. Wouldn't surprise me one bit to find out he's in deeper than he should be." Shrugging, I said, "Not my problem."

Frowning, Amy asked, "Does he know, well, about these dead people?"

Jack laughed. "Oh, yeah, he knows."

I shot Jack a warning glare. We had promised never to divulge the fact the mayor's son had been partially involved in Owen's case. He had witnessed Bob and Elaine's murders, but Owen had threatened to kill his entire family if the poor kid ever told. The mayor had spent years suspecting his son Alex had been an accomplice, using his power as mayor to cover up evidence. Once Owen had been discovered and killed by one of the mob guys helping protect me, the mayor had gone to the district attorney. Everyone had agreed since Owen was dead, no good would come of dragging Alex through the courts, sweeping the incident under the rug. It wasn't pretty, and Alex was finally getting his life in order, but years of psychological abuse from Owen had taken a toll.

"The mayor was able to give us some help with Bob and Elaine's investigation. Along the way, he became privy to our association with Logan. Actually, he also loaned me a few of his security people for protection." I hoped it would satisfy her curiosity.

She listened intently, nodding thoughtfully as I finished my explanation. "I always wondered if the gossip about his mob connections was true. Albert was convinced he was in the mob himself, but I never did believe he was."

"So you like the mayor?" I asked. Probably a good idea to know where she stood, considering my nasty streak concerning the guy flared up at times. No sense upsetting her with the occasional snotty remark about him.

"Oh, dear me, no! He's awfully rude, isn't he? I was downtown at city hall a few years back, and he bumped into me. He almost knocked me down and never even apologized," she said.

I nodded. Sounded about right.

"What's the next move, Jack?" Andy asked.

Jack thought about the question, then said, "I think Mrs. Spanelli would enjoy another visit from Peg and me. Can't do it till later today." He glanced my direction. "Would it work for you?"

I quickly did a mental check on my plans for the day. Other than laundry and thawing a roast for tonight's dinner, I was free for another visit. "Yep. But right now I need a shower."

Andy said, "I need to get to the office. They're probably wondering if I got lost on the way to work." He laughed.

Amy stood up. "When I get home, I'm looking up classes for Peg and me. Wonder if my computer still works; I haven't turned it on in months."

Wow, Amy had a computer; I would have never guessed she even had one, much less knew how to use it. She must have guessed my thoughts by my expression and smiled. "Albert didn't like them, but I was fascinated. So much information at your fingertips! Amazing!"

Well, well, well. She could prove more interesting than I ever imagined.

"Let's get a move on," I declared, pushing back from the table. "I'm heading for the shower." I walked towards the bedroom, hoping everyone, including Andy, would take the hint and leave me alone to enjoy some peace and quiet. They did, and I relished the solitude, working my way through my own morning routine. It was not complicated, and within an hour, I was ready for the day. Maybe. I still wasn't thrilled about those self-defense classes.

Puttering around the kitchen, clearing the small amount of dishes from the morning's social gathering, I jumped when the phone rang. Glancing down at the caller ID, I frowned as I read 'Private Caller.' Shaking my head, I walked back to the sink. Those were usually telemarketers, and I hated those calls. I decided to let the answering machine cope. While dumping dishwashing soap into the sink, the machine clicked on and I heard my least favorite voice.

"Mrs. Shaw? Are you there?" The mayor. What could he want? I hesitated a moment before sighing and making my way back to the phone.

Grabbing it, I said, "What do you want?" My manners went out the window where this guy was concerned.

"Oh, good. You were home."

"Yep. What's up?"

"You remember when you were in my office?"

How could I forget? "Yep."

He paused and then said, "Did you have any of your friends with you by any chance?"

I could sense his uneasiness, which made me itchy. If he was anxious, it spelled possible trouble.

I took a deep breath. "Nope, not to my knowledge. Why?"

Silence greeted my remark. I shifted my stance, glancing around the yard towards the woods. Nope, no Indians. Not for the first time was I grateful for my built in barometer. If I had seen my guys out back, I think I'd have peed my pants. It was that type of day already.

"You sure?" he asked.

"Positive. What's this about? You might as well tell me, and I don't have time for guessing games," I snapped.

"I don't want to say too much on the phone," he answered.

"Oh, for Pete's sake! Just tell me."

"I think someone's here," he whispered. Idiot. Whispering around spirits wasn't going to keep them from hearing you.

"Okay, what makes you think you have an invisible visitor?" I took a quick glance again out back. Still nothing, thank goodness.

"Just a feeling," he continued to whisper.

I opened my mouth for a smart-ass remark but slammed it shut. From personal experience, if you felt something around, it could be an early warning sign.

Sighing, I said, "I'll look into the matter."

I could sense his relief through the phone. I hoped he realized there wasn't much I could do about rogue spirits. I couldn't even control the friendly guys.

"Be careful, and don't wander away from your office today. I'll get back to you if I figure out what's going on,"

"Thanks. I really appreciate your help," he said.

"No problem," I said, trying to remember to be polite.

I hung up the phone with an icky feeling in the pit of my stomach. Finishing the dishes, which didn't take long, I decided Bob could possibly give me insight. For as much as he irritated me, I was constantly surprised by his understanding of certain situations. It was probably unintentional on his part, but his intuition had helped before and might help now.

"Bob!" I yelled.

Nothing. Frowning, I tried again. "Bob!"

Calling for him had always worked instantly before; I wondered if Logan had him on assignment. It would make sense.

Well, hell. Now what? I sat at the kitchen table, drumming my fingers while lost in thought. The air suddenly changed. About damn time.

"What do you think you are doing?" came my mother's voice.

Great. The last person, besides Elaine, I wanted bothering me.

I turned to face her. "I'm sitting here. What are you talking about?" I asked.

"You seem to have a bad habit of butting in where you aren't wanted," she sneered.

"Please clarify," I said, teeth gritted tightly. I threw a quick glance out the window, dismayed to see all my lovely Indians standing at the edge of the woods. Even without my glasses, I could tell they were antsy, shifting their feet, watching the house. Jeez Louise, to make matters worse, I felt a hot flash starting. The day just got better and better.

"You know exactly what I'm referring to! The kid."

Uh-oh. Deciding to play dumb, I said, "Kid? There's a lot of kids in the world. Which kid?"

She threw back her head, laughing. "Evading my questions didn't work when you were a teenager, and it doesn't work now."

My eyes became slits. "How would you know anything about my teenage years?" I snapped as the heat of hormones flooded my body. My mother had chosen the wrong time to confront me. "Listen, lady, you weren't around back then, so why don't you continue your routine and not bother being around now!"

Her eyes widened. "Well, well. Your temper hasn't improved."

I started fanning myself, hoping to lessen the sensation of sitting in an oven. It never helped, but it makes me believe I'm at least doing *something*.

Watching me carefully, she eventually grinned. "Ah, you're having a hot flash. How hilarious."

"Not to me it isn't."

With a malicious grin, she continued, "I don't miss my physical body." She preened, saying, "I'm much happier now."

I shook my head. Her ego never ceased to amaze me. "Yep, you took quite a few years off your appearance by dying."

She tossed me a dirty look and changed the subject. "You need to stay away from Logan. His plans for you tend to be dangerous to your life expectancy." She smiled meanly.

"Whether I hang out with Logan or not is honestly none of your business," I snapped.

Her sick laughter rang through my house. "I disagree." A chill ran up my spine, which helped with the waning hot flash.

My eyes quickly darted to the wooded area out back. She noticed my glance and laughed again. "They aren't there anymore! I took care of the unwanted guards," she declared, gloating.

Frowning at her, I remained quiet. I could see all of my Indians clearly. Why on earth did she think she had disposed of them? Couldn't she look out back and see them, now pacing back and forth?

Even though I had no idea what her problem was concerning my guys, I decided to change the conversation until I had an explanation from Logan.

"What about the girl is so important to you? She's been hurt."

"I know about the incident," my mother snapped. "Her idiot father failed to keep her safe. It's his only job, and he's screwing it up royally!"

Working hard to keep my face from alerting Mom she had just given me a choice piece of information, I said, "Well, I agree, he hasn't done his job very well. She's in the ICU."

My mother stared at me, appraising how much I knew or didn't know. Never good at fooling her, I fought for facial control. It wasn't easy.

"Look, Mom, it's been a long day already and it isn't even noon. I'm in no mood for your crap. Leave!"

Glaring at me, she quickly disappeared. I took a deep breath of relief. I made a mental note to explain to Amy the ability to force a spirit to leave; she would certainly need it if she was becoming part of our team.

"Wow, that was close," said Bob.

I jumped, turning to face him. "Bob! You know the rule! You aren't supposed to scare me."

His face fell. "Gosh, Peg. I made noise before I spoke."

Shaking my head, I said, "Sorry, didn't hear anything." Studying him, I asked, "I called you; why didn't you come earlier?"

"I tried. I couldn't get through," he said, voice quivering a little.

"What? I figured you were doing a chore for Logan."

"Yeah, but it was minor. As soon as I heard you yell for me, I tried to get here, but I was blocked." He shook his head. "Never happened before; it was scary!"

My mouth dropped open as he spoke, fear creeping into my bones. Bob was right; it was scary.

Gathering my wits, I said, "Bob, look at to the woods. Do you see anything?"

He frowned but did as I asked. "Yeah, the guys are standing around looking at the house."

I sighed, shoulders sagging in relief. "Mom was convinced they were no longer there," I said.

His eyes widened. "Wow. Logan must have done something to keep her from seeing them," he said, in awe of Logan's abilities.

I must admit, even I admired this newest trick of Logan's. It was one thing to hide my guys out back from the living; that was easy. But to have the power to hide them from other spirits must take be unique.

"Wow, it's so cool!" gushed Bob. "Sorta like the invisible cloak in Harry Potter."

I frowned. "Bob, those books came out way after you and Elaine had died. How do you know about Harry Potter?"

He evaded my eyes. "I've been catching up."

"Catching up? How, exactly, have you been managing to catch up?" Suspicion was growing inside me.

Bob remained silent; I guess the idiot hoped I wouldn't push the issue. "Bob!"

"Fine," he said, bringing his eyes to mine. "I kept hearing about the books and movies. So I went to the bookstore to learn the order they were written." He stopped, hoping it would be enough of an explanation.

"Go on," I said.

Sighing, he said, "Whenever I find someone watching the movies, I sit with them. Do you know how hard it's been, making sure I watched them in order?"

Shaking with laughter, I said, "Bob, you've made my day! I'm glad you enjoyed them."

With a worried look on his face, he whispered, "Don't tell Logan."

Wiping laughter tears from my face, I said, "Your secret is safe with me."

"Thanks, Peg."

# Chapter 13

"Bob, do you remember the other day when I went to the mayor's office?" I asked, once I had stopped laughing.

"Yep."

"Was there anyone with me? You know, from your side?"

Frowning in concentration, he said, "I don't think so; why?"

Tapping my finger on the table, I said, "He called this morning and has the feeling something, or someone, stayed behind with him."

"Uh-oh, not good," he said, worried.

"Yeah, it's the reason I called you," I said. "Anyway you could find out if someone is hanging out at his office?"

He thought about it for a moment, saying, "Peg, I'd have to run this by Logan. I really can't investigate without permission." He paused. "I'm certain he'll want to know about this though and send me anyway."

I agreed with his analysis of Logan; he more than likely would use Bob to snoop around. The strategy had come in handy in the past.

The doorbell rang before the conversation could continue. "Amy," Bob informed me.

Nodding, I realized Bob's abilities were increasing. *Must be Logan's influence.*

I made my way to the door. When I opened it, Amy stood happily on my stoop.

"Hi Peg. I found some places we can take classes. We have quite a few options!" she announced.

"Come in." I was startled to see she was still a bit disheveled. This wasn't good; wasn't being involved supposed to be engaging her in life again?

"I didn't want to make appointments until I checked with you. I realize your work with Logan has to come first. No sense joining a class we don't have time to attend."

Nodding, I said, "Good point."

We made it back to the kitchen, and I was surprised Bob was still standing near the window.

"Hello, Bob," said Amy. How quickly she had become comfortable with dead people.

"Hey, Amy. Signed up for classes yet?"

Smiling, she said, "Thought I should check with Peg first."

"Good idea. She's got a temper."

"I'm standing right here, guys," I snapped.

Bob looked at Amy. "See?"

Giving them both a sigh of exasperation, I plopped in my chair.

Bob glanced at me. "I'm off to update Logan. You need anything else before I leave?"

"Nope. It was my main concern," I said, throwing a warning look his way. Amy didn't need to know how involved the mayor was in our activities. I'd let Logan decide when she could be included.

With a quick glance at Amy, he nodded, letting me know he got the message. A few months back, it took a sledgehammer for Bob to understand a warning look. I was impressed.

Giving us both a quick wave, Bob faded.

"I find it so fascinating how they disappear., so gradually," Amy remarked.

"Yeah, it's one way to describe it," I said. "I find most of this crap irritating."

She gave me an understanding look. "Yes, I suppose you would."

Now, what the hell did her comment mean?

"Would you like to check out a few of the places?" she asked, indicating the piece of paper in her hand.

I gave her an appraising look. "Sure. We need to stop at the mall first."

"The mall?" she asked, confusion filled her face. "Well, okay. But I'm not allowing you to wriggle out of these classes," she informed me.

What a determined little cuss.

"Fine."

The drive to the mall was filled with her chatter. I learned more about Amy in those ten minutes than I had in all the years we had been neighbors.

"I tried gardening. You would think a science teacher could manage basic gardening, but I never seemed to have a knack."

It takes a knack to pull weeds? I let her babble the entire way.

Happily, I found a parking spot was easily. Amy wouldn't have far to walk, and the last thing I wanted to do was poop her out before we had gotten started with errands.

She continued talking but stopped suddenly as we approached my favorite cosmetic counter. "Do you need to buy something?" she asked.

"Nope. But if you're supposed to be starting with a fresh life, let's give you a new look."

Seeing her nervousness, I reassured her. "Amy, nothing big. Just a little pick-me-up."

"They'll try to sell me something," she said.

"Nope, they're nice guys."

"Mrs. Shaw! It's been a while," gushed Sean, pulling me into a huge bear hug. One of these days, he was going to squish me so hard, I'd pee on the floor. "What are we doing today? You look pretty good."

Shaking my head, I said, "Not me." Pointing at Amy, I continued. "Her."

Sean turned, smiling. His smile fell immediately. "Oh, dear." Taking her hand, he gently guided her to his chair. "Make yourself comfortable." He turned back to me. "Really?" he mouthed.

"Nothing serious, Sean. I thought maybe enough of something to remind her she's still alive."

"Oh, Peg," came a small voice from the chair. "I've never worn makeup."

Sean's eye became as big as saucers. "Never?" he asked, astonished.

"Oh no, dear. My late husband would not allow it," she sighed.

The more I heard about Albert, the less I liked the jerk. Andy had never given me rules to follow. We had simple rules: no comments about hair, weight, or clothes. I have gotten the occasional surprised look if I had grabbed the wrong hair color box at the grocery store, but that was pretty much the extent of reactions.

Sean began studying Amy. "Tell me about yourself," he said. "It helps me decide exactly what I need to accomplish."

Amy nodded. "I am a retired school teacher."

Sean gave her a quick smile. "What subject?" he asked, pulling his comb from a bag behind the counter. As he fussed around her, he kept her talking. She answered every question and after a few minutes, began to relax. Watching her face, I realized she had probably never had this type of attention before, which was another reason to happily hate Albert.

"You have great natural curls," he informed her as he worked wonders.

Blushing, she said, "I never knew quite what to do with them. They have a mind of their own."

Sean smiled. "They are perfect. I'll show you how to control them."

I was grateful Sean used to be a hairdresser but gave it up for cosmetics. He would be able to fix her hair and face at the same time!

Amy beamed, shyly glancing in my direction. I nodded but turned toward the shoe department. How convenient to have them so close to the cosmetics! I wandered over, allowing Amy to have Sean's full attention. I decided she needed some pampering, and I was a distraction since he always wanted to know about my dead friends.

Wandering around, I felt the air change. Jeez, I couldn't grab a break at all today! The hair on my arms stood straight up, which told me Elaine was nearby.

"Not surprised to find you at the mall again," she snipped. "Seems the only thing you do is shop."

I refused to answer her comment, considering I hate shopping with a passion. I seldom hit the mall unless I wanted a pretzel or fabulous pizza. Of course, it meant to earn those treats, I had to walk around every store to justify the calorie intake.

My silence infuriated her, which was fine by me. I hated her, so anything that bothered her, gave me great joy. I picked up a sandal, inspecting a shoe that would never find a home on my foot. Shaking my head at the ridiculously high price for so little leather, I placed it back on the display. *Who pays these prices?* I was a huge fan of half-off sales and, even then, I was picky.

Elaine had noticed Amy and laughed. "Who's the old lady?"

I continued to ignore her. I learned last time how stupid I appeared to everyone when I was apparently talking to myself. It didn't take long to learn my lesson. I seldom opened my mouth to spirits in public. It happened, usually when my temper exploded, but I did try to keep my composure.

Knowing Amy could see the dead made me sweat a little, and I hoped Elaine would assume she would be invisible to the poor old gal. The last thing I needed was for Amy to react to suddenly seeing Elaine. Sean was oblivious to us, and Amy had her face away from me, but Elaine was a mean woman. I had no idea what she had up her sleeve. I continued to meander further from the makeover taking place. I was careful to move slowly, inspecting the displays. Move too quickly, and Elaine's radar would go into overdrive.

"You don't fool me one bit," she announced.

I felt sweat drip down between my boobs. Elaine tended to have that particular effect on me. I remained silent; the added bonus was I knew it was driving the bitch bonkers.

She followed me all the way down the aisle, near the exit. So far, so good. "I know you can hear me!" she screamed.

I flinched but still kept my trap shut. Determination is a strong motivator, and I sure was determined not to allow her to drive me over the edge.

Finally maneuvering us to a corner, right outside the door, I asked quietly, "What do you want?"

"A warning. You need to stay out of this affair."

"Affair? You're having an affair?" I smiled sweetly. Honestly, I was beginning to enjoy our chat, now we were safely away from Amy.

"You know damn well what I'm referring to!" she hissed.

Gosh, I wondered if I was pushing Elaine over the edge. My day was looking up.

"Oh, Peg!" I heard a voice hailing me.

Damn it!

Turning, I saw Amy heading in my direction. I have to admit, she looked tons better once Sean had finished with her. He had managed to tame the wild curls, and the makeup he applied was age appropriate. She beamed with joy. "What do you think?"

I looked past her, spotting Sean waiting for my approval. I grinned, nodding, with a thumbs-up. He had done a great job and deserved high praise.

As she approached, she glanced at Elaine, nodding. "Hi, Elaine." Then she turned back to me, ignoring Elaine completely. I raised an eyebrow, but Elaine's mouth dropped open.

"How dare you!" she snarled.

Amy calmly looked back at her, saying one word, "Leave." I thought Elaine would explode; it was great.

Once the fading image of Elaine was completely gone, I turned to Amy. "You handled Elaine well."

She blushed. "While your friend was prettying me up, Bob warned me. He also explained how I could make her disappear, which was helpful. I don't remember if you had told me or not, but I'm glad Bob made sure I understood."

"Bob warned you?" I asked, surprised. I hadn't even noticed him or felt his arrival. He was gaining way too much aptitude recently. Logan's tutoring must really be intense.

"Oh yes, and he was real careful not to frighten me. I think your friend knew someone had appeared, but he was real sweet about my head moving."

Yes, Sean deserved an award for his kindness towards Amy. "So, you happy with the results?" I asked.

"Heaven's sake, yes. I had no idea what a little makeup could accomplish. All those years, feeling frumpy! I truly never knew." She shook her head.

"Well, you look great," I told her. Not only did she look younger, she also had a bit of spring to her step. Now for some decent clothes.

"We're in the ladies department, so why not look at a few things?" I asked.

"Oh, I couldn't spend this type of money! I already bought some cosmetics. So expensive!" she declared.

I took her firmly by the arm. "Nope. A few new things will do the trick. Trust me."

An hour later, armed with packages, we headed for the car. "I've never spent so much money at one time in my entire life!" she told me, flushed with excitement.

"I hope we haven't broken the bank," I laughed.

"Oh, no. The one thing about Albert, he saved money and made investments rather well."

"Nice to have a sense of security." I smiled.

"Yes. The last time the accountant called, I was somewhere around the million mark. You think it will last me?" she asked, worried.

My chin hit the pavement. Turning to her, I stuttered, "Dollars?"

"Yes, is there something wrong? You don't think it will get me through?"

I slammed my mouth closed and took a deep breath. "Amy, you'll be fine. What makes you worry it isn't enough?"

"Albert was always worried we wouldn't have enough for his retirement. We scrimped and saved until we had enough to start investing. Albert took care of the money. My salary went into the stock market, and his went into his portfolio." *Of course it did*, I thought. I would bet the bank, the jerk figured he'd outlast her.

"How did he die? I'm sorry, I don't remember."

"It's okay. He had a heart attack. Died in his sleep. I slept next to him all night and didn't even know he was gone until I woke the next morning." Her eyes teared at the memory, and I quickly changed the subject.

"Well, you have enough cash flow to live very comfortably for the rest of your life. I don't want you fretting," I told her.

She looked at me with trusting eyes, saying, "Thank you. I've worried for years."

Smiling, I gave her a quick hug as we approached the car.

Once settled in her seat, safety belt firmly attached, she turned to me. "Now, we can check out the self-defense places." She pulled a list from her purse.

Sighing, I held out my hand for the list. Scanning it, I chose the nearest address to the mall. I made it out of the mall parking lot without a lot of swearing. People drove nuts in parking lots, and I've never understood why normal drivers decide a large space of concrete is the place to go crazy.

It only took five minutes to reach the self-defense studio. I parked, glancing around and noticed my favorite drive-in junk-food place was down the road only a few blocks. I tucked the information away, and we headed inside.

I could feel Amy's excitement as she stood next to me, practically bouncing with anticipation. *Jeez, I've created a monster.* Logan could stop torturing himself about her engaging life again. If she got any more engaged, we'd have bigger problems. No telling what she might do with her newfound lifestyle.

The receptionist greeted us with a huge smile. "You ladies looking for lessons?" she asked brightly.

I got tired just hearing the energy in her voice.

"Oh yes," gushed Amy. "Is the instructor here? I have a few questions."

"You can ask me anything you need," the girl answered. "It's what I'm here for."

Amy shook her head, her newly controlled curls wiggling with her determination.

"No. I want to interview the instructor. Your classes are a bit pricey, and I want to know if the price matches the services."

The girl became flustered. Obviously, no one had ever asked to interview the owner.

Holding a finger up, she said, "Just a sec. I'll see if he has time."

While she checked, I looked around the room—plain but not boring. The mats on the floor were probably where customers practiced, I decided. The air smelled clean, so they understood hygiene. I walked over to a table that sat off to one side, filled with brochures. I picked up the first one that caught my eye and began thumbing through it quickly. The pictures showed different classes at work. *Gosh, they did a lot of physical work in this place,* I thought.

"How may I help you," said a familiar voice. I couldn't place it until I turned to the owner.

"Oh, for Pete's sake," I blurted, unable to allow my brain time to control my mouth.

The owner of the voice grinned. "Hey, Mrs. Shaw. Nice to see you again," said Bill.

Amy turned to me, surprised by my reaction.

"Amy, meet Bill. He and a couple of his friends helped me out a few months back," I explained. "Yeah, and saved my life," I didn't add.

Amy looked at Bill thoughtfully for a few moments and then nodded. "The dead body at Peg's house?" she asked.

I looked at her in shock. How on earth had she put it together so quickly?

She smiled at me. "Logic. I taught science, remember?"

I cocked my head at her. "Did Albert know you were this intelligent?"

"Oh, heaven's no!" She smiled. "He never acknowledged the fact I had a master's degree in biochemistry." She shook her head sadly. "I became a teacher because he believed teaching or nursing were the only two professions appropriate for a Christian lady."

"A master's degree!" I asked, shocked at the news. I suddenly realized I had underestimated my new partner. I felt myself turn red, embarrassed I had thought so little of her.

She patted my arm. "Don't feel bad, dear. Most people have no idea. Albert made sure my education was kept under wraps."

I felt anger towards the twit she had been married to for so long. How could he have demeaned her so much? Why had she married such a jerk?

Bill interrupted, saying, "What can I do to help you ladies?"

"I didn't know you ran this place. Since when?" I asked.

"Antonio, Santino and I opened this about five years ago. We knew our time with our other job wasn't going to last forever, and we wanted something to fall back on when we finished up with the family," he said, shrugging. "We have seven locations now."

"Wow."

"What made you decide to take self-defense classes?" he asked.

I opened my mouth to answer, but Amy beat me to the punch.

"In our line of work, we need to know how to protect ourselves."

His eyes grew wide. His grin matched. "Really? And what line of work would that be?"

She narrowed her eyes, studying his face. "I'm sure you are well aware of our line of work."

Surprised, he turned to me.

Shrugging, I said, "I don't know what to tell you. Logan's involved."

"Ah. Which explains everything. Let's go back to my office."

"So you know Bob blew everything," I said, careful not to spill the beans to Amy. Logan could tell her if he saw fit, but I didn't want to complicate matters. I wouldn't be surprised if she figured it out all by herself; I was beginning to understand she was damn savvy.

Bill threw his head back, laughing. "Santino wanted to kill him on the spot."

"Yep. Doesn't surprise me."

Closing the door behind us, he said, "Take a seat, ladies."

Amy pulled a long list from her purse. "I have a few questions."

Smiling, Bill said, "Let's go over your list. I'm sure we can help."

Jeez.

# Chapter 14

Two hours later, Bill ushered us out the front door, smiling. I figured he got a kick out of Amy, plus a big fat check from me. No wonder his smile was huge.

"I'm pooped. Let's head to Treeline," I said. Treeline was a staple in the Akron area—the best hamburgers, great chili, wonderful milkshakes and curbside service. I didn't have to leave the car or talk into an intercom. It was fabulous. When it opened over sixty years ago, it was at the edge of the tree lines, hence, the name. The building was the only commercial property between Bath and the edges of Akron at the time; now, that stretch of road was jam packed with every store you can imagine.

"Oh no, dear. This is the last thing we should be eating. Didn't you hear your friend tell us we needed to have a healthy diet?"

I turned to look at her, not believing my ears. "Amy, I need Treeline. It's an emotional thing."

Shaking her head, she said, "Your aren't doing yourself any favors eating junk food. Your menopause would be better controlled if your diet were healthier."

It was official. I was going to beat her to death. The day had begun with her arriving before my coffee was finished, and now she was keeping me from a juicy hamburger and strawberry milkshake?

She must have deciphered the expression on my face, because she backed down. "One last little treat," she conceded. "Then it's a healthy diet!" she declared.

Obviously, she didn't know me very well yet. I liked balanced meals, but splurging on total junk food was definitely part of my personality.

I happily swung the car into a slot at Treeline, rolled down the window, and waited for the guy to come take our order. The place has run the same way since the day the first hamburger was grilled and was probably the primary source of heart disease in the Akron area. I'd have a salad for dinner, just to even out my odds.

Amy peered through the windshield, reading the menu posted on the brick wall. "What's good here?"

I turned to her, shocked. "You've never eaten here?"

Shaking her head, she said, "Oh, no. Albert always said the food her was too expensive. He felt eating out was a waste of money."

"Too expensive? Treeline?" I asked, amazed anyone had ever believed they were too pricey. "Wow, I've never heard of anyone thinking their prices were too high."

"Yes, I know he was no doubt incorrect, but once he had an idea in his head, he never changed his mind."

Yep, I hated Albert.

"Stubborn?" I asked, as politely as possible.

"That's one way of putting it, I suppose. I've come to believe the man was simply cantankerous."

I laughed. I couldn't help myself. "Okay, works for me."

She smiled, enjoying her own sense of humor. "I'm so glad you know Bill. It will make those classes much more comfortable for me. There are so many scam artists out there; we can't be too careful. It's good to know there are people we can trust."

"Albert tell you that?" I asked.

Nodding, she said, "He didn't trust many people." She cocked her head to one side, thinking. "I don't believe Albert actually liked anyone, other than himself."

Listening to her, I watched the guy approach the window, ready to take our orders. After listing my hamburger, milkshake and greasy onion rings, Amy added her own hamburger and soda.

I turned to Amy after he had gone to turn in our order to the kitchen. "What made you marry him?"

"I did love him—at least I did in the beginning. He was so handsome and tall. In my day, it counted more than it should. Character wasn't something we considered too much." Shrugging, she said, "When you finally realized you're married to a stinker, you find ways to make it work."

"You could have divorced," I said.

126

"Yes, but a divorced school teacher would not be as accepted as it is today. It was unusual enough for a woman to be a science teacher; they were usually men. Art, English, foreign language, or music was acceptable."

I thought about her words for a moment, realizing every single science teacher I had had was a guy. I never realized it until now.

"Divorce wasn't as easy as it is today. Plus, I liked being married. Someone to come home to each day, cook for and share life with. He wasn't always easy, but we did have our moments. It truly wasn't all bad," she explained.

Drumming my fingers on the steering wheel, I found myself fuming. She had accepted her life and made the best of a bad situation.

"You couldn't have kids?" I asked, knowing I might be treading on iffy ground.

"Albert didn't want them. He always said they were too expensive, and we simply didn't have enough money. I had classrooms full of kids. I mothered them instead. It worked out fine, I suppose." She frowned as she talked.

I didn't think it was fine; it was another thing she coped with the best way she could.

"I'm sorry," was all I could muster to say.

Shaking her head, she smiled. "No reason to be. Life works out eventually. I was lonely after Albert died; no one to look after or talk with about the day." She continued. "I'm still here, and Albert's miserly saving has left me in very good shape."

I grinned. She had a point.

Our food arrived, and we dug in happily.

"Oh my goodness," she exclaimed after a few bites. "This is heavenly."

"Yep," I managed with my mouth full of hamburger. "Want an onion ring?"

She eyed them suspiciously. "I'm not sure. There seems to be an awful lot of grease."

"Yep, it's the secret ingredient," I said, handing one over to her.

She took a tentative bite, her eyes closed, and she sighed. "Oh dear, you're ruining me."

I laughed. "We balance each other."

We continued in blissful silence, only our chewing making noise. When the last bite and slurp of drinks had been consumed, we sat back against the car seat, sighing in contentment.

"Maybe this should be a treat every few weeks. It would give us something to look forward to," she finally muttered.

Grinning, I waved the guy over to take the tray out of the window. "Yep, sounds like a plan."

Once we were on our way, she reminded me, "Tomorrow starts our first class with Bill."

Groaning, I nodded. "Fine."

"Could you explain this case a little more? I'm not sure I have a solid understanding," she said.

I squirmed, not sure how much Logan wanted her to know.

"Did you two just come from Treeline?" came a voice from the backseat.

"Hey, Dad," I grinned. "Yep."

Amy turned around. "Hello, Dave. I had never been there before. Must admit, it was delicious."

Dad smiled. "A virgin, eh?"

"Dad!" I stammered. I snuck a quick glance at Amy and saw her face turn red.

"When we get to the house, I've been instructed to bring Amy up-to-date on the case," Dad said, changing the subject quickly.

"Good. I wasn't sure how much information Logan wanted to share. He can be a little peculiar about who knows what."

Dad laughed. "Yeah, he's cautious."

As we swung into the driveway, I noticed Jack leaning against his car. He waited until I had parked and turned off the engine and then started walking over to us. One look at his face told me he was unhappy. I shot Dad a look in the rear view mirror, but he shook his head, "No idea."

I turned to Amy. "Why don't you wait a moment; let me see what's wrong."

She nodded.

I met Jack halfway. "What's up?"

"We have a problem. The mayor is calling constantly. He's freaking out."

"About what?" I asked.

"Pretty sure he's finally accepting the fact Spanelli's nuts. I think his ties to the guy are a little complicated, and he's worried."

I laughed. "Tough beans. He should have thought about consequences before he hooked up with the crazy."

"You think this is funny? He's driving me nuts!" Jack yelled.

I shot a glance at the car and saw Amy's concern. "Pipe down; you're scaring Amy."

Jack ignored me, his arms waving. "Listen, Peg, you aren't the one dealing with His Highness. He's called me all day long."

128

I shrugged, "I've had Amy most of the day, so we're even."

"I'll trade you," he said, calming down.

"Nope," I said, grinning. I patted his arm. "Go back to work. Dad has orders from on high to explain our present situation to Amy. Bringing her up to speed, so to speak."

"I wouldn't tell her your mob guys are actually working on the good side of the fence," he cautioned.

I shrugged. "Not my call, but I agree. She's already met Bill."

Jack gave me a questioning stare.

"He, Santino and Antonio own and operate the self-defense training we are attending."

"No shit! Trying to get out of the family's web completely, eh?"

I grinned. "Sounded like some future planning. They've owned it for about five years, so this has been in the pipeline for a while. Wonder how long they've been working with Logan?"

"I'd bet good money about the same time they opened their business." Jack laughed. "He probably painted quite a vivid picture of their futures."

"Go on, get out of here," I said.

Watching him walk back to his car, I waved Amy to follow me in the house. Waiting for her to make it to the door, I wondered how much Dad was going to share.

Once we were settled at the kitchen table, Dad cleared his throat.

"Amy, sometime in the near future, Logan will clarify the activities we were in involved with earlier this year. But at this point in time, he wants you to focus on this case."

Amy nodded but stayed quiet.

"We know the mayor is acquainted with Mr. Spanelli, but we are pretty sure it is a minor relationship. Nothing illegal, just information concerning investments."

Again, Amy nodded.

"My understanding is Mr. Spanelli is a numbers genius, crazy as a loon, but a genius. His wife hasn't lived with him for quite a while, but she has no contact with their daughter."

This revelation brought a gasp from Amy, but she said nothing.

"There is some mystery surrounding their estrangement, but we haven't figured that part out yet. You may come in handy regarding her situation. We want you and Peg to visit her and see what information you can shake loose."

"News to me!" I said.

"Logan wants Jack in the background for this part; his presence makes her too cautious," Dad continued, ignoring my outburst.

"It's logical," said Amy.

The logic baloney again.

Dad hesitated and then said, "The mayor is aware Peg can see spirits."

"Oh, dear," she said. "Can you trust him?"

"Yep," I answered. "He's too afraid it will ruin his career. Which, in my opinion, is the most important thing in his life."

Frowning, she said, "Surely, his family is more important."

Thinking back to the mess he made of his son's life, I wouldn't have bet the farm on it. "Not sure," I managed to say with a straight face.

"So," began Dad, "any thoughts?"

Amy sat quietly, thinking. Finally, she said, "Mrs. Spanelli more than likely has information that could enlighten us. It would be interesting to know why she has decided not to fight for visitation."

Dad tilted his head, watching her. "How so?"

She tapped a finger against her chin. "If I weren't allowed to see my only daughter, I would have started legal action. She hasn't bothered to go down that avenue." She stopped, and I figured her logic was at work.

I said, "She told me no lawyer would take her case because of threats from the family."

Shaking her head, Amy said, "I suppose that could be the reason she hasn't fought for her daughter, but I'm betting there is more to the story."

Looking at Dad, she asked, "Is he blackmailing her?"

"We haven't been able to determine the root of the current situation," Dad answered. "What made you assume blackmail?"

Looking out the window, she said, "Her daughter. The reason must be strong enough to keep control of her."

Dad shook his head. "Our first thought, also. But, so far, there is no evidence to support the theory."

Amy nodded slowly, continuing to stare outside. Dad and I exchanged glances. I shrugged; I had no idea what was going on in that head of hers.

"I will possibly know more after I meet her. People give away much more than they realize in casual conversation," she said, turning to face us.

I raised an eyebrow. "Really?"

"Oh yes." She smiled. "Whenever one of my students needed to talk to me about homework, or whatever, I was able to learn much more about their home life than they ever knew they were revealing."

"She hasn't been to the hospital to visit the ICU," I volunteered.

Nodding emphatically, Amy said, "Yes, it would follow her pattern."

"She has a pattern?" I asked, surprised.

"Yes, I believe so," said Amy.

"Well, what is it?" I asked.

She shook her head, "I'd rather not say until I meet her in person. I should have a better idea of the situation once I've observed her first hand."

Dad said, "Well, if it helps, Mr. Spanelli hasn't been to see his daughter either."

"What!" I said. "News to me! What a creep."

"She hasn't regained consciousness, has she?" asked Amy.

"Not that I am aware," I answered. "I think Bill would have mentioned it today if she had."

"Very telling," said Amy, turning back to the window. "Peg, can you see the Indians?"

I glanced quickly, hoping they were invisible to me. I was thankful the only the detectable problem was the fact one of the pine trees seemed to be dying. "Nope."

"Is it usual?" she asked.

"It's certainly safer," I said.

"Why?" she asked, confused.

"If I can see them, it means I'm in danger. The fact you see them constantly, probably means, well, you can see them. Period."

"Oh," she said.

I snapped my fingers, turning to Dad. "Which reminds me! Mom showed up today."

Dad frowned. "Not good."

"Yeah, I know. Same old crap, 'leave this case alone.' But it's not the interesting part. She couldn't see the guys out back!" I pointed to the woods. "Did Logan do something?"

Dad laughed until I'd swear there were tears running down his face. How did dead people manage to do this stuff?

Getting himself under control, he said, "He does enjoy driving the opposition a little wonky. So she thinks they are gone?"

"Yep, and she got a great deal of satisfaction from their absence."

"Your mother is dangerous?" Amy asked quietly.

"One way of putting it," I said sarcastically.

"Let's just say, she works for the other side," Dad explained.

Amy nodded. "She always made me nervous."

"You and the rest of the world. God only knows what problems she causes in the hereafter," I said.

"She has a knack for stirring up trouble," Dad said.

Glancing up at the old clock on the wall, Amy said, "Peg, I need to get home. Andy will be home soon, and I'm sure you have things to do. Don't forget our classes in the morning." Turning to my dad, she said, "Dave, always nice to see you."

I walked her to the front door and returned to find Dad watching the woods.

His gaze focused on the guys out back, he asked, "Class?"

Sighing, I plopped in my chair. "Yeah, self-defense classes."

I saw his grin but ignored it.

"Logan must hate me," I moaned.

"Or wants to keep you alive," he said.

"No fair! I'm your daughter; you should be on my side." I pouted.

He shook his head, his eyes never leaving their focus. He said, "I am on your side, Twinkle Toes. I'd like to see you go on living also."

Tears sprang. "Oh, Dad."

We were quiet for a moment and then I asked, "What's so interesting out there? The guys are still there, aren't they?" A fleeting fear drove me to the window.

"Oh, yes, they are certainly there. But so are others," he said quietly.

I looked, but still could not detect any movement.

"Who?" I asked.

"Others. Friends."

"More Indians?" I asked, confused.

"A few, but I'm more interested in the troops they are talking with at the moment."

"Troops? Sounds like a reenactment party," I said.

"Looks like one, but these are the real deal," he told me.

My eye began to twitch. "So," I began slowly, "what does this mean?"

"Not sure. But you can bet Logan sent them."

"I don't like it one bit. It means Logan is sending reinforcements." I could hear my voice become shrill.

"Calm down. Maybe he doesn't want to take any chances this time," Dad explained.

I shook my head. "Not like they can actually do much, physically speaking."

"They can do more than you realize. Antonio took action last time before they could," he said.

"Baloney! Owen had a knife, and other than frantically pacing around, they didn't lift a finger," I snapped.

I shuddered, reliving the scene. Owen came too close to slitting my throat. If Antonio hadn't taken a shot, I'd be a goner.

Reading my mind, Dad said, "They would have stopped him. I think they were waiting for Logan's permission to intervene."

"Just great. So, while I'm almost killed, they have to wait for orders?"

He smiled. "Babe, I think the confusion has been dealt with since then. Logan has more than likely told them to do whatever is necessary to keep you, and now Amy, safe. It won't happen again."

"I can't even spot the extras out there," I said.

"Good. Then they are still your warning signal. If no one is around, and you see them, you know to yell out for all of us, right?"

"I will, don't worry. I'm not very brave, you know," I said.

He smiled. "More than you admit. You're taking those classes."

Groaning, I said, "Don't remind me. Plus the fact Bill teaches them. Actually, all three of the mob guys teach, and rotate their classes. They will all be witness to my inability to defend myself."

"Ah, sweetie, they've already witnessed that fact," he grinned mischievously.

I sighed. "Thanks, Dad."

# Chapter 15

Halfway through the self-defense class, I was gasping for air and sweaty, and I knew I'd be purple from bruises by the time we finished. Somehow, I'd been assigned the role of "attacker." which meant I had hit the floor repeatedly for the past hour. I decided the only information I was personally learning was not to attack anyone. Size of the victim, we had been informed, was not a sign of weakness. Well, I'm short, five foot one on a good day, but so far, my weakness was apparent for all to witness.

Amy, on the other hand, was a good inch shorter than me, not to mention over twenty years more along in life. I wondered if she had always been so short, or if age and time had shrunk her down. Probably a bit of both, I decided. She had also not broken one bead of perspiration. Her eyes were glowing with excitement, and her cheeks were flushed by the exercise. Her curls had returned to their naturally wild state, and I figured she'd have a hard time taming them after the class. She was having a blast. I was glad one of us was happy.

"Mrs. Shaw, come on. Get up," Bill grinned. "We're almost done and ready for a cool-down."

"I've been ready for a break since I walked in the damn door," I muttered.

Bill walked over to my prone body, holding his hand out to help me struggle to a standing position. Grabbing it, I said, "Thanks."

Handing me a towel to wipe down my face, he whispered, "Your friend is fearless!"

Nodding, I said, "Probably years of pent-up anger."

He looked at me, confused.

"She was a high school science teacher," I explained. "High school kids are a real pain in the butt."

His grin returned. "If she could handle teenagers, she'll be fine defending herself in the real world."

"I'm not sure Logan expected her to enjoy this crap so much," I said.

Bill shook his head. "Don't be so sure; he has a real sense about people."

Using the towel to wipe the sweat off my face and neck, I asked, in what I hoped sounded like an innocent tone, "How long have you guys worked for Logan?"

He raised an eyebrow. "You know better than to ask me a question about Logan. If he wants you to have the information, he'll tell you himself."

Sighing, I said, "Chicken."

He laughed. "Yep. I don't purposely piss off the guy. You want to take a chance, be my guest."

I shook my head, handing the now filthy towel back to him. "No, thanks. I irritate him enough now."

He grinned. "Just being yourself?"

"Yep."

"Come on; let's finish the class. You're doing great," he said.

"Oh, yeah, your favorite punching bag."

We walked back to the center mats and began the training anew. I'm pretty sure if I needed to defend myself, I'd be in big trouble. However, I'd gotten damn good at falling.

By the time the class was finished, I was swearing consistently, much to Amy's dismay.

"Peg, you've got to control your language," she told me as we walked out to the car.

"Ha! You weren't the one being slammed on her back for the last two hours!"

"It was fun, wasn't it?"

Fun? Was she out of her mind? I kept my mouth shut and unlocked the car doors.

Once we had buckled, she said, "I had no idea how simple defending yourself could be! Amazing techniques that are so easy, even at my age."

"Such as?" I asked, maneuvering into the traffic on Market Street.

"I think my favorite was gouging the eyes with my knuckles!" she said. I also enjoyed slapping my hands against someone's ears. Who knew the move forced air pressure into the ears?" she said, voice filled with wonder.

I reached up with one hand to massage my ear, saying, "I thought it'd be the ear twisting."

Her eyes sparkled at the memory. "Oh yes, that was a good one. I haven't had this much fun in years."

"Oh, good," I said, sarcasm dripping. She either ignored my snotty attitude or else was oblivious.

"I can't wait for the next class."

I groaned. "We're going again? Don't you think you learned enough today?"

"Good gracious, no! We have to practice, practice, practice. Those moves have to become part of our subconscious so we don't have to think about what to do in an emergency."

"Ah. When is the next one?" I asked, dejected.

Fumbling around for the paper Bill had handed her as we left, she announced, "In two days, same time."

"Another early morning? Are you kidding?" I asked.

"Oh, yes. Then we have the entire day to do whatever else we need."

"Right now, I need a hot shower and another cup of coffee," I told her.

"Yes, I agree. Once we get ourselves cleaned up, we need to visit Mrs. Spanelli."

Where did she find her energy. I was pooped and not afraid to announce it to the world. She, on the other hand, was energized and ready to go, go, go.

"Yeah, I know."

She was quiet, staring out the window. Probably her adrenaline was finally ebbing—I hoped.

"Peg," she began. "I have a question."

"Fire away," I said, flipping the car blinker on for the left turn I needed to make.

"I've been able to see, you know, a few dead people for a while now."

I nodded, watching for an opening to turn.

"Well, why hasn't Albert been to see me?" I heard the hurt in her voice, and knew I needed to tread carefully.

"Amy, their world doesn't work exactly the way we imagine. They have all sorts of activities to do over there. You'd be surprised."

She pursed her lips in thought. After a few seconds of silence, she said, "No, I don't think it's the issue. I'm sure he's joined the wrong side. We don't really change much once we've died, do we?"

"I don't know," I answered slowly. "I think we're given the chance, but we still have the ability to stay the same if we choose." I thought of my mother and Elaine. They hadn't improved one bit with death, and I didn't expect the situation to change anytime soon.

"He wasn't a bad person, really. But he was selfish and enjoyed causing problems." She paused and then said, "You remember the fight about the community center?"

I nodded. "Yeah, a little." I don't like township politics or any other type of politics to be truthful. Let them figure it out—That was pretty much how I deal with local issues. Andy got more involved, but even he is careful. We had to live around these people; they were our neighbors. The less I argue over a stop sign placement or which day my trash got picked up, the better.

"He didn't actually care what happened with the center. He enjoyed causing arguments at all the meetings. It didn't bother him at all that he made people miserable. It was so embarrassing," she said.

I wasn't surprised by the revelation; I had already figured out Albert was a pain in the butt.

"Really?" I asked. No sense making her feel worse.

"Oh, yes. It's why I am positive he isn't doing as well as he should over there," she said sadly.

"Those are his choices, Amy. Don't forget, Dad said he'd seen him around with his church friends," I reminded her.

She waved a hand. "It doesn't mean much. A few of those men were real scoundrels, I can tell you!"

Seeing an opening in traffic, I made the turn. *Not far from a hot shower now,* I thought happily.

Pulling up in front of her house, I turned. "Amy, don't worry about Albert. I'm sure he's fine. You can ask Logan if it will help you."

"Yes, I might." She glanced at her watch with a determined expression. "But now, we need to get busy. We have more important work to accomplish." She smiled, getting out of the car.

"Give me at least an hour," I called after her. Nodding, she made her way into her house. I sat there a few moments, wondering about Albert. Had he joined my mother's group? It wouldn't be good, but, I hoped, it would not be my problem.

Shrugging, I continued home.

Once I had hit the shower, allowing my sore muscles some relief, I indulged in a steaming cup of coffee. The air changed suddenly. I couldn't catch a break.

Turning, I saw Bob standing near the oven.

I sighed. What did he want?

"You didn't seem to be doing very well at your class," he said. "I thought you'd beat some butt."

"Thanks for the encouraging words," I snapped.

Holding up his hands, he said, "I'm just saying."

Narrowing my eyes, I said, "I didn't see you there." His abilities were definitely increasing.

His face glowed with pride. "Yeah, I'm getting really good at hiding, aren't I?"

I looked at the ceiling, taking slow, deep breaths to hold my irritation at bay. Bringing my eyes back to Bob, I said, "What exactly were you doing at Bill's?"

Shrugging, he said, "I was curious. I didn't think Amy would be able to handle the physicalness of self-defense class. Let's be honest, she isn't a spring chicken anymore. How old is she? Eighty? What a surprise! Boy, oh boy, is she ever good!"

"Yeah, I noticed."

He said cautiously, "You need to work on your technique. I noticed you got thrown on the floor an awful lot."

"Bob," I said, teeth clenched, "I was the person they were defending against."

He frowned, saying, "You mean you were the bad guy?"

"Yes."

His face cleared, "Oh. I thought you were just really lousy."

My lips formed a tight, thin line, but I kept them closed.

"Anyway, are you planning on seeing Mrs. Spanelli today?" he asked.

"Yeah, why? Has Logan changed his mind?"

"Nope. Just checking," he said. "Amy going with you?"

"Yes, pretty much the plan," I said. What was he doing? Other than driving me nuts, there was no reason for him to be here as far as I could tell.

"Well, I thought I'd tag along," he said innocently.

I cocked my head, studying him. "Why?"

"Oh, you know. Practice."

"Practice? Bob, what are you talking about?"

He sighed. "Logan thinks I should work on my skills."

"Skills? Which skills?" My patience was already thin, and he wasn't improving it at all.

"Like appearing and disappearing."

"Bob, you are already capable in those arenas. I didn't see you at all at Bill's. It's not the first time you've been able to hide well."

Pride filled his face. "I'm getting real good."

"So what is Logan wanting you to improve?"

He was quiet for a moment and then said, "Allowing people to sense me."

"Instead of see you?" I asked, confused. This didn't make a bit of sense.

"Sort of. Look, there are people like you and Amy who can easily see me. Then there are those who can't see me at all and never think of the afterlife." He stopped, gathering his thoughts, and then said, "But there are certain people who can sense a presence, not necessarily understanding what they are feeling."

I frowned. "Okay, so what exactly is the plan for improving?"

"He's sure Mrs. Spanelli has the sense, but can't see us. We need to find out. If she can, Logan wants to start working with her a little."

"Without checking to make sure she's on our side?"

Bob shrugged. "He must have already researched all sorts of stuff. I don't ask a lot of questions."

"I'd feel better if he was *positive* she isn't a creep," I said.

"Well, *you* can ask him if you want, but I'm not bothering him," stated Bob. "No way."

"Are you in trouble with Logan?" I asked.

"Not that I know of," he said worriedly. "You think he's mad at me?"

"Oh, for Pete's sake! How would I know?"

"Simmer down, I just asked a question."

"Why are you bothering to tell me you'll be there? Lately, you've just shown up," I said.

"Didn't want to startle you. I want her to sense me on her own," he said.

I nodded. "Okay, it makes more sense." What had gotten into him? He seemed out of sorts; I'd keep my eye on him for the time being. I never knew what Bob would do if he got too flustered.

The doorbell rang. "Probably Amy now. You going to be in the car or show up there?" I asked, heading for the door.

He thought a second. "I'll show up. Would you warn Amy not to react?"

"Yep," I said. "Later."

Shaking my head at his odd mood, I opened the door.

Amy had put to good use the cosmetics she bought at the store. Her hair still looked a little wild, but I hoped it would settle itself down once it dried from her shower.

"I'll grab my purse; then we can scoot," I told her.

"Do you think we should call ahead? Maybe make sure she's home?" Amy asked.

"Nope. Something I learned from Jack; don't warn them you're coming, or they might skedaddle."

She nodded. "I never thought about it quite in those terms; I was more concerned with good manners." She stopped and then said, "I guess when you are investigating crimes, manners aren't too important."

I grinned. "Nope, they can get in the way."

Our drive over was pleasant. The air was fresh and warm. The sun was beating down, but it was still too early in the season to melt us as we enjoyed its presence. Winters around here tend to be mostly cloudy, so sunlight is considered a luxury any time of the year—well, maybe not August when the humidity has a bad habit of making the air thick, heavy and sticky.

"Oh, Bob is going to show up, but we can't react, okay?" I told her.

She nodded, "Thanks for the warning. Is there a reason he's going to be there?"

"Working on something for Logan," I said, not willing to explain his relationship with his mentor.

"I think Logan is a good role model for Bob."

I felt my eyes widen. "In what way?"

"Well, Bob is like an overgrown kid in many ways. Logan's quiet nature helps calm him down. It had never occurred to me before, but I guess, even dead, we still have the capacity to mature," she said thoughtfully.

Gosh, I had never considered the maturing angle before. I shot Amy an appraising look. She was pretty smart.

"I have to admit, Bob has calmed down a lot since I first met him," I told her.

"Oh, goodness. He must have been bouncing off walls back then!" she exclaimed.

"Yeah, pretty much. But we also still had Elaine in the mix, and it didn't help," I explained.

We pulled into Mrs. Spanelli's driveway. Parking the car, I looked at the house. My mouth fell open at the sight. Every flower was chopped off or pulled from the ground. Bushes had been cut in half, branches discarded around the yard. Her garden decorations had been smashed into pieces. I felt tears spring to my eyes. It had been such a lovely garden.

We stood at the edge of the carnage, unable to speak for a few minutes.

"This was a beautiful garden at one time, wasn't it?" Amy asked quietly.

"Two days ago, it was spectacular!" I answered angrily. Who could have done this much damage? It was horrible.

Amy began walking through the mess, studying each section of the once-glorious view. She shook her head sadly, saying, "This looks like a temper tantrum to me. So unnecessary."

The front door swung open, and Mrs. Spanelli stood watching us. I looked at her. "What the hell happened here?" I demanded.

Shaking her head, she said, "He went over the deep end."

Amy nodded. "I thought so." She looked at Mrs. Spanelli, "I'm so sorry, dear."

I saw her composure break for the first time on her beautiful face. She sobbed once and then pulled herself together. "Won't you come in and have refreshments. Coffee?"

Amy smiled. "How lovely, thank you." Carefully, she made her way through the wreckage. Reaching the door, she stuck her hand out. "I'm Amy Branch. So nice to meet you."

Mrs. Spanelli took the offered hand and smiled. "I'm Laura."

Amy said, "Like the movie."

Laura Spanelli answered, "Sadly, too much like the movie."

"Movie?" I asked.

"It's an old movie out of the forties. Gene Tierney starred as Laura. What a great film. Otto Preminger directed it; he was such a good director," Amy informed me.

"Never heard of it, and I usually like old movies," I said.

"It's a classic," Amy said.

"Sad, but a good movie," said Laura.

"What happened out there?" I asked, my thumb indicating the mess outside.

Sighing, Laura said, "Anthony was angry." She sighed. "It was to teach me a lesson."

"Angry about what?" I asked. "He must have been more than angry to do so much damage."

She smiled a quick, weary smile. "He only has two moods: very happy, very angry."

I thought about the first time I met him. He was extremely helpful, almost on a high of some sort. Within a few hours, he was totally calm, controlled, and a little bit creepy.

I shook my head. "I've seen him calm."

"Oh, no, what you witnessed is not calm. It's discipline; when he has to control himself, he becomes very contained. Almost robotlike," she said.

Yeah, a robot, that was exactly what he was like the first day I saw the guy.

I continued to study her face. Still beautiful, still a layer of sadness.

Amy openly inspected the room. "Your home is quite lovely, dear. You have wonderful taste."

Laura relaxed. "Thank you." Looking around, she continued. "This house is my sanctuary. I couldn't survive without it."

"Were you aware your husband has not been to the hospital?" I asked bluntly.

Amy gave me a dirty look; I guess for jumping into the business side of our visit so quickly.

"I am not surprised. You must understand, he does not love her. He *owns* her. He and that mother of his treated her as their own private object." She shook her head, disgusted. "I was so relieved when the witch died. But little changed. I honestly think Anthony became worse after she died."

Amy studied Laura and then said, "Dear, he did become worse. Her hold over him was so complete he couldn't cope without her guiding him in every situation."

"Science logic?" I asked Amy.

"No, my psychology training," she answered.

Psychology? Since when did she have training in psych work?

Seeing my face, she said, "I was working on a double major for a couple of years. Finally, I realized my love for science was stronger, so I gave up psychology to focus solely on a science degree."

No wonder Logan had believed she would be an asset.

# Chapter 16

Amy had used our coffee time wisely. She effortlessly pulled Laura Spanelli from the self-induced cocoon she had built for years. I watched, amazed at the conversation.

"Oh, dear," said Amy. "You have had such a hard time. As I listen to your story, I realize my own husband had many of the same distressing traits."

Reaching over to Laura, Amy squeezed her hand. "I know how you feel."

Laura's eyes threatened waterworks, but she maintained control, nodding at Amy. "I love my daughter, but the less interest I show in her, the more Anthony leaves her alone. When he suspects my true feelings, he'll become unpredictable."

"Yes," said Amy, nodding. "I agree. Somehow, your sweet little girl will understand one day."

Laura shook her head. "I'm not so sure. It makes me sick to think she could be emotionally ruined by him. I am convinced insanity runs in the family; his mother was absolutely afflicted." Sighing, she continued, "His constant manipulation of Caterina will warp her totally. No one is there to balance out the situation."

Amy frowned and then said, "Dear, trust she will be protected. I believe there are forces at work to ensure her safety, both physically and mentally."

Laura's eyes sadly met Amy's, and she said, "I don't believe in God; not anymore."

Patting Laura's hand, Amy smiled. "The fact doesn't worry me one bit."

"Did you know she has guards outside her door at the hospital?" I asked.

Laura's eyes widened. "I bet the old man made sure of her safety himself. He hasn't trusted Anthony for years and tried to keep his wife out of Anthony's life as much as possible." She grew silent.

"What was Anthony like in college?" asked Amy.

Laura smiled at the memory. "He was engaging, kind, and had a good sense of humor. Along with his good looks, he was everything I was looking for in a man." Sighing, she said, "Everything changed once we were married. We lived close to his family, and his mother interfered in our lives from the beginning."

"He wasn't around her much while in college?" asked Amy.

Laura shook her head. "Not at all. He never went home, not even during semester breaks. I realized later his father encouraged him to take classes year-round. He had a small apartment not far from campus. To my knowledge, he didn't step foot in the family house for over four years."

Amy nodded her head once. "Exactly what I thought." Seeing Laura's confusion, she explained. "Away from his mother, he was free to be himself. The insanity was still brewing; genetics can be nasty sometimes. Once he returned to the influence of his mother though, he didn't stand a chance. Sad, really."

Laura hung onto every word from Amy. "Do you think he would have been better away from her?"

"Oh yes, dear. She most certainly was corrupting him to her satisfaction." Amy shook her head, sorrowfully. "Such a waste."

I was impressed with Amy's handling of the situation. She had extracted a ton of information from a very guarded woman. My estimation of Logan went up another notch; he had trusted Amy had the personality and knowledge to encourage Laura to speak freely.

I spotted Bob in the far corner of the room, listening to our conversation. As he crept slowly closer to Laura, Amy noticed his presence. She glanced quickly at me, and I nodded as inconspicuously as possible.

"Explain the garden. What set your husband off to destroy the entire yard?" I asked.

Laura eyes moved to the window, allowing her to observe the destruction. "I'm not exactly sure what happened. He showed up earlier, screaming at me."

I narrowed my eyes. "No idea at all?" I pressed her harder.

"No."

Amy shook her head slightly, warning me to back off from this line of enquiry. I felt irritation growing, and I had to work hard not to snap at her.

Bob took another step towards Laura, and I saw her shiver. His face lit up, and he nodded at me. "Thought so," he said, smugly.

I watched her closely.

Amy asked, "What's wrong dear?"

Rubbing her hands down her arms, she shrugged. "Not sure, just had a chill. Odd for such a lovely, warm day." Smiling lightly, she said, "Must be the stress."

Amy said brightly, "You need to work off the stress. Maybe fixing your garden?"

Laura shook her head. "No, I will leave it exactly as it is right now. No sense showing him any signs of restoring his destruction."

"Wise move." After a moment's silence, Amy continued, "Well, Peg and I recently began self-defense classes. Maybe you could join us. It's amazing how wonderful you feel after a good workout!"

I almost fainted. Laura would surely recognize Bill, Antonio and Santino. Not sure if it was in Logan's plan of action, I tried throwing Amy a warning sign with my eyes, but she ignored me.

Laura's brow creased. "I've never thought of self-defense before. Where is this place?"

I noticed Bob's look of shock. So I wasn't the only one worried about the direction the conversation had suddenly taken. Jeez Louise.

"Right up on Market Street! Not more than ten, well, maybe fifteen minutes, from here," Amy announced proudly. "We had such a good time. Didn't we Peg?"

I smiled tightly. "Sure thing."

Bob looked frantic, and I couldn't blame him. But Logan had brought Amy into the situation, so he had to live with where her instincts took us. Tough beans.

Looking over at me, Bob said, "What do I do with this?"

I shrugged. Not my problem.

Bob, in his his distress, had moved closer to Laura unthinkingly. She flinched and caught her breath. I tilted my head, watching her carefully. Her reaction had startled Bob, and his mouth dropped open. "Wow."

She shuddered, saying, "I have no idea what is wrong with me today. I'm so sorry."

Amy, who knew exactly what was wrong, smiled sweetly. "It's okay, dear. You've been under a huge strain for a long time now."

Laura sighed. I realized, with a sudden pang of guilt, how much trauma the woman had silently endured for years. Amy's kindness was not only unexpected but was probably refreshing and much needed.

I shook my head, stunned by the fact in a few short months, I had become aware of so much pain in our little community. It had never once dawned on me the amount of cruelty could existe so close to home. My eyes watered, and I knew my hormones were reacting to the new information. Not exactly my plan of action.

Bob cleared his throat, saying, "I'd better report to Logan. He will be waiting."

I nodded slightly; Amy smiled at his words. Laura was clueless to our brief exchange.

"Tell me about your life since you've lived in this house," Amy encouraged Laura.

Oh, for Pete's sake! Who the hell cared? I endured the dull account of the woman's day-to-day life, which made my routine seem energetic in comparison. Other than my recent activity dealing with the other world, I had viewed my life as an empty nester to be very boring, which worked for me, since I love boring—so uncomplicated.

I tuned out their conversation, allowing my eyes and mind to wander freely. Unlike Anthony's office, which overflowed with family pictures, Laura had not one photo anywhere in sight.

I interrupted their talk. "No pictures of your daughter?"

Laura glanced around the room. "Absolutely not! Even a small picture would remind Anthony to my feelings. As long as I show no interest, he believes I have no love for her."

I nodded. Made sense, given he was manipulative and nuts, not to mention creepy.

"He has a ton," I said, wondering how she would answer.

A sad smile crossed her face. "He actually thinks it makes him appear to be a great father to have those pictures in his office. It never crossed his mind it takes more than pictures to make a man fill those shoes."

Yep, he would believe the pictures portrayed a caring father.

"No artwork here?" I persisted.

She gave me a short laugh. "You've seen Anthony's display."

"It's impressive," I said.

She nodded. "Oh, yes. Which is exactly why they hang there, so every visitor sees them and realizes how much money Anthony had to spend on his obsession."

"He's obsessed with fine art?"

"No! He's fixated with the need for people to admire him and believes those paintings prove his financial worth."

I mulled this tidbit quietly to myself.

"Um, Peg?" Bob said. His meeting with Logan was so short, I wondered if he had been given new orders.

Frowning, I looked over at him and raised an eyebrow.

"Ask her if she has anything in this house belonging to the Spanelli family?" The concern in his voice puzzled me, but I decided if he thought it was important, it wouldn't hurt to ask.

"Laura, this may seem odd, but do you have any objects here which belong to your husband's family?"

"Sure, a few things. Anthony's dad provided the furnishings here and made sure pieces I had admired were included."

I looked back at Bob, who now was pacing. What the heck was wrong with him?

"Could you convince her to get rid of them?"

My fingers began angrily tapping the arm of my chair; they have a mind of their own. I looked at Amy for help and wasn't disappointed.

"If it wouldn't be too much of a bother, could you show us which items belonged to the family?" she asked sweetly.

Why didn't I think of asking a simple question?

"I can't imagine why you would want to see them, but if you think it may be important, sure." Given her love of privacy, I was surprised she agreed.

Amy smiled, nodding her head, but didn't bother to respond. Laura stood, pausing as she glanced around the room. Her natural beauty and elegance was present in her every move, and it was easy to see why Anthony had been attracted to her. The question was what had happened to ruin their relationship? Had his mother manipulated her son to the point of destruction of his family, not to mention his mind? She walked over to the fireplace and plucked a figurine from the mantle.

"This is one of my favorites," she said, looking down at the figure in her hands. "It was a gift from Anthony's father for our wedding."

I looked closer at the figure but didn't see any significance.

"Not what I'm talking about," blurted Bob. "Ask if she has any Spanelli family stuff. You know, stuff that gets handed down through the generations."

Still not understanding what the big deal was, I asked, "Any of their family heirlooms?"

"That's the word!" exclaimed Bob.

"Yes, I have one piece of jewelry that dates back to the eighteenth century, and my end table is from Sicily," she said.

"I hate to be a bother, but could I see them?"

Flustered, she motioned me to follow her into the adjoining room. As she opened the door, I felt a wave of nausea. Uh-oh.

"I knew it!" shouted Bob. "Tell her to throw it in the trash!"

Ignoring his growing hysteria, I asked, "Where is the end table?"

Flipping the light switch, she said, "Over by the window."

Unlike the living room, the color scheme was brighter, less muted. It didn't seem to fit her personality, and I turned to her. "Who decorated in here?"

She laughed. "I was in a rare mood when I picked the colors. Exhilarated to be away from the oppressive house and the family. I have to admit, I never enter this room; it feels off somehow." She looked around the room, her expression guarded. "I should probably change it," she said and shrugged, "but I don't utilize the space, so why bother."

Bob was pacing at the doorway, refusing to enter the room. I frowned at him and then looked back at Laura.

"And the piece of jewelry?" I asked.

"As odd as it may sound, I keep the necklace in here," she said, crossing the room to the window. After opening the drawer to the side table, she withdrew a long box. As she came back towards me, I felt a heaviness surrounding us. This couldn't be good.

"Peg, don't touch it!" screamed Bob.

When she reached me, Laura opened the box, and I stared down at the most beautiful sapphire I had ever seen. It was huge, at least as big as a walnut. The setting had to be platinum, with diamonds circling the stunning sapphire. My mouth dropped open.

Laughing, Laura snapped the lid shut. "I know; it's priceless."

Finally able to speak, I said, "Do you ever wear it?"

"Oh, goodness no. I don't attend galas, and it's a bit much for the grocery store." She smiled. "I always thought it was beautiful, so Mr. Spanelli gave it to me as a house warming present the day I moved here."

"She needs to give it back!" snapped Bob.

I shot him a warning glance; he was beginning to get on my nerves. I had no idea why he was so upset, but his hysterics were becoming a nuisance.

"Have you ever had a chance to wear it?" I asked.

"Once. We went to a charity ball in New York City a year or so before Caterina was born. It was lovely, and I felt like a princess." She smiled at the memory.

"Hmm, how long has it been in the family?" I asked.

"Oh, over two centuries. It was given to the family as a gift, I believe." She shook her head. "I can't remember the entire story. I'm sorry. Is it important?"

"Not sure yet, but every piece of information helps. You never know what tidbit will be the vital part and solves the puzzle." I smiled, hoping to make her more comfortable with my questions. Where was Amy? That woman could extract information from a tin can!

Turning off the light, Laura said, "I'll make a fresh pot of coffee."

I realized she was steering me away from the room but didn't know if it was deliberate or not.

Bob was practically bouncing off the wall as we made our way back to the living room. "She has to dispose of both of those things!"

Ignoring him, I said, "We probably should get going. I'm sure we've taken up enough of your time."

"Oh, it's no bother. I've enjoyed the company," she said. "Amy is such a sweet lady."

No mention of my sterling personality—go figure.

Amy was exactly where we had left her, sitting comfortably. Smiling brightly as we entered, she asked, "Find what you were looking for?"

"Yep. An end table and a beautiful necklace," I answered, wondering what she had been doing while we had been gone. Her eyes sparkled a bit too much to believe she had sweetly sat still for those five minutes.

"The end table is from Sicily?" asked Amy.

"Yes, didn't I mention it before?" asked Laura.

"My memory isn't what it used to be, I'm sorry," said Amy. Losing her memory? Who was she kidding! Her mind was a steel trap. What was the old gal up to?

Glancing at me, then back to Laura, she said, "Could I use your bathroom? We have a few errands to run before Peg takes me home."

"Of course. I'll show you where it is," Laura smiled.

Errands? What errands? Maybe her memory *was* muddled.

"Those two items are a problem," stated Bob, as they left the room.

"So what!" I hissed. "There is no way the woman is throwing them away! They must be worth a fortune."

"I'm just saying," he shot back.

Jeez Louise.

I heard Laura coming down the hall, so I clamped my lips tightly together. No sense taking a chance she would hear me talking with Bob.

"I hope you and Amy visit again soon. I haven't been willing to entertain since I moved here and didn't realize how shut off I have allowed myself to become." She shook her head. "I know it isn't healthy to be alone so much, but I have to be careful. Anthony has a history of being nasty to anyone I befriend."

"Don't worry about us; we can cope with him," I said.

"Never underestimate his temper," she advised.

I nodded, glancing out the window at the destruction his temper had unleashed. I shuddered, hoping my gang of dead folks knew what they had dragged both Amy and me into this time.

I could see Bob frowning and knew he was working through a mental process that was perplexing for him. I had no idea what, until he opened his mouth. "Laura, get rid of those items!" he commanded.

My mouth dropped open as Laura turned white. What in the hell was the moron doing now?

As the poor woman turned to me, Amy walked in the room. "Don't worry, dear; it's just Bob. He's a bit upset about your heirlooms."

My lips clamped back together as I glared at her. "Amy!"

She waved off my scolding, saying, "I had a quick meeting with Logan. Laura is vital to our mission, so I advised him to allow her deeper involvement."

Amy had *advised* Logan? Since when did he allow those in the land of the living to give him advice—not to mention, his actually accepting advice? This was news to me.

Laura put a hand out to the arm of the sofa, trying to steady herself. I couldn't blame her; hearing voices floating through thin air for the first time wasn't fun.

"Bob? Logan?" she asked, barely above a whisper.

Amy crossed the room, reaching Laura as she managed to sit safely on the couch. At least she hadn't hit the floor like Amy had a few days earlier.

Patting Laura's shoulder, Amy continued. "I know exactly how you feel. Take nice, slow breaths, and you'll be fine."

Turning her attention to me, she said, "Logan will be here in a few minutes." She looked over at Bob, "Thanks, Bob. Your suspicions about the antiques were right on the nose."

Bob had relaxed once he heard his boss was showing up soon. "I can't take credit; Logan figured it out and sent me back. Exactly why I returned so fast."

I narrowed my eyes at Amy. "What exactly were you doing while Laura and I were in the other room?"

Smiling brightly, Amy said, "Oh, having a quick chat with Logan. Laura has a few secrets, and Logan knows they are important."

Laura grew even paler. I was impressed; I didn't think a living human could get quite so sickly white and still have a heartbeat.

"Secrets?" she whispered. "What secrets?"

"Oh, my lovely girl," Amy said kindly, "the biggest secret there is for a mother."

Tears streamed down Laura's face. I looked back and forth between the two women. What the hell was going on around here? Somehow I had lost control of the situation.

The air crinkled with energy, and I knew Logan had majestically appeared. About damn time!

"Hello, Laura. It has been a long time since we have seen each other," he said.

# Chapter 17

What? Not only did my mouth fall to the floor, but I felt my knees bend. A second later, I realized my butt was now firmly planted on the floor. Glad I hadn't fallen, merely sat from the shock. I felt my anger growing.

"You mean to tell me she can see you?" I demanded.

"Oh, my God," was all Laura could muster.

Turning to me, Logan said, "Laura and I were good friends at one time. I have guided her most of her life."

"But you were my imaginary friend!" she sputtered. "A childhood fantasy!"

Shaking his head, he explained. "You were exactly what we needed."

Turning to me, he said, "She grew up in an orphanage. No family, no outsiders to interfere."

The heat I felt surging through my body had nothing to do with hormones this time. I was furious.

"Are you telling me you have been using her for years? Do you have any idea of the absolute hell this woman has been through?" I screamed. "Why?"

He regarded me thoughtfully before saying, "I realize you do not understand the severity of the problem. It is normal. If you remember correctly, there is much at stake."

"I don't give a damn about what's at stake! You can't go around using people to get your way!" I pounded my fist on the floor. "My God, Logan, she was a little girl!"

"Yes, exactly the point. She had no entanglements. The situation was ideal," he stated.

"Ideal? Are you kidding me!" I could feel my arteries pounding in my neck; it must have looked like they were about to explode. Fine by me, Logan could deal with me on *his* side of life. Good luck with that one, buster!

Shaking his head, he turned to Amy. "You understand my dilemma, I believe."

She cocked her head, watching him. "Yes, I do, but I also agree with Peg."

Frowning, he looked at Laura. "I meant you no harm. You embodied the perfect scenario for our purposes."

Laura's color had returned to normal but her confused expression hadn't changed. "What is this about? I don't understand at all."

Logan sighed. It must be hell, dealing with stupid mortals. Tough beans.

He looked at each of us, weighing his options. Finally, he began explaining. "The Spanelli family has been a great concern for centuries. We have searched for a solution and believed we had found one with Laura." He paused, his eyes on her. "You were our first *break*, I believe it is called, in the situation. Your circumstances fit perfectly in a plan we had devised many years earlier. We did not move forward without great consideration. To be fair, I had long discussions with many on our side who opposed my idea."

His eyes swiveled my direction. I nodded, not surprised there was a ton of arguing; it must have irritated the hell out him.

"Eventually, I was able to convince my colleagues of the necessity to move ahead with the plan." Colleagues? Since when did Logan have those? I thought everyone obeyed him without question. Good to know.

His focus returned to Laura. "We made sure you met Anthony, and with your natural beauty, it was a high probability he would be attracted to you. We were also working on him to ensure the attraction continued."

I narrowed my eyes. "So you were doing your little whispering trick on him?"

He nodded, either ignoring my sarcasm or missing it totally. Tough to tell with him sometimes.

"It was crucial for a marriage to take place. Once married, Laura would be in the heart of the family; a trusted member." He sighed. "But Anthony's mother interfered more than we had anticipated. Her influence over her son resumed once he returned home with his bride."

"How on earth had you not realized she would meddle in her son's life?" I asked. "It should have been obvious, considering how his father had insisted he didn't return home during his college career."

156

Nodding, Logan said, "That is an astute question. Bella, Anthony's mother, did not hamper the romance, or cause any problems with the marriage planning. From our viewpoint, she would not become an obstacle." He paused and then said, "We were incorrect."

"You mean, *you* were wrong," I blurted.

Without a second's hesitation, Logan said, "Yes."

Satisfied he had admitted his mistake, I nodded. At least the old guy had the guts to own the problem. Too bad it burst another bubble; Logan had the ability to make a bad call, which meant my life wasn't safe merely because he was calling the shots. Crap.

"We have protected Laura throughout her marriage and continue to do so. It is unfortunate Anthony dispatched her away from home. Our mission depended on her being in the house. We had to take alternative actions, which thankfully, have worked in our favor."

Ah, my favorite trio: Bill, Antonio, and Santino. Ideas were flying through my brain as I connected dots.

"So the plans may have changed, but your mission is still working?" Amy asked.

Nodding, Logan said, "Yes. Better than we had hoped." Looking back at Laura, he said, "You have been a great help; this must be understood. There is also another segment which will prove most important." He stopped talking but continued to look deep into her eyes. They widened, followed by her face turning red with embarrassment. I frowned, not knowing what more news there could be so damn important.

"It was a long time ago," she whispered.

"Yes, but an interesting development which we had not considered. I know this has been very difficult for you, but the end is near. Do not lose hope," he said.

His sincerity was obvious, so I kept my big, fat mouth closed. I'd be snotty later, but right now, his concern for her emotional health was legit. Logan wasn't cruel, but he seldom considered the hell he put living people through with his schemes for the *big picture*. I was getting sick and tired of the term and wished I was still ignorant of the grand program.

Laura nodded, tears continuing to fall over her cheeks. Jeez, this poor gal must have been through hell and back.

"What is the other component?" asked Amy.

Laura's eyes closed; she took a deep breath. Either unaware of her tears, or ignoring them, she turned to face Amy. "Our marriage was rocky from the moment we moved near his parents. Youngstown was not my idea of a dream area in which to settle down, but, once back in familiar territory, Anthony refused to be persuaded to leave his family." She shrugged. "I suppose after being gone for so long, he had missed his mother." She paused, shaking her head at the memory. "Not having family of my own to be near, there was little I could do to persuade him."

"What was Bella's main area of intrusion?" I asked.

"Children," Laura whispered. "She was obsessed with having grandchildren. I was sent to specialists across the country after two years of trying to conceive."

Amy cleared her throat, reminding us of her presence, before asking, "Dear, what did all those doctors decide?"

Laura's eyes met Amy's and then grew wide. "You know!" she exclaimed.

"I guessed," Amy answered kindly.

"Know what?" I demanded. I hated when I couldn't follow a conversation.

Laura glanced at Logan, who nodded. Turning to me, she said, "I took every fertility test available; each result was the same. I was one hundred percent healthy. The problem wasn't my reproductive system, but Anthony's. Neither he nor his mother would accept the problem was not with me." She sighed heavily, her shoulders sagged with the memories of her ordeal. "New appointments with new doctors were made after every diagnosis. Anthony refused to be tested; his mother rejected the opinions of the most respected specialists in the country."

"I assume you resolved the problem, considering Caterina is here," I said, still confused.

She darted another glance at Logan then back to me. I felt my stomach flip as realization dawned. I was not naive, but the truth of her situation took me a hot minute to correctly decipher correctly.

"Oh, crap. Caterina isn't Anthony's daughter," I said. "Does he know?"

"Yes and no," was her cryptic reply.

"Well, *that* certainly clears up the matter," I snapped, hoping she heard the sarcasm. Jeez Louise.

"Anthony is a brilliant accountant, but his intelligence has many short comings in most other arenas," said Logan.

"So he didn't figure out the girl wasn't his daughter?" I asked, determined to drag the truth from one of them.

"Oh, dear," exclaimed Amy. "He can still hear his mother, I assume?"

Logan turned to Amy, his expression appraising. She had met his expectations obviously. Nodding, he said, "Yes. May I inquire how you arrived at your conclusion?"

Amy looked up at Logan. "Logic."

He cocked his head to one side, and I could see the wheels spinning in his dead head. Maybe Amy was smarter than he had bargained for when he had decided to enlist her in our weird little army. I smiled, realizing this could become quite fun as time went along. The old gal could give Logan a run for his money.

"Well, I don't use logic very well," I snapped. "So could someone please explain the big mystery!"

Turning her gaze away from Logan, Amy looked at me, saying, "Anthony probably never suspected the child wasn't his—at least until his mother died."

Laura nodded. "Her birth was all the proof he needed the issues had been mine all along."

"What's Bella's death got to do with this?" I asked, refraining from being a snot. At least Amy was willing to lay it out for me.

"Once she was on our side," interrupted Logan, "she acquired the truth. This has caused a great deal of turmoil for us."

Amy nodded, continuing, "Anthony can hear his mother. He is convinced she will help you find the culprit to the accident."

"Yeah, so?" I was a little thick when the situation was this convoluted.

"She knows the girl isn't Anthony's," said Amy. Shaking her head, she said, "I'm sure she has informed Anthony of this fact."

I frowned, mulling through the details. I looked at Logan for a moment before saying, "I thought the other side couldn't see everything clearly. You guys don't have all the facts and figures on your side, right?"

He was quiet for so long, I wasn't sure he had heard me. Finally, he answered. "Somehow, she was given the information. There are enough deceased members of the Spanelli family who would have gladly shared the knowledge." He stopped, watching me closely. I ignored his survey, turning to Laura.

"I'm not asking who the father of Caterina is because I don't want to know. It's your business, unless it complicates my business. Does it?" I asked.

Logan answered, saying, "We are not positive it has any bearing on your case."

"Not positive?" I said, my voice rising. "You mean to tell me it might be a major factor?" I could feel my face flush, and again it had nothing to do with my damn hormones. I was angry.

"Peg," Amy said, calmly.

I glared at her, refusing to defuse my irritation.

"There was no need for you to be troubled with the situation," Logan stated. "Your goal is simple. Find the person who caused the girl's injury."

I narrowed my eyes at Logan, saying, "One thing I've learned from Jack is every piece of information we acquire helps solve the problem. When someone decides to withhold a fact, no matter how insignificant they may believe it to be, it has a bad habit of making my job harder."

Logan nodded. "He is a wise man."

My mouth fell open at his comment. I couldn't believe my ears. "So you realized by not telling me something this important, you could have hindered the investigation?" I pointed my finger at him. "But you decided it was worth it? Who do you think you are?" I demanded. My chest by then was heaving with frustration. My head was pounding, and I wanted to hit him.

He turned to Amy, ignoring my anger. "How insane do you believe Anthony is at this point?"

She frowned, thinking over the situation. "Probably over the edge."

Nodding, he said to Laura, "I want you protected. I will send a team here." He swept his hand towards the destroyed garden. "The destruction demonstrates the fierceness of the man's mind. It does not please me."

I snorted. "Well, good to know."

He shot me a quick glance but continued talking to Laura. "I will ensure your safety. I apologize the situation has become violent."

"What damn good is a bunch of dead protectors for her?" I demanded.

"They have proven helpful to you in the past," he said.

"Yep, as far as getting your attention when the situation was extreme," I shot back.

"It was enough," he said.

I threw my hands in the air, disgusted. "For Pete's sake, Logan. Sometimes a gal would like more than a last-second rescue. It was damn close!"

He acknowledged my statement with a slow nod. "Yes, but you are alive."

"Two more minutes and I'd be with you rather than Andy!"

He gave this a moment's thought and then said, "Yes, it is true. However, the situation was salvaged."

"Peg," interrupted Amy. "Laura could come stay with me. Do you agree it would help?"

I hated to admit it, but no one would think to look for Laura at Amy's. Plus, the Indians could guard both houses.

I sighed. "Yep, it might work."

Logan turned back to Amy. "Thank you for your hospitality. I agree; it would be wise to remove her from this house."

"How do we know he doesn't have someone watching this house at all times?" I asked, not willing to back down.

Logan nodded. "Excellent question. Bob?" he called.

There was a pop in the air, and Bob said, "No one around the area. I searched a square mile. Anthony's back at his house, and no goons in sight." Another pop, and Bob was gone.

"Oh, dear," whispered Laura.

I looked at her with pity. "There's an entire gang of dead people working with us. Indians, Bob, my dad; the list gets longer all the time." I hoped Logan appreciated the fact I didn't mention our mob trio; they may be alive, but they were working on our side.

"Your father is at Amy's house, ensuring no one has learned of her involvement," Logan informed me.

I nodded. "Fine by me."

"Logan," began Amy, "I am convinced Laura should join us in self-defense classes."

"I agree, however it must be done out of sight," he answered.

"What? Private lessons?" I asked.

Logan nodded slowly. "I believe it would be the safest. Three women, each alone, must have a line of defense which relies on no one."

"I'm not alone! I have Andy," I reminded Logan.

He smiled. "Yes, you do have Andy. Is he home every moment?"

I hated when the arrogant snot was right. Of course Andy wasn't home *every moment*; he has a job, and Logan damn well knows it.

"Fine. I'll concede the point," I said, matching his own need to concede earlier. Two can play at being nice.

He smiled, nodding.

"Peg, will you please make the appropriate inquires to our friends?" he asked.

"Yep, as soon as I get home." I smiled. This should be interesting; our mob trio might not be extremely happy to be seen making house calls. Not to mention the fact Laura had no idea they worked for Logan.

"I will explain as much as Laura needs to know and the need for discretion," he replied. Damn, the man read my mind again! Jeez Louise.

"Are these trainers trustworthy?" Laura asked, concerned.

Logan gave me a warning glance as I snorted. "Yes, you may be assured they have my utmost confidence."

Laura nodded. "I'll have to rely on your word. Anthony has friends everywhere."

"Not as many as you have been led to believe," Logan informed her carefully. He glanced out the window, then back at her. "It is his father who owns the hearts of his men, not Anthony."

Laura nodded, thoughtfully. "I believe you are correct. I don't think Anthony commands the respect he thinks."

"True," replied Logan.

We jumped at the sound of Laura's cell phone blaring and stared at the damn thing as if it had dropped from outer space. She reached for the phone, pausing to look up at Logan. He nodded, and she grabbed it. While she was talking, Logan turned to me.

"Peg, I do not want Laura to be informed concerning certain *coworkers*. The less she knows, the less she can accidentally divulge."

I opened my mouth to make a snappy remark when I realized the wisdom of his request. Slamming my lips together, I nodded. "Yep, the fewer people aware, the fewer mistakes."

I shot a look towards Amy. Logan nodded. "Same procedure, for the time being, please."

"Okaydokey."

Amy listened to our short conversation calmly. "It doesn't hurt my feelings, you know. I trust you two."

I winced at her words. Amy might need to know about Bill, Antonio and Santino eventually, but for now there was no need to complicate the situation. Hell, I wouldn't know myself if Bob wasn't such an idiot.

Laura finished her conversation and said, "It was the hospital. Caterina's condition is the same; stable, but still in a coma." She bit her lip, and my heart ached watching her fight for control.

"The hospital calls you?" I asked, surprised.

A small smile appeared. "Yes. Anthony has no idea, but I do have friends."

"Glad someone is keeping you in the loop," I smiled, hoping to encourage her.

Amy squeezed her hand. "You have us also, dear."

I sighed, dragging my butt off the floor. "We might as well get organized. Laura, gather clothes and whatever else you need. The sooner we get you to Amy's, the safer you'll be."

I turned to Logan; he was gone.

# Chapter 18

Once Laura was settled at Amy's house, I skedaddled back home. Amy, thrilled to have someone to fuss over, was busy changing sheets in the guest bedroom, making sure she had enough food in her pantry, and generally going overboard with the whole hospitality ritual. I wasn't sorry to head back to my nice, quiet haven of peace.

As my car found its way up the gravel drive, I sighed the second I spotted Jack. So much for peace and quiet. Parking next to his official vehicle, I noticed the expression on his face and sighed again. I didn't like the scowl that stared back at me, and I dreaded whatever news he had come to share. The day had been full of surprises, and I was in no mood for another shocker.

He waited impatiently as I gathered my purse, phone and keys, his eyes narrowing slightly. I wondered if he knew I was stalling. Probably, he was a detective, after all. Finally opening the car door, I gave him a big smile.

"Hey, Jack. What's up?" I asked. My cheerful chatter had not fooled him one bit.

"I've been calling for the last hour! Where have you been?" he demanded.

Walking up to the front door, I waved my keys around airily. "Oh, you know. Errands."

"Bullshit. You're hiding something!"

I shot him a warning glance and turned to unlock the door. Before I had the key in the lock, the door swung open. I almost had a heart attack until I spotted Andy's worried face staring down at me.

"Andy! What are you doing home so early?" I asked, once I had my breath back.

"Peg! Are you okay? Where have you been? Jack and I have been frantically trying to reach you," he said, his voice cracking as he spoke.

I looked at both men's worried faces and frowned. What the hell was wrong with these two?

"Can I as least hit the bathroom before the interrogation begins?" I asked. Their distress was obvious, and I wasn't in a hurry to hear what had caused it.

Andy stood back from the door, and I sailed through and kept going until I reached the bathroom. Once the door was firmly closed behind me, I took a deep breath. What was going on? I took my sweet time in my temporary sanctuary, but dread filled every inch of my body. When I figured I had wasted enough time, I dried my hands and opened the door. I hoped my stall had given them both time to simmer down a bit.

I could hear them moving around the kitchen as I walked down the hall. Their voices were muted, but I knew they weren't happy campers.

"A cup of coffee sounds pretty good to me about now," I announced, entering the kitchen. I stopped immediately as I spotted Dad.

"Hey, Dad," I said. "I thought you were next door keeping an eye on Amy."

He threw me a tight smile, but there was no humor at all. Not good.

"Peg, what's going on?" asked Jack.

I noticed he had managed to find the pie I had hidden in the fridge, and he sat at the worn table with a cup of coffee. How long had I stalled in the bathroom? He was nice and settled. I knew he was a stress eater, but he needed to be more careful how much pie he consumed during our investigations or he'd be as big as a barn eventually.

Holding my hands up defensively, I said, "It's been a busy day."

Andy watched me, not saying a word, as I grabbed myself a mug and brewed my own cup of coffee. I eyed the pie, which now sat on the counter, but my jeans had been a little tight lately. Not bad, but enough to signal a pound or two had been added to my weight. The trip to Treeline had taken a toll on my waist. I hated standing on the scales, so I judge any snacking by how my clothes fit. Shaking my head, I made the command decision to pass on the pie. Depending on how bad this conversation turned, I might have to rethink the ruling.

Drumming my fingers on the counter as my coffee brewed, I avoided their faces by studying the steady stream of coffee as it filled my mug. When the mug was full, I turned to face the music. Just wished I knew what song was playing.

"Okay, guys, what's the problem?" I asked. Might as well find out what the hell had stirred up three of the most reliable men I knew.

"Peg! For God's sake!" said Jack.

Andy reached out and put his hand on Jack's shoulder in an effort to calm him down. I frowned, 100 percent perplexed.

Dad watched me carefully and then said, "You honestly have no idea what's going on, do you?"

I shook my head. "No idea. I've been with Amy, Logan and Laura most of the afternoon."

Dad's eyes widened. "Logan *and* Laura? In the same room?"

Grinning, I said, "Yep. Long story, but the short version is Laura has known about Logan pretty much her entire life."

Dad shook his head, and said, "I didn't see it coming. Explains a few things on my side though."

He didn't elaborate, and I didn't want to ask. The less I knew about the "other side," the better I felt. Their side got creepy, and the living were bad enough. Dead folks exhausted me.

Andy, his hand still on Jack's shoulder, said, "Sweetie, we were worried. You didn't answer your phone. You promised the ringer would stay loud enough to hear, even in the bottom of your purse."

"I didn't turn it off, I swear. You guys are upset because I didn't answer my phone?"

The three men exchanged glances. "Wait a minute! Jack can see Dad?" I asked, stunned.

Jack was given the ability to see and hear Dad occasionally. Andy had the privilege of always having the capability, but it surprised me Jack had been given access again.

"I thought the situation warranted it," replied Dad, calmer than I would have expected.

"Logan know about this?" I asked, worried Dad would irritate the old Indian.

The question earned me a casual shrug from my dad, which made my stomach turn. "Dad, I can't afford for you and Logan to begin fighting over these things. I need you both focused on my safety!"

Dad laughed, but I knew he understood. Logan was a powerful friend; he was an equally a powerful enemy.

"Don't worry about Logan; he knows me well enough to trust my judgment."

Maybe, maybe not. Logan had his own views, and I didn't always agree with him. I'd have to depend on Dad's assessment of their relationship. My stomach rolled again, and the coffee didn't sound as inviting as it had a moment ago. Glad I had passed on the pie; tight jeans come in handy sometimes.

"So what's got everyone up in arms? Must be more than my not answering phone," I said.

Jack cleared his throat of pie, and said, "Peg, Anthony Spanelli's dad is in town. This could get messy if we aren't careful."

I frowned. "So what? Maybe the reason he's here is the fact his granddaughter is lying at Children's Hospital."

"We think it's more than the girl. Anthony doesn't seem to be thrilled about his father's visit," Jack said. "He's called the mayor a few times, more aggravated with each call. The mayor's about to have a stroke over this and is pressing for results sooner rather than later."

I shrugged. "It would help if everyone involved were more honest. Give me a break."

"Work faster," said Jack. He looked down at his empty pie plate and sighed. "Can I have another piece?"

"Yep," I said. "Help yourself." The more he ate, the less there was available to tempt me. Let his waist expand.

He got up from his chair and headed to the fridge. I was going to have to find a new hiding place if Jack continued eating a ton of pie every time he was here.

"I think Anthony is coming undone," said Andy.

"Yep. He destroyed Laura's garden earlier today. It's a mess," I said.

Jack turned from cutting pie, saying, "Her garden? It was a work of art! Why would he ruin it?"

"Had a temper tantrum," I said, taking a sip of my hot coffee. "Laura was pretty calm about the damage, which tells me she has witnessed this behavior before during their relationship. Surviving his personality for so many years must have been tricky."

I thought about the fertility tests but decided it was Logan's call whether to divulge that particular piece information, considering the situation. If Anthony was aware of his daughter's parentage, life for her would become dicey at best. I didn't need too many people knowing the details and spilling the beans accidentally to the wrong person.

Dad was watching me thoughtfully, and I sensed he knew I was holding back some spicy info, but he kept quiet, to my relief.

"I wonder how squirrely Anthony really is at this point," mused Jack.

I snorted. "Pretty damn crazy, according to Amy." Looking over at Dad, I asked, "Did you know Amy majored in psychology before changing to biochemistry?"

He looked surprised for a moment and then nodded. "No wonder Logan wanted her involved. She brings a specialized talent to the table."

"Yep, the ability to spot a nut miles away."

"There's another issue," said Jack between bites of pie.

I sighed. Of course there was another issue.

"What?" I asked.

"Remember the Marco fellow who relieved one of your mob friends?" he asked.

Nodding, I said, "Antonio, yep. He didn't go back to the office, right?"

"He's the one. Seems his body was found floating in the Cuyahoga River last night."

My mouth dropped open then snapped shut. "Not encouraging. I was hoping he was the culprit of Caterina's accident."

Jack said, "Yep, exactly what I was hoping. It would have been a nice, neat package. He lied to me, so he was number one on my list."

"So you guys were tied up in knots because I didn't answer my phone and Marco gets himself killed?" I asked.

"Peg, be reasonable. We must be pushing someone's buttons," said Jack.

I shook my head. "Not necessarily. Maybe he pissed off the mob somehow."

Dad laughed. "Too many movies."

"Isn't it how they operate?" I asked defensively. "Maybe he secretly works for another mob family. There must be a hundred different reasons the guy got killed."

"I don't like coincidences," said Andy. "You get involved in a case, and in a matter of days, someone shows up dead in a river." His hand was shaking; my heart melted. What a sweetie to be so worried.

Drumming my fingers on the table, I asked, "What do we know about Marco? Is he from around here?"

"Cleveland PD is working on it, but I've got a friend in their department. He's going to call if they ever find out his background," Jack said, finishing off his last bite with a satisfied sigh.

"I don't think he's the one who hurt the girl, but what if Mr. Spanelli thought he was the guilty party? Would he have offed him?"

"He'd use one of your friends for the deed; aren't they his hit men?" asked Jack.

I thought about my trio and then shook my head. "If they are working with our side, I'm positive killing someone isn't on their current job description."

"Good point," said Andy.

I pushed off from the counter I had been leaning against and walked over to the table. Plopping my butt happily on my chair, I said, "I agree this isn't good news, but I'm more focused on Caterina's accident. Anthony is a problem, but our job was to find out who hurt the little girl."

"Right," said Jack. "But we can't ignore the fact the mob is involved."

"Fine, but we still need to focus on the girl. Who hates Anthony enough to hurt his daughter?"

"Everyone," said Dad. "He isn't popular with the family. If it wasn't for his financial magic, I doubt he would have been tolerated."

"There must be more to the story than the fact he isn't liked," I said. "I don't like a lot of people, but it doesn't equate to hurting their kids."

Jack snorted. "Peg, you're talking about normal situations, which this isn't; these aren't your average citizens."

My fingers continued dancing on the table. Something was bothering me, but I couldn't grab hold of whatever was floating around my brain. I was positive I would figure it out eventually, but my last adventure had taught me it could be at the worst possible moment, on the order of a near-death experience. Not a happy thought.

Dad spoke up. "Peg, have you heard from Bella?"

My stomach flipped. "No," I said, slowly. "Why?" Did I want to know the answer to his question?

He pursed his lips, but remained quiet for a few moments longer. Watching him, I felt my head begin a slow, deep thump. I wasn't going to be happy once he started talking.

"We expected her to be very involved with this investigation." He paused. "Anthony also believed it to be true, correct?"

I nodded carefully, hoping to keep the slow thumps from becoming throbs.

The air suddenly crackled, and we all froze in place.

"Wow! A meeting!" said Bob, cheerfully. "Hey, guys, what's going on?"

"Why are you so happy?" I snapped.

"You wouldn't believe how busy Logan keeps me! I've been zipping around everywhere." He beamed.

Good news. It kept Bob out of my hair.

"I've got great news!" He grinned.

"Do you know who ran down Caterina?" I asked.

"Oh, gosh, no. But one person isn't going to be irritating you any time soon," he said.

"Who?" asked Dad.

"Bella!" announced Bob. "She's being detained by the good guys from the Spanelli family."

I frowned. "Dad had just asked me about her; a tad too convenient." Sweat appeared on my upper lip.

Shaking his head, Bob said, "Dave probably had his intuition turned on high. I'm telling you, she won't get away from those guys anytime soon."

Dad was watching Bob, deep concentration showing on his face. His expression didn't give me any warm, cozy feelings.

"Peg, look outside." He commanded. "Do you see your friends?"

"Who's here?" demanded Jack.

*Crap, I forgot he can't hear Bob.*

Bob's expression fell. "He still can't tell when I'm here?"

"Don't take it personally, he barely hears Dad or Logan," I snapped.

His face still registered hurt feelings, but I ignored him.

"Dad, what do you think is happening?" I asked.

Shaking his head, he said, "Not sure, but I don't like it. Check the woods."

I glanced quickly out the window. Sure enough, I could see the Indians and the soldiers. Jeez Louise.

"Yeah," I whispered. "I can see them."

"How defined?" he asked, calm as a cucumber.

I grabbed my glasses from the center of the table and took a deep breath. I shut my eyes, gathering courage to see how clearly the group out back appeared. As I slowly opened my eyes, the air I had been holding in my lungs crept out at a snail's pace.

"Not too clear, actually," I said, relief flooding my body. "It's good, right?"

"Be better if you couldn't see them at all." Dad closed his eyes, shaking his head. His impatience oozed through the room. "Bob," he said, as he opened his eyes, "Where is Logan?"

Bob cocked his head to one side, thinking. Finally, he shook his head. "Have no idea. He gave me a list of errands, and I've been busy running around snooping." He shrugged. "Sorry, Dave."

"Peg, I want you to be extra careful the next few days," he said. "Lock all doors. Don't go anywhere without checking in with someone first. Take extreme precautions."

I felt a shiver run down my spine, but I nodded. "Sure, Dad."

Andy cleared his throat. "Dave, do you think trouble is brewing?" His fear was so thick you could have sliced it with a knife. My eyes watered, knowing his fear was on my behalf.

Dad looked Andy square in the eye, saying, "Anthony's mother had access to extremely negative energies while she was alive." He shook his head, no attempt to hide the weariness. "On our side of things, she not only brought her ability, but it has increased." He looked at Bob. "You may think

Bella can't escape her captors, but it would be wise to alert our forces to boost security around the woman."

Bob looked shocked but nodded. "You got it, Dave." Poof, he was gone. No slow fade, no quick grin before he vanished. Not good.

"You have jails over there," Jack asked in awe.

Dad smiled. "I wouldn't describe our system quite your way, but close enough."

Jack shook his head. "The more I hear about your world, the less I look forward to joining you guys."

In spite of the situation, Dad burst out laughing. It was such a relief to hear his laughter, I almost broke down sobbing. I fought for control and knew I couldn't open my mouth to ask questions or waterworks would begin, which certainly wouldn't help the current status.

Dad turned back to me. "We may need reinforcements, but I'll check with Logan before we make the call."

Reinforcements. I knew exactly whom he was referring to: my mob trio. Hauling in the big guns meant my anxiety could officially climb.

Using a great deal of caution for fear my voice would crack, I said, "Logan has already decided our self-defense classes would now be private and away from their place of business."

Nodding his approval, Dad said, "Wise decision. When?"

I shrugged. "No idea."

The phone shrilled and we froze in place. Looking at Dad, who nodded, I took a deep breath and answered.

"Hello?"

"Peg, I don't mean to bother you, but the woods seem to have an awful lot of people milling around. Is this normal?" asked Amy.

Frowning at her question, I dropped my head. I sure as hell didn't want to take another peek out back, but I knew it was necessary. Raising my head, I realized every eye in the kitchen was on me. "It's Amy. She thinks we have more guys in the woods."

Dad's head whipped around and I could hear him mutter, "Damn." My stomach flipped, and my head started pounding. I forced myself to survey the situation, turning my head slowly to face the window. Yep, we had enough guys roaming around to start a small town. What the hell was going on?

# Chapter 19

"Yeah, it looks like a big party out there," I said to Amy. "Don't worry, I'll find out what's causing the gathering."

"I didn't know quite what to do, so I called," she said, her voice apologetic.

"Yep, you did the right thing. How's Laura?"

"Settling in nicely. Your friend, Bill, called to schedule our lesson. Tomorrow morning at eight," she announced happily.

I groaned. "Eight? Really?" What was wrong with these people?

Amy chuckled. "He knew the time wouldn't make you happy, but it's all he had available."

I frowned, looking at Dad. How were they going to protect me if their own work schedules were full? Reading my mind, which still bothers me, he smiled, whispering, "They'll make time, trust me."

Andy looked confused, so I smiled. "Explain later," I mouthed. He nodded but didn't look happy one bit.

"You two set for the rest of the day?" I asked Amy.

"Oh, yes, I have plenty of food, and Laura is helping prepare dinner. I believe she is quite the cook," said Amy.

Glad someone was having a good time because, I sure as hell wasn't.

"Great. I'll check about the guys out back, so don't worry. Call if you notice anything different," I said.

"Okay, thanks Peg," she said.

After hanging up, Jack said, "I take it there are more folks out there?" he asked, jerking his thumb towards to woods.

I sighed. "Yep, it looks like a damn movie set." I turned to Dad, "I'm familiar with the Indians and British soldiers, but who are the rest?"

Dad, eyes on the woods, said, "Hunters, trappers, along with the odd Viking." He shrugged. "Basically, anyone who ever traveled through this area."

"Viking?" I asked, surprised. "Since when did Ohio have Vikings?"

Grinning, Dad said, "Those guys got around more than historians realize; they made it all the way to Minnesota. You'd be surprised how much history has been wrong."

My mouth fell open. "You've got to be kidding me!"

He shook his head, turning back to the woods. "Nice to know they are back there; they are fierce fighters."

"What good will it do me if a bad guy comes after me?" I demanded. Indians were fierce at one time too. It didn't help me much when Owen had a knife ready to slit my throat.

"The bad guys aren't only in the land of the living, babe. The warriors out back can handle any trouble from our side of the veil, and it's what I'm the most concerned about at this point." He paused. "I've got a call out to Logan. Pretty sure he knows more than we do, but it never hurts to confirm our suspicions."

Well, hell. My life was getting more complicated. Not only did I have to worry about nuts in the land of the living, but this case had the added bonus of nuts from the land of no heartbeats. No wonder Nana and her friends were up in arms, running around, cleaning up the world. Their world sucked just as much as ours. It was not exactly what I had imagined all these years—no more hoping for peace and calm once my life here was finished. I now knew it was more bizarre over there, which was not a calming thought.

Lost in my own dark thoughts, I was unaware Dad had been watching me until he said, "Peg, Logan warned you last time there was trouble brewing."

"Yeah, but he wasn't exactly specific, was he?" I snapped.

"What the hell is going on?" demanded Jack.

"You heard what Dad said! We've got a ton of dead folks milling around, Dad is worried about everything and Logan isn't here," I announced. "It's a wreck with no prospect of improving anytime soon." I threw my face in my hands and groaned. "I was happier not knowing any of this crap!"

"Your happiness is unimportant," came a voice I knew well: Logan's.

Lifting my head, I snapped, "Thanks, buster; nice to know."

He regarded me with serious eyes, which made my stomach tighten to the point of pain.

Shaking his head, he said, "Peg, I do not wish you ill. The stakes are quite high this time. Whether it is comfortable or not, you are part of the solution." Eyeing me, he continued, "You were chosen, but the reason is none of my concern."

I frowned. "Do you know *why* I was picked? No one bothered to explain. Nana showed up, and presto! I was enlisted."

He studied me a moment, his silence causing sweat to form between my boobs. I hated when sweat started, such a disgusting sensation.

"I was not present for any discussion. If you remember correctly, your grandmother asked for my help. I would have become involved eventually, due to the nature of your investigations."

I stared at him a moment, remembering the first time I had met him. The shock of seeing his tall stature, in full Indian garb, had taken the wind out of me. I mentally shrugged; I had been quite new regarding entertaining dead folks, so it was no wonder his presence had sent me reeling. However, I had to admit, the shoulder massage he had given me worked wonders for the emotional stress I was experiencing. Quite soothing.

"Would you have vetoed my inclusion?" I asked.

Regarding me with his piercing eyes, he eventually allowed a small smile to appear. "I have come to appreciate your limited abilities." Cocking his head to one side, he said, "You have surprised me more than once with your unexpected intuition."

I raised an eyebrow. "I take it your comment was supposed to be a compliment?"

A small nod escaped from him, and his smile widened a tad. "Yes. The fact you react to situations on pure instinct is a welcome bonus. I had not anticipated you would possess such strength. It is rare."

Embarrassed by the red I felt flood my face, I jerked my head in the direction of the woods. "So what's with the extra manpower? You expecting more trouble on your side?"

His eyes strayed to the woods and then returned to meet mine. "I do not wish to repeat your last encounter with danger, but I fear there are those on our side who will cause considerable damage if we do not take precautions."

"Your side is the problem in this case? Then why are we involved?" I asked, sweeping my arm to include Jack and Andy.

"Bella."

"Oh crap, I keep forgetting about her." I tilted my head, and said, "Why hasn't she shown up? Bob said she was being restrained, but Anthony is convinced she should have been visiting me by now."

"Anthony is convinced of many things, most of which are falsehoods. He is a fool," snorted Logan.

Wow, I had never once heard him make any type of sound that wasn't regal. Let's face it, snorting wasn't exactly what you expected from someone with his stature. Sort of beneath him somehow.

"Really? He may be a fool, but he is one crazy son of a bitch," I snapped.

"True, he has many mental and emotional obstacles. Sadly, they generate instability, which complicates our mission." He sighed. "He is merely a hindrance; his mother was extremely dangerous while alive. She brought her disruptive powers to our side; they are difficult to control." He gave me a tired look, and said, "We can restrain her to a degree, but it takes many of our resources I could apply more efficiently elsewhere."

His demeanor did nothing to help my frame of mind. If Logan was not happy with our current situation, then it was time for panic. Maybe.

"Should I be scared?"

"Oh Lord," said Andy.

"Wait a damn minute," said Jack. "We can't fight ghosts! We can barely handle the living!"

Logan shook his head. "Those who have crossed through the veil are not your problem; they are mine. You combat the situations they create among the living." His eyes wandered back to the wooded area. "Which is why I have increased your security. It is well known throughout the spiritual world Peg defeated the negative influences Owen had allowed into his life. They had quite a dynamic hold on his mind, which had started in his childhood."

Dad cleared his throat, saying, "So since Peg was successful last time, the bad guys have taken notice of her?"

Logan nodded. "She was, so to speak, the talk of the town."

"I assume it is a bad thing?" I asked.

"From my point of view, yes," he said. "Had you remained anonymous, there would be less danger for you."

"Well, this is just peachy," I said. I rested my head in my hand and groaned. "How much danger to my life are we talking about here?"

Logan remained silent, which set my sweat glands into high gear. Now, along with wet boobs, my entire body was drenched. Jeez Louise.

"How does Mrs. Spanelli fit into this?" asked Jack.

"She is a key player, but not the only key," replied Logan. "I am responsible for her involvement. She will be protected, along with her daughter."

"So who, or what, is the main key? Am I supposed to focus on Laura or not?" I asked.

He kept his eyes on the woods, saying, "She is under the care of Amy; it should suffice for the present."

I lifted my head, squinting at his back. "Amy has gotten a promotion?"

He threw his head back, laughing. I relaxed; there was no way Logan would allow himself so much freedom of expression if the situation was hopeless.

Turning to look at me, he asked, "Does the idea bother you?"

"Heavens no! It is comforting to know you have such a high opinion of her. Makes my life easier," I answered.

"She lacks experience, but her knowledge and teaching background allow her to accept the circumstances easily. I believe you would refer to it as 'going with the flow,'" he said.

I nodded. "Yes, she seems to accept everything calmly, after the initial shock." I stopped suddenly, narrowing my eyes. "Almost as if she expected all of this to happen to her."

Logan turned back to the woods, not responding to my comment. I should have known there was more to the situation than he had admitted.

"You warned her somehow!" I challenged. "How long have you been preparing her?" I wasn't surprised when he refused to answer my question. Logan has a bad habit of manipulating the lives of those he believes could come in handy concerning his own agenda. I was becoming weary of his sticky little fingers in everyone's lives.

"Peg," warned Dad, "Logan has his own way of doing things."

"Well, no one warned me! Nana and her friends just showed up one night and scared the crap out of me! Some type of warning would have been nice."

"You didn't need it," said Bob.

I spun around to face him; how long had he been back?

"What?" I asked, acid dripping from the word. As usual, Bob didn't notice.

"Think about it for a minute. After your initial shock, you've accepted our presence in your life pretty easily. Well, I know you don't like Elaine. Or your mother." He stopped, to give his brain some exercise. "Maybe not even your spirit guide. But, all in all, you've gotten used to us popping in and out," he said. He shrugged, "You've done a good job, and I appreciate your willingness to help." He looked down at the floor, mumbling, "It's changed my life."

I dropped my head in total frustration. How one earth could I stay mad at Bob when he could be so damn sweet? His innocence almost broke my heart—almost.

Logan tilted his head upward, listening to Bob. When he was positive Bob had finished his pep talk, he nodded slowly. "Bob is correct; you have accepted our presence and mission comfortably." He stopped suddenly, cocked his head to one side, and with a quick jerk of his head to the woods, faded with rapid-fire speed. This couldn't be good.

Those of us left in the kitchen shared uneasy looks. Dad cleared his throat, and said, "I think I'll pop out for a moment. Maybe I will be able to find out exactly what caused Logan's disappearance." He was gone before I could argue, and I sighed.

Andy shook his head. "Peg, I don't like what's going on here."

"Ha!" said Jack. "You're not alone. I thought this would be a fast, easy investigation—find who hit the girl. It's turned into a damn circus."

I sat in my chair, head pounding and sweating on overdrive. All I needed now was a hot flash to enter the scenario, and my day would be complete. Thoughts were racing through my mind, and none of them were encouraging. Jack was correct; how had a case that should have been straightforward, gotten so out of control so damn fast? I drummed my fingers on the table, staring at the scars our four boys had managed to produce during their years of homework, school projects and meals. The memories threatened to overwhelm me with emotion.

"Peg."

I looked up at Andy, who had been watching me closely. "It will be okay. Trust Logan."

My eyes filled with tears; I didn't bother stopping the flow. He took two steps to reach me and squatted down next to my chair. Grabbing me in a bear hug, he whispered, "It won't be like last time; we understand more now. Even Logan realizes how vulnerable you are and has expanded your ghostly guards."

"It isn't only my safety I think about," I sniffed. "You, Jack, Amy and now Laura. A lot of people to guard."

Nodding, he said, "Yep. Exactly why it's time to bring in a few more people who know how to protect us."

I pulled away, grabbing a tissue from the box on the table. Blowing my nose, I dipped my head in agreement.

Jack had been sitting quietly, not wanting to horn in on my emotional moment; his own wife battled menopause right along with me. Clearing his throat, he said, "Peg, I'm not going to lie; it's a mess. But all investigations have their frustrations; it's normal. Trust me, out of the chaos comes the answers. Always happens."

I nodded, reaching for another tissue. "Okay, but do all investigations include dead folks mucking up the scenery?"

"Yes," said Logan.

176

Jeez Louise. Back already?

I looked up at him, blowing my nose again. "What?"

He smiled gently. "Peg, every act, every crime, on *your* side of the veil is instigated on *our* side. Good and evil exist here because good and evil exist there." He shook his head. "This has been true from the beginning of time."

I narrowed my eyes. "So the old Bible stories are true?"

He gave me a slight nod. "To a degree, yes. Religion tries to explain truth; some stories are more correct than others. Wars, whether spiritual or physical, are part of nature." He shrugged. "People have become excellent at ignoring what, deep down, their spirit understands." He turned to the window, his arm sweeping the landscape. "Even the trees battle with one another for the sunlight. Some die, others live." Turning back to me, he continued, "You accept the way nature operates as true. The problem arises when mortals refuse to acknowledge the same principles are true for themselves."

I stared at him for a few seconds, then said, "You understood this when you were alive." It was not a question. I realized for the first time why Logan had been so powerful while he had lived. He understood stuff the rest of us ignored.

"Yes," he said. "I was fortunate to be alive at a point in time when surviving did not encompass my thoughts. I spent many hours contemplating the world and our place in this world." He stopped for a moment, then said, "It was enlightening."

"But life was harder back then," I argued. "It took more energy to find food, shelter and safety."

He smiled. "Not as much time as you would think. There were those who had the responsibility for the community, but I was not among them. I had the luxury of quiet contemplation."

I thought about his comments. Looking up at him, I said, "You were a medicine man?"

"Yes and no. I was considered a spiritual leader."

I knew there was more to his story than he was sharing but realized he wouldn't give me any more insight at this point. He was still careful explaining his role while here on earth, and I hoped one day he would share his history with me. But it wasn't today.

I nodded but didn't respond. He had given me the information to help me feel better. I appreciated his words, but it didn't solve our present problems.

"What's next?" asked Jack.

"We have activity. Bella has many family members willing to help her escape her confinement. We have the situation under control, for the moment." He paused and then said, "She is not my main concern. Anthony remains unstable, and his recent visit to Laura's home is not a good sign. He has never been to her house before now."

"I agree," said Jack.

"Yes. It is a concern," said Logan. "When someone behaves differently than usual, the reason is usually from our side."

"Can Bella still talk with him?" I asked. "She's being held back, but I bet she has the capability to communicate."

"I have made her contact with him impossible, but she has many accomplices who could achieve what she cannot."

"Do you want me to drive by Spanelli's house, just for a look?" asked Jack.

Logan nodded. "Possibly, in a while. But I have a greater need of you here."

Jack, throwing me a quick glance, asked Logan, "Trouble here?"

"No. I want to explain Laura's situation. You need to understand why she is so important."

# Chapter 20

Jack's eye grew wide. "Okay," he said, slowly.

"Much to my dismay, Anthony has been given much of the information I will now share. Had it not occurred, I would not feel the need to include you in this matter." He paused. "Laura is very sensitive about the situation."

Jack turned to me, but I kept my fat mouth closed. Logan had more details than I did, so let him tell the story.

"Anthony could not produce an heir, but neither he nor his mother would believe his body was at fault. They sent Laura to specialists for years."

I nodded—no new information here for me. Jack was hanging onto every word coming out of Logan's mouth.

Even Andy was surprised and glanced at me. My mouth remained shut; I had no reason to admit I knew most of the story.

Logan continued. "Bella was making Laura miserable, demanding a baby. Anthony's father watched Bella become more agitated as the years passed."

My heart began to race at this point; it was the first time the old man had been brought up in the matter. Mention of Anthony's dad had to mean something big for Logan to bother including him in the story.

Logan stopped, turned to the window, and studied the sunset as though the colorful sky would direct his words. It must have worked because he continued talking, never taking his eyes from the horizon.

"Bella had been quite a beautiful young girl when her husband met

179

her. The insanity had not overtaken her yet." He shook his head and sighed. "But as the years passed, she began to show signs of instability. Mr. Spanelli worried about their young son. Not quite comfortable with Bella's care of him, he hired a nursemaid from Sicily. Unfortunately, she had little sway concerning the boy. Bella controlled every aspect of the child's life, jealous of even his father's attention towards him." Again, Logan stopped, this time turning back to us.

"It is the reason his father sent Anthony away to college. He was determined to remove the boy from Bella's influence." He paused and then said, "I believe Anthony came close to leading a normal life, but he returned home at Bella's insistence."

I interrupted. "Amy thinks the insanity had already taken root by that point."

"Yes, but away from Bella, Laura would have been the stronger influence. She would have encouraged him to see doctors who would have helped him control the problems to a certain extent." Sighing, he added, "I could be incorrect, but it certainly would have helped had he not had Bella's constant domination."

"I can't argue with you concerning Bella," I said.

Logan gave me a small smile.

Jack asked, "What does all of this have to do with the accident?"

Logan's eyes turned to Jack. "Everything."

Boy, oh boy, his one word sent my stomach into major panic. "Uh-oh, I see where this is going!" I blurted.

Logan nodded. "Yes, I am not surprised."

Andy looked at me, asking, "What is going on here?"

Glancing around the table, I said, "Logan is better at explaining the details, but to speed this along, I'll tell you the most important piece of information." I darted my eyes towards Logan. He nodded so I figured it was okay for me to spill a few beans.

"Caterina is not Anthony's daughter. Legally, yes, but not biologically."

Andy and Jack stared back at me, stunned.

"Well, hell," Jack finally muttered. "Does Anthony know this?"

Logan nodded. "I believe once Bella passed to our side, certain family members informed her."

"Wait a minute," I interrupted. "If Bella was able to communicate with the dead while she was alive, why didn't they tell her this tidbit while she was still here?"

"Excellent question. We worked very hard to keep damaging information from Bella. I will admit, it was a difficult task," said Logan.

"It never dawned on you once she got to you guys, those family members would rush to tell her?" I snapped.

His eyes narrowed a tad, enough to make my stomach flip. Maybe I should adjust my tone of voice once in a while. There was no sense pissing Logan off.

His eyes never leaving mine, he said, "We were assured the security was adequate." He paused, adding, "We were wrong."

My face scrunched as I thought about this news. "So were you lied to? Or did they truly believe they could control Bella on your side?"

Logan's gaze returned to the window. "The circumstances are being investigated."

"There are investigations over there too?" Jack blurted.

Even though I could only see Logan in profile, I noticed his small smile at Jack's outburst.

"Yes, Jack. Even in our realm."

"Shit."

Dad laughed. "Jack, you will never stop being a cop, even when you're dead. Logan will put you to work as soon as you arrive."

"Damnation!" Jack snarled. "I'll never get to retire!"

"Boss, they're ready for you," announced Bob.

His voice startled me, and I said, "Bob, for Pete's sake!"

"Sorry, Peg." He turned back to Logan, waiting for an answer. I watched his expression, which reminded me of a puppy dog waiting for the next command. I wondered when he had started calling Logan "boss." I grinned to myself; it would have been fun to know what Logan thought of the new title.

Logan merely nodded and said to our group, "I will return in a few moments." He was gone before anyone could respond.

"What's with the disappearing act?" Jack asked, irritated.

Shrugging, I said, "No idea. He doesn't tell me much." I looked at Dad. "Well?"

Dad shook his head. "I only know he is planning something. Have no idea what though."

Turning back to Jack, I said, "See? Logan doesn't share with anyone, so don't feel alone. He's a pain in the butt sometimes."

Movement in the woods caught my attention. I slapped my glasses on my face and peered towards the guys out back. The twilight sky made it difficult to decipher exactly what was going on. They were moving about, and I could tell there were a lot of people, but other than all the shifting around, it was a washout.

"Dad, can you figure out what they're doing?"

He didn't move an inch but said, "Nope. None of my business. When Logan wants me to know, he'll tell me."

His attitude surprised me, which must have shown on my face. "Logan can be difficult, and I refuse to get on his bad side. He is running the show; I follow orders. Usually." He gave me a grin, which I returned.

"Aren't you supposed to be guarding Amy and Laura?" I asked him.

Nodding, he said, "I have a few of my own friends over there for the time being. Logan is aware of the fact and approves of my decision."

"Since when does Bob call Logan 'boss'? I almost laughed out loud," I said.

Dad threw out another grin. "The first time he used the term I actually saw Logan's shock ."

I laughed as I pictured the scene. "I bet Bob never even noticed Logan's reaction."

"Nope." Dad paused. "But I have to hand it to the old Indian, he realizes Bob uses the term respectfully. He's accepted the fact Bob is a little, well, unusual."

"He is irritating as hell, but he has a good heart," I said with a grin.

"Yep. Pretty much what Logan sees in Bob. A good heart."

I figured I might as well use the downtime while Logan was away to bring up another sticky subject.

"Dad, what are Mom and Elaine up to this time?"

Frowning, Dad said, "We can't determine exactly what their goals are, but they are under heavy surveillance. Elaine's abilities are growing under your mother's guidance, which has Logan very worried."

"Not good," said Jack. "She was a pain when she lived here. I can't imagine what trouble she can instigate over there."

Dad shook his head. "It's not what she can stir up on our side, but what turmoil she can create in your world that is the real dilemma."

My head started pulsing, and I sighed. "She'll never stop, will she?"

"Doubt it," said Dad.

The phone rang, and we all jumped. I looked over at Dad, who nodded.

"Peg? There's still a lot of activity out in the woods. Should I be worried?" asked Amy.

"Tell her she's fine," said Dad.

"Amy, my dad wants you to know his friends are guarding your property. It's fine. I'm pretty sure Logan has the guys out back under control. If there's a concern, I'll call you."

Her relief was evident. "Thank you Peg. I don't mean to be such a baby, but we are rather secluded."

"Yep, I know. Which is exactly why Logan has us protected. Don't worry." Ha! So easy to say, but I knew from experience, all the dead guards in the world can only help so much.

"Thank you Peg. I'll try not to bother you again," she said.

"Amy, if you get frightened, call me. I understand," I said. I hoped she didn't have a case of jitters in the middle of the night. The phone ringing at 2:00 a.m. would not help my own nerves one bit. To be honest, things were heating up in the investigation. I had absolutely no idea what, but with all the activity in my backyard, I knew something was cooking. I had to trust my goose wouldn't be cooked along the way.

I hung up the phone and looked at Dad. "You sure your friends are reliable? I don't want Amy to get hurt or frightened."

"Yep."

One word was all I was getting from him? Jeez Louise.

Shaking my head, I opened my mouth to be snotty, but snapped it shut when Logan reappeared. The kitchen was really a hopping place today.

"I realize it is your mealtime, but I ask for a few more moments of your time," he said.

Surprised, I glanced at the clock. Sure enough, it was past dinnertime. I looked at Andy apologetically.

He grinned and said, "Pizza sounds good."

Returning his grin, I nodded. Turning to Logan, I said, "Give Andy a minute to order a pizza, then you can finish your story."

Logan's expression was priceless. I doubt he got put on hold often, but I couldn't go without food just because he could. He didn't answer but remained quiet while Andy made the pizza call.

Jack chimed in, saying, "Get the one with everything. I'll split the cost with you."

Our favorite pizza joint doesn't deliver, so I knew Andy wasn't calling Leonardo's. Too bad, my mouth waters thinking about their delicious food. Our second choice had great pizza, but nothing beats Leonardo's. But I knew Andy well enough to know there was no way he was missing a second of Logan's speech to pick up dinner. I didn't blame him one bit.

Andy finished the ordering process and nodded at Logan, who had been watching the procedure with great interest.

"You make a call, and they bring you food?" he asked.

"Yeah, they deliver," answered Andy, surprised at the question.

Logan cocked his head to one side, asking, "Any food you desire?"

"Pizza mainly; other restaurants don't usually deliver food," said Andy.

Logan thought about Andy's answer but didn't reply. After a few more moments of silence, he turned to Dad.

"I trust Amy's property is secure?"

"Yep. Tight as a drum," answered Dad.

Logan gave him a quick nod, then turned back to those of us with heartbeats.

"I apologize for the need to delay our conversation. It could not be avoided."

I was hoping for a bit more information concerning the group in the woods, but Logan kept his side plans to himself.

"Do we need to review our earlier exchange?" Logan asked.

"Nope, Caterina is not Anthony's kid. Pretty straightforward. Right?" asked Jack.

"There is a great deal more to the situation, but yes, you have compressed the information neatly," said Logan.

"What more could there be? I think it's a big chunk of news," I said.

Logan closed his eyes with a pained looked. I smiled inwardly, knowing our lack of concern for details drove the guy nuts. He came from an era when story telling was a big pastime. Today, we want the bottom line and details only if necessary.

I glanced at Dad, who winked at me. He knew exactly where my brain and attitude had gone. Tough beans, Logan.

He straightened his back, pulling himself to his full height, which was considerable. Ah, what a show of strength and command! I knew Logan wanted us to take what he said seriously, and he was probably beginning to feel the meeting was getting away from him.

"I am a firm believer every fact is important in an investigation," said Jack.

I nodded in spite of myself. Jack had taught me details were important, and I knew it was true. Darn it.

Logan nodded. "Yes, details overlooked as minor inconveniences usually are important keys," he said, looking at me. I hate to admit it, but I felt myself grow slightly pink. He had me there. I hate those pesky details, but I knew both Logan and Jack had valid points.

"Why wouldn't Anthony or his mother accept the fact he was the problem concerning pregnancy," asked Andy. "Ego?"

"Partly," said Logan, nodding. "However, it goes deeper than ego. I must stress how important the family line was, and still is, to Bella. She was Mr. Spanelli's second cousin and carried the Spanelli name."

Well, you could have knocked me over with a puff of wind. Jack rubbed his hand over his face, and said, "We're dealing with genetic issues, aren't we?"

"Yes. Insanity is quite strong in the family. Peg is aware of this fact, but I wanted you to have the important pieces of knowledge, Jack. Anthony is not to be underestimated. Laura's garden was destroyed by a man who is not always in control of his emotions." He paused and then added, "If it was a controlled action, his attitude towards Laura has become much darker."

"We don't need the guy to get any worse," said Jack. "I don't like unpredictable." He squirmed in his chair, and I knew he was remembering Owen.

"Amy thinks it was a temper tantrum," I said.

"I hope Amy is correct," said Logan. "Sadly, it is Anthony's normal response to situations."

Andy asked, "You believe Anthony hears voices, right?"

Logan nodded.

"Can you block those voices?"

Logan said, "We block as much as possible. There are many Spanellis who have the ability to communicate with him." He sighed. "We have every available resource engaged in this matter. However, I am convinced he has avenues open, which I'm afraid Bella put in place that we cannot control."

"Bella is the reason for the extra guys out back?" I asked, hooking my thumb towards the woods.

"Yes."

"When this case is solved, is Bella going to continue to be a threat?" I asked, sweat forming on my upper lip. Again.

The question was met with silence, which increased my sweat factor. Logan and Dad exchanged glances, but no one spoke. Not a good sign.

The doorbell broke the tension. I glanced at Dad, who nodded. Andy said, "Good, the pizza's here, I'll get it."

As Andy left to answer the door, I looked at Logan. "So Bella *could* haunt me forever?"

"Not forever, only until we contain her. She is restrained at this point, but her powers are quite strong."

Jack's cell phone began singing the theme for Darth Vadar of *Star Wars* fame. I looked at him, asking, "Who the hell is calling?"

He grinned. "The mayor."

I laughed out loud.

"You going to answer it?" I asked.

"Nope, let it go to voicemail. The guy has called a million times today and I'm sick of him," said Jack, sliding the phone back in his pocket.

Andy came cruising back into the kitchen with two pizza boxes. Bless his heart, he had ordered me my very own pepperoni pizza. I didn't like pizza piled high with anything other than pepperoni. He and Jack could enjoy their own messy pizza, while I happily would plow through mine.

We spent the next few minutes getting plates, iced tea, and napkins organized. Logan and Dad quietly watched the proceedings. I'm pretty sure Logan was irritated by the interruption of food but wisely kept quiet until we were seated back at the table.

"Please eat your meal while I continue to explain the situation."

Like I would have waited! Ha! I didn't realize how starved I was until the aroma of fresh pizza hit the air. We dug into the food, nodding at Logan to talk.

"Laura was experiencing extreme anxiety due to the insistence of Bella and Anthony she must be the one with the reproductive problems. There was little she could do at this point but continue seeing special doctors." He paused. "It was a very painful time for her."

"You were watching this entire scenario, weren't you?" I demanded.

"Yes," he sighed. "I had no power over the situation, but I was protecting her when I could."

"So who's the real father?" asked Jack, between bites of pizza.

The doorbell rang again. We all looked at one another, then Andy said, "Probably the pizza delivery boy again. He forgot Peg's salad."

*Salad? Andy ordered me a salad? What a sweetie.*

He left to answer the door, and Jack looked at Logan. "Well?"

I heard a voice in the hall and knew it wasn't the delivery boy. Turning to Dad, I raised an eyebrow. He face remained neutral. Uh-oh.

Jack asked again, "Logan, who's Caterina's real father?"

"I can answer your question," said a voice from the kitchen doorway.

We all turned and froze. Standing in my kitchen door was the old man himself, Salvatorio Spanelli.

I hate to admit it, but I think I peed my pants, just a little.

# Chapter 21

"Hello, Salvatorio," said Logan.

"Logan," nodded Mr. Spanelli.

Oh, for Pete's sake, those two knew each other. This was getting to be a bloody circus. Logan had more connections to this case than he had led me to believe. The stinker.

Never having seen him before, I studied the old man's face. To be honest, I was surprised how little Anthony resembled his father. While good-looking, he was tall and about fifty pounds overweight. His hair was almost entirely gray but had a few patches of dark brown sprinkled around his head. It was so unfair men looked distinguished sporting gray hair, while women merely looked old.

Jack had taken a big bite of his piece of pizza moments before Mr. Spanelli had entered the kitchen. When I looked over at him, I had to stifle a laugh. Hot mozzarella cheese was now stretched from his mouth to the plate where he had dropped his pizza. Totally unaware of the cheese connection, he stared at our new arrival with horror. It was not a good idea for the chief of police to be rubbing elbows with one of the biggest mobsters in the state of Ohio. His reputation was well known. Back in the heyday of Ohio's Mafia, he had been quite influential in every area of life imaginable. Politics, journalism, religion, and education. Hard to believe, but Mr. Spanelli was a huge fan of higher education, donating millions of dollars to the state universities for decades.

Logan turned to Dad, nodding a silent message. Dad, acknowledging the action, returned the nod and immediately disappeared. Frowning, I wondered where Logan had sent Dad, but I knew better than to ask. Logan didn't necessarily agree with me about sharing information and kept his secrets as he desired.

Andy looked at me, not sure what our next move should involve, considering we were new to entertaining gangsters. I took a deep breath and then offered, "Cup of coffee?" It was the best I could think of under the circumstances. I sighed, embarrassed at my lack of social knowledge for these situations. Maybe there was a book I could read about entertaining members of the Mafia.

The doorbell rang again, causing Andy's body to jerk slightly. Maybe it was the pizza boy with my salad this time. Andy glanced at me; all I had to offer him was a quick shrug. Turning to make the trek back down the hall, I could hear him muttering under his breath. I felt sorry for the poor guy; this case had taken a few weird turns, and even Andy doesn't like *too* much excitement in our lives.

Jack had finally noticed the cheese string connecting his face to the table and growing red, used two fingers to disconnect himself from the plate of food. He glared at me, but I had no control over my guest list at the moment. This was Logan's gathering, and I had no idea in what direction we where headed. I raised my shoulders at Jack's expression, hoping he understood this wasn't my party.

Hearing the voices coming back down the hall, I was surprised to recognize Amy's. Frowning, I looked into Logan's eyes, trusting the blaze of heat I knew they were emitting would signal my frustration at the lack of information. He returned my stare but remained silent. Damn him.

As the voices became closer, I noticed Mr. Spanelli stiffen as he heard their conversation.

"I have no idea why Dave instructed us to come over," said Amy. "I'm so sorry to barge into your home this way."

"I'm sure Logan was the instigator, so don't worry yourself. It's not an intrusion," said Andy.

I spotted the trio as they rounded the corner and was not surprised by Laura's reaction. She had not expected Mr. Spanelli to be standing in my kitchen doorway. Halting, she said, "Hello, Sal."

After a quick glance at Logan, he turned to face her. "Laura." One word, but it said everything. She moved at lightning speed to his side. "Anthony knows about Caterina."

Nodding, Mr. Spanelli reached a meaty hand out to squeeze her shoulder. "How much?"

Shaking her head, tears cascading down her face, she said, "I'm not sure." She looked up at him. "Thank you so much for the guards at the hospital."

The penny dropped. My merry trio of pseudo-mobsters were to protect Caterina *from Anthony*. No wonder he hadn't been to the hospital! The situation was becoming quite intriguing. From the furious look on Jack's face, he had come to the same conclusion. I decided it would be wise to intervene at this point before the poor guy exploded.

I stood and headed for the coffee machine. "Mr. Spanelli, I'm making Amy and Laura a cup of tea. Would you like some?" My tone was dripping with kindness; out of the corner of my eye I saw Jack turn his glare my direction. Ignoring his temper, I began the routine of making tea. It gave me something to do and a certain amount of control over the whole mess. Logan might be calling a few of the shots here, but it was *my* house!

"Please take a seat. Andy, could you bring in a couple more chairs from the garage? Jack, why don't you finish your dinner and I'll get the pie out of the fridge." Someone ought to enjoy the pizza, because my stomach wasn't in the mood to be filled with spicy ingredients.

Amy took her own action, for which I was grateful. Joining me in the kitchen, she said, "Everyone make yourselves comfortable while Peg and I get the refreshments gathered." Noticing no one following our lead, she said firmly, "We will all be in a better frame of mind if we conduct ourselves appropriately." Clapping her hands smartly, she continued, "Now. Come on, Mr. Spanelli, take Peg's seat. Laura, you sit next to him." It must be her teacher's voice, but she got their butts in gear. No wonder she was able to teach teenagers for so many years; people responded to her assumed authority.

Off to my side, I noticed Logan's eyes twinkling. Probably one of the reasons he had Dad drag Amy over was her teacher's attitude. If I hadn't seen it with my own eyes, I would never have suspected she had the gumption to tell a mobster to plop his butt in a chair. Laura reached out for Mr. Spanelli's hand as she sat. He protectively covered her delicate one with his own thick, beefy hand. I shook my head, wondering what other surprises Logan had up his sleeve.

Once the tea was ready, along with pie cut and served, Logan began speaking in his quiet tone. Nodding toward our mob guy and Laura, he said, "Thank you both for coming together. I am aware you have kept yourselves at a distance from one another for many years." He nodded at them both, then said, "It is no longer necessary. Anthony may not have all the available information, but it will not be long before he acquires information you have hidden so successfully."

"Thank you, Logan, for protecting them. I will not forget your help," whispered Mr. Spanelli.

Logan waved his hand, as if to brush away the statement. "I was responsible for your predicament. I thank you for accepting my guidance; you could have taken a different course of action."

Spanelli shook his head. "I would have made a mess of the situation, and you understood what was at stake."

"Your mutual admiration society is all well and good, but someone needs to explain what the hell is going on around here," I said, fuming.

Logan raised his hand, stemming the flow of my anger. "Yes, I realize you do not possess all the facts. My hope was it would not be necessary to indulge your curiosity, but matters have forced me to decide all of you needed to be aware of the details." He paused, looking at Spanelli. "Salvatorio, they need to be informed. I apologize."

Spanelli, turning white, nodded. "Yes." His grip on Laura's hand tightened. Laura drew a quick breath but nodded.

Logan looked out towards the woods, which didn't thrill me at all. Nodding to himself, he turned back to us, saying, "The workings of Mr. Spanelli's profession are complicated."

Jack snorted, shaking his head. "One way of putting it," he said.

Logan turned his eyes on Jack, making the poor guy squirm.

"Much like kingdoms, there is the question of succession. The bloodline must be continued." He glanced around the group, making sure we followed his storyline. I was lost as hell, but Amy nodded her head.

"I thought as much," said Amy softly.

"Ah, yes. I had faith you would discover facts through your use of logic," replied Logan and smiled at her.

Her logic stuff was beginning to irritate me. "You never told me!" I accused her, hotly.

"Oh no, dear. I realized quite quickly what was at the bottom of Laura's anxiety, once Logan had informed me of Anthony's, well, problems concerning procreation." She actually blushed.

"Well, that makes one of us!" I snapped.

Andy held his hand up. "Mr. Spanelli, you are Caterina's biological father?"

"Wait a minute," I said, rubbing my head. Damn the headaches these investigations cause. "You two had an affair?"

Laura exclaimed, "Oh my God."

Mr. Spanelli shook his head. "No, no." He paused and then added, "Logan advised I donate my sperm."

I felt my eyebrow rise to my hairline and stayed quiet. No response came to mind, so I gladly kept my trap shut.

Jack had been listening intently, and asked, "Why?"

Spanelli sighed. "It is important in our line of business…" He paused, quickly shooting his eyes to Jack, "For my son to have a child. The longer they tried and the more doctors Laura was forced to see, the more obvious to anyone with half a brain, Anthony couldn't reproduce." He stopped, using his free hand to rub his face. "Logan and I talked over the consequences I faced with either not having an heir or Anthony discovering who was the true father of Caterina."

Logan intervened, saying, "We chose the path of least consequences." Shrugging, he said, "If Bella had remained alive, our plan would have succeeded."

"How do you figure?" asked Jack.

I could see his fascination with the information and bet he hated himself for being intrigued.

"As long as Bella was on earth, we blocked her access to our side. Once she died, it became difficult to keep the secret from her." He shook his head, saying, "The outcome has been disappointing."

"But Bella doesn't know, right?" I asked.

"Her suspicions are strong," he said.

"Now wait a damn minute!" snarled Jack. "How long have you two known each other?"

"Most of my life," came the quiet response from Spanelli. "As a child, I was different from the family. Even though I was next in line to take control once my father died, I wasn't interested in the business."

Logan nodded. "This family has been a problem for centuries. Salvatorio was the first member we felt could be effective for our endeavors."

Andy had been leaning against the counter, and he straightened suddenly. "You're the reason the mob activity in Youngstown has all but disappeared!"

Holy cow! Logan sure as hell had his fingers in a million different pies. Jeez Louise.

"Partly; I can't take all the credit." He looked at Logan. "We believed removing our various business channels would reduce crime in the area. We hadn't counted on the gangs filling the void." He shook his head again. "Sorry, Logan."

"It will be handled efficiently, friend. Do not concern yourself; your part has been accomplished."

*Friend?* Wow, that was the first time I ever heard Logan use the term. The notion of Logan having friends never entered my head. Learn something new every damn day.

Laura spoke for the first time. "I had no idea you had known Logan for so long. Did you know I knew him as a child?"

Spanelli's face told her the answer.

Logan looked up at the ceiling. My gaze followed his eyes. I hoped he didn't see any cobwebs. Since the last case, I've tried to keep a cleaner house. It was a revelation how much dust I had ignored for the past few years, but my new visitors certainly noticed. I didn't need any further discoveries about my housekeeping abilities. I quickly sneaked a peek at the corners of the ceiling, relieved at the apparent lack of spider webs.

Turning to Logan, Spanelli said, "Logan, why didn't you tell me?"

I almost laughed at the question. Logan gave out as little information as possible. Friend or not, there was no way Logan was sharing one bit more than he absolutely was forced to give. This moment was one of those rare instances where he found himself sharing more than he had anticipated. I didn't feel sorry for him. He had created the mess, he could clean it up himself.

His eyes slowly returning to Mr. Spanelli, Logan quietly said, "I had to protect all involved. Salvatorio, you are aware this was a sensitive situation." He nodded towards Laura. "She had to be shielded completely." He stopped, lost in his own memories. "When you and I discussed the strategy, it was done with utmost care. Concealing our meetings became increasingly difficult." He smiled at the old mobster. "You have many family members who have crossed through the veil of time; very few of them are friendly to our mission."

I had been leaning against the counter, watching Jack's face. His confusion was obvious, but he kept his mouth shut, trusting he would figure out it all out eventually. I hoped he could remain calm as we heard the rest of the story. I had an icky feeling in the pit of my stomach this was heading to a messy revelation.

Laura spoke up, startling me. "Sal, I believe our decision was correct. I have no regrets."

Her comment brought quick tears to the old mobster's eyes. "Anthony has become very unstable in recent years. I have been very worried for both you and Caterina."

Logan nodded. "Anthony was disappointed his child was not a son to carry on the family name. His obsession, largely due to Bella's influence, has created difficulties." His eyes slowly turned to Laura, "You are aware he has had many women in his life?"

She nodded but remained quiet.

Logan, returning the gesture, continued. "A son, even outside of marriage, would have inherited everything from Anthony. So sure of his ability to father a child, he had become frantic to find a woman to bear him a son. He has failed but refuses to believe the problem lies with him." Logan shook his head. "I had not anticipated this particular complication. Bella has much to answer for eventually."

192

"Bella?" I asked. "Anthony is nuttier than a fruitcake; why is she to blame?" I tossed Mr. Spanelli a quick apologetic glance and then asked, "Did she egg him on to have another kid?"

Logan turned to me, nodding. "She encouraged him to find a woman who could have a male heir to ensure the family line would continue. Bella was, and still is, obsessed with the Spanelli name continuing through future generations."

"So," said Jack, "she's as looney as her kid?" He didn't bother with an apologetic glance at Anthony's dad. At this point, Jack was fuming.

"Chief Monroe, the situation is complicated," Logan responded softly. Wow, he never used Jack's title, so I knew it was a signal, warning Jack to stay calm. It didn't work.

"Everything with you is complicated," exploded Jack. "If you shared all the information from the get-go, we'd be able to do our jobs more efficiently!" His fist pounded the table, causing the plate with his half-eaten pizza to jump.

Logan remained quiet. It didn't mean he agreed with Jack, merely that he wasn't allowing himself to get into an argument at the moment. The old Indian had enormous self-control, which was not exactly how I would have described Jack's mood at the moment.

"I have a question," said Amy. She had the teapot in her hand, and was walking to the table to refill the cups. Her composure helped lower the tension in the air, but not by much.

Logan raised an eyebrow, nodding at her.

Topping off everyone's cup of tea, she said, "Mr. Spanelli, I don't wish to intrude on your private matters. But I need to ask you one question." Setting the pot on the table, she looked squarely into his eyes. "Are you adopted?"

My mouth fell open, and I wasn't the only one in the room to react.

"What the hell!" Jack moaned.

Once I had gathered my wits about me, I shut my mouth, glancing quickly at Logan.

Andy had been watching patiently, but now asked, "What makes you ask, Amy?"

She cocked her head, her expression thoughtful. "I have come to appreciate Logan's predicament."

"Well, how nice of you," snapped Jack.

She shot him a quick warning glance; her teacher posture kicking in, I supposed. I stifled a giggle, watching Jack's lips slam shut, but a defiant expression crossed his face.

"Logically speaking," began Amy.

I groaned at her mention of her damn logic. I was rewarded with a stern look from her; I followed Jack's example and shut my mouth to keep from offering any further noises.

Amy resumed speaking, "The goal is to rid the area of crime, correct?" She looked at Logan for the answer. He nodded but wasn't about to earn her teacher's glare himself. He didn't even make a sound.

She cocked her head to one side, saying, "We know the Spanelli family has caused problems for centuries." She stopped, looking at the aging mob guy. "I'm sorry, I don't mean to offend you. But, facts are important."

"Yes," was all he dared say.

Amy had us feeling like we were in tenth-grade science class.

Nodding, she continued. "Insanity runs in the family, so it is one of the problems to contend with through the years." She paused, deep in her own logical mind. No one spoke, while she worked her way through the maze of thoughts.

"Logan decided the best course of action was, quite simply, to rid the family of the insanity problem as the first step." She looked back at him. "Correct?"

Eyes twinkling, he nodded but still had the common sense to remain silent.

She focused her eyes on Mr. Spanelli, asking, "How old were you for the adoption?"

"An infant," he said, watching her, fascinated by her analysis.

She nodded again, "Yes, it was best." Again, she was quiet, connecting the dots in her mind.

Her fingers began dancing along the rim of the teapot. No one dared uttered a sound, watching her, enthralled with her reasoning.

"No one knew you were adopted. It was a secret." No questions, but firm statements.

Mr. Spanelli's eyes grew wide. "How did you know?"

Amy cocked her head to one side, and I knew exactly what was about to come out of her mouth. "Logical analysis."

Logan finally asked, "How did you arrive at your conclusions?"

"Logically speaking, it was the best input for the desired output." Seeing our confused expressions, she added, "Once I knew *what Logan's plan entailed,* I worked back until I found the best possible *scenario to accomplish his goals.* Simple, really."

Simple? I'd known Logan a few months longer than Amy, and simple was not how I'd describe his short- or long-term goals—too many levels, layers, and contingencies for my taste. He liked complicated plots; I liked boring and easy.

"What are Logan's plans?" asked Andy.

Shrugging, Amy said, "To rid the area of crime, which includes evil. A tall order, in my opinion."

"So you concluded Mr. Spanelli, here," Jack pointed at the old man, "was secretly adopted, because Logan wants evil out of Ohio?" He shook his head. "I don't get it."

Smiling, Amy said, "Logic explains everything."

# Chapter 22

"Logic, schmolic," snapped Jack. "How the hell did you arrive at the conclusion Mr. Spanelli here…" He pointed his finger at the topic of conversation. "…was secretly adopted?"

"Chief, start the thought process at the end of Logan's plan; not the beginning," said Amy, walking back to the kitchen to start another pot of tea. I'm not sure how many people were actually drinking the stuff, but the pot was empty. Someone must have been swallowing it, but I sure as hell didn't see them in action.

Dad intervened before the conversation took a turn for the worse. "Jack, Amy realized Logan wanted to end the mob's rule in northeast Ohio. He chose Mr. Spanelli years ago to help accomplish his goal. The fact Mr. Spanelli was adopted would enable the gene pool to have a chance of weeding out the insanity. It would probably takes generations, but Logan plans for the long term."

"Okay, I follow you Dave. But what about the kid?" asked Jack.

Dad opened his mouth to answer, but Logan's raised hand stopped him cold. "Chief Monroe, genetics play a very large role in this story." Uh-oh. Twice Logan had used Jack's title instead of his first name. I glanced at Dad for help defusing Jack's anger, but Dad was too intrigued with the drama playing out right in front of us to notice my concern.

"Fine, but it doesn't explain what the hell—" He stopped.

I watched as his face changed from anger, through confusion, to realization dawning. He looked at Logan, "She doesn't carry one cell of actual Spanelli blood."

Logan beamed as though a prized student had solved a difficult problem. Nodding, encouraging Jack's train of thought, he said, "Exactly."

"So while the name can continue, even though she isn't male, the insanity genes won't," said Jack, as his brain caught up with the rest of us.

"Yes. Today, even though a woman marries, she may retain her maiden name. Women in most ancient societies did not assume their husbands' names, unless they chose to do so. It is not a new thought, though many believe the practice is original with this generation." Logan smiled as he finished.

I decided Logan finds our modern world humorous. We tend to think we are smarter than all the previous cultures, but, as history proved, we are just as stupid, arrogant, and selfish. Sad as it was, some things never changed.

"Okay, but it doesn't solve the problem! Anthony is still nuts, crime is everywhere, and we still don't know who the hell hurt Caterina!" said Jack. His frustration was on the rise, but Amy stepped in quickly.

"Oh, but we do know who hurt the poor child," she chided Jack. "Think."

Jack turned to Amy. "Who?" he demanded.

"Think it through, Jack. You have proven yourself through the years to be a man of great investigative abilities. I have confidence in you," she smiled. Ah, her damn teacher mode again. Amy could quite easily become a thorn in our butts with this attitude.

Jack's face grew beet red with frustration, and I couldn't blame him. His phone rang, which gave everyone a good reason to take a deep breath and relax for a moment.

Grabbing the phone from his pocket, he frowned as he read the caller ID, which was unnecessary as we sat through another few seconds of the Darth Vadar music. "The mayor," he announced to no one in particular. Sighing, he answered the call. We gave him the courtesy of staying quiet for the duration.

Once he had ended the call with a curt reply, I said, "Well, what did His Highness want?"

Before Jack could answer, another voice interrupted us.

"Anthony's lost it big-time," a breathless Bob reported as he snapped into the kitchen. As he glanced around the table, he spotted Mr. Spanelli, and Bob's face grew as red as a tomato. I sorta felt sorry for him.

His eyes searched frantically for Logan, and once they landed on his mentor, they stayed glued. "Sorry, boss, but Anthony just threatened the mayor. The guy is up in arms, and I can't find Anthony anywhere."

I could feel his panic and felt a few twinges of my own surfacing. Andy, who had been casually leaning against the kitchen doorframe, straightened.

Looking over at Dad, he said, "What can I do?" He instinctively guessed Anthony was looking for Laura.

Jack pulled his cell phone back out and called the station. "I want an APB out on Anthony Spanelli immediately. Consider him armed and dangerous."

He tossed the phone on the table and leaned back in the chair. "It will help, but I'm sure Logan has a more efficient idea."

I noticed Mr. Spanelli on his own cell phone and guessed he was calling reinforcements of his own.

Dad's worried frown did nothing to improve the mood around the table. Looking at me, he said, "Peg, take a peek out back."

Sweat immediately beaded on my upper lip, but I nodded. Taking a deep breath, I turned to face the window. My shoulders sagged as I spotted not only the Indians who had guarded me for months, but the British soldiers and trappers, alongside the Vikings. Jeez Louise, there was a lot of manpower out back. Too bad they were all dead.

My physical reaction told Dad all he needed to know. Turning to Logan, he said, "Do we separate people or keep them all in one spot?"

Logan considered the question a moment and then said, "Keep them together. I believe Salvatorio has called in his reinforcements." Turning to the old mobster, he asked, "Correct?"

Mr. Spanelli nodded. "They should be here soon."

"It will be easier for them to guard one house rather than two," said Logan, glancing out the window. "Peg, is it possible for you to allow Laura and Amy to stay here?" His tone of voice alerted me to the fact he wasn't really asking, more along the lines of a polite order. Under normal circumstances, his attitude would have pissed me off, but these weren't normal circumstances.

Andy piped up, saying, "They can stay in the boys' old rooms."

Nodding his head, Logan said, "I believe having both women in the same room will be safer."

Frowning, I said, "Well, the boys shared bedrooms growing up. I'm not sure bunk beds will be comfortable." I looked over at Amy's aging body, shaking my head. "I can't see either of them enjoying the top bunk."

Laura spoke up, saying, "It would work. I can take the top."

Amy's eyes glittered with humor. "Sleeping in a top bunk would be exciting! I've never gotten to experience bunk beds before!"

I groaned. The last thing I needed was hearing a thump in the middle of the night as Amy plopped on the floor from such a height. Before I could argue with her, the doorbell rang.

As Andy turned to answer the door, I threw Dad a questioning look. Shrugging, he pointed to Mr. Spanelli. It must be the old man's help arriving,

I decided. I could hear voices coming back down the hallway and recognized Santino's laughter. Relief flooded my system; I was glad the mobster had called people I not only knew but liked and felt comfortable having around the house. Bill, Antonio and Santino entered the kitchen ahead of Andy by a step or two.

They noticed Laura's presence at the table, but only Bill reacted with a faint look of surprise. His face quickly returned to his normal serious expression as he turned to face Mr. Spanelli.

"Sir," he said. I guessed the one word was the mob 'hello.'

The old man nodded and outlined the situation with rapid-fire confidence. It was obvious he had been giving orders most of his life and was comfortable with the role he played. Once he had explained the situation, they began discussing the best strategies for protecting the house and property.

Jack's face was as red as a beet, and he finally exploded.

"Wait a damn minute! Protection is police business, and you three will complicate our efforts!" he shouted. The veins in his neck were bulging and I knew he was going to blow apart any minute.

"Chief Monroe," explained Antonio, "we have advantages in these situations. You have to follow the letter of the law for court reasons; we don't." Couldn't get a more straightforward statement. Watching Jack's reaction, I knew he didn't like it one bit.

"Jack," I said, trying to ease his anger, "we know from experience, they don't break any rules they don't absolutely need to break."

He snapped his mouth shut so hard I was surprised his lips didn't split from the force.

I would have reminded him of their allegiance to Logan, but I had no idea what the old mobster knew. No sense giving away a secret if I could help it. I had noticed they were ignoring all the dead folks in the room, which led me to believe their boss may not be aware of their association with Logan. Never could tell with these guys.

To lend some aid to the mob guys, Andy said, "They've done pretty well in the past, so I trust they will continue in the same manner."

I'm pretty damn sure Jack wasn't thrilled to be reminded it was Antonio's actions which saved my butt a few months ago, but Andy's statement helped lower my friend's blood pressure a little. Jack remained silent but did concede a curt nod, acknowledging Andy's words. I sighed with relief; I really wasn't in the mood for someone to decide to throw a temper tantrum in the middle of this mess.

Seeing Jack's reaction to Andy, Antonio turned back to his boss. "We partially discussed the plan on the drive over here. Is there any further information we need at this point?"

Shaking his head, Mr. Spanelli said, "Not now; maybe later. Anthony has gone off the rails. I know he has threatened the mayor, which isn't a good sign. If I know my kid, he is having a royal meltdown." He sighed. "No telling what he'll do next."

Antonio nodded, turning to me. "Mrs. Shaw, the plan is much like last time. One of us in the house, two of us outside. No one is allowed to answer the phone unless it's one of us. Agreed?"

"Yep," I answered quickly. "I hope it will go better than the last time you guys were here."

His glance slid to Laura and Amy. "Which room will you ladies be occupying?"

Their eyes flew to me.

"Down the hall and first door to the left," I said.

"Windows?" he asked.

"They face south, towards the back yard," Andy chimed in. "Is it going to be a problem?"

Antonio glanced at Bill and Santino then met Andy's eyes. "Better than the front. We will be stationed in the back and can keep our eyes on the window. Is it locked?"

Andy frowned. "I have no idea." He headed towards the bedroom to check the window in question, Santino following closely behind.

The nonbreathing crew in my kitchen had remained silent throughout the exchange. I looked at Dad, but he shook his head, putting a finger to his lips. I allowed my head to return a slight nod and then looked back at Bill. He had noticed my silent communication with Dad and grinned at me. I couldn't help but grin right back at him. This could become a three-ring circus if we weren't careful.

"Um, Peg," said Bob.

Damn, I had forgotten all about him. I finally spotted him squeezed tight in the far corner of the kitchen, obviously trying his best to remain unnoticed. He had succeeded as far as I was concerned. He must be nervous, not to start a conversation with the hired guns. Or maybe Logan had threatened him with consequences the next time he pulled the stunt in front of people who may not have been aware of the connection. Logan could be scary, and Bob was definitely scared spitless of him sometimes.

Everyone in the room stiffened, afraid to acknowledge the voice in the corner. I shot him a glance that could have melted an iceberg. He got the message. Even Amy wouldn't glance at the corner. A room full of adults, pretending no one heard the voice from the corner was ridiculous, but it allowed the facade to continue.

Waiting for Andy and Santino to return from the bedroom, we remained silent. Not sure why, but you could have heard a pin drop. Finally, I heard their voices as they headed back toward the kitchen.

"Good as it can be," Santino said to Antonio. "Small, but a determined person could get through."

"Anthony's not tiny," said Bill.

Santino shrugged. "Depends on how much he wants in the house." Pointing at Laura, he asked, "Anthony know she's here?"

Every eye turned to me, and I looked at Logan, who shook his head.

"Don't think so. Why would he?" I said.

Antonio nodded, lost in his own head. Probably trying to decide if his plan had any holes in it, which I hoped to God it didn't.

"Any way we could put motion sensors out there?" I asked.

Antonio gave me a rare grin. "The way things are shaping up, it may be a good idea. You need more protection than I had anticipated." Then he shook his head. "No time now, though. Plus, I don't want my security guys out here working on the property. Anthony knows them by sight, and it would be a dead giveaway Laura was here."

Mr. Spanelli's face went white at Antonio's words. I didn't blame him. The longer Anthony had no idea where his wife was, the better it was for all of us.

The phone shrilled, making us all jump. I knew from experience I couldn't answer the phone, but neither could the trio. Anthony knew their voices too well. We stared at each other, deciding how to handle it.

Andy said, "Let the answering machine pick up."

Antonio wasn't happy, but he nodded. "This time only. No sense someone thinking the house is empty."

Crap, he had a point. I looked at Logan, who nodded his agreement.

"Fine, but who's going to have the job of answering it the next time it rings?" I demanded. "We can't let every call go unanswered."

"Bill, there's a recorder out in the car," said Antonio. Bill smiled as he left to do Antonio's bidding.

"What good is a recorder?" asked Andy.

Moving my stacks of papers around to make room for his precious recorder, Antonio answered, "Whoever is guarding the house will be able to listen to the caller when Mrs. Shaw answers. If it isn't Anthony, we can relax and continue on as usual. If it is, we'll be able to give Mrs. Shaw pointers on how best to answer any inquiries he may have for her." Shooting his boss a quick glance, he added, "Anthony can be sneaky, so we have to be prepared."

Mr. Spanelli didn't argue with Antonio's statement; he didn't even acknowledge it had been made. I nodded, relieved. Should the creep call me, I would have help deflecting any questions concerning Laura.

Andy must have felt exactly the same because he came and squished me in a huge bear hug. My eyes filled with tears, either from his support or hormones. It was a toss-up which was the culprit, and I didn't care, but his hug made me want to pee. Jeez. My bladder was beginning to become a problem.

Jack sat and watched with interest as Bill set up the recording device. "Is this legal?" he asked.

Bill cut his eyes to Jack, grinning.

Jack sighed but didn't pursue the issue.

I checked the caller ID, but it came up a private caller. When you need the darn things, they don't help much at all. We heard the answering machine pick up the call and recognized a telemarketer blaring out from the speaker. I hit the end button, cutting off the call. I hated those calls but was relieved this time.

Out of the corner of my eye, I noticed Bob trying to get my attention. I ignored him; let Logan deal with his irritating butt.

Amy cleared her throat, saying, "Mr. Spanelli, do you have any idea what Anthony could be planning?"

The old man shook his head. Sadness enveloped his whole body, and as a parent, I felt sorry for him. He had worked so hard to protect Anthony from Bella, but her emotional control over her son was too strong in the end. Mr. Spanelli had lost the fight, and I hoped the plan Logan had for the family worked. Caterina could grow up to be a powerful player in the family business and lead them down a legit road, which would solve many problems for the entire group. We just had to get rid of Anthony somehow.

Bob was starting to make frantic arm waves, so it was becoming pretty hard to ignore him any longer. I gave him a "What now?" look, but he was almost exploding with anticipation.

Suddenly, the air sparkled with energy. The entire room went still as we darted our eyes around, trying to spot the source.

"So you folks are having a meeting?" came the nasty voice behind me.

I twirled around, only to see Elaine's face smirking at me. I almost threw up but held it together enough to snap, "Why the hell are you here?"

She laughed. "To see what you losers are up to!"

I had to hand it to my mob guys, after their initial reaction of complete stillness, they went on about their business as though they had no idea Elaine was in the room. It was pretty impressive, considering the fact if they could talk with Bob and Logan, it was a good bet they could easily hear other dead folks.

Even Laura and Mr. Spanelli remained out of the conversation, but the old guy did slide his hand away from Laura's. It was a telling move, in my opinion. He must have had a sixth sense Elaine was evil, and Bella didn't need any further evidence of the friendship those two had acquired through the years.

Amy broke the silence. "Why, Elaine, we aren't up to anything in particular. Too bad I can't offer you some tea, but I'm not sure you could actually drink it." She smiled sweetly as she ended her remarks, but I wasn't fooled. This was Amy being mean and nasty; I loved it.

Elaine's eyes narrowed as she honed in on Amy, but if she thought she was scaring the little old lady, she was wrong. Amy held the gaze and it was Elaine who looked away.

*Ha! What she gets for trying to intimidate a school teacher.*

Elaine focused her attention back on me. "Has your mother been here yet? I was supposed to meet her."

Oh, for Pete's sake. Just what I needed.

# Chapter 23

The news my mother was supposed to show up soon did nothing to improve the tension in the room. My mob trio, while not acknowledging Elaine's presence, skedaddled out of the kitchen faster than I would have ever thought possible. They recognized a bad situation when it hit them in the face.

Glancing at Dad, I was relieved to see I wasn't the only one unhappy with the news my kitchen would soon have more dead than breathing people filling it to the brim. Those without heartbeats were beginning to overtake my life, and I wanted the pesky beings out of my living space. I opened my mouth to demand Elaine leave, but Logan raised his hand to stop my words.

Turning to Elaine, Logan smiled. It wasn't a welcome smile, more like I'm-going-to-make-your-existence-miserable smile. I could feel the sweat forming again on my upper lip, and maybe even a teensy bit down my bra. Yuk.

"Elaine, how nice to see you again," he said.

Even Elaine wasn't stupid enough to think he was serious. She cautiously nodded at his words but wisely kept her annoying mouth closed—a small miracle but one I'd take with happiness.

"It is surprising you and Nell are interested in the Spanelli family," he paused a moment before adding, "Very intriguing indeed."

I noticed goosebumps forming at the nape of my neck; his tone was not threatening, but I swear there was underlying menace coating each word. If Elaine and Mom thought they could outfox Logan, they were nuttier than the average person.

"Perhaps you could explain your involvement?"

It may have sounded like a question to the dumb bitch, but I knew it was a demand. Logan's commands could be really sneaky.

Bob chose this moment to be a complete moron—no surprise there. Clearing his throat, he said, "Elaine, I don't trust you, so get out of here."

Her eyes never left Logan's face, but she laughed as Bob spoke. "You have no authority over me! What a jackass!"

I swear I could actually see Bob shrink a little; I didn't feel sorry for him. When Logan was in command, you stayed out of the conversation.

Logan ignored Bob's comment, saying, "It is not wise to be involved in matters that do not concern you."

"What makes you think this family doesn't concern me? They are a huge part of our plans, and we don't need you meddling in our affairs. Maybe you should think about keeping your nose out of our business!" Elaine declared.

What an idiot! Even if I was batting for their team, I would be able to recognize Logan's power. Hell, it dripped from him as thick as molasses. The air rustled again, alerting us to a new arrival. No shock, it was Mom.

"Hello, Peg," she said to me. Looking around the full room, she said, "Quite a party you have here."

Spotting Dad, her eyes narrowed. Leaning against my wall, he gave her a slow nod but didn't bother wasting words.

"Hello, Nell," said Logan.

She stiffened hearing his voice—smooth, silky, and totally scary. Mom wasn't as stupid as Elaine; she knew how dangerous Logan could be for her. Maybe it was her length of time over in Deadsville that had taught her a thing or two. I wasn't so sure Elaine would ever learn those lessons; her arrogance might cost her in the long run.

Nodding, Mom said, "Hello." Looking at Mr. Spanelli, she continued, "You think you can change how this family works for us?" She laughed. "We've had them for centuries!"

I glanced quickly at the old man, feeling sorry for him. He sat straight in his chair, pretending he couldn't hear her words. Logan had taught him well; we didn't need the bad guys knowing Mr. Spanelli had the ability to hear the conversation. Amy reached over to Laura, squeezing her arm to reassure her. I couldn't tell from Laura's expression if her capabilities allowed her to hear Mom and Elaine, but it wouldn't have surprised me one bit if Logan had allowed those abilities for both of these people. Dad was correct; Logan's plans reached far into the future.

Logan gave Mom a small smile. "Yes, your friends have had much control over this unfortunate family. The question is why?"

Mom gave him an airy wave of her hand. "You are well aware of the plan. The more chaos, the better. It doesn't take much to stir the pot of corruption, discontent, and greed."

Logan appeared to be considering her words. "Yes, sadly, you are correct. Human nature has not progressed. I am hoping to change the situation."

"You can't change human nature!" Mom laughed.

Tilting his head to one side, Logan replied, "You are possibly accurate in your assessment. However, there is a chance, small though it may be, of even a limited progression, which could change the entire world." He shrugged. "It does not hurt to make the effort."

"You're wasting your time," smirked Mom. "People don't change."

Logan must have had enough of her crap because the next thing I knew, he announced, "Both of you, leave."

The air changed again but this time for the better. A heaviness, which had accompanied both women, was gone in a split second. The relief in the room was noticeable, and I for one, was grateful Logan had got rid of them.

Laura had held herself together so tightly when Mom and Elaine were gone, she sagged against Amy, sobbing. Mr. Spanelli's eyes filled with tears, watching her fall apart. My heart went out to both of them, and I marveled at Amy's ability to soothe Laura effectively. She might not have had kids of her own, but the woman had a mother's heart.

"There, there, dear. It's over." She comforted Laura, stroking her head softly. "They're gone."

My throat tightened watching Amy care for her new friend. I realized she would have made a wonderful mom, and my feelings towards her husband Albert didn't improve. What a jerk.

Logan watched the two women, satisfied with the situation. I was beginning to understand he had brought these two together for more reasons than solving the problem of crime families operating in our area. Jeez Louise.

The phone blasted our individual thoughts right out the window. I almost peed my pants with the shock of noise. I shot Logan a glance, but his eyes were glued to the hall doorway. Sure enough, I heard footsteps moving fast as lightning coming towards the kitchen. Santino, while calm, had made good time getting his butt back to us before the second ring of the phone. Crossing to the recorder, he nodded at me, indicating I could answer the phone. He pushed a button as I said "Hello?"

"Mom? Hey, we are planning a trip soon. What's the name of the hotel we stayed at when we went to Fort Lauderdale?" asked Adam, our firstborn son.

My shoulders sagged with relief, but irritation was fast to take over my emotions.

"Adam? It was twenty years ago! I can't remember," I snapped.

"Simmer down; ask Dad; he'll remember," he said.

Shaking my head in disgust, I looked at Andy.

Grinning, he said, "The Waterfront."

I relayed the information, and my oldest son said, "Yes! That's it. Tell Dad thanks. Hate to make this short, but our dinner just got to the table. Love ya."

We? Our? Was he dating someone new? Who was she? Every question a mother asks herself began flying through my brain.

Dad interrupted my thoughts. "Peg, I'll check her out for you."

Wow, I hadn't realized the entire room was watching my face, correctly interpreting my thought process.

Andy grinned. "Sweetie, maybe he has finally found a girl he wants to have around for longer than a split second."

I felt tears forming and was surprised by the reaction. I usually didn't care who the boys were dating, but Adam's tone of voice told me this could be more than a new flame. I didn't want to be one of *those* mothers—the interfering, nosy, aggravating women who tried to run their sons lives. Bella was exactly that mother, and look at her kid.

I looked over at Dad. "Promise?"

Grin still firmly in place, he nodded. "Yep."

I took a deep breathe. "Okay, I'll be fine."

Andy shook his head but kept quiet. He knew I'd process this new situation and make peace with the fact my boys were no longer kids but maturing adults. It was the worry though; they were still in the *maturing* phase. Could we trust their judgment? I hoped so.

Santino did an about-face to return to his post when the phone rang out again. Thinking it was Adam again, I reached for the phone, but a hand stopped me. Logan had physical abilities in our realm, but he seldom used them. The fact it was his grasp restraining my arm gave me goose bumps. He nodded at Santino, who reading Logan's expression correctly, said, "Second ring, Peg."

Sweat bypassed my upper lip and went straight for the boob area. Yuk. My stomach was flipping around so much I was afraid it would empty its contents on my kitchen table.

The second sound we were anticipating rang out, and, with a look at Logan for confirmation, I took a deep breath, saying, "Hello?"

"Mrs. Shaw? Yes, this is Anthony Spanelli. I hate troubling you at home, but do you have any information for me?"

Logan shook his head, informing me not to share anything at all. I agreed but was nervous I would accidentally spill a bean or two. I decided to throw the entire situation on Jack. He was more experienced than I was by a long shot.

"I'm so sorry, Mr. Spanelli. You need to call Chief Monroe. I personally have no information for you. The chief oversees the investigations and is in better position to give you answers." I thought it sounded pretty good, and I was relieved to see Logan nod his approval.

There was a pause and then his voice changed. "Mrs. Shaw, I believe you know more than you are admitting."

My throat constricted, hearing the edge now in his voice. I felt my eyes widen, and I looked at Logan. We had the conversation on speaker, and the reaction from everyone in the room, dead and alive, was a collective gasp. Jack looked at me, eyes narrowed, shaking his head. He reached over and hit the mute button, then said, "This guy is off the rails. Don't tell him a damn thing!"

Santino was frowning, and said, "I agree. Stall, deflect, but don't give him any information."

"Mrs. Shaw?" came the now oily voice.

Jack's eyes met mine. He nodded once and then hit the button again, now allowing Anthony to hear me.

"Yes, Mr. Spanelli?" I managed to keep my voice steady; I had absolutely no idea how I accomplished the feat, but I sounded normal.

"You should be careful lying to me. It would not be healthy for you to withhold information from me."

I could feel the panic rise in my entire body. Sweat was forming in places I didn't know it could, and I tasted bile in my mouth—not a good situation.

Logan frowned, which did nothing to improve my reactions. I heard him in my mind telling me to ask Anthony a question.

"Mr. Spanelli, what makes you think I know anything? I'm not the police, and Chief Monroe isn't in the habit of giving civilians sensitive information."

I was thankful my words had the ring of truth. Logan was an excellent coach in these matters. I began to settle down, knowing Logan was basically in the driver's seat and I was merely along for the ride, repeating the ideas forming in my brain. This was not the first time I was grateful Logan had many avenues of communication.

I noticed out of the corner of my eye Dad was no longer casually leaning against the wall but standing straight, eyes darting back and forth between Logan and me. Somewhere in the back of my mind, I realized he was waiting for orders from Logan. Santino reached down to press the mute button and turned to me.

"We need to know what makes him think he can get information out of you. Why didn't he call the Chief?"

I nodded, knowing the request was more for Logan than me, but since we were all still playing the game of secrecy regarding my trio's involvement with the Indian, I focused on Santino's face. "Yep, got it."

Once the mute button had been pressed again, I asked, "Mr. Spanelli, what on earth makes you feel I have the chief's confidence regarding the department's investigations?"

His laughter echoed through my kitchen, affecting each one present. The insanity rang through the sound, and the old man almost groaned aloud. Thankfully, Santiono reached over, gently covering the mobsters mouth with his right hand, while he leaned down to whisper soothing words. It was enough to allow the father of the deranged son to pull himself together. I wondered briefly if we should remove him from the kitchen, but Logan's focus wasn't on his friend's misery.

Dad and Logan made eye contact, and through their silent shorthand, a message must have been relayed because in a flash, Dad was gone. I knew Logan had sent him on some type of errand but was surprised how fast Dad returned. His expression was grim.

Anthony's laughter subsided, and as he gathered himself to answer, a thought blazed through my brain and I sighed. "Bloody hell," I whispered.

Andy lifted an eyebrow, but I shook my head.

"Mrs. Shaw, do you recall I mentioned my mother would help?"

"Yes," I said slowly. Damn it, I knew what was coming next.

"Well, she may not have appeared to you, but she does to me!"

"Okay," I said, determined to make him completely spill his own beans.

He giggled, then said, "She told me *you* know all the answers."

I sighed. Yep, exactly what I thought he was going to say.

"Well, I'm sorry, but I don't know all the answers. I wish I could help you, but I'm a consultant, not a member of the police department."

He chuckled. "I believe my mother over you, Mrs. Shaw."

Santino began giving me a sign of cutting off the conversation. I nodded, thankful someone finally thought this ordeal should be over and done.

"I really can't help you, Mr. Spanelli. I am busy at the moment, but if I do find anything I believe you should be aware of, I will call." I hit the off button and happily collapsed against Andy's chest. His arms swallowed me in a protective hug, and it felt great.

"I admit it is time to *lay the cards on the table*, I believe is the saying," Logan said, glancing at me.

"Yep," I said.

Turning to Santino, Logan said, "Please have your partners join us." I felt my eyebrow move north, but no one else seemed to react to the fact the old Indian had spoken directly to Santino.

Santino nodded and talked into his shoulder. Wow, they bought new equipment since the last time they protected me. The microphone was so well hidden, I couldn't even see a wrinkle in his well ironed shirt.

We waited in silence for the rest of my mob trio to make their way from the yard to the kitchen. You could have heard a pin drop until Bob spoke. "Is it just me or is this Anthony guy really nuts?"

Poor Mr. Spanelli stiffened at the words, but I'm not sure anyone else noticed.

After what seemed an eternity but in reality was about a minute, I heard the side door open and quiet voices making their way to our gathering.

Antonio and Bill entered and nodded at the old man and Andy but ignored the dead folks.

Logan began speaking, and the shock on everyone's face was plain as day.

"I have examined my options carefully. The time has come for everyone gathered here to be aware of certain facts." He paused, looking at each face, before continuing.

"Some of you, I have known for years." He looked at Mr. Spanelli, Laura, and even Amy.

"Others have become part of my world more recently." His gaze turned to Andy, Jack, me, and the mob boys.

"Each one has understood the need for us to work together, breaching the veils which have been in place for millennia. There are now as many people living on earth as a total for its entire history. Many people equal many problems."

"Wow, I had no idea!" exclaimed Bob.

Logan ignored the remark and continued. "A tiny percentage of people causing problems if the total population is small is quite manageable." He sighed. "But the same small percentage today causes complications. It is no longer easily contained."

"What percentage?" asked Amy. always the scientist, but I had to admit it was a good question.

"Even one percent creates great dilemmas."

Amy calculated quickly in her head, and blurted, "Logan, that's over seventy million people who disrupt society!"

He nodded. "Yes. A great deal of evil to contain effectively."

Looking around the room again, he sighed. "It was not my intention to deceive those of you here, but I have carefully chosen my aides on this side of the veil." He paused a moment before continuing. "I am pleased with my choices."

"Are you saying all of us..." Laura's hand indicated everyone in the room, "...have had contact with you?"

"Yes. Each one of you is a trusted ally, and I have been cautious concerning your knowledge of one another." He gave us a small smile. "It was possible I could have selected poorly. Safeguarding your involvement from one another controlled any problems inadvertently caused if one of you were persuaded by the enemies to join forces with them." He shrugged. "I offer no apologies, only explanations."

I smirked; of course Logan wouldn't offer apologies!

"So," began Mr. Spanelli, "these men who work for me also work for you?"

"Yes," Logan stated simply.

Bill closed his eyes briefly, before directing them straight at Mr. Spanelli. "Boss, we took what we believed were the correct actions."

"Incredible!" sputtered the old man.

"Uncle Sal, Logan had us look at the bigger picture rather than focus only on our little piece of the pie. You have to admit, he was right," said Santino.

The old mobster looked surprised. "I'm not upset. Quite the opposite."

Antonio tore his gaze from the backyard to face his boss. "You're not angry? Why not?"

His boss drew in a deep breath, releasing it slowly. "I have trusted Logan most of my life. He has never led me down the wrong road. If he thought my knowledge of you three helping him would compromise the situation..." He shrugged, "...I accept the fact."

Antonio shook his head, clearly surprised by the reaction.

"Bella remains a problem, however," said Logan.

"Wait a minute. I thought you had her under control," I said.

"Under control, but she must have discovered a weakness somewhere in the mist I created surrounding her," Logan said.

"Mist? You can make mist?" asked Jack.

Oh for Pete's sake. Jack was obsessed last time concerning mist. Personally, I had never witnessed any type of mist when dealing with my dead folks. Jack couldn't believe they didn't arrive through some sort of mist. It took forever to convince him otherwise.

Logan frowned. "Yes, it is usually very effective."

Pointing a finger at me, Jack said, "I told you there was mist involved somewhere!"

Jeez Louise.

# Chapter 24

Once we had finally gotten everyone settled, including Mr. Spanelli, the household was quiet for a change. Andy and I sat at the kitchen table, too emotionally spent to say much, but it was comforting to have a few peaceful moments with Andy. I was glad I had clean sheets for both spare bedrooms. Amy and Laura agreed for the night Laura would take the top bunk. If they were still here the next night, Amy could have her turn. I appreciated Laura's sweet nature convincing the old gal the bottom bunk would be easier in strange surroundings should she need to visit the bathroom in the middle of the night. I'm not sure whether Amy agreed with Laura, but she didn't put up much of a fight. Maybe the day's excitement had pooped her out to the point arguing was too much trouble.

Logan decided Mr. Spanelli should stay as well, so he took the last available bedroom. I felt a tad bad the old mobster had to sleep in a bunk bed, but I couldn't supply him with the luxury to which I assumed he was accustomed. Oh well, life sucks sometimes. I had to hand it to him; he seemed to appreciate our efforts on his behalf and quietly thanked us for caring for his safety. Logan wanted all of us in one house, so here we all were, tucked in and guarded by my favorite trio.

"I want to express my thanks for your willingness to accommodate my wishes in this matter," Logan said, once he had given us a few moments together.

Sighing, I said, "Not many options I can see."

Shaking his head sadly, he agreed. "No, I believe our precautions will prove necessary."

Andy looked over at him. "Necessary?"

"He may not present himself tonight, but eventually Anthony will be a problem," Logan answered.

Frowning, I said, "So I'll have house guests until Anthony is caught?"

The last thing I needed was to babysit a house full of adults. Kids were bad enough, but adults have grown accustomed to their own routines and tended to get cranky when those routines were disrupted. I should know; I was the worst of the bunch.

Before Logan could answer my question, Bob popped back into the kitchen. I hadn't even noticed he had left, so his return startled me.

His eyes locked on Logan and he said, "We've got her locked down tight as a drum! It wasn't easy, but we did it!" His face glowed with excitement, proud to be able to announce good news.

I guessed correctly he was referring to Bella, and I could only imagine how difficult it was to get her back under control.

Logan's nod was slow and thoughtful. "Where was the breach?"

Bob waved a hand. "One of the guys guarding her had gotten distracted, so an itty bitty spot was open—well, at least thinner than normal. But once we discovered his problem, it was fixed in no time at all."

I sat listening, wondering what exactly had gotten thinner—and how did someone Logan trusted to guard Bella somehow get *distracted*? I watched his face and knew by his expression this fact was irritating the dickens out of him.

"This is disturbing news. I will deal with the individual when Anthony is contained."

Bob's face paled at Logan's words. I had no idea how Logan would *deal* with whoever dropped the ball, but I wouldn't want to be in that person's shoes.

Logan turned to face the window. His expression was guarded, but you could see those wheels spinning as he thought of the ramifications concerning Bella's contact with Anthony. Andy and I exchanged quick glances, knowing deep in the pit of our stomachs Bella might have stirred the pot to the point Anthony was totally nutso. Not good news for our team.

Sighing, Logan turned to us. "Bella has agitated Anthony. Now she has no ability to contact him further; we must face the possibility he will become extremely flustered." He stopped, turning back to Bob. "You are confident she is contained?"

Bob sputtered, "Absolutely!"

Logan's eyes darted to Dad, who nodded and poofed out of the kitchen. I could bet money on where he was headed. Logan wanted to assure himself Bella was sealed good and tight.

Turning back to Bob, Logan said, "Please guard the girl. I do not trust hospital security, and our other usual bodyguards are here with us."

Bob nodded, saying, "Yes, sir!" He was gone before I could blink, probably happy to be out of Logan's presence. Even though I suspected Bob was still leery of Logan, his pride in his job was obvious. Logan wasn't someone to irritate too often, and Bob had a bad habit of being pretty damn irritating, even on a good day.

Logan turned his gaze back to the window. It was pitch-black, so I wasn't sure what he was seeing. Of course, for all I knew, dead people can see in the dark. It wouldn't surprise me and made a certain amount of sense. If they can pop in and out of my kitchen, it stood to reason they had tons of skills I hadn't gotten around to contemplating. I knew for certain Logan had advanced skills even Dad couldn't match.

I heard the side door quietly open and close and footsteps heading our way. Bill's face was grim.

After a quick nod in our direction, he faced Logan.

"We sent a couple of guys over to Laura's house, just in case Anthony decided to show up there."

Logan nodded. "Wise decision."

"A minute ago, they reported in and said someone was prowling around the property. Even though they were careful, he must have heard them. Whoever it was has stealth. He was able to avoid our guys and got away before they could catch him."

"Anthony?" asked Logan.

Bill hesitated. "Not sure. Where would the guy obtain enough skill to evade highly trained men?" Shaking his head, he continued. "Anthony does have his own loyal group of family men. Could have been one of those guys."

Logan nodded. "Yes, the scenario is logical."

Since when did Logan start caring about logic? Amy was rubbing off on him. Jeez.

Andy asked, "Did they get into the house?"

Bill shook his head, saying, "No way. We have the house locked down tight."

Logan turned to me. "Is this a time of the day Laura would be in bed?"

Frowning, I said, "I have no idea what time she goes to bed, but it's past my bedtime. So, yeah, good possibility she would already be asleep. Why?"

Thinking through the problem, he said, "A dark house too early in the evening would point to the fact she was not home. However, if this is a time many people would be sleeping, no one would question a dark house."

Hmm, good point.

"Well, it's time for me to join the rest of the house and hit the hay," I said, with a yawn the size of the Grand Canyon.

Logan nodded, and smiled. "Good night."

Andy and I happily made our way down the hall and headed for bed. Once I stretched out, I realized how exhausted I was and sighed, contented to be in bed. Andy was snoring before I could even get comfortable. As I drifted off to dreamland, I heard an unfamiliar noise. I shot straight up, heart pounding, sweat forming in yucky places. Listening to the sound, I realized it was Amy wandering down the hall. She was probably making a midnight run to the bathroom; I made plenty of my own middle-of-the-night potty runs, so I smiled and plopped back into my pillow. She seemed to be taking so long I decided I might need to check on her when I heard the toilet flush and her slippers slapping against the floor as she made her way back to the boys' room. I was glad Andy and Bill had gone over to her house and gathered the women's nighttime garb so they would be more comfortable. It had been so long since we had anyone sleeping in the house other than ourselves, I wasn't used to the noise people make as they move around what must be unfamiliar territory.

Allowing myself to drift off again, I heard the side door open and close, Bill's voice faint as he relayed whatever information he had to Antonio. I knew Santino was stationed out by the woods but didn't know what schedule they had decided to keep this time; last time, it was a couple of hours at each station. Antonio didn't want anyone to become comfortable with his or her position. I guessed he worried they wouldn't be diligent enough, which I thought was ridiculous; these guys were professionals and I trusted them.

Now aware the trio could communicate with Logan, I wondered if they could also see my merry band of characters out back. It wouldn't surprise me unless Logan had blocked the ability from them for some reason. I had to force myself to quit thinking about the entire situation and took a deep breath, hoping it would help send me to dreamland myself.

A few hours later, roused from a deep sleep, I heard a thump from the living room. My first thought was one of the guys had dropped something. My second thought was I would be bloody mad if they had managed to break something I really liked. I didn't hear anything further and decided Amy was making herself a cup of tea. I had no idea why my brain came to that conclusion, but it made sense somehow. Turning over, confident Amy was in the kitchen making noise, I felt myself relax. It was short lived.

"Peg, I think someone is in the house," came the whisper from Amy, standing at my bedroom door. "I didn't want to scare Laura, so I was quiet."

Heart pounding, I reached over to wake Andy. He slept so soundly, you had to really shake him, but he surprised me.

"I heard her," he said, legs swinging over the side of the bed.

"How long have you been awake?" I asked, as quiet as I could muster.

"Not long; heard something." He was reaching for his robe when we heard another thump, followed by a quiet cuss word. Definitely not one of my guys.

By that time, my pounding heart was so loud I could barely hear myself think.

I had a brilliant idea, which was a surprise. I didn't usually think well under stress.

"Bob!" I called out in the loudest whisper I could manage. "Bob!"

We heard a soft pop in the corner, and Bob was there, hand over his eyes.

"What are you doing?" I asked, exasperated.

"I'm not allowed in your bedroom. I'm not sure you're dressed," came his frantic whisper.

*Oh, for Pete's sake. He picks now to worry about manners?*

I pulled my robe on, and said, "We are all decent."

He separated his fingers only enough to check the truthfulness of my statement. Satisfied he wouldn't see a stray boob, he let his hand drop from his face.

"What's up?" he asked.

"Could you go check who's in the kitchen? We heard noises," I whispered.

He frowned. "Sure. Be right back."

Another soft pop announcing he had gone on my errand for him. Andy opened his mouth to say something when we heard another pop.

"Oh my gosh, Anthony is in the house! How did he manage to get inside?" announced my breathless spy.

Andy and I stared at Bob in shock. Amy made a clicking noise with her tongue; I wasn't sure what the sound meant, but I bet it went back to her teaching days. She turned quickly and headed across the hall, back into the boys' bedroom she now shared with Laura.

"What happened to our guards?" Andy asked, his voice barely audible.

Shaking his head, Bob said, "I didn't see any of them. Want me to go look?"

I hesitated a moment before answering. "Yeah, maybe you should. Did you notify Logan?"

"Oh yeah! Immediately," said Bob before he disappeared to discover if my favorite trio was alive and well.

We could hear cautious movement from the kitchen. Anthony must be looking for something specific to stay in one room for so long, but I had no idea what he thought he would find. There was no paperwork declaring we had guests for the night or their identity. I heard a door softly open from further down the hall and realized Mr. Spanelli had awakened. I hoped he would size up the situation fast and stay silent. A moment later, his head appeared, peering around our door.

"Trouble?" he asked faintly. So the old guy had a sixth sense when there was a problem—good to know. He moved a bit further into the doorway.

"Yep." I noticed the robe Andy had loaned him barely closed in the front, and his T-shirt was the old tank style. It reminded me of scenes from movies made in the forties; Humphrey Bogart came to mind for some reason. Well, Bogie with a potbelly. I didn't allow my eyes to drift further down for fear of what they would see—no sense having the image seared into my retinas for eternity.

Giving us a quick nod, he turned and padded back to his temporary quarters. I wondered if the bunk bed was comfortable enough for him but decided it didn't matter under the present circumstances. Unless we somehow controlled Anthony, we might all be headed for Deadsville.

I heard the side door open and close. Andy reached for my hand, squeezing tightly. "Maybe he left."

"I'm not moving until Bob gets back with a report," I whispered.

The words were barely out of my mouth, when I heard a faint pop in the air. "Logan's on site. Anthony is poking around outside. Wonder what he is looking for," Bob said.

Grabbing the phone and Andy dialed 911, which suited me just fine. After giving the police the information we believed someone was prowling around our yard, and the address, he hung up and smiled.

"They are on their way. Jack told them if we called, they were to move their butts pronto. Nice to be friends with the chief of police."

It wasn't long before I heard the crunch of car tires on the driveway. Amazing what you can hear in the dead of the night. Sound must carry well in the night air. A few minutes later, there was a knock on the door.

"Bath Police," came a voice from the other side of the door.

Andy sprang out of bed faster than I had seen in years. Maybe we weren't as old as we thought. I pulled my robe tighter around me and followed close behind. Opening the front door, Andy asked, "See anyone?"

"There are signs of someone tromping around out back. Any idea what they were doing?" I didn't recognize the officer and decided he must be one of the new guys. He was young and really tall, well over six foot, but it was his shocking red hair that really caught my attention. Wow, I hadn't seen hair so red in years.

"And you are?" I asked.

"Sorry. Officer MacMillian." His tone was professional but nervous. What had Jack said to his guys about us?

"Want a cup of coffee?" I asked.

He seemed surprised by the questions, but I noticed his shoulders relaxing. "Thanks, but better not. The chief might not like it."

"You're new to the department?" I asked.

"Yes, ma'am."

"Unless you are having a busy night, have a cup of coffee. There is enough of a nip in the air, it would do you good to have something hot in your system," I said. I decided having a cop in the house was my best bet. "Come on; follow me."

Unsure of how to handle the direction the conversation had taken, he did as he was told.

I slapped a little plastic coffee pod into my fancy brewing system and turned to face him.

"If Jack says anything, tell him you came in to explain what you found," I said.

Grinning, he nodded. "Okay, sounds like a plan."

As he made himself comfortable at the kitchen table, I asked, "Black? Cream? Sugar?"

"Sugar," he answered, looking around the room. "You need to fix the wallpaper before it peels clear down to the floor."

I felt my eyes narrow, but before I could make a rude comment, he continued, "I worked my way through college fixing older homes. I could glue it back for you; it'd only take a few minutes."

All irritation flowed completely out of my system. Here was a kid willing to fix the wallpaper!

"We should have taken care of it years ago," I said with a shrug. "You get to the point you don't even see it anymore."

He laughed. "Yep, heard it a million times. My next day off, I'll stop by with my tools. Only take a jiffy to get it back in place."

"You don't need to go out of your way," I said, hoping like hell he wouldn't take my comment seriously.

Waving his hand, he said, "No problem. Payback for the coffee."

"It's a deal," I grinned.

"Ah, I thought I detected the aroma of coffee," said Amy, padding in the kitchen. "A nice cup of hot tea is what I need." Turning to our new friend, she asked, "Well, Officer, what did you find?"

"Would it be possible for me to have a cup of coffee?" came Mr. Spanelli's voice from the doorway.

Jeez Louise, I hadn't planned on a middle-of-the-night party.

"Sure, come on in and make yourself comfortable," I said, hoping my smile looked genuine.

"Officer?" Amy persisted.

Glancing at me for approval, which I gave with a quick nod, Officer MacMillian said, "No one was there, but there was evidence of someone, or something, prowling around." Turning to me, he asked, "You sure it wasn't a raccoon."

I looked at the messy paperwork sitting on the corner of the kitchen table, shaking my head. "These papers weren't disturbed when we went to bed. Whoever we're dealing with was in the house first."

His eyebrows shot up. "What! No one told me there was an intruder!" He made a move to get up, but I waved him back down.

"By the time we called, he had already gone outside."

A movement in the corner of the kitchen caught my eye. Turning, I saw Bob hopping from one foot to the other, which reminded me of the boys when they had to pee but wouldn't take time out from playing.

I was pretty sure our visitor couldn't hear Bob but decided not to take any chances. I made Mr. Spanelli's coffee then excused myself for a moment.

Once down the hall, I turned to Bob. "What?" I demanded.

"Andy must have gone out back to check on things and Anthony hit him on the head," Bob announced.

I felt my head spin and reached for the wall for support.

"Where?" I asked.

"Out back. He's breathing, but out like a light," he said.

"Go get Amy and tell her what happened; she'll grab the cop," I ordered, heading for the door.

"Yep," he said with a pop of air.

## Chapter 25

I found Andy moaning in the front yard by the bushes. At least he was regaining consciousness; I could breathe again. Kneeling down next to him, I cradled his head in my lap. I could feel the warmth of blood seeping onto my robe. For a moment, I thought I was going to faint but took a deep breath of the cool night air. It helped, but I would be glad when reinforcements joined me.

I could hear voices and running feet coming my way. I heard Amy's voice say, "Mr. Spanelli, wake Laura. I need a cold, wet compress immediately. Officer, call for an ambulance." Her authority wasn't to be questioned, and I was grateful for her commanding tone of voice. No one argued with her; those years teaching must have really ingrained a bossy attitude. Damn good thing!

While the two men scurried off to perform their given duties, Amy said, "Peg, it's fine. He's coming around and probably has a nasty bump on the head."

"Um, Peg?" came Bob's quavering voice.

I frowned, "What?"

"The ambulance is going to be busy when it gets here. I found the guys who were guarding you," he said.

My stomach threatened to heave, but I fought the urge to puke. "Well? Are they alive?" I snapped. I could get a bit cranky when scared spitless.

"Santino is still unconscious but breathing normal. Bill is moaning, but…" he stopped.

Oh, god. Antonio. My savior.

"Is Antonio alive?" I asked, dread filling me.

"Barely," came the soft reply. "Barely."

Amy jumped up with the agility of a twenty-year-old. "Bob, show me where Antonio is right this minute."

"Around the corner," Bob told her.

"Come on; I may need your help," commanded Amy. Bob followed her, looking back at me. I gave him a faint smile. If anyone could help Antonio while we waited on the paramedics, it would be Amy.

Laura came rushing out with a cold, wet washcloth and a blanket. I found the cut on Andy's head and carefully placed the sopping cloth against the growing bump. Laura wrapped him tightly with the blanket. I was irritated to notice, even awakened from sleep, she looked gorgeous. Life was so unfair.

"He'll be in shock if it's bad enough. I know enough to cover up people who are hurt but not much else," she told me with sorrow.

"When this is over, we should all take first-aid classes." I gave her a grim smile.

Andy started stirring again, and, to my relief, his eyes fluttered open.

"Peg, my head hurts," he mumbled.

"Thank god!" I blurted, tears streaming down my face. Until that moment, I hadn't realized how frightened for his life I had been the past few minutes.

The ambulance came flying down the drive, and I was relieved to see them. I heard another vehicle skid to a stop and recognized Jack's police car. Wiping the tears and snot from my face with the sleeve of my robe, I looked at Laura.

"Go see if you can find Amy so we can direct them to Antonio, please," I said.

"Yes," she answered.

I watched her run toward the back of the house and turned my eyes to the EMTs. Jack ran over to me.

"Peg? What the hell is going on around here?" he barked. Jack got as cranky as I did when he was scared. It was nice to know I was not the only one who couldn't remember manners under stress.

While the paramedics took over Andy's care, I kept hold of his hand and gave Jack the scoop concerning our most recent excitement.

"Anthony got into the house somehow. We heard him, but then he left through the side door. Bob…" I shot a quick glance at the paramedic nearest to me, then back at Jack, "…helped.

"Bob?" the paramedic asked. "Is he hurt also?"

I almost laughed, but was afraid it would turn into hyena hysterics and forced myself to stay focused.

"No, but there is a man around back who is seriously wounded," I answered.

He jerked his head to his partner, who took off at a run.

Jack reacted to the news quickly. "Who?"

"Antonio," I said sadly.

Jack looked down at the ground. I know he didn't necessarily approve of my mob guys, even if they were helping Logan, but it had nothing to do with the fact he was well aware Antonio had saved my life a few months back, and he did respect him for the help.

"To be on the safe side, I want to transport your husband to the hospital for a CAT scan," the paramedic said, as he finished bandaging Andy's head.

"Yep," I said. "I appreciate it."

"We have another ambulance on the way to transport your friend," he said. Maybe Antonio wasn't as injured as we had feared.

Nodding, I asked, "Do you know how he is?"

"Not yet. My partner will be back as soon as he has the guy stabilized."

I felt fresh tears stream down my face and dug around my robe pocket for a tissue. One good thing about having kids was you learned to always have tissue close at hand, ready to wipe a snotty nose. After so many years, it had become habit.

Laura came running around the corner. She reached the guy working on Andy, saying, "Your buddy needs you when you're done here."

"Just finished," he said, patting Andy's arm. "Pretty sure you're going to be fine." With those words, he was off and running, supplies in tow.

Jack's face was grim. "If Anthony recognized those three, he must have figured out Laura is here."

Shaking my head, I said, "Not so fast. Those guys were here once before, and it had nothing to do with her."

"Yeah, but Mr. Looney Tunes doesn't know," he said.

"Why do I always seem to be dealing with crazy people," I moaned.

Andy laughed and then said, "Oh gosh, it hurts."

Squeezing his hand, I said, "Hang in there, sweetie. Once we get you to the hospital, they can make sure everything is okay."

He returned my hand squeeze with one of his own, saying, "I'm fine. Head hurts, though."

"Andy, did you hear Anthony at all?" I asked.

"Nope, not a peep. One minute I was inspecting the front yard, getting ready to head out back. I was worried about the guys." He stopped and said thoughtfully, "I do remember being nervous, roaming around the yard alone. I hadn't even bothered to tell you I was heading outside. Not too smart."

"Nervous? Why?" I asked.

"Just a feeling, I guess. If Anthony got past the guys, I knew we could be in real trouble. I trust them a great deal, you know."

"Well, he has training from somewhere!" snapped Jack. "You don't sneak up on three professionals easily."

"Bella," came a soft voice. Logan.

"Bella? What the hell does she have to do with Anthony's training?" I heard myself snap at him.

"A trip to the old country following his graduation from school," said Logan. "I was concerned regarding his experience. She must have had a great deal of help from our side to shield the true reason behind the graduation gift. He was at the perfect age to be heavily influenced."

"What, around eighteen?" Jack asked.

"Yes. The age when most men feel invincible," he smiled. "It has been true for millennia." Sighing, he continued. "I am convinced he was trained with the family's elite men."

I thought back to my own boys at their graduations, believing they were bulletproof. Each one went off to college thinking they had all the answers to life. All four had graduated college knowing they had a few answers at most. But the lessons it took for them to come to the realization, at times, gave me nightmares. I was thankful they had survived their immaturity and grown into pretty nice people—most of the time.

I was sure whatever Anthony had learned during his summer training had planted seeds in his squirrelly mind, which had taken years to develop into the mess we were having to cope with today. I could feel the anger at Bella growing. How dare she purposely twist her son onto a road of insanity. Even if she was nuts herself, it was no excuse.

"You were wise to call Bob," said Logan.

"I couldn't think of another option," I said. A thought flew into my head. "Oh, my gosh, he was supposed to be guarding Caterina!"

Logan smiled. "Yes, but he called for a replacement before he left the hospital. He is learning."

Ah, which was why I'd had to call him twice. Nodding, I said, "Good for him. Is Caterina okay?"

Logan looked off to the tree line. "She will be soon."

Logan was holding back information, but I decided to keep my fat mouth closed. He had his own ways of dealing with predicaments, and I was slowly learning his plans had an ordered sense to them. I just wished some of his decisions didn't put my own life and those of people I cared about in danger. The long view of his could be a pain in my butt.

Amy came charging around the corner, face grim but satisfied. I sighed in relief; if it was bad news about Antonio, she wouldn't wear that expression.

"Hello, Logan. Jack." Turning to me, she said, "He'll live. It was a close call, but they got the bleeding under control."

I looked at her hands and clothes, which were covered in blood. She must have held him much the same way I had held Andy. I felt the tears start again.

"No time for tears, young lady," she told me. "We still have to transport both Andy and Antonio to the hospital." She looked around the driveway. "Where is the second ambulance? Andy, you look fine, so I will tell the paramedics to use this one and you can follow in the second ambulance. If it ever gets here!" she said, turning quickly, pounding back to her patient. Antonio would never live this down; his friends would tease him about Amy's contribution for years to come.

The paramedic came running around to us. "Gotta grab the gurney. The old lady is one tough nut," he said, breathless. "Was she an officer in the military?"

"High school science teacher," I said.

"Ah, explains her commanding nature." He grinned.

We waited quietly until they returned with Antonio, motionless on a gurney. His face was white as snow, but at least he was breathing. They loaded him into the ambulance and made their way out of the drive. The second ambulance still hadn't arrived, which was strange.

"Wonder if we should shove Andy in my car and go to the hospital ourselves?" I asked.

Jack grabbed his phone from his jacket pocket, punched in a couple of numbers, and barked, "Where the hell is the ambulance?"

His face dropped. "What? When?"

Andy and I exchanged glances.

"Damnation! Why didn't someone call me? I'm on my way." He ended the call and jammed the phone back into his pocket.

"Family fight on Hametown Road. Big, huge, bloody mess. Sorry guys, but I've got to go," he said, heading for his car.

Amy took charge at that point. "We need to get Andy out of this cold air and some hot tea in him."

Nodding, I managed to stand and earned a stab of pain in my legs. They had fallen asleep with Andy's head resting on them, and movement sent pins and needles soaring through both legs. I shook them a little, hoping to speed the process. It worked but not by much.

Laura took one of Andy's arms, and I grabbed hold of the other. Amy led the way, and we made it into the house where the warmth felt so good I almost peed my pants. If this continued, I'd be in adult diapers soon.

"A nice cup of tea is just the ticket," said Amy, leading us down the hall towards the kitchen. She opened her mouth to continue as we approached the doorway, and stopped suddenly. Uh-oh, I thought. Not good.

"Come in, please," a voice told us.

I looked and saw poor Mr. Spanelli sitting rigid at the table, his eyes focused on the floor. I knew the voice, and I wasn't at all happy—Anthony.

Amy set her mouth in a firm line, and we headed towards the voice. Laura and I sat Andy down at the table with as much care as we could. He reached for my hand, squeezing it for reassurance. Well, we were in a pickle for sure this time, and I didn't need to look towards the woods for confirmation.

I looked at Anthony's hand, seeing the gun for the first time. I knew next to nothing about guns, but this sucker was big. Noticing my gaze, Anthony laughed. "Oh yes, I have a gun." Looking at all of us, he said, "Well, well. The whole gangs here. My dear father and also my loyal wife." His face gave me the creeps; eyes wide, pupils pin points.

Amy started for the sink, but he said, "Where do you think you are going, old lady?"

"To make Andy a cup of hot tea," she answered, sweet as pie.

His eyes narrowed, but he nodded. "Nothing else! Understand?"

"Of course," she said meekly. She went about the chore of gathering the teapot and tea. She turned on the burner for the hot water.

"Don't get any ideas about throwing hot water," Anthony warned.

Nodding, she gave the appearance of fear. I narrowed my eyes, watching her carefully. Either the evening's excitement had pooped out the old gal, or she was up to something. I was betting she wasn't tired but plotting. She continued puttering around the kitchen, getting a cup and saucer out for the tea. As she opened the refrigerator door, Anthony screamed, "What are you doing?"

I flinched at the pitch of his voice but remained silent. This was Amy's show, and I wasn't interfering.

"He needs a piece of pie. Peg keeps pie in the fridge. Sugar is good for shock," she answered, again the meek tone dripping off every word. Anthony must have been as dumb as a brick not to see through her charade.

He thought about what she said for a moment and then said, "Yes, I'll allow it."

Yep, dumb as a brick. But to be fair, who would worry about an eighty-year-old woman?

"But no one else!" he declared.

Amy nodded and turned to her self-assigned duties.

My eyes darted over to Laura. I noticed her face as she watched Anthony; if those muscles became one bit tighter, they'd snap like a twig. Mr. Spanelli never took his eyes off the floor, where I hoped he wasn't discovering some new flaw I would have to fix later.

"How nice to see the two people in the world who have made my life miserable stuck here, while I have control over whether they live or die," Anthony sneered.

I could feel my anger starting to grow but clamped down on it, forcing myself to control the impulse to smack his face. No sense ruining Amy's plan of action because I couldn't keep a rein on my emotions. Hormones or no hormones, I was responsible for my own stupidity and tried to keep it to a minimum. I wasn't always successful.

My eyes darted to Amy, but she was ignoring Anthony. Busy slicing the pie, she acted as though he wasn't in the room. She must have nerves of steel. Maybe being married to Albert all those years had taught her how to ignore the asses of the world. Or maybe she was perfecting whatever plan she had cooked up to save us all. I decided my best plan of action was to watch the old gal carefully and hope I'd be able to follow her lead when and if she made a move.

I wasn't thrilled with Anthony's nervousness and decided a little distraction wouldn't hurt—at least I hoped it wouldn't screw up Amy's plan.

"Anthony, how on earth did you get into the house earlier?" I asked. To be honest, I really was interested in his answer.

He laughed. "It was easy, you really should have an alarm system installed."

I admit I had to agree with him. If he had been able to get in with guards outside, our security was in hot water.

"But you knocked out three men; how was it possible?" I asked, hoping his arrogance would compel him to brag. It worked.

"Ha! Those men think they are elite! *I*, Anthony Spanelli, am elite! I was trained by the family's most prestigious combat forces." He acted as though he had been handpicked for the training, rather than sent by his mother.

"Combat forces? The family has a combat group?" I asked, intrigued in spite of myself.

Nodding his head emphatically, he continued. "Oh, yes! The Spanelli family is famous for our exclusive training. Our men have fought in wars throughout the centuries and have received many high awards. It is important for enemies of the family to be in fear of our forces!"

I nodded, hoping he believed I agreed with him. I thought he was nuts, but he didn't need to know it. I mean, jeez Louise, this wasn't the old country.

"Look at my father; does he project a strong presence? No! I will take control of the family business and continue the Spanelli name with fierceness. My father has become soft in his old age. He does not have the strength of character to run this family."

Wow, talk about delusional. Mr. Spanelli had more strength of character than his son would ever understand or appreciate. Anthony wanted to live the glory days of centuries past, while his father understood the need to move away from the violent history. A legitimate family business could make millions and be free of worry about interference from the law. Anthony wanted the blood and gore of history to continue.

In his excitement, he had taken a step forward, waving the gun around like a banner. Amy saw her chance and took advantage of his position. As quick as lightning, the old gal whirled around, grabbed the gun, and with her free hand, gouged his eyes with two fingers. I jumped up from the table and let my right foot find a home in Anthony's groin. He went down like a block of cement, groaning. Mr. Spanelli joined us and pushed his son's head to the ground, holding it in place.

"Could I have some type of rope, please," he asked, as calm as a cucumber.

I thought frantically for a moment and then remembered a jump rope I had bought a few years back. I admit I was trying to stay in shape; it lasted about two days. I ran back to the bedroom. I had to rummage around the closet longer than I had expected, but finally was able to find it under Andy's sweat pants. Grabbing it, I ran back to the kitchen. Mr. Spanelli had his knee in Anthony's back to keep him under control. He was relaxed and in control. Anthony continued groaning, but his father ignored the discomfort his son was experiencing. I handed him the rope, and Mr. Spanelli quickly tied his son's arms. I was amazed at the speed with which the old man was able to accomplish his goal. Within seconds, Anthony was secure.

Mr. Spanelli looked down at his son. "You are not the only member of the family to be trained by the elite members of our clan. You mistake calm order and sound business decisions for weakness. It has always been your downfall."

I turned to Laura. "Please call the police."

White-faced, she nodded, reaching for the phone. "I think there's an officer in the back, but I'm not sure where he's gone."

Amy calmly placed Andy's pie and hot tea in front of him. "You need to get this in your system. We'll head to the hospital once the police have finished here."

Andy looked at me and then down at his pie. He shrugged and started eating.

# Chapter 26

The police finally left, and we still hadn't gotten Andy to the hospital. Even though he was feeling better, I wouldn't relax until a doctor told me he was fine. The sun was peeking through the scattered clouds, and we had survived the ordeal. We sat around the kitchen table, exhausted, but safe.

Jack sat, head in his hands.

"I can't believe it happened again!" he moaned.

"Jack, you weren't even here this time," I said. "It makes no sense for you to feel guilty."

He lifted his head, looking me square in the eyes. "Peg, we fight these situations together. The fact I wasn't here makes it worse."

"Jack, you were doing your duty as leader of the police department," Logan told him. Ah, he was using his name again, rather than the title of 'Chief.' Things must be getting back to normal.

"I'm so sorry about everything," said Laura. Her face was still white, but damn, the woman looked beautiful even after the night we had endured. It was so wrong someone could consistently look so fabulous, no matter what the circumstances. Even her disheveled hair looked stylish. Something was perverse with the universe. I'm just saying.

"You have nothing to apologize for in this matter," Logan told her. "I chose you for this endeavor. You have performed excellent in all respects."

Laura shook her head but didn't reply. Logan smiled at her and then turned to Mr. Spanelli.

"Thank you for achieving our most difficult goal. Neutralizing Anthony must have caused you great emotional pain."

The old mobster looked out the window and then back at Logan.

"I realized a long time ago I had lost Anthony. The years of shielding him from Bella didn't protect him in the end." He sighed. "Last night was a relief, to be honest. It was an end to the misery he has caused so many people I love." He glanced at Laura and allowed a small smile. "I hope Anthony is put away in an insane asylum. I will pay for the best care, but he needs to be committed for his own good."

"I believe it would be a wise course of action," said Logan, a note of sadness in his voice. "I am sorry, old friend, we could not prevent Anthony's decline."

Mr. Spanelli shook his head. "It was a long shot, but worth the effort even though we weren't able to achieve the goal. If the plan had worked, it would have saved us all a lot of trouble. When even the Cleveland Clinic's mental health specialists couldn't help him, I knew we had lost the fight."

I couldn't think of anything to say, so I kept my mouth closed. I did feel sorry for the old guy; I was starting to really like him. His relationship with Laura was unusual; she was the mother of his daughter and the wife of his son. Could it be any more complicated? Their bond was strong, and I wondered if they were romantically tied.

Logan turned to Andy. "You behaved foolishly." The rebuke was mild, his voice kind. "Please remember we have many miles ahead of us in this battle. Do not act alone again."

Andy's face flooded red, but he nodded. "I agree."

Logan's attention passed to Amy. His smile was genuine as he met her eyes. "I am pleased with your work. Thank you for your dedication in this matter."

Amy's cheeks flushed, but her eyes flashed. "I have a question."

Logan nodded. "Yes?"

"Where were *you* while Anthony was terrorizing this household?" she demanded.

Logan was taken aback by her anger. Cocking his head to one side, he studied her face. After a few moments, he said, "I do not answer to you, but I will explain. There are many battles ongoing. This was but one and rather minor." He pointed to the woods. "They were in charge."

"Ha!" she snorted. "They did absolutely nothing, Logan. They're *dead!* We had four men down and came close to having more carnage right here in this kitchen."

"They performed more duties than you realize." His voice had an edge to it, but I was enjoying Amy's anger. Poor Logan. He now had two women whose tempers would explode occasionally.

"It remains to be proven! Bob did more to help than the rest of you," she snapped.

"He is assigned to be Peg's helper. I would expect him to assist in any way necessary. I cannot always be here for you," he said, shrugging. "I have many helpers."

"Fine and dandy, but you dragged all of us into this war. You are responsible for our safety to a degree. At least until we have more experience." She wasn't backing down. Wow.

"I am not accustomed to being questioned," he stated flatly.

"Which is your problem," she said, turning back to her task—more tea. Jeez. The woman must have made gallons of the stuff by now.

The building tension was broken by a soft *pop* in the air.

"Boss," said Bob, excitement pouring out of him, "it's time."

We looked at one another. "Time for what?" I asked.

Logan smiled. "Laura, Salvatorio, please make your way to the hospital. Caterina is waking."

A sob escaped Laura, and Salvatorio grabbed her hand instinctively.

"Come on," said Jack, standing. "I'll drive you both down there." He looked at me. "We'll talk later."

I nodded. *Talk? About what?* I wondered.

Watching the three of them rush out the door, a thought emerged.

"We still didn't discover who ran Caterina down," I said.

"Oh, Peg!" said Amy, turning to face me. "Anthony did it!"

"What?" Both Andy and I said.

"No way!"

Nodding her head as she continued puttering around with the tea, she said, "I realized he was the only one who had a motive to hurt the child."

I felt my eyes narrow. "Why? Did he figure out he wasn't her father?"

She waved a hand. "His arrogance would never allow a thought along those lines to enter his head. Even if it had, he would have dismissed it immediately." She stopped, and said slowly, "Bella may have suspected, but I don't think she could have convinced Anthony of the truth. Even with her power over him."

"But why would he run down his own daughter?" asked Andy.

"His need for a son was overwhelming. Even though Caterina could carry on the family name, he wanted a boy. The poor little girl meant nothing to him—no emotional ties at all." She shook her head, sad at the thought a father could feel so little for his child. It hit me, as a motherless woman, Amy would feel real anger over Anthony's actions. He had what she had always wanted, and it meant nothing to the self-absorbed jerk.

"Still doesn't explain why he hurt her. He had a ton of pictures of her in his office at the house," I said, a little snottily, I admit. I was tired, and Amy was taking her sweet time explaining.

Leaning against the counter, she said, "His hatred for Laura had become dangerous. He blamed her for their lack of more children. Even though she had stayed far from the child as her only way to protect Caterina, Anthony instinctively knew Laura loved the girl. To hurt Laura, he had to hurt Caterina." She shrugged.

"But what about the threatening letters he received?" I asked.

"He wrote them himself," she said, confident in her analysis.

Frowning, I asked, "You sure?"

"Oh, yes." She looked at Logan. "Correct?"

Logan nodded, his eyes twinkling.

"You've known all along!" I accused him.

"I suspected—true it was a strong suspicion, but correct in the end," he said.

"Well, I've got a few questions of my own. Don't you dare even think about fading out before we clear a few details up about this case!" I declared, fuming.

His eyes narrowed a tad, but he nodded. "Proceed."

Tapping my fingers on the table while I gathered my thoughts, I glared up at him. "Who was Marco? What was his role in this mess?"

"Ah, Marco." Shaking his head, Logan continued. "Poor Marco. He was loyal to Anthony from childhood. Bella had introduced them when they were quite young, hoping I am sure, one day Marco would work for her son. He followed Anthony's orders without question."

"But he's dead now," I said.

"Yes, Anthony killed him in a fit of rage." He nodded in Amy's direction. "I believe you call it a temper tantrum."

"Yes," she said. "The poor man died because Anthony had a bad day?"

"Marco took the brunt of Anthony's anger. I did not anticipate the event," replied Logan.

"Okay, one mystery solved." I thought a moment and then said, "The mayor is convinced some spirit was in his office. Any idea who it was?"

Dad cleared his throat. "Um, sweetie?"

I frowned, turning my attention to him. When the hell had he shown up?

"Well, it was me." He held his hands up as I sputtered.

"I wanted to make sure he wasn't double crossing us." Shrugging, he said, "I listened to a few of his phone calls, realizing he was just trying to cover his own butt and was no real threat. I was only there the one afternoon. Really spooked him, huh?" he finished with a grin.

I shot him a grin of my own. "Yeah, freaked him out for sure."

"Another question answered. Okay, Dad told me the guys out back…" I jerked my thumb towards the woods, "…could actually have physical contact with anyone trying to harm me. If it's true, why didn't they help us with Anthony?"

Logan sighed. "I have given them abilities to handle anything on the property but failed to include *inside* the house, which will be rectified before I leave this morning. As for the men outside, my men had no orders for anyone other than you, Andy, Amy, Laura, and Salvatorio."

"You forgot the *inside*? Those guys out back didn't pay attention to anything happening in here?" I asked, stunned.

"My decision was based on Owen's actions in the garden. I admit, with your security detail, I had not anticipated anyone entering the house who could cause harm. Again, I was wrong."

Wow, Logan had to admit to another bad decision. He was probably as grateful as we were this case was over and done.

"Andy was outside when he was attacked. Why didn't the dead help?"

Logan nodded. "Andy was in the front of the house and out of their sight. They were watching Anthony while he was in the back." He shook his head. "I will ensure my orders of protection include everyone who works with us."

Deciding to move on with my questions before he scooted out of here, I said, "What about the gorgeous sapphire and end table Laura owns? I can tell you right now, those suckers have major negative energy attached to them."

Nodding, Logan said, "Excellent question. Those items will be dealt with properly. Salvatorio and I have discussed them. He was quite stunned to learn of their power but realizes objects have the ability to carry dangerous energy. They will be disposed of in a way which contains the negativity, which I will handle personally."

My face fell. "The beautiful stone is going to be destroyed?"

"It may be beautiful, but it possesses much evil. It has been in the family for centuries, gathering evil with each generation."

"Wow," was all I could think of to say about the items. "Okay, last detail. What's with Bob testing Laura to see if she can *sense* him, when you knew full well she has had contact with you when she was a kid! Plus, why do you have Bob giving me information you know I already have found?" Another thought hit me. "How much *whispering* are you doing in Caterina's life? Has she really been in a coma, or are you involved there, too?"

Smiling, Logan began fading.

"Logan! Get back here!" I shouted, watching his form become fainter.

I heard Dad laugh. "He's not going to answer those questions. You're lucky he allowed any at all."

"Peg, I'm tired. I'm going to bed," said Andy, rising from his chair.

"Oh, Andy, we never got you to the hospital!" I moaned.

"I'm good, really. Headache is gone, vision fine, and I don't want to puke. I'm pooped though."

I watched as he headed towards the bedroom, fearful he really needed to see a doctor.

"He'll be fine, dear," said Amy. "I've been watching him. His eyes cleared up rather quickly, and he sounds quite good. We'll keep an eye on him for a day or two."

"You a doctor now?" I snapped.

She smiled. "Nope, but not stupid either. It's basic first aid."

I glared at her but kept my mouth shut.

"I'm off, babe. Logan has asked me to be there for the wrap-up meeting later today," Dad informed me as he faded. "Love ya!"

Wrap up meeting? There was a meeting to wrap up this case? Did they do it every time? Jeez Louise.

Amy and I found ourselves alone in the kitchen. I looked out back, testing my vision with the gang near the wood line. Nope, no evidence my dead crew was out there guarding the house and its occupants. I sighed, happy in the knowledge I couldn't see them, so all was well.

A faint *pop* filled the air. Now what? I turned to see Nana. Well, it was about damn time!

"Nana! Where have you been?" I demanded.

Waving a hand, she said, "I've been busy. Hello, Amy, nice to see you."

Amy smiled. "It's nice to see you again; it has been a long time." Turning to me, she said, "I'll make us a nice cup of tea."

Shrugging at her suggestion, I said to Nana, "Busy doing what?"

"You'd be surprised how much has been happening on our side of things. You sure know how to stir the pot!" she said, rubbing her hands in glee.

Frowning, I asked, "What pot did I stir? I've been trying to stay out of trouble, solve a simple accident, and not get killed in the process!"

"Well, you are the talk of the town! Taking down the Spanelli crime family!"

Talk of the town? Notoriety was not what I wanted; I pretty sure I wanted to be invisible to their side of life.

"I didn't *take down* the Spanelli family! Amy did most of the work, I only kicked him," I said.

Ignoring Amy's part entirely, she continued, "Your kick was a doozy from what I heard. Right in the—"

I stopped her before she could finish. I didn't need Amy to be embarrassed by Nana's crass vocabulary.

"Enough! It was one kick. Plus, it doesn't end the Spanelli business. Anthony is the only member of the family going to jail." Since I wasn't exactly positive Logan wanted everyone, including the nonheartbeat group to know Mr. Spanelli was on the side of good, I decided to be careful what information I shared.

"Well, it caused quite a bit of excitement, even if it was one kick." She pouted.

Shaking my head, I said, "Nana, I'm pooped. Is there a special reason you are here?"

"Wanted to check up on you, sweetie. Make sure you were okay. I'm real proud of you!" she beamed.

I smiled. "I'm fine, Nana. Thanks for stopping by, but I need to get some sleep."

Nodding, she said, "I'll be by again. Love you," she said as she faded.

I sighed heavily. I wasn't sure her visits were necessarily healthy for me. Each time she dropped by, I found myself in hot water.

Amy had been quiet for Nana's visit. Turning to her, I said, "Sorry about her. She's a little too enthusiastic about my involvement."

Amy laughed. "Exactly what grandmas are supposed to do! But I'm glad we are going to those self-defense classes. I told you they would come in handy."

"Yep, you sure called it right. How'd you know?" I asked.

Shaking her head, she said, "I didn't, but at our age, we need all the training we can get." She turned back to her task.

At *our* age? She included me in her group? Jeez.

She puttered over to me, setting a fresh cup of tea in front of me. "Drink up, it will make you feel better."

I looked down at the tea with little interest. A coffee drinker myself, tea didn't quite meet my standards.

Seeing my expression, she laughed. "You'll enjoy it, I promise."

Shrugging, I took a sip. Wow, did it have a kick!

Amy grinned. "Told you so!"

"What the heck is in here?"

"It's a hot toddy. A little tea, a little honey, a little more whiskey. I found the bottle under the kitchen sink and decided it was exactly what you needed."

"It's great!"

"Drink up, then get to bed. If you don't mind, I'll borrow the spare bedroom again. Not sure I could make it back to the house, I'm so tired."

Nodding, I finished my special drink, looking forward to a warm bed and a long nap.

# Letter to Readers

**T**hank you for reading *Midlife Chaos*. This is the second book in the *Peg Shaw* series.

I was experiencing the joys of hot flashes when I first begin to write about these characters and their adventures. I noticed that the characters, like the hot flashes would show up at the most inopportune moments, demanding their story be told.

I hope you are enjoying Peg Shaw's adventures as much as I love telling these stories. I love introducing the new characters, like Amy, and seeing the reactions of the readers. The new characters have a way of just showing up for me and I have to introduce them to you.

Each character appears all by themselves and I seldom know why they decided to join the story. I've learned to let them have free reign. I feel privileged they allow me to tell their stories.

Bob is still my all-time favorite spirit. I love his enthusiasm, even when he trips on his own personality. I have a real soft spot for him; he makes me smile every time he pops in to create his own particular type of chaos. He's more of a hero than he realizes.

I have great respect for Logan. His wisdom, power and sense of responsibility are what makes him important to me.

I would enjoy hearing who your favorite characters are. Drop me a line at suehawleyauthor.com and tell me who captured your heart and why.

*Sue Hawley*

PS – If you enjoyed this book, I would love it if you go to Amazon and post a review.

PSS – Sign up on my website and I will add you to the list of people to notify when Peg and the Deadsville gang have a new release.

# About the Author

Author Sue Hawley proves that writers become writers by reading. With little formal writing instruction but years of avid reading, Sue Hawley began writing a series of cozy mysteries. Her stories surround the adventures of menopausal Peg Shaw who sees dead people. "The first one almost wrote itself," Sue said of *Hot Flashes Cold Cases, which she wrote in 12 weeks*. "My sister, who is now my biggest fan, loved it."

When asked where she gets her ideas, Sue explained, "Characters show up when they are ready. It's not something that can be forced." She goes on to say "One day I was writing about Peg when a character showed up ringing the doorbell. I had no idea who was going to be on the other side of that door when Peg answered it. It turned out to be Amy, someone who has been important to Peg ever since."

While working on other writings, Sue began to publish the first three books in the *Peg Shaw* series. Even though the process of publishing proved difficult at times, undeterred, Sue pushed forward and found publicist Sandy Lawrence. Their business relationship quickly turned friendship and has been a solid foundation to push Sue's writing to become an Amazon best seller.

Raised in Pasadena, Texas, Sue is a graduate of Sam Rayburn High School. She has always been drawn to books, a love passed down by her mother. This love of reading she passed to her each of her five children.

While in her early twenties, Sue met her husband Jack through her oldest sister. After a brief engagement, they were married and moved into Jack's family home, built by his great-grandfather. They are the fifth generation to live in the farmhouse, dating back to the 1800s. Many renovations to the old farmhouse, five children and eleven grandchildren later, they are still going strong.

Always challenging herself, Sue took part in a national writing event. "I signed up for the annual NaNoWriMo event (National Novel Writing Month) and challenged myself to write 50,000 words by Thanksgiving." By maintaining a rigorous 8:30am to noon daily writing schedule she met her goal. "As I wrote about one character, new characters kept popping up. I like some of my dead characters more than the living ones," she admits.

Mostly self-taught, Sue has read a lot about how to develop a back-story and develop characters. On her writing table, she is surrounded by the world of her characters and their stories, all on 3" x 5" index cards or sticky notes attached to her corkboard.

Writing from her farmhouse, Sue says, "I am very happy on my hill. I'm not a joiner; I'm a rather private person." However, she maintains, "Everyone has a story. Write your story."